LORD ARGYLL TURNED TO JENNY WITH A DECIDEDLY WICKED GLEAM IN HIS EYE.

"Alone at last, my bonnie lass."

Well, that didn't take long, Jenny mused. In any case, she still had the advantage.

She batted her eyes. "Please temper your words, my lord. The ladies are bound to return in a moment."

"A moment is all I need, lass."

She knew she should pretend to faint, or at the very least wilt. But as Jenny looked into Lord Argyll's eyes, she somehow didn't care about the ruse anymore. She slipped her arms around his neck and pressed her lips to his.

She had half expected her brazenness to shock or repel him. But he ran the tip of his tongue along the fullness of her lips until she shuddered.

Jenny pulled back. "You...are not the gentleman you pretend to be, my lord."

He laughed deeply. "And ye are not the lady you pretend, either..."

Also by Kathryn Caskie

Rules of Engagement

Lady in Waiting

Kathryn Caskie

NEW YORK   BOSTON

Copyright © 2005 by Kathryn Caskie
Excerpt from *A Lady's Guide to Rakes* copyright © 2005 by Kathryn Caskie

Cover design by Diane Luger
Cover illustration by Tony Russo
Hand lettering by David Gatti
Book design by Giorgetta Bell McRee

Warner Books

Time Warner Book Group
1271 Avenue of the Americas
New York, NY 10020
Visit our Web site at www.twbookmark.com

Printed in the United States of America

First Paperback Printing: January 2005

10 9 8 7 6 5 4 3 2 1

For my sister Jenny Byers,
the original Jenny Penny.

Acknowledgments

I must thank those generous souls who assisted in bringing *Lady in Waiting* into being.

Dr. Kenneth Hylson-Smith, of Bath, England, for his willingness to share his great knowledge of the history of Bath Abbey.

The very patient docents from the Bath Preservation Trust, who graciously answered my numerous very odd questions about Number One Royal Crescent without batting an eyelash.

My dear friends and fellow writers, Deborah Barnhart, Denise McInerney, and Pam Palmer Poulsen, who dropped everything to read and comment on my manuscript before publication.

Nancy Mayer, for helping me with Regency-era facts. Any mistakes are completely my own.

My editor Melanie Murray, who encouraged me to let my imagination soar.

And my wonderful friend and fellow author, Sophia Nash, who, besides being there every step of the way, taught me the true joys of retail therapy.

Author's Note

The Featherton sisters' Bath home, Number One Royal Crescent, actually exists to this very day and several of its rooms are open to the public through the generosity of the Bath Preservation Trust.

The house itself is actually quite famous, and *The Bath Chronicle* records on September 27, 1787, that Princess de Lambelle, *Lady in Waiting* to Queen Marie-Antoinette of France, stayed at Number One Royal Crescent.

Between the years 1814 and 1823, there are no records of who actually occupied the house, so of course I immediately moved the Featherton sisters, their niece Meredith, and their staff into Number One.

For purposes of this story, I took some liberties with room layout, placing the dining room next to the study. In actuality, a wide entrance hall divides the two rooms. I also placed the drawing room on the ground floor, when it exists on the next level.

For more information about Number One Royal Crescent, please visit my Web site where I have posted some photographs, or contact the Bath Preservation Trust for Number One Royal Crescent, Bath, An Illustrated Guide and Souvenir; or *The Royal Crescent in Bath* by William Lowndes, The Redcliffe Press, Bristol, 1981.

Lady in Waiting

Prologue

Scientific Diary of Miss Genevieve Penny
20 December, 1817

I have made an important scientific discovery—one that will change my life forever.

By crossing two particularly vigorous varieties of Mitcham peppermint, I have produced an essential oil of unmatched potency. Alas, which two varieties, however, I have no memory, having no mind for storing such dreary details. Hence, the introduction of my exquisite new scientific journal with fashionable marbled facings, satin page mark, and soft leather spine. I purchased it today, along with a gorgeous cairngorm brooch I saw in the window of Bartleby's, which has fast become my favorite shop on all of Milsom Street, if not all of Bath. But I digress.

Through a most fortuitous accident, I found that this particular oil has the curious effect of causing the skin to flush with youthful vigor immediately upon contact. Thus far, there have been no ill side effects, therefore I shall commence blending a half-dozen gallipots of the peppermint cream for the Featherton ladies. No doubt they will be pleased, as will the shopkeeper at Bartleby's, for the guinea the Feathertons will likely gift me must be applied directly to my overdue shop bill before I am barred from the establishment forever.

Chapter One

Bath, England
January 2, 1818

Genevieve Penny spun around and stared, quite unable to believe what she was hearing. "What, pray, do you mean she used the cream down *there*? My God, Annie, it's a *facial* balm. Did you not explain its intended use to her ladyship?"

"Course I did, Jenny. I'm not daft." Her friend, an abigail like herself, punctuated her words with a roll of her eyes and settled her plump behind on the stool before the herb-strewn table. "But how could I have known Lady Avery and the viscount had a more *amorous* plan for the cream?"

"And now she wants a pot of her own?" Jenny nervously tucked a loose sable curl behind her ear. "I gave the Feathertons' cream pot to *you*. My gift was meant to be our secret. I never intended for the cream to find its way above stairs."

Above stairs? What an awful thought. Jenny's stomach

muscles cinched like an overtight corset and she gasped for a breath.

What if the Featherton ladies learned of her little gift born of supplies *they* paid for—blended in *their* own stillroom? Heaven forbid. She might find herself out on the cobbles without a reference! Where would she be then, hawking oranges on the street corner for her daily bread?

She seized Annie's shoulders. "You did not tell your mistress that *I* gave you the cream."

"Nay, of course not. Said a friend gave it to me." But as she spoke, Annie's keen eyes drifted across the table to the sealed clay gallipots on its edge. With a twist of her ample form, she broke Jenny's grip and made her way across the stillroom.

"Have some made up, do you?" Prying open the lid, Annie lifted the pot to her nose and, as she breathed deep, let out a pleased sigh. "Well, my lady wants two pots of the tingle cream to start—"

Jenny's cheeks heated. "Lud, stop calling it that! It's *not* tingle cream. It's a peppermint *facial* cream."

"You can call it what you like, but I tried a dab myself. You know . . . *there*." Annie flushed crimson and looked away. "And I own, Jenny, the way it tickled me below . . . positively *sinful*. I do not doubt it revived my lady's desire."

Jenny heard Annie return the clay gallipot to the table, but then she heard something else. Her ears pricked up at a faint but unmistakable jingle of coins.

As Annie turned around, she withdrew a weighty silken bag from her basket and pressed it into Jenny's palm. "My lady bade me to give the maker this, *if* that maker could be persuaded to oblige her with two pots today."

Jenny loosened the heavy bag's satin tie and emptied ten gold guineas onto the table. It was a fortune for a lady's maid like her. A blessed fortune! Her blood plummeted from her head into her feet and she sank onto a stool, unable to stop staring at the gleaming mound of riches.

"You do have two spare pots, don't you, Jenny? Her ladyship would be most displeased if I returned to the house without her cream."

Jenny nodded absently and pushed two of the three gallipots forward. This was certainly not the use she intended when she blended the cream. But what else could she do except oblige? This was more blunt than she'd ever seen in her lifetime.

"Jolly good. Knew you'd come around." With great care, Annie wedged the pots into her basket and covered them discreetly with a square of linen. "Must run now. Haven't much time, you know. I'll be needing to dress Lady Avery for the Fire and Ice Ball this eve."

"Of course." Jenny glanced at the rough-hewn table and the lone gallipot sitting amid the crushed nerbs. "Only one left," she muttered to herself.

Annie set her fist on her fleshy hip. "One? You mean that's all you have—at all? Well, dove, if I was you, I'd set about making more of that tingle cream right away."

"Why should I need more?" Jenny raised her brow with growing suspicion.

Beneath the snowy mobcap, Annie's earlobes glowed crimson. "Well . . . I *might* have overheard Lady Avery telling Lady Oliver about her thrilling discovery of an amazing cream. Of course, I knew she was talking about the tingle cream. And, Jenny, Lady Oliver was *most* interested."

A jolt raced down Jenny's spine. "You do not mean others in society know of this? Lud, this is a disaster."

"Oh, Jen, you're getting all foamy for nothing. What's so wrong with an abigail making a few bob on the side? Who knows, a society connection could be the very thing to catapult your sales and help you remove yourself from debt for good."

Jenny forced a snort of laughter, but as the idea settled upon her, she became very still.

Criminy. The idea was intriguing, even if a little mad. But the more she thought about it, the more enticing the suggestion became to her.

No, no, this was ridiculous. She couldn't possibly produce enough pots to clear her accounts—not without getting the sack from her employers.

Could she?

Rising, Jenny walked to her supply cupboard, twisted the wooden door wedge, and peered inside. She was keenly disappointed at what she saw—or rather at what she didn't see. The cupboard was nearly bare. She'd need more emulsifying agent. Plenty more. Gallipots too. Of course she'd have to distill some more Mitcham peppermint.

This was going to be *real* work.

But she would do it. In fact, if she worked very hard, she might even come to terms with her accounts before the last spring leaf unfurled. If not before. She had a society connection, after all.

"Jenny, are you listening?"

She looked up blankly.

"I need to stop by Bartleby's and retrieve some ribbon for my lady. Care to join me?" Annie scooped up a guinea from the table and flipped it spinning through the air. She grinned as Jenny opened her palm and caught the coin before it hit the table.

"Why not." Tossing the glittering coin atop the pile, Jenny cupped her hand and neatly corralled the ten guineas in the silk bag. She looked up and flashed a jubilant smile.

Annie laughed. "Won't the shopkeep be gobsmacked when you actually *pay* ten guineas on your account?"

Jenny winced a little. "Well, maybe not the *full* ten. I think I might stop by the apothecary and fetch a few more supplies."

Annie's eyes widened with excitement. "Does this mean you're going to do it—start a business?"

"A business? Oh, I don't know." Moving to the wall hooks, Jenny crowned herself with her new velvet bonnet, then swept her perfectly coordinated pelisse over her shoulders. "But it can't hurt to have a few more pots of . . . *tingle* cream on hand, now can it?"

Muffling their giggles so they wouldn't be overheard above stairs, Jenny and Annie headed out the door in the direction of Milsom Street.

&

"The man is entirely unreasonable!" Jenny jerked the handle hard, slamming Bartleby's shop door behind her. "Eight guineas I paid him, and still he wouldn't let me put the pearl earbobs on my account." With envious eyes, Jenny glanced down at Annie's neatly tied packet of ribbon.

Annie stuffed the parcel into her basket and drew the

linen doily overtop as if purposely hiding it from Jenny's view. "You must owe him an awful lot."

Jenny shrugged. "I suppose. But I am a loyal customer. He should have more faith."

"Can I ask . . . how much do you owe?"

"I don't know really. Dropped all his notices in the dustbin. After all, he needn't remind *me* that I owe him payment. It is not as if I've forgotten."

"There's Smith and Company too, don't forget. What was it you put on account there?"

"A black bear muff. You should buy one. Most fashionable this season." Jenny wrinkled her brow as they walked. "I should have brought it today. Would have kept my hands warm as embers."

Annie sighed. "And then there's the jeweler on the Lower Walk—a quartet of garnet buttons, wasn't it?"

"Now you must admit *those* were a bargain. All I need to do is replace the shell buttons with the garnets and my pewter gown will be transformed. Why, I've actually saved the cost of a new gown simply by buying the buttons. Really very economical."

Annie stepped before Jenny and caught her shoulders. "Just look at you, Jenny. We're headed for the markets and you're wearing a pelisse of apple-green kerseymere, vandyked with satin! Why do you do it? What need have you for fine gowns and trinkets? You are wasting what little money you earn on this nonsense. You are a lady's *maid*, Jenny. Not a real lady."

"I *am*." Jenny caught Annie's wrists and yanked them from her. "Or I would have been . . . had my father married Mama. He was a highborn gentleman, you know."

"Yes, I do know. But, ducks, he *didn't* marry your

mother, and you are not a lady, no matter how you dress and adorn yourself."

Jenny was about to snap a retort when the sun's reflection off a large shiny object momentarily blinded her.

When her eyes refocused she found herself looking at the most exquisite, certainly the most modish, carriage she'd ever seen in Bath—or even London.

"Will you look at that, Annie? Have you ever seen anything so grand?" Jenny started slowly toward the conveyance, feeling quite incapable of stopping herself. "Come on, I have to see inside."

"Jenny, *no*." Annie ticked her head toward the first pairing of ebony horses. "The footman. He's bound to stop you."

"Oh, botheration. You can keep him busy for me. Come on, Annie, be my friend and chat him up, while I just go and have a tiny peek inside, all right?"

"Jenny, you *can't*."

But Jenny's boots were already upon the cobbles and she was making her way to the far door.

Once Jenny heard the sultry tones of Annie's voice mingling with those of the footman, she crouched low and skulked around the gleaming carriage. Rising up, she peered wide-eyed through the door's lower windowpanes.

To her delight, the carriage was empty. Now, if only the door was . . . she pressed the latch down, and the door opened. Jenny smiled and gave a wink to the heavens, for someone up there was certainly looking out for her this day.

The scent of new leather slipped through the crack

and she greedily breathed in its essence. Oh, this was better than she'd hoped.

And what with the door being open, this was practically an invitation to slip inside, was it not? Besides, it would hurt no one for her to indulge herself for just a moment.

Jenny glanced warily in both directions, then, confident she'd not be seen, put her foot on the step and eased herself inside.

Oh, it was all simply glorious. She was almost giddy with pleasure as she ran her hand over the interior walls, resplendent with a gold-pressed crimson silk that perfectly set off the dark burgundy leather benches.

Eagerly, she fluttered her fingertips over the leather-squabs, which were quite easily as soft as fresh churned butter. She eased herself back, allowing her bonnet to settle against the headrest. "Oh, *yes*," she purred. It was like resting on a cloud.

Jenny had just closed her eyes, imagining herself being whisked to the Upper Assembly Rooms for the Fire and Ice Ball, when she heard a man's stern voice.

"Madam, might I be of some assistance?"

Startled, Jenny snapped her eyes wide open and jerked her head upright. She blinked into the cool afternoon light streaming through the open door. Outside the opposite side of the carriage stood a huge, kilted gentleman, who was stooping down and peering back at her.

Don't panic.

Just stay calm.

But already, as she stared back into the man's dark brown eyes topped with scowling brows, she could feel her heart slamming madly against her ribs.

Lud, what must he think? She knew what she would

think if she found a strange woman relaxing in *her* town carriage. Well, if she had one. She'd think the woman was quite mad. Or . . . maybe a thief.

A thief? Blast! What if he called a constable?

"I believe ye have mistakenly boarded my carriage," the Scotsman said with a controlled level of gentility that surprised her. "Might I help ye find yer own, my lady?" He leaned back then and glanced down Milsom Street, grimacing slightly when he realized no other fine conveyance was parked upon the cobbles.

"Oh, I—" But no other words were coming. Lord help her. *Think, Jenny, think.*

Then, inexplicably, the perfect explanation planted itself in her mind. "Kind sir," she managed, lifting her hand weakly to her brow. "Pray, forgive me. My head began to swirl and I needed to sit down. The sensation came upon me so quickly, I was forced to seek my ease inside your carriage."

"Och, I see." The Scotsman seemed to take to her words immediately, and his eyes softened with concern. "Has it passed—the spell, I mean?"

She nodded her head and offered a thin smile. "Indeed it has. Just this moment, in fact." Furtively, Jenny laid her hand on the door latch and pressed down. The door sprang open. "I am sorry to have troubled you. I will go now."

A look of surprise lit the Scotsman's eyes, and quite suddenly he disappeared from the far door.

Jenny heaved the carriage door beside her open and leapt down, hoping to escape, but the Scotsman had already circled around and caught her elbow before she could flee.

"Please allow me to assist ye by offering a ride to yer home."

A few yards away, Jenny could see Annie, her eyes wide and mouth gaping, standing with the footman near the lead pair of horses.

Jenny turned back to the Scotsman. "No need, sir." She wrenched her elbow from his grasp. "My abigail can escort me. I own, I have fully regained my strength and my residence is not so far away. Again, I am sorry, sir. Do excuse me."

With that Jenny shot up the flag way, hooking Annie's arm as she passed and dragging her along with her.

"Very well then. Good day," the gentleman called out in a confused tone as the two women scurried around the corner on their way to Queen Street.

"Lord above! You're mad, Jenny. I told you not to do it," Annie lamented. "But no, you climbed inside the bloody town carriage anyway."

Jenny slowed her step and stilled. "I know, Annie, but the carriage was *so* lovely. You can't imagine how extraordinary it was. I only wanted to board and see what it felt like to travel like a lady of the *ton*. Just for a moment."

"When are you going to give up your impossible dream of becoming a lady? Do you not see the trouble it causes you? You owe half the shopkeepers on Milsom."

Jenny looked away and shrugged, then urged Annie forward up the walk. "I am well aware of my financial circumstances. But I'll find a way to pay my debts."

"Well, you had better, before Bath's markets send the constables after you for stiffing them."

Jenny focused on the swish of her skirts and the rhythm of her boots as she walked, anything to keep from looking her friend in the eye. Annie was right, of course.

But this time, she might actually be able to do something about her debt. The cream could solve all her worries.

Reaching inside her reticule, Jenny retrieved the two guineas she had left. "Come on, Annie. I need to stop at the dispensing apothecary on Trim Street. I have some supplies to purchase."

⚜

Later that afternoon, above stairs, Jenny tightened the laces of Miss Meredith Merriweather's ball gown, then tossed the back of her mistress's skirts into the air so she could see the luminous effect the sheer, rose-festooned overdress created.

"Oh, you look like an angel, Miss Meredith." Jenny smiled, proud of her own handiwork. "You'll be the envy of every lady in attendance."

Meredith chewed her lip, and twisted a thick coil of copper hair around her finger. "I'm just not sure, Jenny. I think I might like the saffron gown better. Anything but white. Everyone wears white. This is my very first ball—and even though I've not come out yet, I want to look my best. What do you think?"

"Both gowns are lovely, miss. And you know as well as I that 'tis the woman inside that makes the gown beautiful."

"I suppose . . ."

Jenny folded her arms across her chest. Meredith was

damned lucky to be allowed to attend any society event—even in staid old Bath. True, young ladies often were permitted to hone their social skills in the spa city before later coming out in London, but Meredith was a real hoyden.

Meredith peered at her reflection in the cheval mirror, then whirled around to face Jenny who stood behind her. "I wish I could see them both at the same time." She arched her brows expectantly.

"What do you mean?"

"You and I measure for size more closely than the Brunswick twins. Will you not slip into the saffron gown, then we can both go downstairs to the drawing room and let my aunts choose which is best suited for me."

"Oh, no, I couldn't possibly." Jenny knew she ought to protest more strongly, owing to her position in the household, but goodness, she could barely restrain herself from dashing to the bed and throwing the gown over her head that very moment!

Meredith took Jenny's hands into her own and pushed her bottom lip outward in a pretty pout. "Please, Jenny. For *me*?"

Jenny glanced down at the floor, as if considering the proposition. She counted to ten, for anything less would not be convincing, before returning her gaze to her mistress. "Oh, very well. But only if you explain to your aunts that this was *your* idea, not mine. Wouldn't want to cause trouble with the ladies, you know."

Meredith giggled at that. "What a thing to say, Jenny! You've been part of this household since you were a child. Why, they think of you more as a daughter than a lady's maid. Now, raise your arms for me."

Jenny laughed as Meredith assisted her into the saffron gown. "This exercise will likely all be for naught anyway, for I doubt the gown will fit my form." But of course, she knew it would.

Perfectly in fact.

For more than four days after Mrs. Russell, the modiste, had completed the gown for Meredith, Jenny had secretly sequestered the finery in her own small chamber. Each night she'd withdrawn it carefully from her trunk, eased into it, adding the requisite citrine earbobs and pendant she'd acquired from Smith and Company, then slipped up the stairs to peer by candlelight at her reflection in the cheval mirror.

Meredith tied the lacings off, then stood side by side with Jenny. They both blinked into the mirror with astonishment.

Jenny could not help but stare at her reflection in the cheval glass. In the daylight, the gown emphasized the golden highlights in her ordinary brown hair, and the vibrant greens in her hazel eyes. La, she felt positively regal.

She felt . . . like a lady.

"Oh, Jenny," Meredith gasped. "You're . . . *beautiful*. I mean it. I always thought you were pretty, but . . . just look at you. You look like a princess."

It took Jenny a moment to find her voice. "Well, I don't look like the old Jenny Penny anymore, that's for certain." She gave a small laugh as she turned and dropped a pronounced curtsy to Meredith. "So pleased to meet you, Miss Meredith. I am Lady Genevieve, Countess of Below Stairs."

Meredith laughed, then turned Jenny to face the mirror once more. "You are truly beautiful."

Jenny bowed her head, hoping the ridiculous tears swimming along her lashes would remain in place.

"We must show my aunts. Come!"

"Oh, no, Miss Meredith, I don't think—" But it was too late. Meredith snatched up her hand and within a blink Jenny found herself being whisked down the stair treads to the drawing room.

In any other household, an abigail caught for whatever reason in her lady's clothing might well be dismissed on the spot. But Jenny knew she had little to fear in the Featherton home. No, her employers, two peculiar old spinsters, had as strong a penchant for mischief as their grandniece Meredith, and would surely delight in the diversion of seeing their maid trussed up in a gown of the first cut.

Giggling uncontrollably, Meredith threw open the drawing-room door. "Aunties, may I present my dear friend, Lady Genevieve." With that, she propelled Jenny through the doorway and into the center of the drawing room.

In an instant, Jenny regretted setting foot outside Meredith's chamber. Regretted leaving her bed that morning. For her employers, the grand ladies, Letitia and Viola Featherton, who might have enjoyed Meredith's game under more intimate circumstances, were not alone.

There, standing before Jenny, was a towering, dark-eyed, kilted gentleman. The very same Scot, in fact, whose carriage she had had the audacity to invade only two hours earlier.

Both of the elderly Featherton ladies, who had come to their feet the moment Jenny entered the room, were wearing like expressions of pale shock.

The Scotsman lifted a sardonic brow as he slowly surveyed Jenny from boot to crown.

"My lady," he said, in the deep, dulcet tones of the Highlands. "I am so verra pleased to make yer acquaintance"—amusement played briefly on his lips—"*again.*"

Chapter Two

Jenny couldn't move. Sweet Mary, what was she to do now?

Her gaze lurched from the huge Scotsman and fixed on the drawing room's doorway. There Meredith stood, grinning mischievously.

Why, the young miss was enjoying this! And why shouldn't she? Her clever pranks at Miss Belbury's School for Girls had prompted many a letter from the stern headmistress threatening to pack Meredith in a trunk and set her off for home on the very next mail coach.

Lady Letitia crossed the drawing room and laid her pudgy gloved hand around Jenny's bare arm. "How nice to make your acquaintance *again*, did you say, my lord? No introduction needed then?" The old woman lifted a white brow as she awaited his response.

As Jenny stared blankly at Lady Letitia, she saw an unmistakable gleam in her employer's faded blue eyes. *Oh, no.* She'd seen that look before—whenever the two Featherton sisters were about to stir up a touch of excitement.

The Scotsman abruptly moved closer, his looming presence all but stealing the breath from Jenny's lungs.

"The lady and I met briefly in Milsom Street earlier this afternoon." He paused then, and Jenny could feel his sharp gaze upon her. "It seems she suffered a bout of dizziness and was forced to retire to my carriage until she found her feet again."

There was a wryness to his tone that Jenny didn't quite care for. Surely he realized she was not truly a lady. Just what was he trying to do—see her sacked? She tried to glare at him, but how could she, what with him looking at her so intently?

He was different, this gent. Unlike other highborns in Bath, the Scotsman didn't seem to care a lick about his appearance. He was wearing a kilt for goodness' sake. A kilt! No one wore a kilt in England! No one. Still, he looked damned good in it, what with his long muscular legs.

His shoulders were broad and around his slim waist hung a badger sporran. His dark brown hair was shorn quite fashionably, but pieces hung carelessly about his forehead, brushing his brows and all but commanding her to gaze into his sable-hued eyes. Even Jenny had to admit, he carried off the rugged look quite well.

Lady Viola lifted her ebony walking stick, plunged it into the Aubusson carpet, and aimed her frail body in Jenny's direction.

The sudden movement forced Jenny to recall her predicament. And remember it, she did. It was all she could do not to groan as the old woman moved beside her and wrapped her thin, knobby fingers around her other arm.

And there Jenny was, trapped between her employers in the most horrid situation she could ever imagine.

"Dear, did you suffer a spell?" Lady Viola asked her

with genuine concern, but before Jenny could answer, the old woman looked to the Scotsman. "I, myself, suffer from spells of a sort. But I must own, since I've begun taking the waters at the Pump Room, and soaking in the baths, my health has greatly improved."

"Indeed it has, Sister. My gout has all but disappeared as well." Lady Letitia leveled an amused gaze at Jenny. "Mayhap *Lady Genevieve* should join us when next we visit the baths?" She widened her eyes at her sister Viola, then tipped her head toward Jenny, as if she believed no one would notice.

Lady Viola did not miss her cue. "Oh, pray, do forgive us, my lord. Whether or not you and the *lady* have met, a formal introduction is due." She cleared her throat, and glanced nervously past Jenny at her sister Letitia.

"Lady Genevieve," she began in a quivering tone, "may I present Callum Campbell, Sixth Viscount of Argyll."

Jenny blinked. She was just introduced as *Lady Genevieve*. My heavens! Did they actually think they were going to get away with this? There was no conceivable way he was ever going to believe that she was a real—

"Lady Genevieve," the Scotsman said. "I am charmed."

Good heavens.

As the viscount bent in a low bow, Jenny noticed the hem of his kilt rise several inches in the back and couldn't help but wonder if what one of the scullery maids told her about Scotsmen and their kilts was true.

Jenny looked up and as her eyes met Lord Argyll's

penetrating gaze, her mind went utterly blank. Just what did one say to a viscount anyway?

Just then, she felt Letitia's firm elbow in her side. "Curtsy, gel."

"O-oh, quite right," Jenny muttered as she dropped a perfectly serviceable curtsy.

Lady Letitia quickly slapped a plaster on Jenny's social gaffe. "Lady Genevieve is a dear friend of Meredith's . . . from Miss Belbury's school. Although she is some years older, she took our dear Meredith under her wing immediately and for that Sister and I are forever grateful."

An amused giggle came from Meredith's direction, earning her a reproachful gaze and a finger-summons from her great-aunt Letitia. "This young rapscallion would be my grandniece and charge, Miss Meredith Merriweather."

Meredith slunk into the room and sank into a half-hearted curtsy. "Good afternoon, my lord."

Jenny fixed her gaze on her shoes. Lud, the lies were mounting so quickly she was not at all certain she could remember them all. Why were the ladies doing this? It made no sense at all.

"I am pleased to have made yer acquaintance, ladies, but I fear I have other business to attend to this day." Lord Argyll tipped his head at Jenny and Meredith.

Finally, Jenny sighed inwardly, more relieved than anyone would ever believe. The Scotsman was leaving and this wretched game of her dotty employers would be over for good.

"Mayhap we shall meet again . . . at the ball this eve?"

"Of course you shall, my lord. We've been anxiously

awaiting the Fire and Ice Ball for some weeks now."
Lady Letitia looked straight at Jenny. "*All* of us."

Jenny felt her eyes bulge in their sockets and she half
feared they would burst from her head. "But I cannot—"

"Decide which gown to wear?" Lady Viola interrupted. She patted Jenny's arm reassuringly. "Pish posh.
No need to think on it any longer. The saffron gown is
perfect."

As the manservant, Mr. Edgar, entered the room and
saw Jenny, his wild gray eyebrows shot toward his hairline. But somehow, he remained otherwise unaffected
by her surprising appearance in the drawing room, and
solemnly handed Lord Argyll his hat.

"Do you not agree that the gown is beautiful, kind
sir?" Lady Letitia asked as she gestured to Jenny. "Lady
Genevieve appears undecided."

Lord Argyll studied Jenny then, taking in every detail
of the gown, then a slow smile eased its way over his
lips. "A more flattering gown ye'll never find, Lady
Genevieve."

Suddenly Jenny felt a warm fluttering in her middle
and a blush swept her cheeks. She gazed up coquettishly
through her lashes. "Oh, surely you jest, my lord."

But at her words, meant only to glean another com-
pliment, the viscount glowered at her. "I assure ye, my
lady, I never speak *anything* but the truth. You may take
my words as gospel."

Jenny was stunned by the sheer strength of his response. "Oh! I—I beg your pardon, my lord. I only
meant—"

"I agree with Lord Argyll," twittered Lady Viola.
"The gown suits you perfectly. I vow you and young
Meredith will be the talk of the ball."

No doubt, Jenny thought. Jenny Penny, lady's maid, mingling with the *ton* at the Fire and Ice Ball at the Upper Assembly Rooms. That alone will send the *ton* into an uproar. Still, she had to own, she was exceedingly excited by the prospect.

Over the next few minutes, Jenny paid little attention to the ensuing conversation. For if the ladies were serious about allowing her to go to the ball—and of course they were, for such an exploit was just the sort of thing that sent their blood racing—Jenny had a bucket full of preparation awaiting her.

Her knees wobbled beneath her flowing skirts in anticipation. Oh, how she longed to rush below stairs and begin her toilet.

She'd bring the gold-shot tapestry reticule, of course. Oh, and she had to wear the red satin mules with the marigold trim. She smiled at the thought. There were lovely, and surely the most voguish shoes she'd ever possessed.

But then her smile tightened into a grimace. What was she thinking? It was a ball, for heaven's sake. One cannot wear mules for dancing!

She knew this from experience, for one eve she'd tried dancing in them in her chamber. Within three steps, one mule flew from her foot and slugged that awful scullery maid, Erma, in the head. Didn't really hurt her though, and besides, it was her own bloody fault. Had she knocked before entering, she might have spared herself the goose egg on her noggin.

So no mules—she'd have to wear slippers. But the only pair she owned were castoffs from Meredith's oldest sister, Eliza. They were adequate, of course, but they did nothing to set off the fine saffron gown.

Jenny chewed her lip. If the viscount would be good enough to *leave*, perhaps she'd have a few moments to slip into one of the shoemaker shops.

At the sound of a masculine chuckle, Jenny broke from her musings and looked up to find Lord Argyll eyeing her. "I see I am delayin' the ladies from their ball preparations."

"Oh, no, my lord," Lady Viola protested.

And though the Featherton ladies tried in earnest to persuade Lord Argyll to extend his visit, he bid them all farewell and disappeared through the doorway to the street.

Jenny for one was pleased the handsome Scot was gone. He was right, she had much to do. The first of which was slip back into her work clothes so she could begin to dress Meredith, a task she dreaded, for when it came to clothing selection, the young miss was habitually unable to make up her mind. With an audible sigh, she turned her gaze upon Meredith, who had just hiked her hem to her knees and raced to the front window to watch the viscount board his town carriage.

With a squeal of delight, Meredith whirled around, her face positively aglow. "Jenny is truly coming with us to the ball?"

A mischievous grin lifted the whole of Lady Letitia's face. "Indeed she is. Did you not see the way Lord Argyll looked at her? He was smitten with Jenny, I tell you."

Jenny felt the pads of her ears heating. "If the viscount was smitten, as you suggest, my lady, it was by *Lady Genevieve*—and she does not exist. Had I walked into the drawing room as myself, Jenny Penny the lady's maid, he would not have paid any heed."

Lady Viola shook her head. "No, no. His attraction was clear and I daresay, so was yours, Jenny."

Jenny felt her cheeks grow hot. *Her* attraction? What was she talking about?

Lady Letitia leaned forward. "You do fancy Lord Argyll, gel?"

Looking up, Jenny met her employer's gaze. *Oh, no.* She'd watched the two old ladies turn the household upside down when they'd gotten it into their heads to find matches for Meredith's older sisters. Is this what they had in mind for *her*? *How intriguing.* "He is every woman's dream."

"But is he *your* dream, Jenny?" Lady Viola awaited her answer with bated breath.

"Oh, yes. *Of course*," Jenny muttered softly. *If saying so gets me to the ball this eve.*

Lady Viola beamed. "So, Cupid's arrow has been drawn from the quiver. But you are right, dove. The difference in your stations is great, and being a peer, I fear he mightn't allow himself the opportunity to know a gel in service."

A look of worry fell over Meredith's eyes. "She's right, Aunt Letitia. Once he knows who Jenny really is, he won't wish to court her. He'll never see past her apron and know the true woman inside."

Pausing, Lady Letitia considered Meredith's words, then her round face brightened like a beacon. "The solution is simple. We do not reveal Jenny's true identity until we are sure she's snared the Highlander's heart."

Jenny looked helplessly from one Featherton lady to the other. There was no way she could maintain a masquerade of this sort for more than one eve. "Please do not think me ungrateful, my ladies, but have I no say in this?"

Lady Letitia took her hand and squeezed it. "You want to go to the ball, Jenny. I can see it sparkling in your eyes."

Of course, she longed to attend the ball—to be a real lady and live the life she'd always dreamed of, but this matchmaking scheme of theirs was insane. She raised her eyes to her employer. "Perhaps for one night. Beyond that—"

Lady Viola broke in. "Beyond that will be up to Cupid." She glanced at Letitia, and the two old ladies began to giggle excitedly.

Jenny gave a worried look to Meredith.

"Don't fret, Jenny. I'll help. Just follow my lead and you'll be fine." Meredith smiled hopefully at Jenny, then hugged her aunt Letitia. "Such fun this will be, Aunties—but you both are *mad*. Mad I tell you! That's why I love you so much."

Yes, the two old ladies were mad if they thought they could pull this off, Jenny silently agreed.

But out of this night's folly . . . a lady would emerge.

No sooner had Jenny removed the glorious saffron gown and had begun to dig through her bedside table for the earbobs she intended to wear than her summons bell jingled on its iron coil.

"Oh, perdition," she murmured as she wriggled into her black service gown and stuffed her hair beneath a white cotton cap. "I have a ball to prepare for, and those ladies well know it."

Stealing a glance at her image in the small oval looking glass sitting on her table, she raced up the stairs only to be stopped by her mother, the Feathertons' housekeeper.

"Go back down and fetch your sewin' basket, Jenny. The Widow McCarthy popped by to visit the ladies and snagged her hem on the step."

Jenny narrowed her eyes. "And she wants me to mend it? Why can't she go home and have her own girl have a go at it? Haven't I got enough to do this day?"

Her mother glared back at her. "Look at you all high and mighty today." She flicked her fingers outward. "'Tisn't up to you to question Lady Letitia's directives. So go on. Hurry now. It doesn't take much to get the widow's ire up, and every moment you delay will make it that much worse for you."

With a huff, Jenny returned to her small, windowless chamber for her sewing basket and scampered back up the stairway. When she entered the drawing room, the twig-thin widow, who appeared not more than ten years older than herself, rudely snapped her fingers at her.

"Here, gel. The hem."

Jenny nodded and turned for the footstool, but the young widow reached out with her clawed fingers, clutched her apron, and reeled her close.

"Haven't got all day. Just kneel down and mend it."

From the corner of her eye, Jenny saw Lady Letitia snarl and open her mouth to speak, but Lady Viola, her countenance pinched in a worried look, shook her head vehemently and her employer said nothing. *Too bad*, Jenny thought. *The crow really deserves to be knocked down a few steps.*

Ignoring Jenny completely, the widow resumed the

conversation. "So why is the viscount in Bath? I mean, a Scottish viscount, *here*. It's not an everyday occurrence, is it now?"

Lady Viola appeared even more unnerved by this comment and looked to her more courageous sister for a response.

"He did not say," Lady Letitia began. "His mother was a relation, and we cared for her for a time in her youth. His visit to us was purely obligatory, I assure you."

Jenny glanced over at Lady Viola, and saw her release her pent-up breath. Now that was interesting. There was something they weren't saying. Maybe even *hiding*.

Well, soon enough she'd get to the truth of it all. It would be like a little mystery. What sport!

"Perhaps he's come to Bath for a wife," the widow offered as a pleased smile stretched her tight lips. "He's quite handsome, isn't he? At least, he appeared so from what I saw through my window. Rich is he?"

Neither Featherton responded, only stared back at the widow in shock.

Well, blow me down. The widow must have buried her husband as half a man, for she certainly had his stones today. Even Jenny knew such a direct question was entirely inappropriate and, not to mention, ridiculously stupid. For goodness' sake, didn't she see his sleek town carriage? Of course he had money. One didn't come across a carriage like that every day.

Just a few more stitches and she'd be done. Pity. It was quite diverting to sit here, invisible as air, and listen in on *ton* gossip. Jenny slowed her needle's movement to a snail's pace.

Then the widow started up again, in that whistling nasal voice of hers. "You'd tell me if he was, searching for a wife I mean. Charles, God rest his soul, has been gone for two years now. 'Tis about time I reentered the marriage mart, wouldn't you say? And Lord Argyll, well, a lady could do far worse. *Ouch!*"

Jenny looked down and saw her needle protruding from the widow's ankle. *Lord have mercy.* In one swift movement, she pried it out.

"Ouch! You stupid girl!" the widow howled. "You've stabbed me, and now I've got blood on my new stocking."

Lady Letitia wrenched Jenny to her feet, then yanked her behind her. "Of course I will reimburse you for your stockings. 'Twas just an accident."

"An accident? A scratch might be an accident. A poke. But half the needle's length was in my ankle!"

"Oh, no, madam. 'Twas only a quarter of an inch at most." Jenny produced the needle. "See, the blood only goes up to *here*."

"Dear me! Below stairs, Jenny. Quickly now," Lady Viola whispered.

Jenny nodded. "Truly, I didn't mean—"

"*Now*, gel," Lady Letitia ordered.

"Yes, my lady." Jenny disappeared into the passage and started down the stairs.

She really hadn't meant to jab her. At least . . . she didn't *think* she meant to. But what right did that old bat have to put her claim on *her* viscount?

After all, she saw him first—and he was her voucher to the ball!

Dressed in Meredith's glowing saffron ball gown, Jenny strode through the kitchen on her way to her mother's chambers. Two scullery maids snickered as she passed them by.

"Look at the fine lady. Off to the ball, she is, like one of the Quality," Erma, the younger of the two, announced loudly so that anyone below stairs might hear.

"Thinks she's better, she does. But she ain't. She mightn't have grime under her nails, but she's as low-born and coarse as the rest of us." The two maids chuckled at that.

Jenny stilled her step, but did not turn around to face them. She wouldn't let them rile her. She was a lady after all and as such was above such petty remarks.

Straightening her shoulders she rounded the corner and entered her mother's chamber.

Her mother, who was sitting in her worn tufted chair before the low fire, looked up as Jenny opened the door.

Jenny grinned and raised her arms outward as she spun around in a joyous circle, allowing the dress's full skirts to lift with the momentum, before drifting gently down to her sides once more.

But instead of smiling with pride, as Jenny had expected, her mother only frowned, then set back to plunging her needle into the crisp linen napkin on her lap.

"Mama? How do I look?"

Her mother exhaled but did not look up. "You know very well. You look ridiculous in that gown."

"W-what?" Jenny shook slightly at this. "I thought you would be happy for me. Tonight my dream is coming true."

Then she turned her reddened eyes upward.

"Thought I'd be happy? *Happy?* You are making a fool of yourself, child. Why, all of below stairs is abuzz about it. Why can't you let this dream die, child? Why can't you accept your lot in life—you are a lady's maid. 'Tis a coveted position in service. You should be proud. 'Tis nothing to be ashamed of!"

Jenny shook her head as she walked to her mother and knelt down. "Mama, I am grateful for everything. And I am not ashamed of being in service. But you are right. I am not content. I want more. I deserve more."

Two burning dots appeared on her mother's pallid cheeks. "Because of your father's position in society? Bah! Jen, you are not of his ilk. You are in service and the sooner you come to accept this, the better off you will be."

Jenny rose slowly and moved to the small wooden box sitting on the bedside table. Opening it, she removed a gleaming opal brooch and turned back around.

"Oh, *no*," her mother exclaimed, leaping up from the chair. She snatched the brooch roughly from Jenny's hand. "You're not wearing it this eve."

Jenny bristled. "But my father gave it to me."

"Which is exactly why you are not going to wear it. I'll not have it said I encouraged your nonsense. I won't!"

Heat collected in the corners of Jenny's eyes, and she spun around and raced for the door, but when she reached it, she looked back over her shoulder. "'Tis only for one night, Mother. You needn't worry. By morn my dream will be ended and I will be simple Jenny Penny, the lady's maid, once more."

The short distance to her chamber never seemed so great. She sat down on her narrow bed carefully, so as not to crush the gown, and waited in silence for her summons above stairs.

When the great clock in the upper passage finally toned the hour, Jenny quietly gathered up her pelisse and reticule and met the Feathertons and Meredith in the entry hall.

As the Feathertons' town carriage ambled across the hill toward the Upper Assembly Rooms, Jenny watched her breath crystallize in the cold air. She drew her pelisse close over her shoulders. She should have worn something warmer, more appropriate to the weather, but the pelisse, trimmed with a bit of the whitest ermine, was the more stylish wrap of the two she owned.

Meredith, on the other hand, had insisted on wearing a horrid wool shawl, more determined to remain toasty warm than to be fashionable.

Chattering excitedly with her sister about the evening's grand possibilities, Lady Letitia sat directly across from Jenny, her gout-plumped feet resting on the only brazier in the carriage. Jenny kicked off her shoes and slipped her stocking-wrapped toes forward to steal a little warmth, but guilt got the better of her. The whole reason they were in Bath was to soften the effects of her employer's gout, and she knew she should not begrudge the old lady her comfort.

Spying Jenny's outstretched toes, Meredith nudged Jenny in the ribs. "Put your slippers back on, Jenny. You're a lady tonight, remember?" she whispered to her.

Jenny hurriedly shoved her feet back into her slippers, before either of the prattling matchmakers took notice, then glanced about the cab in an effort to distract herself from a growing case of nerves. She'd ridden in the conveyance before, but tonight it was as if she were seeing it for the first time. The walls were green, but devoid of ornamentation, and the leather squabs were hard. No doubt stuffed with straw. Such a contrast to Lord Argyll's plush town carriage.

Instantly her mind centered on the handsome Scotsman, who she was sure would ask her to dance. This unnerved her more than a little for she only knew three or four dances, and those were of the country variety that she learned on the arm of dear old Mr. Edgar. She had not a clue what sort of dances the Quality of Bath would prefer and at this moment, she wanted to not think about it. Lord above, she had to concentrate on gathering her courage just to walk through the door of the grand Upper Assembly Rooms.

"Now, Jenny, all of Bath society will be mingling at this event. Do take care to avoid drawing undue attention to yourself. A lady is demure, her movements graceful and understated. Do you understand, gel?" Lady Letitia leaned forward and seemed to rest her heft atop her large, pillowy bosom as she awaited Jenny's reply.

"Oh, heavens, Sister," Lady Viola quipped, "Jenny has been living in our home for years and has no doubt had opportunity to observe the two of us. Of course she understands." She blinked her round watery blue eyes at Jenny. "Don't you, dear?"

"Yes, of course, my lady." Jenny lowered her gaze as she delicately folded her hands atop her lap. For she could not meet either of the old womens' eyes as the coming lie unfurled from her tongue. "I've already decided to fashion myself . . . I mean, Lady Genevieve, in the gracious image of the two of you." Rather apprehensively, she raised her eyes.

Both of the Feathertons grinned broadly.

"Oh, please," Meredith murmured, but thankfully for Jenny, neither of her great-aunts seemed to hear her.

The carriage pulled to a jerked halt, thrusting Jenny forward and sending her beaded reticule to the floor. She leaned down to retrieve it and as she did, the carriage door opened and the footman extended his hand.

Oh, goodness. She wasn't ready! How could she ever imagine she could play a lady true? Jenny's startled gaze flew to Lady Viola, who rose, took the footman's hand, and climbed out of the carriage into the night. Lady Letitia and Meredith followed, and soon Jenny found herself shakily lifting her gown to carefully walk through the ice-encrusted mud toward the door of the Upper Assembly Rooms.

She should have thought to wear pattens to raise and protect her shoes, for no matter how carefully she proceeded, flecks of wet earth splattered upon her slippers and they would never, ever be the same. But such was the price of fashion.

As they passed through the columned doorway, Jenny removed her pelisse and looked about for a coat hook.

Lady Viola winced at this. Taking Jenny's upper arm in her hand, she guided her to the crew of awaiting footmen who were collecting wraps from ladies and gentlemen as they entered.

Oh, of course. How stupid of her, Jenny chided. If this ruse was going to work, she had to remember to think and act like a lady, not a coarse maid.

Jenny squinted in the bright light. Even in the column-ringed octagonal entrance hall candles were not to be spared. A great crowd of people momentarily mingled as they converged in this space, before passing through the double doors and disappearing into the grand ballroom.

Lud, who'd have thought there would be so many gentry in all of Bath—or even all of London!

Lady Viola tightened her grip on Jenny's arm for support and guided her in the direction of the ballroom. Jenny could scarce stop her head from swiveling as she gaped at the grand decor, the voguish fashions—and some pitifully dated gowns as well—and enviable glittering earbobs.

Then suddenly, through the doorway of the card room, she spied none other than Lord Argyll. As if she'd called his name, he caught her gaze and smiled warmly. A nervous flutter battered about Jenny's insides as she watched him turn and walk toward them.

But then, her party entered the ballroom, and he was gone from her sight.

Huge glittering crystal chandeliers, the like Jenny had never seen or even imagined, dominated the ballroom. *My word.* She gulped down the swell of emotion rising in her throat as her eyes began to sting with tears. *I am standing in a real ballroom.* She looked over her shoulder as they moved deeper into the assembly room, and noticed that over the doorway was a wide balcony set into the wall, and in it eleven musicians overlooked the massive ballroom. Around the perimeter were two rows of cushioned settees filled with older madams and gents, while stretches of wooden benches provided respite for giggling young ladies and their beaus.

Yards of pale blue and silver silk swathes were

draped from the ceilings and across the high narrow windows, making her feel as though she were in a magical land where anything was possible.

But for her, it already seemed as if anything was. For she was standing in the ballroom of the Upper Assembly Rooms, waiting for a handsome viscount to lead her in dance.

Lady Viola released her arm at last, and Jenny began to turn in a circle to take in the stunning grandeur of the ballroom, when suddenly she felt her hand brush something warm and furry. In her confusion, her fingers, of their own accord, instinctively gripped and prodded the fur.

She whirled around completely and found herself facing Lord Argyll, who was dressed most handsomely, but very unfashionably, in a coat, kilt, and—*oh, heavens*—a blasted fur sporran that hung centered over his—*no, it can't be.*

No.

Please, someone tell me I didn't just brush my hand over his sporran. Over his—

Heat filled Jenny's cheeks and she squeezed her eyes shut.

"Good eve, Lady Genevieve." And then he leaned close and his deep voice buzzed in her ear. "Surprisin' how soft badger can be, aye?"

Chapter Three

How mortifying! Had anyone seen what she had done? Seen her grip his . . . *sporran*?

"Oh, Lord Argyll," Lady Letitia twittered. "How lovely that you found us."

Jenny felt a row of bony fingers on her upper arm, holding her in place and preventing her from dashing from the ballroom. "Why, Lady Genevieve was just commenting on how much she would desire to dance and here you are. How fortuitous."

The Scotsman arched a dark brow. "I've never been one for proper dancin', but fer ye, Lady Genevieve, I would be pleased to make an exception." He offered up his muscular arm and without thinking, Jenny instinctively took it.

Blast! What was she doing? *Surely I will be found out the moment the music begins.*

But then, the violinist set free his song and to Jenny's delight, couples took to the floor for a country dance. Why, glory be, she actually knew this one!

Jenny beamed at Lord Argyll, then turned as they waited for the right count to begin and let her eye wander the great room.

Heavens. Was it her imagination, or was every high-browed eye focused on her?

She tried to follow the visual path of one particularly bug-eyed miss. Why, it almost looked like the chit was gazing at Lord Argyll—and not at her at all.

Jenny glanced appraisingly at her dance partner. Oh . . . of course! Everyone was likely focusing on Argyll's shocking kilt.

And then the viscount took her hands and drew her forward down the line. Together they whirled in a circle, sending her hem, and heaven forbid, *his* as well, flaring up behind them.

The brows of several matrons slammed the upper rims of their dowdy turbans. Still, their interested gazes trailed the handsome Scot down the column again, as wry smiles budded on their lips.

Jenny smiled too, her keen imagination creating what her own eyes had not the fortune to see.

Gads, dancing was enjoyable. She should do it more often. Why on earth had she worried so? The steps were the same as those she danced below stairs, on the off occasion that Mr. Edgar approved any sort of celebration —which wasn't often, what with all the work piling up the minute anyone looked away for an instant. Jenny watched the other young ladies demurely twirl and dance through the archway of arms.

Obviously she needn't have worried at all. Why, were she to cast judgment, she would have to say that her skill was far superior to those studied in the art of dance. Their movements seemed so restrained, so staid, compared to her own. Lud, they weren't even smiling!

Well, their loss, Jenny decided as she kicked up her

heels gaily and raced forward to pass beneath the bridge of clasped hands.

Even Lord Argyll noticed her natural affinity for dance. She could see it in his eyes and his amused grin. *They* were having fun, and isn't that what dancing was all about?

But then, the music ended. Drat it all. And here she was, just beginning to truly enjoy herself.

Lord Argyll raised his forearm to her. A broad smile still lingered on his lips and playfulness she hadn't seen before lit his eyes. "Shall we return to yer duennas?"

"If we must." A sigh fell from her lips as he guided her to the Featherton ladies.

Blast the rules. She desperately wanted to dance again. "I do hope you will ask me to dance another time, Lord Argyll. I own, we make a fine pair. Did you see everyone watching us?"

The corner of his mouth twitched the very moment they rejoined the Feathertons and Meredith at the perimeter of the dance floor. "I did indeed, my lady."

"And I don't think it had to do with you not wearing anything under your kilt either," Jenny added matter-of-factly.

"Oh, my heavens!" Lady Viola wavered and leaned against her sister. "*Spell . . .*"

Lord Argyll, appearing somewhat startled, assisted Lady Letitia in dragging the frail old woman into a chair along the wall.

Meredith dashed forward and snared Jenny's arm. "Come with me, please."

"What? Is something wrong?" Jenny asked as Meredith hauled her through the wide doorway into the octagonal foyer.

"Jenny, you simply can't mention things like men's under things . . . or lack of them . . . in proper company."

"Oooh, I see. Well, you're quite right." Jenny nodded her head. "But I don't think anyone, save your aunts perhaps, noticed my slip, do you?"

Meredith's eyes widened and she held her breath for a moment. "Oh, surely not. 'Twas likely just me. Still, I thought it worth a mention."

"What did you think of my dancing? I've had no proper training, mind you, but I thought I did quite well."

"Yes, your dancing was very . . . uh . . . *enthusiastic*," Meredith stammered.

Jenny grinned appreciatively. "Why thank you, Miss Meredith."

As the two young ladies slipped back into the assembly room, Jenny noted with some shock that their neighbor, Lady McCarthy, blocked the only pathway back to the Feathertons and Lord Argyll.

The widow showed her teeth as she recognized Miss Meredith and moved forward to greet her.

Oh, perdition. Jenny's breath snagged in her throat. For certain she would be recognized! 'Twas not more than four hours since she'd been summoned above stairs to mend the widow's loose hem. Four measly hours! Why, 'twas not even enough time for her needle stab wound to crust over!

As Meredith and Lady McCarthy exchanged pleasantries, Jenny averted her face and affixed her widened eyes to the floor. Lud, she had to get out of here. She lifted her eyes a smidge and sought out the double doorway. But then the widow's attention was upon her.

"Miss Meredith, would you do me the great honor of introducing me to your companion?" the widow asked. "I do not believe I've had the pleasure."

Jenny looked up and shot Meredith a horrified gaze.

Meredith appeared somewhat confused by the blatant look of alarm on Jenny's face and it was several seconds before she could summon her voice. "Uh, Lady McCarthy, this is my dear friend—"

"From Miss Belbury's School," Jenny blurted.

". . . Yes, from school, Lady Genevieve d'en Bas."

Jenny stared into the woman's eyes, so frightened that it took a nudge from Meredith to remind her to drop the widow a curtsy. "Madam."

"Charmed." Then the woman studied her for several overlong moments. "Lady Genevieve, have you been in Bath long? I have the distinct impression we have crossed paths."

Jenny was aghast.

Thankfully though, Lady Letitia had taken notice of the potential problem and was charging forward to take matters in hand. "Oh, good eve, Lady McCarthy. I see you have met Lady Genevieve. But I do beg your pardon. My sister has succumbed to a spell and I have come to fetch the young lady to her side. Do excuse us, please."

Jenny grinned. Lady Letitia was ever so brilliant, for the next thing Jenny knew, she was being pulled quickly away from the overly curious widow, leaving Miss Meredith behind as a distraction.

Meeting the widow could have been a complete disaster, save for her quite convincing performance as the refined Lady Genevieve. But it wasn't *really* a performance, now was it? Had her father placed a ring on her mother's finger, she *would* be Lady Genevieve. Not a cowering imposter, but a lady true.

Lady Letitia led the way, at a rapid clip, toward her sister and Lord Argyll. But not so fast that Jenny could not catch a snippet of conversation between the two matrons they were passing.

"A kilt! Can you believe the nerve of that Scotsman? Why, his father would turn over in his crypt if he had any idea of what the current Lord Argyll is about."

Jenny stopped midstride and turned to look at the two starched matrons. *What the current Lord Argyll is about? Another piece of the mystery, is it then?*

Lady Letitia jerked her arm and urged her onward.

"Did you hear what they said, my lady?" Jenny asked. "What do you think they meant?"

"Oh, I'm sure I don't know. Nothing probably. The viscount's kilt is causing a bit of a stir, but I see nothing improper. Just Bath gossip, I expect. One needs something diverting now and again to keep madness at bay in this sleepy little town."

Jenny grinned at that. At least to her way of thinking, the Scottish viscount was a most welcome diversion.

Barely a moment after returning and seeing Lady Viola fully herself again, Jenny found her arm atop Lord Argyll's and headed for the dance floor once more.

A waltz was called. Jenny could scarce believe it. A waltz in staid old Bath. And she had not an inkling how to begin. "I—I haven't permission to dance the waltz," she blurted.

Lord Argyll only chuckled at that. "Since when have ye fashed about obtainin' permission to do anything?"

Oh. Of course. The carriage incident. A little smile lifted her lips. "Now, now, my lord. You do not know me so very well as to make such a sweeping and, dare I say, ungentlemanly comment. One might take you for a rake."

"Several have." He lifted a brow as if waiting for her reaction.

"Have they?" An admitted rake, was he? A real lady would consider walking from the floor immediately. But for some reason, his admission of being less than a gentleman intrigued her all the more. In fact, it made her belly do a little flip. "Well, I definitely should not dance the waltz with a known rake."

"'Tis not as if the Upper Assembly Room is Almack's." With that, he pulled her into his arms as the music filled her ears.

A shiver of pleasure raced southward, as his hand slid around her, rested in the middle of her back, and they began to move together. *La, the waltz is wonderful!*

Still, she could certainly see why permission should be obtained. Why, she was a woman of three and twenty, and her sensibilities were positively aloft.

But who could blame her? Lud, here she was in a handsome, tall Scotsman's arms, feeling his kilt brush against a place that would make a fresh-faced debutante blush. Knowing that between her and his . . . sporran was naught but one delicate layer of paper-thin silk and one of threadbare cotton. Heat suffused her cheeks, and elsewhere as well, at the decadent thought.

"But I have not danced the waltz before."

"Och, dinna fash. Ye are doin' quite weel. Just hold on to me and let me lead ye where I might."

Jenny nodded dumbly and tightened her hold on his muscled upper arm. *Criminy*. Even through his coat, it felt as hard and thick as a fire log.

As he whirled her around the floor, she lifted her chin and peered upward, surprised when she met his heated gaze. But she did not look away. Instead, she plunged into those warm eyes, as deep and brown as the mouth of a river in spring. And there she swam, as the music played on, barely aware of the crowd ringing the dance floor, blurring and fading until there was nothing but him, and her.

And sensation. Her body was highly aware of every place that his body touched.

"Ye're beautiful," he told her in the honeyed tones of the Highlands.

"You're a rake."

"Aye, I am. But I dinna lie." His eyes were smoldering. "*Ever.*"

Blood raised into her cheeks, heating them.

"'Tis our last dance. Another would declare more than I intend—right now."

Jenny pinned him with her gaze. *Right now?* Just what did he mean by that? But since he seemed to be waiting for her to respond, she nodded. She must look like an idiot to him. Always bobbin' her head up and down. How she wished she knew what else to do—what to say! She was so clearly out of her element here.

"So when might I call?"

"C-call?" she stammered.

"Aye. If ye'll be remainin' in Bath a wee bit longer."

"Oh." Jenny frantically searched the ballroom for the Featherton ladies. This was only to be for one night. *One.* She could never maintain this ruse for more than a few hours—could she?

But Jupiter he was handsome. Why just the sight of him made her belly swoop and her legs quiver like quince jelly. Still, he was a rake. A rake who, for some reason, fancied *her*.

To what end though? She had to concede that it was entirely possible that he saw through her guise—saw her for the servant girl she truly was. Worry plummeted into the pit of her stomach and sat there as heavily as a wedge of Cook's foul Candlemas cake. He likely thought her a light skirt, one with whom he could take his bodily pleasure, then walk away without thinking nary a thought.

Like her father had done with her mother.

Bah! What was she thinking? This was too ridiculous.

Besides, she reasoned, after this eve the ladies would have had their fun, and the novelty of dressing her up like a princess and sending her off to the ball to meet the handsome prince—err . . . *viscount*—would surely have lost its sheen.

Oh, perdition. She didn't want this dream of being a proper lady to end! This is what she was *born* to. A grand lady was who she was meant to be.

Then, quite suddenly, Lord Argyll's expression changed. The cocky roguish grin was gone. "Fergive me, my lady. I've fergotten me place."

What? What is he going on about now? He's done nothing wrong. Or am I too coarse to realize it? Best feign displeasure. Yes, that's it. Jenny screwed up her features until she felt she had attained a fair approximation of being appalled.

But the corner of the viscount's mouth twitched, leaving Jenny to wonder if he'd figured her out.

"I should have asked yer duennas fer permission to call on ye."

Yes. *Yes!* If he asked the ladies—showed a bit of interest in her—then perhaps they might consider allowing the game to continue . . . for a short time anyway.

She smiled brightly up at him. "I should very much like an interview. But of course, the decision is *entirely* up to the Featherton ladies. My future is in their capable hands."

Criminy, if he only knew how true that statement was.

As the music ended, and Lord Argyll, the *gorgeous* Lord Argyll, escorted her back to the Feathertons and Meredith, Jenny's heart pounded louder than the kettledrum in the orchestra.

Oh, please, *please*, grant his request, she chanted inside her head, as if doing so could mentally compel the two dotty old ladies to bend to her will.

But as they reached the fold, Meredith snatched up Jenny's hand and hauled her several steps away. Jenny stared back as Argyll began to speak to the ladies Letitia and Viola.

No, *no!* She wouldn't be able to hear anything from where they were now standing. She looked longingly toward the Feathertons and Argyll.

"Jenny," Meredith began. "I've spoken with my aunts and, well, you will never believe this but—" She sucked in a breath so deep that even over the murmur of conversation around them Jenny could hear Meredith's corset creak. "They have agreed to allow you to continue on with Lord Argyll."

Jenny narrowed her gaze. "What *exactly* do you mean by that?"

"They see the affection you and the viscount already

have for each other. And lud, you know that matchmaking is their grandest passion in life."

Jenny nodded at that. Their fervor for orchestrating love matches was every bit as consuming as hers for shopping.

"And, well . . ." Meredith's pupils grew impossibly large. "They intend to see the two of you engaged!"

"Did you say . . . well of course you didn't . . . ?" Jenny suddenly felt faint. "*Engaged?*"

"Yes, engaged. Can you imagine what fun this will be?" Meredith bounced on her heels. "But, la, we have so much to do. You have so much to learn. We've already decided that a dance master is first on the list— but only to *refine* your repertoire. And of course, you will need a new wardrobe. At least two or three gowns for evening events, and a walking frock or two . . ."

After the phrase "new wardrobe" Jenny barely heard another word. Well, except the bit about three gowns and a walking frock.

A little tremble of excitement raced through her. Could this really be happening? Was her grandest dream coming true—at least for a short while?

No, surely she *was* dreaming. Of course. As Meredith rambled on, Jenny caught a bit of the flesh inside her cheek between her upper and lower teeth and bit down hard. "Ouch!"

Meredith startled at her outburst. "What is it? Are you well?"

Jenny's lips slid away from her teeth and she beamed back at the girl. "Perfectly."

How could she be otherwise? Somehow, her dream had slipped through the bonds of her imagination and taken solid form.

Still smiling, she turned and caught Lord Argyll's gaze.

"Soon," he mouthed.

Soon, Jenny echoed, and a pleasurable prickle danced across her skin.

The next morning, Jenny sat in the drawing room, waiting impatiently for the two Featherton ladies, who watched her from the settee, to begin. She fidgeted with her mob cap, tucking away a loose curl, then set about smoothing a wrinkle on the sleeve of her gray cambric work dress. It was all she could do not to thrum her fingers on her knee or nervously pick at her nails. But a lady would have more control, and therefore, so must she.

"Jenny, dear," Lady Viola continued softly. "What we are about to undertake is fraught with risk. If you do not follow our instruction to the smallest letter, our project will be at an end. The persona we carefully craft for you will crumble and the lot of us will no doubt be run out of Bath, despite our current standing in society."

"No one, and especially not members of the *ton*, likes to play the fool," Lady Letitia added, somewhat sternly.

Jenny swallowed deeply. "I understand, my lady."

Lady Letitia lifted a brow and stared hard at her. "We are not asking that you understand, gel. You've always been headstrong. We are not blind to the fact that you often see rules as . . . pliable, shall we say?"

"Dear," Lady Viola began, "what Sister is trying to say is that we need your assurance that you will do nothing without our direction."

"That's right, gel. *Nothing*. You are unschooled in the ways of society. What may pass for acceptable on the street or below stairs may draw ridicule from the *ton*."

Jenny nodded. "I understand, my ladies, and I vow to do as you direct." *No matter how bleedin' crazy it might seem*, she added mentally.

Why, they could ask her to attend a ball with a birdcage on her head and she would do it. For without them, her dream of becoming a lady would be just that—a grand, but unreachable dream.

Broad smiles grew on the two Featherton ladies' painted-on lips.

Lady Letitia dislodged her ample bottom from the settee and, with the assistance of her walking stick, came to her feet. "Well then, shall we begin?"

A little glow began to bloom inside Jenny, an energy spreading through her like the wake of a flame. She sprang to her feet. "I am ready." A giggle erupted between her lips. "It's as though I have been preparing for this all my life."

Just then, Meredith entered the drawing room with a massive bundle of dresses, hats, and wraps. When she reached the center of the room, she tossed them into the air and let every last piece cascade to the Aubusson carpet.

"'Tis no use, Aunties," Meredith said forlornly. "I thought at least something would suit Jenny's needs, but nothing does. See for yourself."

The two ladies lifted their brows and peered over their noses to the scattered pile on the floor.

"What about the ruby gown?"

Jenny snatched it up off the floor and examined it.

She wrinkled her brow. "Begging your pardon, my lady, but the cut is for a young girl, not a woman grown."

When the Feathertons exchanged meaningful glances, Jenny quickly amended her words. "But I can remake the gown. Why, all I'd need is a few scraps of sarcenet and a length or two of satin ribbon."

Instantly, Jenny felt Meredith's arm about her waist.

"You are so clever, Jenny. And 'tis a good thing too. You need a serviceable wardrobe quickly, and it will take more time than we have to set a modiste on the task."

Jenny felt her spirits plunge. She'd been daydreaming all morn of exploring the fabric and millinery shops for fashionable swathes of velvet and silk crape, from which she would have made modish gowns of the sort she'd drooled over in *La Belle Assemblée*, and Lady Viola's odd castoff issues of *Ladies Monthly Magazine*.

She looked at Lady Viola then, dressed in the ladies' signature lavender color, but clearly in what was modish at least ten years past! Why, to look at her, you'd never know the old miss studied fashion as carefully as Jenny herself.

The corner of Jenny's mouth lifted as she remembered finding a French magazine jutting from under the settee cushion and suddenly it all made sense. The prim Lady Viola fancied fashionable *underpinnings*. She knew she was right. Had to be. Why, she'd ask her mother about it the first chance she got, since it was she, for some odd reason, who exclusively assisted the lady with her dressing.

Edgar entered the room with a gleaming silver tray just then, and though he kept his eyes focused on Lady Letitia, Jenny felt his cool disapproval of her. It mustn't sit well to see one of his staff lounging with the above stairs crowd, chatting as if she were their equal.

No, she was sure it didn't sit well with *anyone* below stairs. Devil take 'em. Devil take the lot of them.

Her blood was half-blue, was it not? She deserved this chance, more than anyone below stairs. And if anyone challenged her about it, she would tell them so directly. Jenny gave her head a good hard affirmative nod.

When she looked up again, Lady Letitia had lifted her lorgnette before her eyes and was reading the vellum card Edgar had presented her. Her smile grew very broad, and she looked up at Jenny.

"Well now, you made a fine impression on Lord Argyll at the ball, my dear Jenny. He wasted not a moment securing the interview he'd requested. He shall call at four in the afternoon—tomorrow."

Jenny felt a shudder work its way down her body. "Tomorrow?" *Tomorrow*. Good heavens! She had so much yet to do.

Edgar cleared his throat and Jenny was startled to find him standing directly before her, now thrusting the silver salver before her nose. Hesitantly, Jenny lifted the missive from the tray and opened it.

How odd. It was written in Mr. Edgar's own hand. But the scrip was dark, as if written in haste . . . or even—*gads*—anger.

Annie and a footman are waiting below stairs. See to them as soon as you are able.

Jenny glanced sheepishly up at Edgar and gave a quick nod. Something must be dreadfully wrong. Mr.

Edgar didn't usually permit his staff to have visitors. Lud, what was Annie thinking?

"Can you be prepared, Jenny?" Meredith was asking as she lifted the sleeve of the ruby gown Jenny was holding in her lap. "By four tomorrow?"

"Well . . ." She supposed she could repiece the gown into something more modish, and wear it for the viscount's interview.

But it would need something. *Yes*—the garnet buttons. She'd need a bit of cream satin too, or maybe gold ribbon. *Criminy*, she needed to get to the shops, that's what she really needed to do, and in a hurry. Who knew how long it might take her to find just the right accents?

Jenny gave the dress a dubious look, then glanced sidelong at Lady Viola and sighed. "Well, I *might* be able to rework the gown—if I had no other duties this day or on the morrow. But of course, I have so much to do . . . like seeing to Miss Meredith's mending, and the laundry—"

Lady Viola turned her attention to Mr. Edgar, who was staring wide-eyed with thin lips agape at Jenny in all her audacity. "Jenny will be excused from her duties this day and tomorrow, Mr. Edgar. Please see if Mrs. Penny can fill in, and if not, engage a girl from town to assist."

Edgar nodded, then with a chilly parting glance to Jenny, one that made her skin ice over, he turned and left the room.

This was hardly the Edgar she knew and loved. Hardly the man who'd practically raised her alongside her mother. But then, she'd never disrupted his household and staff before either. Why couldn't everyone just be happy for her?

She deserved this chance, by golly. *Deserved* it!

Lady Letitia caught her sister's hand and squeezed it enthusiastically before turning her faded blue eyes on Jenny. "There, 'tis all settled, gel. Off with you now. Got a bit of sewing to do if you are to be ready to receive Argyll tomorrow."

Jenny leapt to her feet. "Thank you, my ladies. Thank you so much!" Not knowing what else to do, she dropped a curtsy to them both, which obviously did not have quite the desired effect for it set the two old ladies into fits of giggles.

Then, she dashed off to the servants' passage and went below stairs to see why Annie had come around.

Chapter Four

"That's right, ducks," Annie excitedly announced to Jenny. "I'll be needin' six gallipots of the tingle cream today, and Horace 'ere, he'll be needin' two."

Jenny was stunned. "But . . . I haven't got any more."

The gleam in Annie's eyes faded. "But I was with you when you bought all the supplies yesterday. Told me you were going to set up the pots that eve."

Jenny's gaze fell to the floor. "I know, but last night . . . well, I went to the Fire and Ice Ball instead and—"

Annie roared with laughter. "Did you now? And which gown did you wear? Your black sack dress, or the brown with the cotton apron? I must say, I hope it was the brown. Sets off the green in your blinkers."

Jenny stared straight into Annie's eyes. "I wore Miss Meredith's saffron silk."

The merriment dissolved from Annie's face at once. "You aren't havin' me on, are you, Jenny?"

"No. Oh, Annie, you can't believe it. Last eve, my grandest dream came true—I became a lady. A *real* lady."

Annie slumped on the stool. "But how?"

Jenny drew up the other stool and told Annie the amazing string of events that led up to that very moment. "So you see, Annie, I only have until tomorrow to remake this gown. I haven't got time to set up any pots tonight either. I am sorry."

Horace, who stood with hat in his hands, shifted his weight from one foot to the other. "But, Jenny, my master sent me to Annie special for the *tingle cream*. I can't go back without it. I just can't."

Jenny laid a gentle hand on his shoulder. "But I haven't got a single pot to spare."

Horace pulled a small leather bag from his waistband. "He gave me a few shiners to pay. See?" He emptied the bag into his palm.

"Yes, but—" Jenny stared at the stacks of gold coins in the footman's hand and a shiver of excitement skimmed her scalp. Why, with Horace's money she could buy all the ribbon and the slip of cream satin she needed to remake the gown.

Horace emptied the coins back in the bag, sighing all the while. "Well, if you haven't got any . . ."

Suddenly she recalled the pot of peppermint facial cream sitting unopened on Lady Letitia's dressing table. The solution was simple. She could *borrow* that one, and replace it with another in a day or so. It's not like there weren't other pots and bottles on the table. Why, her employer would never notice.

A bright smile lit Jenny's face. "On second thought, Horace, I might have just *one* pot left. I'll be back in a tick." With that, she lifted her skirts to her knees, raced up the back stairs, and slipped into Lady Letitia's bedchamber.

Her heart beat loudly in her ears as she stealthily

padded toward the cherry dressing table. Heavens above, if she was caught sneaking around that would certainly be the end of her dream.

Her hand shook like a rain-spattered fern as she reached out for the pot and concealed it in the folds of her cambric work frock.

As she tiptoed back below stairs, guilt pummeled her insides. But, she reasoned, she was doing it for the ladies anyway. If she was not dressed appropriately, the Feathertons' matchmaking game would fail, now wouldn't it?

When she reached the kitchen, she removed the pot from her gown and held it out to him. "Here you go, Horace."

The footman grinned broadly and reached for it, but she snatched her hand back for a moment. "Remember now, *no one* is to know where you bought the cream. Do you understand? It must remain our secret."

"I understand, Jenny. Annie already made me swear on me mum's head—and she's got a cold on her chest just now. So you can rest easy that I won't give you up."

"Very well then." Lifting the pot in her palm, she opened her hand and allowed Horace to take the cream.

"Ah, my thanks, miss. My master will be most pleased . . . as will the mistress." Horace winked then.

Clearing her throat, Jenny lifted her brow and gave a glance to her empty palm, still poised midair before the footman.

"Oh, yeah. 'Ere you go, Jenny."

Her fingers closed around the bag of coins and she smiled to herself. Now she could buy exactly what she needed for the gown. She opened the bag and peered giddily inside. But then she paused a moment in thought, and withdrew a single crown. "Here you go, Horace. Take this, for your mum."

The footman's eyes widened as he accepted the money. "Thank you, miss. Thank you!"

Jenny shrugged. "You earned it. Brought me the business, after all."

Annie folded her arms over her ample chest. "So what about my pots, Jenny? *I* brought you some business too."

"I suppose I'll have to make some more. Tonight, after the ladies are abed," Jenny sighed.

Odsbodikins. The production of the cream would take *hours*.

Jenny sank onto a stool and rested her head in her hands. Lord above, this was going to be a long night.

❦

"Here you are! Get up, Jen. It's already seven, and here you are sleeping the morn away."

Jenny raised her head from the stillroom table and blinked up at her mother, who was staring angrily down at her. "Seven?" Jenny murmured as she stretched her arms above her head and yawned. "Already?"

Her mother thrust several folded notes before her.

Jenny stared blankly down at them. "What are these?"

"You know very well what these are. Snatched them off my lady's morning salver before she could open them!"

Jenny stared down at the addresses and noticed that not a one was intended for her, but rather for Lady Letitia. "What are you thinking, Mother. I can't open Lady Letitia's letters."

"Well you had better, and do something about what's written inside. What if I hadn't been there to take them? What if she'd actually read them?"

With slow deliberation, Jenny opened the first letter, noting that the return direction did seem familiar somehow.

She looked at the heading. Why, it was from Smith and Company. Jenny read on and a sudden cold chill crept over her skin. She looked up with horror at her mother. "It can't be. Oh, no!"

"Again and again I've warned that your excesses will get you into trouble. And now it has. Your unpaid accounts are being sent to your employer for payment. And not just one either. There are two others beneath that."

Jenny looked at the directions on the other letters. "Marbury's Millinery. Oh, dear. Wait a moment. What is this? Darnfield Ironworks?" She looked up, somewhat cockily at her mother. "This one clearly isn't for me. I've never been to the ironworks."

Mrs. Penny snatched the letter from her and tore it open. "One pair of pattens." The rigid words were still in the air when her mother shoved the bill back at her. "*Yours.*"

Pattens? Jenny thought back for a moment and suddenly remembered the days last month when it seemed to rain forever. Why, she ruined two pairs of slippers that week alone. Would have muddied even more than that too, had she not put the pattens on account. "*Oh, now I remember. My mistake.*"

Mrs. Penny folded her arms across her chest. "So

what are you going to do about your debts? I can't stop the notices from reaching the ladies forever, you know."

Pulling a brittle, dried peppermint leaf from her tangled hair, Jenny gestured to the twenty pots sitting at the end of the table and smiled up at her mother. "Simple. I'll sell these and pay off my debt at Smith and Company."

"And why would anyone want your homemade facial cream? Hmm?"

Jenny raised her shoulders and let them fall. "I cannot say. But for some reason, the *ton* is beginning to take to them. They've become quite popular. In fact, thus far, I've been able to sell every pot I've made." *And then some*, Jenny silently added with a little wince, remembering the pot she owed Lady Letitia.

Mrs. Penny lifted a dubious brow. "Then for goodness' sake sell them today, *if* you can, and settle your debts." With that, she turned and stomped from the stillroom.

"Yes, Mother," Jenny droned as she leaned back on the stool, one-handedly gripping the table for balance, and tossed the notices into the smoldering fire.

A thumping at the door drew Jenny's gaze upright again, to where Erma, one of the horrid scullery maids, stood. Her arms were folded across her chest and she was looking down her hatchet-shaped nose at Jenny.

"You've got visitors," she spat, mockingly adding a curtsy to her announcement. "*My lady.*"

Scowling at the maid, Jenny rose and brushed past the wretch.

When Jenny arrived at the kitchen door, she was surprised to find not only Annie, but at least three other abigails and two footmen, all from the finest houses in Bath.

Surely they weren't *all* here for the cream. But then she caught notice of the small bags in their hands. Her heart leapt.

"What's all this about?" Jenny schooled her features and looked to Annie for a reply.

Annie glanced down at her boot, and seemed particularly interested in a long scrape along its edge. "We've come for some cream—if you've got some more, that is."

Catching Annie's arm, Jenny pulled her forward. "What happened to our secret? You've got all of bleedin' Bath standing outside the door!" she whispered in her ear.

"'Twasn't me. I swear. I only told Gretchen here," Annie admitted with a nod to the plump girl with red curls.

Horace edged forward. "I only told Old Tom."

An elderly man made his way forward. "Annie told me that the cost was a half guinea. But I told my master I heard the cream was a guinea. Thought I could pocket a *halfer* for myself."

Jenny exchanged a confused glance with Annie, who waggled her eyebrows at her, urging her to play along.

"I was hopin' to do the same," squeaked Gretchen.

Jenny stiffened. She never really set a price for her cream, but if they could easily get a guinea . . . *Hmm.* Maybe she could ask for— "The pots are one guinea each," she blurted before she had time to think.

There was a collective groan, then the group folded in among itself and Jenny suddenly wondered if she'd asked for too much. In fact, she was about to drop the price to three crowns, when Annie moved to the front of the throng again.

"A guinea it is." But then Annie paused. "*But* you sell the pots only through those in service. And we decide how much we'll sell them for to our masters. Does this work for you, Jenny?"

Jenny bit her lips and sucked them into her mouth to prevent a joyous cry from bubbling out. She nodded, and excused herself to gather up the pots she'd made, taking care to set one aside to replace the pot she'd nicked from Lady Letitia's dressing table. Quickly depositing them into her harvest basket, she hurried back to the door.

An excited giggle slipped from her mouth as Annie exchanged a palmful of guineas for the six pots of cream Jenny owed her. Then she turned to fill the other servants' orders. Only one minute later, her basket was nearly empty—only four spare pots of cream remained—but her hands were full . . . of money.

She was going to be rich. *Rich!* Why, just today, she was making fifteen pounds. It was a fortune!

In no time at all her debts would be paid in full. Soon, shops would open their doors to her again. And with a full purse, the keeps would surely offer her a cup of tea, or sherry, like they did when someone of the Quality entered their establishment. And she would sip her beverage quietly while all the latest fabrics were paraded before her.

Yes, it was all quite clear to her now.

A lady she would be—in her own way. If not through birth, or marriage—for it was ridiculous to believe the Feathertons' scheme to engage the viscount would ever survive the light of day—then by her own hand.

Jenny smiled brightly to herself, quite liking the notion.

Jenny opened her bedside table drawer and fished inside for her gloves. Instead she found a stub of candle, wound with tag-along pieces of scarlet thread, three shell buttons from her gray morning gown, and the crumbs of a biscuit she'd smuggled home in her reticule from the Fire and Ice Ball.

Blast! Where were her gloves? They couldn't have walked off on their own.

Oh, it was those wretched scullery maids. She just knew it. Erma probably sneaked in that afternoon and stole them while Jenny had been shopping for the ribbon she needed.

Jenny started for the door, ready to twist the chit's fool head off for thievery, when she saw Meredith at her chamber door.

"He's here!" Meredith bounced on her toes, hardly able to contain herself.

"Already? But it's not even four yet."

"Still, he's in the drawing room with my aunts. But don't you worry, Jenny. Once you appear, they've promised to disappear for a time."

"But I can't see him now. Those scullery maids have made off with my gloves."

Meredith's eyes sparkled with mischief. "You are missing your gloves? Really?" Then she pulled a parcel from behind her back. "Then maybe you can make use of these."

"What have you done, Miss Meredith?" Jenny smiled

as she took the parcel and sat down on her bedstead to open it. She could scarce believe her eyes. There inside the wrappings were the most beautiful, certainly the softest, ivory kid gloves she'd ever seen. She looked up at Meredith, feeling her eyes fill with wet heat. "Oh, Miss Meredith. They're lovely."

"I'm sorry you thought the maids took your gloves. I had to borrow them to make sure of the fit." Meredith grinned. "No harm done though . . . right?"

Jenny laughed as she eased her hands into the cool satin-lined gloves. "No harm done."

Meredith drew Jenny up from the bed and smoothed down the deep red gown. "I can't believe what you've done with this dress. If I didn't know better, I'd think it'd come straight from France."

"Well, don't look too closely. I haven't had time enough to do a proper job. The dress is barely tacked together."

Meredith cringed. "Best not move around too much then."

"Exactly my thought." From the grin on Meredith's face, Jenny knew she expected a giggle in response, but she just couldn't manage it. The thought of her gown unraveling before the viscount was all too horrifying.

Gingerly lifting the dress, Meredith glanced up at Jenny. "Do you need help dressing?"

Though amused at the irony of the lady offering to dress her own maid, Jenny shook her head. "I'll be fine, really. But thank you."

"I'll wait for you above stairs. Try to hurry above stairs though. Don't want to keep Lord Argyll waiting."

Jenny's heart pounded in anticipation as she eased herself into the gown. Then giving a pinch to both her cheeks, she took one last appraising glance in her oval looking glass and headed above stairs.

Meredith was waiting for her in the entry hall. "Much more appropriate! I'll leave you here. Good luck, Jenny." Meredith leaned close and gave Jenny a quick peck on the cheek. "Just make sure *this* is the only kiss you receive, young lady."

Jenny nodded and watched Meredith disappear down the passageway. She laid her hand on the door handle and was about to enter the parlor when she heard the viscount's deep voice.

"I know 'twas a long while ago, but if ye can remember anything, anything at all, it might have meaning. She was yer kin, she must have come to call."

Jenny pressed down the handle and allowed the door to open just enough to peer inside.

Lady Viola blanched at the question. Within the time it took Jenny to open the door another inch, Viola's face actually became as white as her snowy hair.

Just then, however, Edgar, who'd somehow sneaked up behind her, reached over Jenny's head and pushed the door wide.

Jenny glanced up and gasped at the look in his eye. She'd been caught spying on her employers. Edgar was sure to inform her mother—as if she wasn't already in enough trouble with her mum.

As the door swung wide, Lady Letitia caught notice of Jenny and used her appearance to redirect conversation. "*Lady Genevieve*. Lord Argyll has come for an interview. Do come in, gel, and sit down."

Immediately Lord Argyll came to his feet and looked into Jenny's eyes in such an interested way that she actually colored.

"Yes, ma'am," Jenny muttered, then made her way to the settee.

Within seconds, Edgar stood before her with a silver tray of sherry. His aged eyes were blazing. Jenny glanced at Lady Viola, who nodded to the diminutive glasses.

Jenny lifted the stem of the crystal glass between her fingers, tossed the amber liquid down her throat, and replaced the empty crystal on Edgar's tray with a smile. But her smile fell cleanly from her lips as she noticed the look of horror on both the Feathertons' faces.

From the corner of her eye, however, she saw the viscount's mouth twitch with amusement and decided that perhaps her blunder had not been so great after all.

Lady Letitia made an exaggerated point of looking around the room. "Oh, dear, the sherry is nearly gone. Perhaps you will join me, Sister, in locating one of the special bottles Father kept."

"Why can't Edgar—" Lady Viola began.

"Oh, *no*. He would never know which I meant, Sister. Though he could fetch it down for us once we've identified the correct bottle." Lady Letitia waggled her thick white brows and threw a meaningful glance in Lord Argyll's direction.

"Oh! Of course you are right." Lady Viola turned to the viscount. "How could Edgar know which bottle you meant? Silly me."

One corner of the viscount's mouth lifted, but he nodded and rose as the ladies departed the room with Mr. Edgar. When the door closed behind the trio, Argyll turned to Jenny with a decidedly wicked gleam in his eye. "Alone at last, my bonnie lass."

Well, that didn't take long, Jenny mused. Did he

think he unnerved her? Well, he was sadly mistaken. She'd fended off more roguish footmen when she was a girl of ten and four. No, the challenge he offered her now would be pure sport. For she had the advantage. He thought her to be a proper lady, an innocent, something Jenny, for better or worse, was not. And besides, there was no chance in the world that the viscount would ever truly make an offer for her, so why not have a little fun?

Jenny batted her eyes. "Please temper your words, my lord, the ladies are bound to return in but a moment."

"A moment is all I need, lass."

She knew that to maintain the ruse the ladies had concocted, she should faint, or at the very least wilt at the thought of his overt gesture. But then, her dress might come apart . . . and as she looked into his eyes, glinting with the sparks of passion she longed to ignite, for some reason she didn't care about the ruse anymore.

Maybe it was the sherry that warmed her belly, maybe 'twas her below stairs upbringing. But something made her mind forget what was proper, and in the next instant, Jenny reached out and carefully slipped her arms around the viscount's neck. And pressed her moist lips to his.

She had half expected her brazenness to shock him, to repel him. But it seemed to do neither.

His arms eased around her waist, then one hand slid slowly up her back, coming to rest at the nape of her neck. He held her mouth close as he ran the tip of his tongue over the bow of her top lip, then down along the fullness of her lower lip. Then he slipped it inside her mouth, exploring the soft slickness inside, swirling his tongue with hers, until she shuddered and felt a seam beneath her bosom come open.

In an abrupt jerk, Jenny pulled back and quickly crossed her arms beneath her breasts, covertly pinching the seam closed with her thumb and index finger. "You—you . . . are not the gentleman you pretend to be, my lord."

He laughed deeply, wickedly then, a sound that sent goose bumps over the whole of her body. "And ye are not the lady you pretend either."

Oh, dear. Had her impulsiveness destroyed the game so quickly? Her thoughts tangled in a nest of worry. "May I ask exactly what you mean by that, my lord?"

He chuckled at that. "Oh, dinna fret, dear one. I dinna doubt yer lineage. But there's a most unladylike passion inside of ye just waitin' to be freed."

"You overstep, my lord." Jenny did her best to appear appalled, as she knew she should be.

"Ye may call me Callum," he told her in that low husky voice of his. "All me lovers do."

"*Callum,*" Jenny whispered huskily, quite unintentionally.

"And what shall I call ye?"

And the word slipped out unbidden again. "Jenny."

My heavens, what am I saying? Jenny stared at him as if truly seeing him for the first time. And indeed she was. "I—I have *no* intention of becoming your—your *lover.*"

"Dinna ye, Jenny? Yer kiss told me differently."

Still gripping the loose seam with her left hand, Jenny poked her right index finger outward and met his muscled chest, which she used as leverage to push away. "You are a rake of the first order."

"Aye, but I told ye as much when we met. And I believe ye know, for I admitted as much, that I never lie."

Just then, the door opened again and the Featherton ladies emerged from the passageway.

"Here we are, and with the *special* sherry!" Lady Viola sang out.

Callum whirled around to face them. "I fear I must take my leave, fer I have some matters to attend to."

A dual sigh fell from the Featherton sisters' mouths.

"Shall we meet again, my lord?" Lady Viola asked sweetly. "We are taking the waters tomorrow noon, a little later than usual. Mayhap we will see you then?"

Callum's mouth lifted into a crooked smile. "Perhaps, my lady. Perhaps indeed."

And, as seemed to be his way, he departed abruptly with nary another word.

Good riddance, Jenny thought. She wasn't about to have her life ruined by a blue-blooded rogue—the way her mother's was. And the longer he remained in her presence, the more likely that became.

If only he wasn't so damned handsome.

Chapter Five

Impossible! Gentlemen and ladies, all bathing . . . *together?* Jenny wondered if her mother knew about this. Or Mr. Edgar! Maybe if he was aware that the *ton* saw nothing wrong with bathing together, then he'd stop threatening the kitchen girls with the sack just for kissing the footmen.

Dressed in what Jenny took to be the appropriate bathing uniforms, baglike marigold frocks cord-cinched beneath their bosom, she and Meredith wheeled Lady Letitia to the steps, helped her down into the steaming water, then eased into the blissfully warm water themselves.

Though the bathing gown she'd borrowed from Meredith was itchy upon her skin, the hot bath felt grand, especially on a day as bitingly cold as today. Though, Jenny had to admit, she felt a bit silly strolling chest deep in the Roman baths with a flat basket of medicinal herbs and flowers floating before her, anchored by a wide ribbon about her neck. And to polish the ridiculous look, she was still wearing her best bonnet atop her head. All the ladies were. And most of the gentlemen wore their beaver-skin top hats. The whole event was just a hair north of idiotic if you asked her.

And this "treatment" was supposed to cure what ails you? Bah! What folly. Someone was a having a grand joke on the *ton* and they were actually *paying* for the privilege.

Still, without fail, Lady Letitia made her way to the baths several times a week—for her *gout*. In fact, it was the very reason they'd packed up the London house and come to Bath—for the supposed medicinal waters.

Eating a little less would make for a far better cure, Jenny decided. It couldn't help the mistress toting all that weight around.

The wake from a passing couple nearly upset Jenny's floating tray, but she remembered her ladies' instructions and remained as serene and genteel as if she were standing in the Upper Assembly Rooms—instead of chest deep in water that smelled like boiled eggs.

A warm hand pressed against her back, almost caressing her, and Jenny smiled expecting to see Meredith as she turned. But halfway around she saw the young miss now sitting at the water's edge, splashing her feet in the water and annoying everyone around her.

"I like the way yer wet gown hugs ye close, lass. Makes it easier to imagine ye as the Good Lord made ye."

"*You*," Jenny snarled. She whirled around, causing a tight whirlpool to encircle her and raise her hem about her thighs. She shoved her gown back down into the murky depths.

"We did agree ye'd call me Callum," he whispered in her ear.

"Leave me. *Please*. The ladies are bound to see you."

"And I would think they'd be quite pleased. It canna be a secret to ye that they desire a love match between us."

"So they might, but *you*, my lord, have absolutely no intention of offering for me." She glared up at him. "I am not as naive as you would believe me to be. I know your true intentions, and they involve a bed, not a ring."

Callum grinned at that, but her accusation did nothing to urge forth the gentleman inside. Instead, one wide hand cupped Jenny's bottom. She gasped, unsure what to do, as he pressed her forward through the water, at such a rate that a wake spread out behind them, until they reached a wide column near the corner of the bath.

Then, the wicked viscount disappeared from sight. A horrible thought entered Jenny's mind, and she stared down deep into the water below. Then she thrashed her feet and kicked her legs below the water's surface. But he wasn't there.

With suspicion, her eyes lit upon the wide column and she slowly peered around it. Just on the other side, the sound of water dripping, as if from a wet shirtsleeve, told her she'd found him. Well, she wasn't going any closer. Now that she knew where he was, she'd just back away quietly.

She eased one foot behind her, and shifted her weight to it. Then a hand shot out and caught her wrist.

Startled, Jenny yelped as Callum dragged her up against the column, where they'd not be seen by anyone. At once he cupped his hand over her mouth, overturning the basket of flowers and breaking the ribbon as he did so.

Her eyes wide, Jenny panted against his hand. Her

breasts rose and fell against the rock-hard surface of his chest as he held her firmly against the stone column.

Then he smiled at her. Oh, it was a wicked smile that one might expect from Bath's own Don Juan, the great seducer of women.

Jenny steadied her breathing and when he finally removed his hand from her mouth, raised a mocking brow at him.

"What game is this, Argyll?"

He lifted his own brow at that. "No game at all. I quite enjoyed yer kiss last eve, and thought to have another."

"Did you?" An unexpected thrill raced across Jenny's skin, and to her horror, she felt her nipples harden against her coarse wet frock. "Well, my lord, I shan't be gifting you with another."

"I wasna askin' fer a gift." He stared hard into her eyes and her breath grew deep and fast again.

His tongue ran over his lower lip, and he leaned in, tilting his head down to kiss her.

Ohhhh, my God . . . save the King. Jenny's thighs were suddenly aquiver and she felt her arms wrapping around him. Her fingers clutched at his soaked marigold shirt, then rode along his broad shoulders.

Beneath the water, she felt his hardness intimately pressing against her and without thinking, she raised her leg, wedging it in the crease behind his knee, as she nudged him more firmly against her.

He released her mouth then, and stared with surprise at her.

Mortification swept over Jenny, but there was no way she was going to give him the satisfaction of knowing this. So instead, she raised her chin and, with a cheeky flick of her brows, flashed him a triumphant smile.

"Why, Lady Genevieve, such a paradox ye are." Then he smiled back at her. "How verra intriguing."

Jenny shook a bit, but recovered her wits quickly. "I merely wanted to let you taste"—she leaned forward, and as she softly brushed his lips, heard him sigh— "what you will *never* have."

She forced a cool laugh then, slammed her hands against his chest, and shoved him backward and under the water. "Good day, my lord," she crooned saucily as she rounded the column and made her way back to Miss Meredith.

❧

An hour later the ladies were dressed once more and strolling into the famed Pump Room to partake of the waters.

Jenny pressed the crown Lady Letitia had handed her into the attendant's palm, then passed a cup to both her employers and Miss Meredith before tilting her own to her lips.

She sniffed it first, smelling its salty essence, then took a small sip of the warm water that set in motion a deep involuntary gag. How vile!

She looked at the two old women, then at Meredith, who was pinching her nostrils shut in order to down the water.

How could the Featherton ladies drink this swill? It tasted like hot seawater. *Thick*, egg-smelling, hot seawater! Well, she wasn't about to have any more of it, and she didn't give a fig that it cost three pence for a tin cupful!

Plastering a demure smile upon her lips, Jenny strolled to the window and paused at the foot of a potted palm, which she secretly watered with the most expensive water in all of Bath.

As she turned, she had to marvel at the expansive room. Or rather at those inside. Ladies and gentlemen of substantial wealth and evident refinement mingled with one another while sipping the water. And not a one winced or cringed at the foul taste. *Extraordinary*.

But even more amazing were the fashions the women wore. For if Jenny was not mistaken, Lady Marshall was wearing something she herself had only just read about in the *Mirror of Fashion*—the English Witzchoura.

It appeared to be composed of superfine lilac and white cloth, and lined with what had to be the finest china silk. Its purpose was to shield the wearer from the inclemency of the weather, while preserving the gown worn under from being rumpled. Jenny marveled at Lady Marshall's modish appearance, for the Witzchoura formed a most elegant covering for days or even evening parties.

She'd barely had time to take in the utility of the Witzchoura when she noticed another woman wearing the most divine cornet cap of blond lace and scarlet silk velvet she'd ever seen.

Oh, why hadn't she thought to bring her scientific journal to make notes? 'Twas almost as if *La Belle Assemblée* had sprung to life in the Pump Room, and here she was without a means to record her observations.

And then she saw it and knew at once she must have

it. A girl, scarcely older than Meredith, strolled past her in a gown of paisley gauze, trimmed with soft white fur and black cording all around it. The dress was of moderate length, revealing white satin shoes that perfectly matched the young lady's kid gloves. The sleeves were full and appeared to fall gracefully over her shoulders, displaying, in a tasteful way of course, the girl's bust and back. Jenny stared as long as propriety would allow, drinking in every tiny detail and trying her best to commit it to memory.

"'Twould look all the more lovely on ye, my dear," came a voice inside her head.

"I know . . ." she answered dreamily, only belatedly realizing that the voice was not inside her head at all— but coming from the wicked viscount who was now standing beside her!

Lifting her skirts an inch from the floor, she walked to one of the grand windows and peered out, hoping that if she ignored the Scot he would leave her alone. Maybe even retrain his eye on some other worthy quarry.

Despite her intention to pay him no heed, her heart thudded inside of her, and willing herself not to turn around became dreadfully difficult. But she couldn't allow herself to do it. That would only encourage him and show him her discomfort. So instead she stared ever forward.

There, outside a few feet from the window stood a little man, not much taller than Jenny's midthigh.

Well, he was certainly unique, wasn't he now?

She leaned her forehead upon the cold glass and studied him. His clothes were wrinkled, and stained, but free of any rips or tears. Gleaming in the thin light, a tiny top hat sat upon his overlarge head, which was shaped, oddly enough, like a balloon Jenny had once seen at an ascension in London's Hyde Park.

But probably the most remarkable thing about the little man was that he was practically barking at three members of the Quality, all of whom were sneering back at him.

Fascinated, Jenny watched as the three finely dressed individuals, two dandies with walking sticks and a woman wearing a rich scarlet turban, left the little man in the street and entered the Pump Room.

Something didn't feel right about them. As she heard the doors open, Jenny was compelled to turn around to look at the three. But when she did, Callum was standing right there before her wearing that cocky, crooked grin of his.

Jenny grimaced, and bent to the side to look past him at the trio, who were now moving toward the pump.

Upon closer examination, the three individuals were not nearly as fashionable as Jenny had first believed. The woman's gown was considered quite modish—at least five years ago, Jenny noted—and the jewels that sparkled at her throat and wrist were clearly paste. But it was her shoes, or rather her walking boots, that gave Jenny pause. There was nothing fine about them at all. In fact, the scullery maids in the Featherton household wore finer leather goods.

Bypassing Callum, Jenny absently followed the odd trio through the Pump Room, watching them, studying them.

"Leavin' me for another, are ye, lass?" came the Scotsman's low voice.

Jenny looked across at him and an idea entered her mind. She'd be far less conspicuous in her study of the newcomers were she on the arm of Lord Argyll. And so she flashed him her prettiest smile and settled her hand on the forearm of his coat sleeve—this time taking great care not to accidentally miss and brush his fur-covered sporran.

But as that precise thought chased through her mind, her eyes inadvertently glanced at the badger bag hanging low beneath his waist.

Callum's dark brows lifted with amusement. "Would ye like to see what's inside, my lady? Then perhaps yer curiosity will be sufficiently sated."

Heat all but burned Jenny's cheeks, and her gaze quickly searched the Pump Room for Miss Meredith and the ladies. She spotted them on the far side of the room, watching her and Lord Argyll. Jenny turned a brilliant smile upon him. "I should much prefer a spin about the Pump Room, my lord. If you care to oblige me."

It pleased Jenny that without a smart retort or otherwise roguish gesture, he raised his arm and politely crooked his elbow for her.

As they strolled slowly through the high-ceilinged chamber, the sun breaking through the windowpanes to create a chessboard pattern on the floor, Jenny realized she felt perfectly at ease with the wicked viscount.

Odd though, wasn't it? The man goaded her more than any other she'd known. And even though she'd kissed more than a few valets and footmen in her time, only Callum's kiss seemed to have the power to rock her senses.

Bah, no more thinking about kissing and such, she chided herself. Wanton thoughts might tempt wanton actions and she did not want to risk duplicating her mother's plight—being left with child with no means of support.

But as Callum folded his left hand protectively over hers, and the side of her breast pressed firmly against his solid upper arm, all she could think about was peeling away his coat and shirt and seeing him naked but for his kilt—the way she'd seen him in her dreams of late.

Oh, she had too much of her mother's blood in her. The sort that made a girl desire things she should not. In fact, it would not surprise her in the least to learn that she was part gypsy, or maybe even half French. Now *they* were a passionate lot, weren't they?

The more she thought about it, the more it made sense. Of course she was French. That would explain so much—her fascination with the latest gowns . . . her desire for men . . . or at least, one man.

The one walking beside her.

Tiny beads of sweat began to collect like seed pearls along her brow as she tried to think of something, anything, besides Callum . . . in his kilt. Blast him. He most likely knew what the sight of his muscular legs did to a woman, and being the rake he certainly was, knew too about the lusty stirrings the vision caused beneath their shifts.

"Why are we pacin' the woman in red?" Callum asked beneath his breath.

"What?" Without realizing it, Jenny had aligned herself parallel with the little man's suspicious lady friend. "*Oh, her.* I fancied her frock and wanted a better look at it."

But the woman was all too aware of Jenny's scrutiny and now looked back, with a snarled look on her pinched face.

Was I that obvious? Jenny turned away from her. She smiled brightly at Callum, and tugged his arm, turning him to the right. "But now that I've seen it, I realize it doesn't suit me at all."

Callum lifted a dark brow and looked over his shoulder at the woman, who was not even pretending not to be ogling them.

Of all the raw nerve.

Then, suddenly, a shrill scream pierced the relative peace of the room.

Jenny swung her head around to see an elderly woman holding a long cord in her hand. "My reticule! Someone has taken my reticule!" she wailed, holding the frayed handle up for everyone to see. "You see, it's been cut!"

At once, Jenny looked for the woman in red. She was standing with one of the gentlemen she'd entered with, looking positively aghast.

Where was the other gentleman—the more effeminate one in foppish dandy's garb? Jenny's gaze sorted through the crowd, but he was nowhere to be seen.

Jenny dropped Callum's arm, hurried to one of the tall front windows, and peered outward.

There, directly on the other side, stood the little man. He lifted his hat and bowed to Jenny in a most mocking manner.

Jenny was sure he was involved. She had to tell someone. Whirling around, she nearly plowed into Meredith.

"Oh, thank goodness. Look, Meredith." Jenny poked her figure at the window. "I think *he* might have done it."

At her words, a purposeful expression passed over

Callum's face. As he dashed through the doorway in the direction of Bath Abbey, his muscular legs pumping, an excited thrill shot straight through Jenny's body.

How mortifying! All it took was a slight flick of his kilt and her heart went all to pitter-patters.

Meredith widened her eyes, and turned her head from left to right. "Who are you speaking of, Jenny? I don't see anyone."

"What do you mean? *Him*!" Jenny followed her own finger with her gaze, but there was nothing there but a smudged windowpane. "But he was just there! A tiny little man, barely taller than Lord Argyll's knee and he was wearing a huge top hat."

Meredith giggled. "Oh, Jenny. You are having me on. And to think I actually believed you for a moment." Then she leaned close to Jenny's ear. "Mustn't play games about *this* though. Everyone is quite shaken by the crime. We have a thief within our fold, you know."

"Of course, you're right." Jenny nodded her head. "Though the stir is rather exciting, isn't it?"

Meredith brought her fingers to her lips and giggled like a girl of six. "I must admit, it *is*!"

"Now, now, gels." Lady Letitia clapped her gloved hands, making a sound like clopping draft horse hooves as she walked slowly toward them. "The excitement is over and I for one am thoroughly exhausted from it all. Best be off."

Lady Viola tapped her cane to the floor as she pivoted in a circle. "I daresay, Lord Argyll is missing. Where do you suppose he's gone off to?"

"I think he might have seen the thief, for he went dashing from the establishment with nary a backward glance," Jenny offered. "He might have been after the tiny little man. No bigger than a wee elf, he was."

Lady Letitia looked at her then as if she were mad. "Well, if his quarry is so small he will have no difficulty catching him up. Still, I am not inclined to wait for him to produce . . . *an elf.*" She winked at her sister, then with a whirl, she turned her ample form to the door. "Besides," she added as they walked, "the constables have no doubt been summoned, and I vow that all will be put to rights in no time at all. This is Bath after all and nothing, but nothing nefarious ever occurs here."

Jenny cast a wayward glance at Meredith. "She's right, nothing ever happens in Bath." Meredith grinned conspiratorially back at her.

As the Featherton ladies departed the Pump Room, and began to board their custom double-wide sedan chair, Jenny chanced a look over her shoulder hoping to catch a glimpse at the woman in red.

Heaven forbid. She could not believe it. The woman was watching her . . . still. Jenny's eyes widened in her head as the woman dropped her a sloppy curtsy and the gentleman she was with swirled his hand in the air before bowing.

"Who was that?" Meredith asked as she wrapped her arm around Jenny's and led her to the doorway.

"I'm sure I don't know," Jenny said, glancing back once more over her shoulder. She narrowed her gaze at them. "But before the week is through, I intend to find out."

Meaning to change out of her day gown, for she did not wish to soil it as she completed her house duties, Jenny made her way below stairs. Before she even reached the last tread, her mother was before her, arms folded crossly over her chest.

"Do you hear that, Jenny? Do you?"

"Do I hear what?" But before the words were even cleanly out of her mouth, she did hear something. Cackling laughter mingled with low male voices—coming from the kitchen.

"Get in there right now and take care of this. I promised Mr. Edgar it weren't going to happen again, and so it shan't. Do you understand me, gel?"

At first, Jenny hadn't a notion what her mother was prattling on about. Everything became clear, however, the moment she reached the kitchen.

Annie.

And at least a full baker's dozen of service staff from all over Bath.

The moment they saw her, the crowd rushed forward, pinning Jenny against the chopping block.

"Hang on now. Hang on!" she shouted. "Please, just give me a moment."

The gaggle of maids, footmen, and even a manservant from the Oliver residence backed away and their requests fell to a mere murmur.

"That's better," Jenny said quietly. "Can I take it you've all come for a pot of tingle cream—just nod if you have."

As she glanced at their faces, all but the manservant bobbed their heads.

"And you, sir. You haven't come for a pot?"

"No," he droned. "I've come for three pots." An amused giggle rose up from the throng.

"I've only got four—" Jenny had begun when the crowd rushed her again. Elbows toting baskets jabbed from side to side, and small pouches of coins were dangled before her face as the servants each vied for the four remaining pots.

Gads, her mother was right. This could not continue. But she was not willing to give up the money. She needed it too badly.

"Stop!" Jenny cried as a plan emerged in her mind. "I will fill all your orders soon enough, but you must be quiet. *Please*."

When every tongue went still, Jenny emptied the winter squash from a harvest basket and set it atop the chopping block. "I will set this basket outside the service door each night. If you wish to purchase a pot, place a stone inside. By morn, I will leave a pot for every stone. Take your pot and leave one guinea for each pot ordered. You are on the honor system. If I do not find one guinea per pot, I will cease filling orders. Do you understand?"

Annie settled her hands on her hips. "You heard her. No one comes inside or even raps on the door. You place your orders in the basket or not at all. Pass the word."

And so it was settled. It would be easier this way.

Or so Jenny thought, until late that eve when she found *twenty-six* stones in her basket outside the service door.

Chapter Six

Muted gray light crept through the square stillroom window leaving the table where Jenny rested her head shrouded in shadow. She blinked her eyes open, only half aware of the great clock in the upper passage proclaiming the sixth hour. "Oh," she groaned. *Morning already.*

Wearily, she raised her head. As she pushed up from the table, her hand brushed one of the thirty pots of peppermint cream she'd managed to complete during the night. Jenny stretched out the sore muscles in her arms and yawned.

Lud, she was exhausted. How long had she slept? Maybe an hour?

From the corner of her eye she glimpsed the lavender gown she needed to remake lying pitifully untouched atop her sewing basket. The gown was another castoff from Meredith, requiring quite a lot of work to become even marginally stylish, but Jenny desperately needed another gown if she wanted to preserve her lady's guise. She loosed a long sigh. There just weren't enough hours in the day to complete her lady's maid duties, pot the cream, and see to her own needs as Lady Genevieve.

Dutifully she wedged the thirty pots into the long, sturdy harvest basket and opened the door to set them outside.

Jenny lurched as a cold breeze rushed at her, along with five members of Bath's service staff who'd been patiently waiting on the stoop.

"Good morn, Jenny!" a parlor maid called out in a voice as bright as a golden guinea.

Heavens, I must look a fright, Jenny thought, and fretfully tucked the hair hanging in her face behind her ears.

"I've made four extra," she announced abruptly, "in case any of your needs exceed your orders."

"I'd hoped to coax another from you, Jen. I'll take a spare." Horace, the toothy footman, stepped forward and emptied his leather bag into Jenny's eager hand.

Two guineas. *Two*, and the day had barely begun. Jenny felt almost giddy. After no more than three minutes, she left the two unsold pots in the basket and went back inside with twenty-eighty guineas in her hands.

She was rich, *rich*!

Jenny pranced into the kitchen, her mood as light as a gossamer overdress.

Well, today she'd celebrate by engaging Mrs. Marshall to craft a French-inspired gown. She'd even pay the modiste to rush the order, since goodness knows she could well afford the extra fee now. She still had a week's worth of cream supplies after all, and could always pay down her shop debts later. What difference would a few days make anyway?

Besides, rushing the gown to completion was not just an indulgence. It was a bleedin' imperative—for who

knew when the Featherton ladies would grow tired of
their game and put an end to her forays into society?

Her eye touched upon the girlish lavender gown atop
her sewing basket. She'd better get started on that frock
right away. As she snatched the pile up, Jenny was immediately reminded of her tiredness, for with each step
forward the meager heft of the sewing basket sent
painful spasms into her back.

Then an idea exploded in her mind. Of course! Now
that she had a couple guineas, maybe she could steal a
little time from the Widow McCarthy's sewing girl next
door. Yes, she could pay her to repiece the gown, to her
own specifications of course.

Opening the door to her small chamber, Jenny didn't
dare look at her bed for fear it would woo her between
its warm covers. Instead, she picked up her boar's bristle hairbrush and her small looking glass, intending to
tidy up a bit. But when she smiled into the mirror, all
lightness and cheer drained away at the glimpse of the
dark circles ringing her eyes, and the sickly pale pallor
to her skin.

Criminy, she looked positively ghastly. Why didn't
she keep one of the pots of facial cream for herself?
Surely, no one needed its rejuvenating effects more than
she this morn.

Jenny raced from her chamber, through the kitchen,
and flung open the service door. Her gaze dove into the
basket.

Blast! The two spare pots were gone.

Instead, two homespun coin bags lay inside—along
with *nine* stones. Gads, not more orders!

She moaned at the thought of another sleepless night.
Slipping her fingers around the basket handle, Jenny

trudged through the kitchen, past the two nosy scullery maids, and back to her chamber.

She was never going to survive. Why, her eyelids seemed to be just waiting for her to blink, so they could close for a good four hours.

Who would have thought being a lady would be so terribly hard?

§

By the time the clock struck the tenth hour, Meredith was finally dressed and sitting at the dining table breaking her fast with the two Featherton ladies. Their voices were confined to mere whispers, but with just a little effort Jenny managed to hear enough to know that the matchmakers were busily hatching yet another way to lure Lord Argyll to their house.

By half past ten, Jenny's morning ironing was completed, or at least so it would appear if anyone were to check. In truth though, she'd only ironed three of Meredith's shifts and used them to cover the wrinkled clothing still in the basket.

Still, she'd not be needed again until just before tea, and so Jenny decided to make use of this rare gap in duties to take care of her own most pressing sartorial needs.

Her eyes flashing warily around her, Jenny stole her mother's woolen cape from the hook near the service door and laid it around her shoulders.

It itched against her arms and neck like a marching army of ants. But she had to borrow it, for the cape concealed the huge, puffy bundle of Meredith's hand-me-down lavender frock long enough for her to slip next door.

Lud, the cape was so hideous. Jenny could hardly bear to see herself clothed in it. And so, before leaving, she pulled from her wardrobe the satin hatbox from Matilda's and placed atop her head the most splendid velvet bonnet she owned. That way, she reasoned, if someone saw her, their gaze would be so riveted by her lovely bonnet that they'd never ever notice the horrid cape.

Stealthily, she made her way next door and through the service door where she met Molly, the widow's sewing girl, who, as Jenny had hoped, was more than eager to earn a few coins beneath her employer's notice.

With that task undertaken, Jenny headed next for Trim Street to place her dress order with Mrs. Marshall, and then finally she was off to Bath's center.

Truth to tell, Jenny couldn't wait to near the Pump Room. She wasn't going *in* of course, not dressed as shabbily as she was, but rather she planned to loiter outside, waiting and watching.

She had quite convinced herself that the mysterious woman in red, the one with the scrappy worn-out shoes, and her two gentlemen friends would be there, and some wicked plan to rob Bath's finest would be afoot.

As she walked past the Pump Room, she lingered at the front windows, but there was no sign of the terrible trio.

Keenly disappointed that no entertainment was to be had, Jenny finally spun on her heel in the direction of Royal Crescent. There was ironing still to be finished, slippers to be cleaned . . . and cream to be blended in the stillroom—secretly of course. Those tasks would have to provide her excitement for the day.

Suddenly, the sky cracked open and a bone-chilling rain began to fall. Jenny tightened her mother's wool cape closer about her shoulders.

The rain was heavy and within moments she was soaked through to her chemise.

Then she smelled something foul. She sniffed the air and realized the smell was coming from herself.

Oh, perdition, the wet cape was starting to make her reek like a sodden sheep.

She glanced angrily up at the low gray sky as she splashed her way across the Abbey Church Yard. There were no signs of blue anywhere, and if she did not seek shelter, she would soon catch a horrid cold upon her chest. And that would be the end of the grand Lady Genevieve.

All of Bath's service staff would come to her funeral, Jenny mused. Of course they would, and during her burial, not a shirt in the entire city would be ironed, not a meal prepared or a fire lit. At the notion, she smiled a little as she quickened her pace.

The *ton* would be confused and outraged at the work stoppage, and the interest of the mysterious *on-dit* columnist would be pricked.

Jenny's brows raced toward the bridge of her nose—for this event would mark her downfall. Being the curious sort, the columnist would no doubt investigate the hushed background of the great lady, who was so admired by those in service. The columnist would dig and pry and snoop. And in the end, he'd expose her for the maid she was. What a horror that would be!

What would Callum think of her then?

She squinted her eyes and looked around. Bath Abbey was just ahead, though through the gray veil of cold, lashing rain, the peaks of its soaring spires were no longer visible. It was a trick of light and mist, certainly, but the carved angels ascending the abbey's twin ladders to heaven appeared this day to have a chance of reaching their ultimate destination at last.

Since the morning service had concluded at least two hours prior, Jenny slipped inside to prevent her death and ultimate exposure as a lady's maid.

Her boots echoed loudly as she moved forward down the long open aisle. Sitting quietly upon the bench along the wall, Jenny gazed upward at the exquisite fan-vaulted ceiling above the altar, and at the brilliant stained-glass shields in the clerestory above the nave, and smiled.

It was deliciously peaceful here, and quiet. Here she could be alone with her most sacred and intimate thoughts . . . and ponder the cut of her next ball gown— for surely she would need another soon.

The sound of a cough lured her gaze toward the front of the abbey. Through one of the arches, nearly hidden in the shadows beneath the great glass windows, stood a very tall man.

Good heavens! Jenny leaned over her knees for a better look. Was he wearing a kilt?

With slow deliberation, she rose from the bench, and balancing on the tips of her toes, lest her heels touch the floor and announce her approach, she slunk through the archway toward him.

His back faced her, but as she neared there was no doubt that the imposing figure, with strong broad shoulders and well-muscled legs, was indeed Argyll.

She watched curiously as he ran a trembling hand down the names carved in the memorial tablets along the abbey wall.

His finger stopped abruptly upon a phrase inscribed beneath a skillfully carved marble cartouche of a delicate angel perched above a parted drape. Jenny edged closer to read what had so intrigued him.

In memory of Olivia Burnett Campbell,
Lady Argyll of Argyll, Scotland,
who departed this life in the flower of her age
at Bath on the 3rd of January, 1802

"Your *mother*," Jenny gasped involuntarily.

Callum whipped around and stared at her. His penetrating gaze was fierce, and his skin was soaked and hair dripping, like Jenny's own.

She reached out to him, wanting to comfort him, but his hand shot outward and grabbed her wrist roughly, preventing her tender touch.

Locked in each other's gaze, his hard and unyielding, hers fraught with compassion, neither moved.

Then something seemed to crumble inside of the great Highlander. His grip loosened, the ferociousness in his eyes disappeared, and he lowered his trembling hand to his side.

It was all Jenny needed. She opened her arms and he fell into them, needing to be held as much as she needed to offer him solace and comfort.

She squeezed her eyes closed and held him tightly, so close that even through the layers of wool coat and cape between them, she could feel his heart thumping.

There in the east aisle of the abbey, they clung to one another, their soaked clothing dripping into puddles on the marble floor.

In that moment, something grew inside Jenny and made her warm. Holding Callum in her arms felt so right. *He* felt so right.

Raising her fingers up to his cheeks, Jenny turned his face to her, made him look into her eyes. Droplets of water broke from strands of hair clinging to his forehead and fell upon her face, as she raised herself onto her toes and kissed his lips softly.

Despite the chill and dampness and the shivering of their bodies, his mouth was warm and welcoming. And as they kissed, slowly, gently, Jenny's body heated where they touched, as surely as if she were standing before a fire.

Their mouths parted, and they each gasped a small breath.

Callum stared down at her, and his lips began to move as if there was something he wanted to tell her. But no words came forth.

Instead, he pulled her tight against him once more, and kissed the top of her head. Jenny closed her eyes and pressed her cheek against his sopping coat, knowing somehow deep within that as soon as she released him, this moment—their connection—would vanish.

And she didn't want it to end . . . ever.

As if this thought had conjured their parting, she heard from the rear of the abbey the familiar sound of the reverend clearing his throat. "The rain has ended, my children."

Callum drew back from her and stared as if seeing her there for the first time. With a startled look in his dark eyes, he backed away, then turned and hurried from the abbey, leaving her standing in the aisle alone.

Jenny smiled politely at the reverend and bowed her head while passing him on her way outside.

As she exited through the arched doorway, Jenny raised her gloved fingers to her lips and relived Callum's kiss in her mind.

What had just happened? Though she couldn't put a name to it, something had changed in the depths of her soul, warmed within her, and she knew for certain that things would never be the same between them again.

As she reached the square, fingers of soft light cut through the cloud cover and etched a pathway upon the cobbles. She had just stepped onto the slick, wet pavers when movement to her right caught her notice.

There, leaning against the corner of a building, was the tiny man. Somehow, his clothes had remained dry, and he was leisurely eating a crumbling bit of Sally Lund bread.

Jenny stopped walking. Why, he was grinning at her. "Good afternoon," she called out tentatively.

But the little man said nothing. Instead, he raised his hat from his oddly shaped head and tipped it to her. Then, he leaned on his outer leg, and with a slight limp, disappeared around the corner.

Jenny followed, eager for a little adventure, after all. As she rounded the corner, however, she was completely dumbfounded. She looked down the empty street in both directions. The little man was nowhere to be seen.

"And just where have you been?" her mother snapped the very moment Jenny opened the service door and entered the kitchen.

Jenny shrugged off her wet wrap, hoping her mother wouldn't notice it belonged to her, and slipped it on a hook beside the fire to dry. She daren't tell her mother where she was . . . or that she had been with Callum. That bit of information would not sit well with her at all. "I . . . had errands to run, and was caught in the rain. Had to wait it out."

"Well, change into your black and whites and get yourself above stairs. The ladies wish to have a chat with you, right *now*."

"With me? Did they say why?"

Her mother folded her arms tightly across her chest. "And why would they confide in me? Just hurry yourself along if you want to keep your position, gel. The ladies have been waitin' three-quarters of an hour already."

༜

A mixture of apprehension and dread filled Jenny's belly as she scratched on the drawing-room door a few minutes later and waited for admittance.

"Come in, gel, and take a seat," came Lady Letitia's voice. "We've been waiting for you all morn and have a matter of great concern to speak about with you."

Jenny did as she was bade, and sat nervously across from the two Featherton ladies.

Lady Viola leaned forward. "Child, are you playing our game because you enjoy mingling with the *ton*? Or because you feel some affection for the viscount?"

Jenny's eyes wedged to the right. There was a right answer, the perfect reply to appease them enough that they'd allow the game to continue . . . if only she could find it.

"No, gel, I shan't have you ponder the question and tell us what you *believe* we would like to hear." Lady Letitia leaned close as well. "Look to your heart."

Against her better judgment, Jenny raised her gaze then and spoke without thinking of the consequences. "I do love playing the lady. For me, 'tis a dream come true."

Lady Viola slumped back against the settee with a forlorn sigh.

Rising, Jenny moved before the fire in the hearth and stared pensively into its licking flames and opened her heart. "But today, well . . . something changed inside of me."

Lady Letitia rose and laid her hand on Jenny's shoulder. "What do you mean, gel? What happened today?"

Jenny turned around, and reluctantly recounted her brief, yet emotional encounter with Callum in the abbey.

By the time she finished, great tears were rolling down Lady Viola's cheeks, cutting white tracks through her powder and rouge.

A knowing smile laced Lady Letitia's lips. "You *love* him."

Jenny looked up at her, and shook her head. "I didn't say that."

"You didn't need to, my dear." Lady Viola sniffed back her tears and dried her cheeks with the handkerchief her sister gave her. "But it is clear nonetheless. You mightn't even know it yet yourself, Jenny. But from what you've told us, your hearts met in the abbey.

Maybe only for a moment, but it won't be the last time, I promise you that." She leaned forward and held Jenny with the most potent of gazes. "Why, I have a notion that the two of you are falling in love."

Jenny flinched at that. *Preposterous*. They shared a moment of tenderness. She eased his pain. She paused then. Was there more to it? Was she falling in love with Callum?

The sound of hands clapping drew Jenny's gaze to Lady Letitia, who was prancing, as best she could given her heft and swollen ankles, around the drawing room gleefully. "'Tis exactly as we'd hoped, Sister. A love match in the making—a *real* love match!"

There was a rustling sound at the drawing-room door, then it flew open and Meredith backed into the room, her arms laden with a huge parcel. "It's here, Aunties. Come and see!"

At once the ladies set aside their views on Jenny and Callum's attraction, much to Jenny's relief. Lady Viola struggled to her feet and the three women joined Meredith around the polished mahogany table in the center of the room as she tore the muslin wrapping away.

With a gasp of pleasure, Jenny stared at what lay before her. There beneath the scraps of muslin was the most beautiful evening gown she'd ever seen.

She couldn't help herself. Jenny had to touch the fabric.

Snatching it up, she shook it from its folds and marveled at the creation. The evening gown was made of vibrant midnight-blue sarcenet draped over an icy white satin slip. The waist was short in accordance with all the latest fashion magazines, and topped by a daringly low bodice. The cropped, full sleeves cascaded over the shoulders, and fell deliciously low in the back. Around the waist was a sash of blue satin ribbon fastened in a petite bow in the back.

Were she to wear this gown, no one would be able to take their eyes from her. And most especially not Callum.

Jenny lurched with surprise.

Callum? Lud, where had that thought hailed from? That notion came quite out of the sky, didn't it?

Tucking the distracting thought in the back of her mind, Jenny held the dress up to her shoulders to view it more carefully. The gently flared skirt was ornamented with a deep trimming of net, and finished with ruched rows of more blue satin, which would produce a light, ethereal effect, particularly when Callum swirled her around in the ballroom. Lud. There he was in her thoughts . . . *again*.

Once more, Jenny tried to put her thoughts of Callum aside and instead focused her attention on her new gown.

Golly. That was assuming the gown was meant for her.

Oh, it had to be. Just had to be. It was the most gorgeous thing she'd ever seen!

Well, she wasn't about to wait around to find out while her heart was already claiming it for its own.

"Your gown is lovely, Miss Meredith. Though I daresay," she added cleverly, "I would not have chosen quite this shade of blue for you." Then she glanced sidelong at Meredith who laughed in response.

"No, silly. Aunt Viola had the gown fashioned especially for *you*."

"For me?"

Lady Letitia chuckled to herself. "Come now, gel, you know you have need of it."

"We are not too old to recall the feel of wanting to look fetching for a beau." Lady Viola smiled warmly.

Jenny's innards somersaulted. Oh, this was too wondrous to be true. The gown was hers. *Hers!* "Oh, thank you, my ladies. Thank you ever so much."

"No need to thank us, my child. You have no idea the happiness you are bringing us." Then Lady Viola's eyes widened and she slapped her fingers to her lips.

This odd reaction was not lost on Jenny. It was almost as if Lady Viola had erred and said something she shouldn't have. But Jenny couldn't think what that might have been.

Lady Letitia hugged her sister to her. "Now, now, Viola, you've done nothing wrong by simply admitting the joy we glean from observing love in blossom."

Lady Viola smiled meekly then and nodded her head. "Quite right."

Still, Jenny watched the old woman's countenance carefully. Something wasn't being said. Oh, how she wished she had the gumption to probe deeper. But she knew she had to remember her place.

She was a lady's maid in the household. Nothing more.

Jenny glanced down at the dress once more and smiled with delight.

Meredith gave her a little nudge. "Well, go on. Run and try it on. I am quite beside myself waiting to see how it will look upon you."

Jenny smiled so broadly that her cheeks actually smarted. With the gown hugged tightly to her chest, she dashed below stairs.

❦

Not a full day later, the opportunity to wear the midnight-blue evening gown presented itself. Lady Viola had extended an invitation to Lord Argyll to join her and her sister, Meredith and Lady Genevieve in their private box at the Theatre Royal.

While Jenny had certainly seen the theatre's imposing entrance on Beaufort Square, she never dreamed she would ever attend a performance there. Let alone in a gown that could have inspired an entire page of description in *La Belle Assemblée*.

That night, their party entered the Feathertons' private box, one of only twenty-six, Jenny noted proudly, through a private home adjoining the theatre. A suite of retiring rooms, including a saloon, adjoined the private box to ensure the occupants complete and luxurious comfort.

In fine gentlemanly fashion, Lord Argyll assisted the two Featherton ladies to their seats. Within an instant, Lady Letitia's plump finger directed Meredith to sit between them, a measure no doubt intended to more easily monitor the untamed young lady's conduct.

Only then did Jenny realize that she and Callum were to sit behind the others, quite out of sight of the Feathertons' watchful eyes.

Had this been any other eve, this situation would have suited Jenny quite nicely. But not tonight. Despite the fact that she was clothed in the most exquisite gown in Bath, Callum had hardly glanced at her.

It wasn't hard to discern why, after their emotional exchange at the abbey. Still, understanding his reasoning did nothing to make his inattention easier to bear. For now, when she craved his notice more than ever, he was all but ignoring her.

Ridiculous tears began to fill Jenny's eyes, and she turned away from the viscount, pretending to peer through the gilt lattices separating the Featherton box from the next. But when the play began, this ploy was no longer feasible, and she focused her blurred eyes on the cast-iron pillars at the edges of the box. Soon, her tears threatened to breach her lower lashes and she was all but forced to study the fancifully painted ceiling in order to maintain her dignity.

Bah! Why was she acting so foolishly? She should just wipe her eyes and concentrate on the stage play. After all, she'd never seen one before, and it would serve her well to imbibe a little culture, now wouldn't it?

And so, without looking away from the ceiling, she loosened the cinch of her reticule, and jammed her fingers inside for her handkerchief. Unfortunately, her new and therefore rather stiff kid gloves made her perception by touch virtually nonexistent and she was forced to peel down one glove and remove it completely to accomplish her aim.

Then he touched her.

Callum's own bared hand grasped hers and squeezed it reassuringly. Without thinking of the tears poised in her eyes, she tore her gaze from the ceiling and looked at him with astonishment.

With the downward momentum, two heavy droplets spilled over and splashed her cheeks.

Suddenly Callum held his own square of linen before

her, and she took it gratefully. It felt warm in her hand and she pressed it to her eyes to dry them.

Oh, *no.*

He didn't take it from his . . . Jenny glanced sidelong in time to see Argyll fastening the sterling buckle upon his sporran. *Oh Lord above, he did.*

When she looked up again, she saw that he had followed her wayward gaze. He grinned at her, and ran his thumb along the side of her hand.

Jenny gasped, a tiny bit too loudly, for Meredith glanced over her shoulder at them, and upon seeing their bare hands clasped, let out a giggle.

Blood coursed beneath Jenny's skin into her cheeks, heating them, and she knew for certain that even in the low light, her face was aglow with embarrassment.

This was too much to endure. And here she had such high hopes for her lovely evening at the theatre.

Now there was no question. She had to leave her seat to compose herself, if only for a few minutes. Jenny glanced behind her at the rear opening of the box and plotted her escape. *No one will mind at all*, she told herself. *I'll come right back. I just need a few moments alone to collect my wits, that's all.*

"Excuse me, will you?" she muttered as she replaced Callum's hand to his knee. Before he could stand, she slipped quietly from the box.

Jenny wandered aimlessly through the anterooms until she found a small saloon outside what she took to be the ladies' withdrawing room. As she closed her eyes and exhaled, she allowed herself to fall into a high winged-back chair where she planned to spend the next five minutes trying to clear her muddled senses and return a modicum of normalcy to her life.

"It's very hard to obtain," came a woman's voice from behind the chair. From the volume, Jenny determined they must be standing just inside the withdrawing-room door.

"I've managed only one pot of the peppermint cream, but that was only because I told my housekeeper I would pay up to ten guineas if needed."

Jenny straightened her back in her chair and her eyes went wide. *She'd pay a tenner?* And here she was only charging one.

"Well, I simply must have a pot," came another female voice.

"You know, it's rumored that the cream is made by a grand lady. *Lady Eros*, the service staff calls her. I've heard, from a *very* reliable source, mind you, that the herbs she uses for the extract can only be harvested when the moon is full. That's what gives it such power to . . . you know . . . *excite*. Unfortunately, that's also why the love cream is so hard to acquire."

I only harvest it by the light of the full moon? Jenny laughed softly to herself. She had to hand it to the service staff, they were a creative lot. A grimace took hold of her mouth then. And a greedy lot too. *Ten guineas*.

Well, maybe it was time to raise the price. She'd have to think on that one.

Lud, she wasn't about to stay up all night for a measly guinea if the Quality were willing to pay ten! Or . . . would they pay even more?

Jenny came to her feet, rounded the chair, and opened the door to the withdrawing room. "I beg your pardon, but I couldn't help hear you both discussing the cream . . . err . . . the *Lady Eros* cream."

The two matrons looked at Jenny with suspicion.

Jenny turned abruptly, purposely sending her skirts swirling about her legs in hopes that the sight of their beauty and quality would convince the ladies that she was . . . well, their equal. "I just wondered, do you think if I offered . . . perhaps *fifteen* guineas, that I might be able to acquire a pot?"

"But, dear," the older of the two women began, "why do you need the cream? Surely one so young as you—"

Raising her hand, Jenny quieted her and whispered her reply confidentially. "Oh, then you've not heard? It works its magic on *gentlemen* too."

Both women's eyes grew large as they exchanged excited grins.

"No, we hadn't heard," the younger of the two said. "But I thank you for sharing that keen bit of information." She turned to her companion. "My William could certainly use a touch of the cream. Do you think your gel can find me a jar?"

"I don't know, but I can ask. I've often wondered why the pots can only be purchased through those in service. You don't suppose they are stealing them?"

As the ladies turned away and started toward their box, Jenny asked herself that very question. If the pots of cream were so coveted, perhaps she should consider asking Mr. Bartleby to sell them for her at his shop on Milsom Street.

Then maybe she wouldn't have footmen and maids dropping stones in her basket at all hours of the day and night. For, if that kept up, the Feathertons were bound to learn of her secret.

Jupiter.

Chapter Seven

"You rang for me, my ladies?" Jenny stood motionless and tried very hard to focus on the Featherton sisters instead of on her mother who stood alongside the breakfast table with a steaming pot of chocolate in her grip.

"Yes, gel." Lady Letitia lowered *The Bath Herald* to the table and laid her lorgnette atop it. "Sister and I were just discussing a most interesting mention in the *on-dit* column this morn. The 'Strange But True' column . . . you know, the one written by the secret columnist."

"R-really, my lady?"

"Indeed. And due to your own stillroom activities, we thought you might find it of interest." Lady Letitia lifted her lorgnette again and with a shake repositioned the newspaper before her eyes.

"*According to a certain Lady D. and a Lady A., Bath's Quality, and indeed Cheltenham's as well, have fallen under the spell of a mysterious* crème d'amour *reportedly produced by one of their own, a well-respected yet anonymous peer who has chosen to be known simply as 'Lady Eros.' Who is this lady, this columnist begs to inquire, and what is the magical ingredient of this sought-after tingling cream that transforms ladies and gentlemen alike into Lady Eros's all-too-willing sub-jects?"*

Jenny inadvertently stole a glance at her mother, whose face had become as snowy as the linen cloth upon the table.

Lady Letitia lowered the paper and looked up at Jenny too.

"I—I don't know what to say, my ladies," Jenny stammered.

"We thought this tingling cream sounded quite a lot like your peppermint facial balm," Lady Viola twittered.

"D-did you?" Jenny swallowed deeply.

The chocolate pot began to shake noticeably in her mother's hand. "Ah, more chocolate, my ladies?" she asked, as if that small interruption would rescue Jenny from this disaster. As if anything could!

With a flick of her hand, Lady Letitia waved Mrs. Penny away. "Like the columnist, we too want to know what extracts and oils are used in the cream. We've tried to acquire a pot, and have used the pre-scribed channels."

"Indeed," Lady Viola offered. "We've put both Edgar and your mother to the task, but thus far we have been unable to locate a single pot."

"A-are you asking me to locate a pot for you, my ladies?" Jenny asked, hoping to divert any blame from herself.

"Yes, but there is more," Lady Viola said in a confidential tone. The old woman beckoned Jenny closer and closer still until there was less than a teacup's width between them. "We'd like you to find a pot, but then we'd like you to break it down into its components to discover its receipt."

"Ohhh, I see."

Lady Letitia broke in. "Then we'd like you to make up a couple of pots . . . for Sister and me. Of course, your activities must not be disclosed. For the cream, you realize, is meant to be used . . . *below stairs*, if you take my meaning."

Jenny nodded uncomfortably. "I do indeed, my lady. You can count on my discretion."

Lady Viola smiled broadly. "Well, then, it's settled. How soon can you begin?"

"Right away, my lady." Then Jenny lifted a wry brow. "But then . . . I already have so much to accomplish today, what with Miss Meredith's ironing needin' to be done . . . and her slippers needin' to be cleaned . . . oh, and the mending."

Lady Viola lifted a diminutive silver bell from beside her bread plate, and rang it.

Responding to the summons, Mr. Edgar walked into the room, then smiled brightly at Lady Viola, who, even beneath her face powder, blushed becomingly.

"Jenny will be relieved of her duties today, and tomorrow as well," the frail old woman told him.

Jenny did not miss the grimace on both Mr. Edgar's and her mother's faces.

"*Tomorrow* . . . as well?" Jenny asked, trying to disguise the smile on her mouth. Why, things were turning out quite well, weren't they now?

Lady Letitia smiled up at her. "Indeed, gel. After *so* enjoying himself at the Theatre Royal"—she bobbled her eyebrows meaningfully at Jenny—"Lord Argyll has invited us *all* to join him tomorrow for a day jaunt to Dyrham Park and, if the weather warms as predicted, an alfresco nuncheon as well."

Lord Argyll said he enjoyed himself? At the thought of him, Jenny got a warm tingling feeling all over, almost as though she'd used a dab of cream.

Yes, after making a complete goose of herself last eve at the Theatre Royal, she could make good use of a casual outing with Callum to rework her dropped stitches.

"I was thinking, child, that Meredith's lavender from last season might be just the frock for the occasion," Lady Viola added. "She gave it to you, did she not?"

Jenny began to pick at her cuticle as she thought about it. The frock was next door with Molly being reworked. She supposed it was possible the sewing girl would have it pieced by now. She did seem quite anxious for the guinea Jenny had promised her for the work.

"So much to do, isn't there?" Jenny gave an exaggerated sigh. "But I'll manage it somehow, my lady, for a fine idea it is indeed."

As anticipated, the day was exceedingly mild, and felt to Jenny more like an early spring day than one of midwinter.

As Lord Argyll's sumptuous town carriage roared down the dusty road, closely followed by the Feathertons' carriage, Jenny proudly unclasped her new Witzchoura and swept back its flowing sides to reveal her remade lavender frock. Jenny had Annie to thank for the Witzchoura, for she had spotted the cape in the window of Mrs. Russell's shop only this morn, and had deftly persuaded the modiste to put it on Jenny's account.

Jenny glanced up at Lord Argyll, who sat across from her and Meredith, who had fallen asleep from the rock and sway of the carriage ten minutes past, and now was drooling from the side of her half-open mouth.

But none of this mattered to Jenny. As long as Meredith was counting Suffolk sheep in her dreams, Jenny was as good as alone with the handsome Scotsman. Only this time, she would remain in control of her emotions and rein in any skittish bursts of panic.

"My, it is getting rather warm in here, is it not?" Jenny pushed her cloak from her shoulders in order to better reveal the bust-flattering neckline of her walking dress.

"Perhaps not so warm as ye claim. There is still a bracing catch to the air, lass. This ye know." He leaned forward, then glanced at Meredith and lowered his voice.

"But we aren't truly speakin' of the weather. Ye want to know if I think that yer gown flatters ye, aye?"

Jenny felt taken aback at that. "Must you always be so blunt, my lord?" She wrenched her head around and stared out the window at the passing countryside.

"I canna abide lies, and seek to speak only the truth. And truth to tell, yer frock flatters yer form nearly as well as the blue gown ye wore last eve at the Theatre Royal."

A burst of excitement lit through her. "You mean the midnight blue. It's new, you know. A gift from the Featherton ladies. Oh, it *was* gorgeous, wasn't it?"

Callum gave a small laugh at her exuberance. "Not half so lovely as the woman who was wearin' it."

Jenny felt a glow within. He really thought she was

lovely. He said it himself, after all, and he *always* told the truth.

She fought to restrain the upward pull of her lips, not wishing for her pleased ladylike smile to expand into the full, village-idiot grin that truly captured her elation.

As she gazed upon Callum, she wished she too could say exactly what she thought, without concern for the consequences.

Firstly, she'd tell him if he insisted on wearing a kilt, he should learn to keep his legs together. Not that she could see anything scandalous, for she didn't allow her gaze to dwell in those shadows. The fact remained, however, that she *might* be able to see what lay beneath his sporran if she did not divert her eyes. She was a lady after all.

Or at least *pretending* to be one.

She looked up into his cozy brown eyes and at his far too handsome face. Though it was still morn, already the dark beginnings of a beard had begun to crop up along his jawline, chin, and above his lips. But this only made him more arresting for it befitted his rugged Scottish nature entirely.

And, were she to speak her mind just now, she'd tell him she found him more striking than the sapphire bonnet with the silver plume she glimpsed at Bartleby's.

And that, beneath his clothing, judging from what she'd had the wanton pleasure to feel, she was sure to find a well-muscled body more perfectly cut than the center stone in a diamond ring . . . the one in the second display case to the right at Smith and Company.

Callum lifted a bemused brow, and Jenny realized he was clearly aware of her scrutinizing gaze and her obvious inventory of his person.

Heat flowed into her lobes, and suddenly she longed for her straw bonnet with its wide ear-sequestering silk ribbon ties.

He grinned, obviously aware of her discomfort. "Why, I believe ye fancy me, Jenny."

She swallowed the hard lump that formed in her throat. "What a wretched thing to say to a lady, my lord."

He studied her for some moments before speaking again. "Och, dinna fash. 'Tis quite all right, for I fancy ye as weel. But ye know that already."

Jenny disliked feeling so completely tilted from her footing. "I suspect, being the rogue you are, you've *fancied* a great number of women over the years."

He laughed at that. "I find ye verra attractive, 'tis true. But ye intrigue me as weel. Ye're verra different, Lady Genevieve, from any other gentlewoman I've ever had the pleasure to know."

A cold hand seemed to squeeze Jenny's insides. He thought her . . . different? Well of course he did—because she *was* different. "W-whatever do you mean, my lord?" she somehow managed to ask.

"I'm not sure what I mean exactly." Remaining silent for some seconds, he seemed to ponder his reply as he peered back at her. "Ye are . . . like this day, a warm spring breeze, yearned for and welcome, but so out of place in the depths of winter."

Golly. That was really nice. She had to admit, she especially liked the "yearned for" part. Liked it quite a lot.

Oh, she wished Meredith had been awake to hear what he'd all but admitted. Just so she could be sure she wasn't contriving the whole thing in her mind.

Jenny fashioned a demure smile for him. "How kind of you to liken me to a spring breeze."

"I dinna say it to be kind or to flatter ye . . . I meant only to explain myself." He flushed a little then and looked out the window, which struck Jenny as being entirely out of character for such a strong and imposing man.

"I understand . . . *Callum*."

The instant he heard Jenny utter his name, he turned back to her, his eyes lit from within, making her heart flutter.

My, my . . . if she was not mistaken, the viscount had just dropped his roguish flag and hoisted his true colors.

She could scarce believe it.

"We'll be arrivin' soon." With deliberation, he reached out his fingers and lifted Jenny's hand from her lap. He looked deep into her eyes. "Will ye walk with me, alone—if yer duennas will allow it, of course. I wish to explain what happened in Bath Abbey."

"Of course." Her voice sounded unusually high and nerve-strangled. "Anything you wish."

No more than five minutes later, the carriage slowed and halted, but Jenny's heart still galloped at breakneck speed.

"Here we are, Dyrham Park," Callum announced as the stairs were let down. He practically leapt from the cab and promptly drew in an astonishingly deep breath of the fresh country air.

Somewhat apprehensively, for she'd never ever set slipper outside the cities of Bath or London, Jenny took

Callum's proffered hand and started down the steps. But as her foot touched the earth beneath her, she realized her apprehension was all for naught, for the landscape that stretched out before her was certainly the most beautiful she'd ever seen.

Lush gardens tumbled toward a manor house to her left, while to her right ran a wide swathe of grass sloping toward what appeared in the distance to be a water garden.

It must have taken quite a lot of money to maintain something like this. For it was simply gorgeous, and here it was the bones of winter.

Meredith emerged, blinking and sleepy, from the carriage and came to stand next to Jenny. "Oh, jolly good. Plants. Loads of plants," she droned. "At least *you* will be in paradise, Jenny."

Callum's attention caught. "Do you study flora?"

Jenny opened her mouth, but Meredith answered in her stead. "Lady Genevieve is quite the botanist. She's always fiddling with some plant or another."

The viscount turned and looked at her in astonishment. "I hadna any idea yer interests included botany."

Jenny shrugged and with a faint smile, turned away. She wasn't about to discuss her experiments with plant extracts. That'd be all she needed for Callum to connect her with the Lady Eros *on-dits* in the newspaper!

Walking to the edge of the road, Jenny stooped and quickly categorized several of the plants and shrubbery before her.

This place was amazing. Why, she couldn't even imagine the gardens in the spring, blooms would be everywhere. Oh, she'd have to come back then. She'd just have to find a way.

Her excitement burst forth in an exultant giggle and it was all she could do to keep from lifting her skirts and skipping across the sweeping lawn.

The Featherton carriage rolled onto the gravel a moment later and the two elderly ladies stepped out into the daylight.

"Lovely, just lovely," exclaimed Lady Viola.

Two footmen rounded the carriage with several baskets and coverlets and looked at the ladies for direction.

"Over there, I think." Lady Letitia gestured to a low, sun-dappled outcropping of stone.

"Isn't it peculiar. A day warm enough for a picnic — in January. Perhaps after our meal, Lord Argyll will be good enough to show Lady Genevieve the exterior of the manor house. I recall the structure is quite commanding."

"Well, I, for one, am positively famished. My mind has been riveted on the thought of Cook's pigeon-pie and apple dumplings."

Lady Letitia's stomach gave a loud, deep growl, which sent her and her sister into fits of laughter. "You see," she struggled to say through her pants of laughter. "What did I tell you? Even my belly is calling for the pies. Come, let us dine."

❀

While Lady Viola argued the wisdom of her sister taking a third serving of apple dumpling, Meredith wandered off toward the water garden, and Jenny and Callum walked toward the manor house.

As they rounded a natural hedge of boxwood, a large

spotted animal with great horns bounded out of the trees and seemed to charge straight for them.

With a yelp of fright, Jenny yanked her skirts to her knees and took off running down the path.

"Jenny, stop! What's wrong?" Callum called out.

Though she could hear his rapid footfalls behind her, she daren't look back, not with that *thing* coming for her!

A moment later, Callum seized her left arm and whirled her around to a stop. "Why are ye runnin' away? 'Twas just a wee fallow deer."

Jenny looked around him at the animal now grazing on the stubble of grass jutting up from the cold earth. Was he blind? There was nothing wee about *that* creature.

She studied the graceful animal as her breathing slowed. So that was a deer. Lud, she must seem the goose. But how could she be expected to know what a deer looked like? She'd spent her entire life in the cities of London and Bath after all. In fact, the only deer she'd ever seen was a roast of venison skewered on the kitchen spit.

Callum waggled his brows at her. "Ye're afeart of deer?"

"Don't be daft. Of course not!" Jenny shook his hand from the sleeve of her Witzchoura and folded her arms over her chest. "The beast just . . . startled me, 'tis all."

"The beast. Och, I see." Amusement still glowed in Callum's eyes, but he politely dropped the matter and instead surveyed the rolling hills in the distance until she fully gathered her wits about her.

He offered Jenny his arm once more and together they retraced their steps toward the manor house.

"Isn't the land beautiful?"

"Aye. 'Tis almost like being at hame in the High-lands." Callum breathed the air deep into his lungs as they walked, almost as if hoping to catch the scent of heather in Dyrham's breeze.

"Do you miss Scotland?"

"I do. But I have me work here and until 'tis done, I'll not be goin' hame."

"Really?" Here was the opening in the conversation Jenny had been waiting for—her chance to piece to-gether the mystery of Lord Argyll. "What sort of work?"

Callum stopped walking altogether. He turned Jenny to face him fully, and exhaled a long sigh before speak-ing. "I came here, to Bath, to learn about me mother."

Jenny knew better than to speak, for to do so might put a halt to Callum's willingness to provide more in-formation.

Callum cupped her elbow and led her to a waist-high retaining wall just out of view of the Feathertons, then lifted her up to sit upon it.

"When I was but a lad, I awoke one day to find my mother leaving. Every trunk she owned, every portman-teau, was filled with her things." His words were slow and deliberate. "I knew she wasna coming back and I ran to her, cryin'. I begged her not to go or, at the verra least, to take me with her. But she wudna."

In Callum's eyes, emotion collected, and his voice grew husky. "She told me she would come back—come back for *me*. But her eyes were red, like she'd been sheddin' tears all the night before."

He took each of Jenny's hands into his own and pressed them tight as he stood before her. He swallowed deeply, but said nothing more.

"And did she come back?" Jenny asked in a small voice.

"Nay. I never saw her again." His voice was so low, she hardly heard what he said.

"After a few weeks, my da told me she'd died."

"How awful for you."

"Awful, aye. But not true." Callum set his gaze to the horizon. "One night, I found a letter she'd written to me in his chamber, and then another a month after that, and I knew fer certain he had lied."

Jenny gasped before she could stop herself, but Callum continued on.

"Though I was but a wee lad, I called me father a liar and threw the letters at him. That's when he struck me, his Lord Lyon signet cuttin' into me face."

Unconsciously, he brushed his cheek with his own fist. When he drew his hand away, Jenny noticed, for the first time, a whitened scar just above his cheekbone.

"I dinna cry and I wudna take back my words. So he struck me again, until he drew blood. And so it continued over the years. Until one day, I finally believed his words, for I knew me mother would have never allowed me da to hurt me fer so long." He fumbled for her hand again.

Tears burned in Jenny's eyes for him. She pulled her right hand from his grip and raised it to his cheek, tracing the scar with her fingertips.

Meaning only to kiss his scar, Jenny leaned forward, but Callum jerked back and turned his head away from her.

How she wanted to hold him in her arms, and kiss the pain away. But it was clear he would not have her pity, her sympathy. Or even her comfort.

"Callum?" she whispered.

Slowly he turned his reddening eyes toward hers.

"The day I found you in the abbey—"

He sighed and distractedly focused his attention on a gray stone near his boot. "Even after all these years, though I had no reason to believe it, something inside of me held out hope that she still lived."

Abruptly Callum stepped back from her, and as he straightened his back, steeling himself for the words to come, he let her left hand, the one he still held, fall to her knee.

"Me father died late last year, and when I went to Argyll to settle his affairs, I found a passel of letters from me mother, hidden inside his desk. Three years' worth of letters. *Three*."

Jenny slid down from the ledge and took a step forward. Callum raised a hand, tilting his head away from her sad gaze.

"Allow me to finish."

Jenny tipped her head forward once, and he continued.

"The letters told of her life in Bath, visits to the Pump Room, tea with the Feathertons, but little more—except that she held out great hope that she would be coming home soon."

A notion suddenly sparked in Jenny's mind. "She was ill. Dying."

"I believe she was."

"But she never told you. Never told your father?"

"She never told me, but I was little more than a bairn. But me father knew. In several of the missives, me mother mentioned that she hoped me father explained it to me . . . in such a way that a wee lad could understand her need to leave." He paused, and Jenny uttered the words he could not say.

"But he didn't explain it to you." Her throat felt tight as she spoke. "Instead, he told you that she had died."

"Aye." Callum stepped backward before meeting Jenny's gaze once more and looked down the curved road to where the Feathertons sat. "When ye came in from the rain and found me in the abbey, I had just found my mother's memorial stone."

Clear understanding dawned on Jenny. "And at last you knew for certain she was gone."

Heedless of his wishes, she rushed to Callum, clasped him in her arms, and held tight. "Oh, Callum, I am so sorry."

He pulled his shoulders back and tried to gently break from her grasp, but she wasn't about to let him go. Not now.

Why else would he have told her what he had? He needed her comfort. Whether he realized or not, he needed *her*.

Slowly, she felt his arms raise up and wrap around her, and the span of his wide hands press against her back, pushing her body tightly against him. Jenny lifted her head from the mound of his chest, and turned her face upward to look at him.

He was already looking at her, and what she saw in his eyes made her tremble within. In all her life, she'd never seen anyone so vulnerable.

As if he sensed her acknowledgment of his emotional state, he cupped her chin with his palm and pressed his lips against hers. He kissed her roughly then, a punishing kiss, the sort a rake would ply, but she didn't pull away.

For she knew what he was doing. He sought to raise the wall around him once more, and banish his feelings of weakness by driving her away.

But it would not work.

"I'm not going anywhere, Callum. I am here for you and you cannot drive me away. It's far too late for that." She looked him straight in the eye. "I know you are not the rogue you pretend."

Releasing her from his arms, Callum stared incredulously at her. "I pretend nothing. Truth and honesty are everything to me. 'Tis the way I have chosen to live."

"Then be truthful with yourself." She pinned him with her gaze and stood firm in her footing, knowing that what she was about to say would shake the both of them. "You need me and I am here for you. But unlike others you have cared for in your life, I won't leave you."

Like a crack of blinding lightning from the sky, her words seemed to shatter him to his core. He stared, in shock and awe of what she said, before turning and walking alone toward the manor house.

What had she done?

Jenny turned to the wall and rested her head atop her folded arms. When she had told Callum she would not leave him, she had meant it with all of her heart.

Now, despite her pure intentions, she realized too late the error of her words.

For though she may have intended to stand by Callum, to comfort him, dare she think it . . . *to love him*, he would never accept her.

Not when their entire relationship was grounded in a lie—the one thing Callum could not abide.

Lifting her head, she pushed a dangling lock of hair from her eyes, and was surprised to feel damp tears cooling on her cheeks.

Was it too late for her to admit all and hope he could forgive her? Or was it too soon—for though she was falling in love with Argyll, she could not be sure that his feelings for her ran quite so deep.

Oh, what was she to do?

"Jenny? What's wrong?"

Turning her head, Jenny saw Meredith standing just behind her, her brilliant copper hair gleaming in the bright sunlight.

She lifted a hopeful smile to her lips, knowing she could not confess to Meredith, or the Featherton ladies. They would only try to help, each in her own misdirected way.

No, Jenny knew she had to find her own way if she was to salvage any piece of her budding relationship with Callum.

And so, without a word, she linked arms with Meredith, and slowly walked down the road toward the carriages.

The journey back to Bath that early afternoon was brutal, at least for Jenny. Owing to a thin strip of gray clouds on the horizon, Callum suggested an early close to their picnic. Of course Jenny knew that the supposed coming storm was just an excuse to see the day through. The clouds were as thin as her old lace chemise and

quite unable to carry the sort of storm he warned the
Feathertons about.

And if she had any doubt as to his true intentions,
which she didn't, all was made abundantly clear when
Callum announced he would ride up top with the coachman, leaving Jenny alone with Meredith inside.

When they arrived at the Featherton household, Lord
Argyll bid Jenny no more than a polite good-bye before
quitting to return to his own lodgings.

"Is all well between the two of you?" Lady Viola
asked as they entered the house and deposited their
wraps with their footmen.

Jenny looked up at the two old ladies, who were
waiting expectantly for her reply. Knowing their penchant for creative matchmaking of the most extreme nature, there was no way she could tell them the truth, but
neither did she wish to lie. So she settled for the next
best thing—a half truth. "H-he kissed me," she said as
modestly as possible. "I suppose I am still a little
shaken."

The Feathertons whipped their heads around to look
at each other, their faces positively beaming with delight.

"You must come into the drawing room and tell us all
about it!" Lady Viola caught Jenny's arm and urged her
forward.

"No, my lady, *please.*" Jenny remained firm in her
stance. "My senses are still overwhelmed, and I need a
bit of time to understand the great emotions I am expe-
riencing. Would you mind if we chatted later . . . once
I've had a bit of time to reflect?"

Lady Letitia moved her walking stick forward and
hugged Jenny close. "Of course, gel. One's first taste of

love is often a mite difficult to digest. Give your feelings time to settle. But when you are ready, we'll be waiting."

And Jenny knew they would be.

But when she descended below stairs, eager to be alone with her thoughts, someone was already waiting for her. Her mother.

"Well, I am glad you've returned because there is something for you outside the door. Go on, have a look." Tapping her foot impatiently, her mother lifted her brows and puckered her lips as Jenny walked to the service door and depressed the handle.

Inside the basket outside the kitchen door were— *mercy*.

"No need to count. I've done it for you. There are thirty-two."

Thirty-two stones. Thirty-two orders for her to fill this eve.

Jenny gasped for air.

Chapter Eight

As she strolled down Milsom Street later that afternoon, Jenny peeled off her right kid glove and pressed
the back of her cool hand first to one cheek, then the
other. "Feel my head, Annie. Do I feel overwarm to
you?"

"Honestly, Jenny. You are making far too much out of
this." The pair paused for a moment on the flag way.

Prefacing her fever test with a roll of her eyes that
did not escape Jenny's notice, Annie removed her own
glove and slapped her palm to Jenny's forehead. "No,
ducks, you feel fine."

"Well, something is wrong." Jenny expelled a long
sigh. "I mean, here I am shopping, with loads of money
in my reticule, and I feel nothing. *Nothing.*"

"Nothing?" Annie looked at her with some concern.
"Not even a bit of excitement, a little tremble of anticipation? We're almost to Bartleby's you know."

"I *know.* Look, look down." Jenny pointed at her
boots. "My step hasn't even hastened—not one bit!"

"Now that ain't normal. At least not for *you.*"

And it *wasn't* normal for Jenny, not at all! She adored
shopping. Dreamed of shopping. Lived for shopping.

But today, she couldn't care less about pillaging the shops of Bath.

"Maybe you're just distracted," Annie offered. "How many pots do you have to set up tonight?"

"Thirty-two."

Annie smiled then. "That's all it is then. You're just worried about such a large order. You'll be up all night long, I reckon."

"I suppose you might have something there," Jenny muttered. Of course, Annie wasn't right. The work, though exhausting, wasn't what was weighing on her mind. Wasn't what was distracting her so fully that she couldn't enjoy visiting the shops on Milsom.

Her mind was on Callum and the lie of all grand lies that threatened to destroy any potential for love.

Worse yet, she still didn't have the slightest notion of how to remedy the situation.

Confess her lie now, before love has fully set up, and she will lose him.

But wait for love to grow, so both their hearts are bound, then confess, she will lose him still. *Perdition.* What was she to do?

She had hoped that running her fingers over fabric and baubles would be enough to distract her from these thoughts—for it never failed to overtake her mind before—but it didn't divert her this time. Not at all.

"Jenny. I say, *Jenny?*"

She looked up and saw Annie holding Bartleby's door open for her.

"You are in bad spirits." Annie shook her head as Jenny entered the store. "Why, you almost passed by your favorite shop."

With a forlorn sigh, Jenny stared blankly into a glass case full of new silk scarves.

"Now, they're nice aren't they? Just your style too," Annie added. "And here, look at the sign. Straight from London, they are."

Jenny nodded. She knew she really ought to have one of the scarves, even if she had no desire to make a careful comparison just now. She had the money after all. But as she blinked down into the case, nothing appealed.

Well, the red one with ivory border was nice. She could make do with that one. And maybe, just maybe, the simple act of buying something would shake her from her melancholy mood.

As Mr. Bartleby, the shopkeeper, came around, Jenny pointed at the scarf and opened her mouth to speak when another customer rudely interrupted.

"I'll take the red one."

Bartleby bent and touched a rose-hued scarf to the left.

"No, no. *That* one!" the woman insisted, poking her finger on the other side of the glass.

Jenny could not believe it. The shopkeeper was reaching for *her* red scarf with the ivory border!

"Stop!" Jenny very nearly shouted. "That one is *mine*. I saw it first and I was next to be served." She turned to the rude woman, a ready glare already set on her face. But when their eyes met, Jenny's knees nearly buckled beneath her.

It was the woman dressed in red that she saw at the Pump Room only the other day! "*You*," she hissed.

The woman behind her, who was at least a hand taller

than Jenny, sneered down her nose. "I asked for the scarf first. It is *mine*."

Jenny snapped her head around and snatched the scarf from Mr. Bartleby with her left hand, while digging inside her reticule for a coin. Then she handed both to the shopkeeper.

"Here you are, sir. You may wrap it up. I shall take it with me now."

To her astonishment, the man just shook his head. "I told you not to come back here—without all the money you owe on your account."

Jenny held up her reticule. "But I have paid you for the scarf."

"Can you pay off your account?" he replied in an odd voice that made her think his nose was blocked.

Blast! She had plenty of blunt with her, just not quite enough to pay off her account. "Not completely, but I can—"

Mr. Bartleby smiled as he wrapped the scarf in a length of brown paper.

Jenny turned around and gave a satisfied smirk to the woman behind her.

But then the shopkeeper did the unthinkable. He passed the parcel over Jenny's head to the woman from the Pump Room.

"Why, thank you," the woman said, casting a laughing glance at Jenny as she tossed a gold coin to Mr. Bartleby.

Jenny's eyes went wide with absolute disbelief. Her facial muscles went slack and her mouth dropped open of its own accord.

"Come back with the whole account payment," the shopkeeper told her, "and I will be happy to do business with you again. Meanwhile, I'll apply the guinea you gave me to your debt."

"Ah!" Jenny exclaimed as she caught up Annie's arm and started for the door. "Well, I never!"

"I know you never—never *pay*, that is," the shopkeeper called out with a nasty chuckle as Jenny exited the establishment.

❧

After visiting the dispensing apothecary for the supplies she needed, Jenny headed back to Royal Crescent. Eighteen more stones were piled in the order basket by the time she reached the house that evening. She nearly cried when she saw the teetering pile.

By morn, after spending her nocturnal hours toiling over a steaming cauldron, then setting up the blend of moisture cream and essential oils into no less than fifty gallipots, Jenny was exhausted.

Still, she sat in the drawing room with her employers, hands folded in her lap, patiently awaiting the dance master.

Lady Letitia peered at her through the quizzing glass she wore on a golden chain about her neck. "Heavens, gel, you look positively ashen this morn. Did you not sleep at all?"

"Oh, Sister. How insensitive you can sometimes be. 'Tis obvious she has not slept, and who can blame her? Lord Argyll kissed her yesterday. A gel's first kiss is a momentous occasion."

At the comment, Mr. Edgar, who had just delivered a tray of tea and biscuits, cleared his throat loudly. "I beg your pardon, my ladies," he murmured. "Just a dry tickle."

I beg your pardon, indeed. Jenny shot a barely masked scowl at him. *Go ahead, Mr. Edgar, tell the ladies that their protégée has kissed at least a half-dozen footmen on the Royal Crescent alone. I'm sure they'd be quite interested in that.*

Lady Letitia smiled empathetically at Jenny. "I do understand. Are you fit enough for a dance lesson this morn?"

"Oh, yes, my lady. Wouldn't miss my lesson for anything, for I do not wish to embarrass either you . . . or Lord Argyll."

The old women exchanged pleased glances.

"Lord Argyll is a fine, fine catch, if I do say so myself," Lady Viola informed her. "His father was Lord Lyon, you know."

Jenny felt the skin above her brows wrinkle. "But Callum Campbell is the Sixth Viscount Argyll . . . *Argyll*, not Lyon. What am I not understanding?"

A guttural laugh burst from Lady Letitia's lips, making her sister spill a grand splash of steaming tea on the silver salver. "No, no, gel. The title 'Lord Lyon' is an esteemed elected position in Scotland. 'Tis he who records and monitors Scotland's heraldry and governs her ranking peers."

"He worked for years to acquire the position, much to his wife Olivia's hardship and dismay, I'll have you know. And in the end, the assembly unanimously elected Callum's father, Lord Argyll, to the position."

"Oh, that is a great honor." But something about this revelation did not meld with Callum's view of his father. And so, Jenny decided to take the opportunity presented to her and delve a bit further into the Argyll history. "His family, therefore, must have been very important to Lord Lyon."

"More likely his family name." Lady Letitia snorted. "The standing and continuity of Argyll was always foremost in his mind. In fact, it was his most earnest desire to see his son marry and produce an heir before he died."

"As we all know, that hasn't happened—yet." With a trembling hand, Lady Viola passed her sister a cup of tea. "Oh, Jenny, dear, do not think the viscount is disinterested in marriage, for I do not believe this to be so."

"That's right," Lady Letitia quipped. "He just hadn't yet met you, gel." She whooped with laughter again, nearly spilling her tea upon her outdated lavender gown.

When Lady Viola offered her tea, Jenny took it graciously and made a point to smile at her and her sister as if in agreement with their assessment of the situation.

Only Jenny's intuition told her there was something more to Callum's continued bachelorhood. She remembered hearing the two women discussing Callum's exploits at the Fire and Ice Ball and how the former Lord Argyll would be tossing in his grave.

No, there was more to Callum than the Featherton ladies were telling her.

And she planned to know what it was.

Ten pots were still left in the basket that morn. *Ten!* Jenny came back inside and closed the kitchen door hard behind her. But as she did, she caught notice of the scullery maids grinning.

"Did you put the extra stones into my basket?" she asked.

They only cackled gleefully, then grabbed up their ash buckets and dashed out of the room.

Seething mad, Jenny slammed her basket down on the table.

Those conniving wretches had better run. They'd played a jolly good trick on her, they had. Made her stay up at least an additional two hours last night filling their false orders.

Oh, they made her so bleedin' angry! Why, she would certainly be within her rights if she was to wring their thick necks.

Today was not the time for the maids to pull their little stunt. Jenny's mood had been blacker than soot for two days already, for since her day jaunt to Dyrham Park there had been no card or communication of any kind from Callum. *None*.

Thankfully for her, however, the ladies were well aware of this, and had already taken matters into hand.

Yesterday, they had sent around invitations to an intimate dinner party. Lord Argyll was the first on their guest list, but the ladies also admitted to extending their hospitality to at least one other. It wouldn't do to have it appear the rout was merely a ploy to position Callum before Jenny again. Which it was, of course.

A spinet player and a small quartet had been engaged to provide just the music to showcase Jenny's newly acquired dance steps. Yes, the ladies had already gone to quite a lot of trouble to bring Jenny and Callum together.

Most amazing, however, was the new gown that had just arrived from Bristol.

When Jenny opened the parcel, she had to applaud Lady Viola's classic sense of style even if she never seemed to ply it on herself. The luxurious gown was made of fine dove-gray silk, and had short puffed sleeves as light and sheer as summer clouds. A gossamer overdress, iced with silver threads and tiny fresh pearls, overlaid the bodice and skirt that seemed to sparkle and shimmer in the candlelight.

Still, even the surprise of such a wondrous gown did little to lighten Jenny's mood. And she knew nothing would, until she was sure of her standing with Callum.

Crossing her arms over her chest, Jenny looked at the ten gallipots with disgust at first, but then her outlook suddenly brightened. Dashing into her bedchamber, she pulled open the drawer in her bedside table and drew out a slightly dog-eared but still serviceable piece of foolscap, as well as a frayed quill pen and a glass pot of ink. Within moments, she had penned her message.

Lady E. regrets that she will be unable to fulfill more than ten orders this eve.

Smiling for the first time that day, she affixed the note to the handle of her order basket and set the lot outside the kitchen door.

Jenny nearly skipped back to her chamber and plopped down on her bed. *Finally*, she would get some sleep this eve.

As she lay on her back, she reached over, picked up her oval looking glass, and peered into it.

Oh, my word. Her face was as wan as a ripening rain cloud! She could not wear the dove-gray gown this eve.

The "just risen from the grave" look wasn't apt to draw Callum back to her.

What could she do?

Jenny sat bolt upright in her bed as the solution occurred to her. *The cream.*

Snatching up her ink-soaked quill, she raced outside the kitchen door and scratched through the phrase "ten pots" on her foolscap note and changed it to "nine."

Then she lifted a pot of the cream and carried it to her chamber. If a dab could bring back youthful vigor to the Featherton sisters' ancient faces, then a palmful might be just what was needed to raise her from the realm of the dead.

Gleefully, she scooped out a handful and smeared it over her cheeks, under her sleep-deprived eyes and across her forehead. Since she could not go about her daily chores with the tingle cream looking like white wave caps all over her face, she decided to lie down on her bed and rest for ten minutes while allowing the cream time to do its magic.

Who would miss her a mere ten minutes anyway?

"What in the king's name are you doin', gel? You can't be sleepin' the day away when there is a party to prepare for this eve!"

Jenny blinked her lids open. *Criminy.* Her eyes were stinging something fierce. Must have gotten a bit of the cream in them.

"Good heavens, Jenny. What have you got slathered all over your face?"

"Oh, a bit of my cream. Thought it might put a glow in my cheeks for the rout this eve."

But the horrified look on her mother's face told her the cream had done much more than that.

Hurriedly, she grabbed the oval glass and looked into it. Peering back at her was a red, swollen-faced beast, the like she'd never seen before! The oval slid from her hand and shattered on the floor.

"Oh, Mother, what shall I do?"

The housekeeper shook her head. "I don't know, child. You're the chemist. But whatever you decide, you best do it quickly. The ladies . . . they've sent me to fetch you."

⚜

Lady Viola gasped loudly as Jenny entered the drawing room. "Lord have mercy, child, what have you done to your face?"

"I—I was . . . testing my own blend of the cream. You know . . . the *below stairs* cream," she fibbed.

Lifting her quizzing glass to her eye, making it appear like a blinking bulbous fisheye, Lady Letitia studied Jenny's face from close range. "Oh, dear. Doesn't look good. Not good at all. Have you tried cold water to bring down the swelling?"

Jenny nodded futilely.

"Course you have." Groaning her displeasure, Lady Letitia returned to the settee to sit beside her sister.

Lady Viola wrinkled her brow and chewed her lower lip. "But why were you testing it . . . on your face?"

Why indeed? Jenny wondered. "Um, you see . . . Oh! I peered into the cauldron while the extract was steaming. Yes, that's it. I had no idea the blend was as powerful as it was."

"Oh, of course," the two ladies chimed in unison.

Jenny glanced at the japanned chair near the fire, and Lady Letitia motioned for her to take it. "I cannot see Lord Argyll like this," Jenny complained. "I just cannot."

Rising from the settee she and her sister shared, Lady Viola caned her way to Jenny. "But, my dear, 'tis too late to withdraw the invitation. Our guests will arrive in a few short hours."

Bobbing her head, Lady Letitia agreed. "Cook's nearly finished preparations for the meal. I am afraid the party must commence as planned, gel."

"Perhaps there *is* something we can do." Lady Viola's eyes brightened. "The rout can be an Arabian Nights party and we can all wear veils." Her eyes were large as she nodded her head, hoping to gain consent.

"Don't be daft, Viola." Lady Letitia gestured to Jenny. "Look at her swollen eyes. Veils would not conceal them. Besides, how would we eat?"

"Well, I do not hear you coming up with any solutions," Lady Viola muttered in a decidedly hurt tone.

"Give me a moment, if you will." Lady Letitia lifted her full bottom from the settee and began to pace. "Darkness is our only option, the only cloak that will conceal her face."

"What? Beggin' your pardon, my lady, but how can anyone entertain in the dark?" Jenny asked, for as far she could see, this was not a possibility at all.

Lady Letitia grinned mischievously and laughed from deep within her belly. "Oh, there is a way. Have no doubt."

A shiver of foreboding raised the wispy hairs on Jenny's forearms.

Just what wild scheme did the old lady have in mind this time?

⚜

Jenny, whose eyes had grown accustomed to the near total lack of light, watched helplessly as Mr. Edgar opened the door to Lord Argyll, who promptly stumbled in the darkness across the threshold.

"Spare a candle, me good man?" he asked, glancing into the drawing room where a lone candle burned.

Lady Letitia burst through the shadows and suddenly appeared behind him. "Welcome to our night of mystery and the *metaphysical*."

Visibly startled, Callum whirled around. "Lady Letitia. Good eve. An evenin' of . . . what did ye call it?"

Lady Viola, dressed in ghostly white, suddenly appeared at his elbow, which caused him to start.

"The *metaphysical*, my lord." She took his arm then, and giving a quick glance at Jenny, who still lurked in the gloom of the corner, escorted his lordship to the drawing room.

Oh, she couldn't follow them. Heavens, with all the powder and rouge the ladies had coated her face with, she had to look positively ghastly, even in the dimness.

"Come on," Meredith whispered to her. "I am going to read Lord Argyll's fortune. I can't wait to see his face when I mention *you* as his future bride."

Jenny breathed an exasperated sigh. "Oh, yes. I am sure he will believe the notion came upon you as a result of contact with the infinite."

"I've been practicing my trance in the cheval glass for twenty minutes. Do you want to see? I roll my eyes back in my head, then I just . . ."

Oh, my word. When would this night be over?

When Jenny glanced into the drawing room, she could just make out Lady Letitia waving at her to join them. So Jenny did the only thing she could, and ignored her employer, pretending instead that she didn't see her.

"Oh, there you are, Lady Genevieve." Lady Letitia beckoned again. "Come, come in. You too, Meredith, for our own Lord Argyll has arrived."

When Jenny smiled, however, she was sure she felt the powder and cream mixture on her face crack, and a small wedge detach. *Oh, no.* Her face was falling off!

Callum turned, but somehow in the thin light, she missed that he had bowed and she continued to walk forward.

"Oof!" she bellowed as his head raised up and punched her breasts skyward.

"I do beg yer fergiveness, Lady Genevieve. Most clumsy of me. Ye're not hurt are ye?" She felt his gloved hands on her arms, and she became aware of him looking her up and down.

"I am quite fine, my lord. No need to trouble yourself over me."

Just then, the brass doorknocker slammed against its rest, and the entire party turned to see who had arrived next.

Mr. Edgar collected the guest's wrap and directed her into the darkened drawing room.

"Good eve," came a familiar woman's voice. "I have come."

Jenny stood frozen to her spot. It was inconceivable. What were the Featherton ladies thinking?

It was the offensive widow from next door! Her evening of horror was now complete. Nothing else could possibly go wrong. There was nothing left, was there?

Then one of the scullery maids appeared at the door, candle in hand, and crooked her finger to Jenny.

Mr. Edgar, long legs taking abnormally lengthy strides, was bearing down on the girl fast. Even in the darkness it was clear the girl was worried, and no doubt would not have dared near the drawing room if something wasn't terribly wrong.

Jenny raced through the door and pulled the maid toward the passage to the back stairs before Edgar could reach her.

"Oh, Jenny, you're in it now." The maid's eyes were wide.

"What's wrong, Erma?" Jenny asked quickly, before Mr. Edgar could nab the scullery maid and pull her below stairs.

"It's Mr. Bartleby, from the shop. He came in through the kitchen door and is waitin' for you below stairs."

Jenny froze.

"He said, if I didn't find you and bring you to him, he would come above stairs and hunt you down 'imself."

"Surely he is having you on," Jenny rationalized.

A low nasal voice broke through the darkness behind her making her skin freeze.

"I assure you . . . *Lady Eros*, I am not."

Chapter Nine

"*Lady Eros?*" A painful throbbing drummed beneath the thin skin of Jenny's temples.

Hearing Bartleby's words, Erma spun around and dashed down the stairs, taking with her their only source of light. In the retreating candlelight, Jenny could see little more than a pale blur of the man's face before her. A twinge of fright raced across her scalp, making the roots of her hair prickle and raise up.

"I—I don't know to whom you are referring," she managed to add, but her words were thin and her voice shook with panic.

"I think you do," Bartleby replied evenly.

Mr. Edgar's tall lanky form cut abruptly between them and he spun to face Jenny, protectively shielding her from the rude shopkeeper. "My lady, you are wanted in the drawing room."

"Thank you, Mr. Edgar. I shall come presently."

Mr. Edgar pivoted slightly and stared down at the shorter man for several long seconds. Jenny heard Bartleby nervously wet his lips as Edgar hovered over him before stepping away and heading back to the drawing room.

"Mr. Bartleby, as you can see, I am otherwise engaged." Jenny struggled against the childish urge to duck down the stairs and hide beneath her bed. But she couldn't leave. She had to get the shopkeeper out of the house before he drew more notice and ruined everything for her. "If you do not mind, I shall call at your shop on the morrow to discuss whatever matter you find so important."

Hoping against hope that Bartleby would simply leave, Jenny turned around to follow Edgar into the drawing room, when the shopkeeper's fingers wrapped around her upper arm and squeezed tight.

"Sir, you forget yourself!" she shrieked, a little more loudly than she should have, for her knight in shining armor was inside the passage at her side in an instant.

"Might I be of some assistance, Lady Genevieve?" Callum asked, forcefully knocking the shopkeeper's arm from Jenny's. He moved his towering body within a breath of Bartleby, forcing the shopkeeper to look straight up to meet his piercing gaze.

Bartleby began to sputter, his threatening tone reduced to a mere mouse squeak. "I—I was just . . . well, her ladyship had admired a scarf at my establishment, but someone else acquired the item before she could purchase it. Just wanted to let her know that I'll receive another by week's end and shall keep it for her if she's still interested in purchasing it."

Jenny was impressed with Bartleby's alacrity with a lie, but that did not excuse his brash behavior this night.

"'Tis all right." She laid her hand on Callum's coat sleeve and he twisted at the waist and turned his chest toward her. "I informed Mr. Bartleby that I shall make every effort to visit his shop on the morrow."

She stepped beside Callum and wrapped her arm around the crook of his elbow as she spoke to Bartleby. "If that is all, Mr. Bartleby, would you please excuse me so I may return to the party?"

Mr. Bartleby bobbed a quick, nervous bow, then disappeared into the stairwell that led to the kitchen below.

Callum leaned his mouth near Jenny's ear as they started through the open door to the drawing room. "What was that all aboot?"

Jenny sighed, but turned a smile upon him. "Honestly, my lord, I do not know . . . exactly. But let us put him from our minds for we have a great surprise in store for you."

"Indeed we have." Meredith raced to the doorway and snatched Callum's hand. "Come with me, Argyll, and I shall predict your future. Oh, come now, do not hedge. My predictions of the future are startlingly accurate. You will see."

Even in the light of a single candle, no one in the room could have missed Meredith's pronounced wink in Jenny's direction.

After supping on roasted venison, a culinary choice Jenny could have done without after their trip to Dyrham, the small party returned to the drawing room for a supposed rousing demonstration of the metaphysical. Or rather, they settled for Meredith and her bag of inane party tricks.

Still, Jenny was grateful, for without Meredith's willingness to perform, the chandeliers would be glaring down on her red and puffed face at this very minute.

While Meredith positioned the young widow into a japanned chair, preparing to attempt Dr. Mesmer's famed mind control, Callum led Jenny to the settee, which was conveniently, for Jenny's hot and cracking face, located just out of the reach of candlelight.

In fact, they sat in absolute darkness.

Instead of causing Jenny worry, the idea that no one could see them was most titillating.

Like sun through a window, she could feel the blissful warmth of Callum's body beside her, could hear his slow breathing, and yet she could not see him. But neither could anyone else, a point on which he was obviously aware, for he took her hand in his, turned it over, and rubbed his thumb from her palm to the pads of her gloved fingertips.

Jenny shivered, and afterward felt a little embarrassed at her visceral reaction.

"Jenny," Callum whispered ever so softly.

The sound vibrated in her ear and tickled her, bringing a smile to her mouth.

"I am sorry aboot walking away from ye at the park. 'Tis no excuse, I ken, but I wasna ready to hear the truths ye spoke. Can ye fergive me?"

She turned her face toward his to reply and, not realizing he had moved his own closer, was surprised to feel her lips brush his firm lower lip.

She didn't know if he meant for their mouths to touch at all, or if he was urging her to lean in to truly kiss him. It really didn't matter. She *wanted* to experience his kiss again.

Needed to.

And in the ebony cloaked drawing room, she would.

She directed a wary glance across the room to where

the Featherton ladies sat in the candle's tight, circular glow.

Sure that they would not be seen, Jenny turned her body more fully toward Callum and ran her hand up his broad chest, then over the rough whiskered skin along his jaw. Her left hand slid through his tousled hair, and without even a nod to propriety, she slid her hand behind his neck and pulled his mouth to hers.

Callum's breath hitched, and belatedly, Jenny realized the boldness of her desire had surprised him. Somehow, though, deep within, this pleased her immensely and emboldened her further.

Suddenly she felt strong, large hands reach around and lift her body effortlessly. Her eyes went wide in the blackness and she felt Callum settle her atop his lap. But she could not protest. Darkness might cloak even the most salacious actions, but it could not mute words.

Now it was Jenny's turn to gasp as she became aware of the hard bulge upon which she now sat.

"This is unseemly, Callum. We are not alone," she whispered, instantly forgetting her shock as he traced the rim of her lip with the tip of his tongue, making her feel drugged and oddly drowsy.

"Shh. No one can see us, lass."

More than hearing his words, she felt them breathed hotly upon her lips, coaxing her mouth open so she might catch each one.

At once, she was obsessed with the desire to feel the contours of his body. She leaned firmly against him, pressing harder and harder as his tongue slid inside her mouth.

She felt his fingers flutter eagerly over her waist, and excitement surged inside of her as she imagined his hands touching her elsewhere. Then, as if she had willed it into occurring, his fingers began their slow climb upward over her bodice.

When his broad hand cupped her breast, she wanted to moan aloud, and indeed would have had his mouth not devoured the breath the sound rode before it escaped her.

Callum's hand moved agonizingly slowly, his fingers spreading wide, until through the gray silk, his thumb and forefinger came together around her hardened nipple and squeezed it gently.

Jenny's eyes snapped wide, and she pulled away from him, retreating to the far edge of the settee. He had supposed too much.

There were others in this room after all and only the veriest rake would dare attempt such a scandalous thing.

Oh, my word. Why had she not realized it? A wash of heat suffused her cheeks.

She had thought he was being genuine. Letting her come close, letting himself feel something for her.

But she had been wrong, hadn't she?

The walls around his heart stood ever stalwart and unbreachable.

The rogue had returned to his keep.

But then his hand reached for hers again, and gave it a reassuring squeeze. "I am sorry, Jenny. My passions got the better of me and I regret it. I want ye, want ye somethin' fierce, but I dinna wish to lose you."

She turned her head back to consider him, to see if the truth glistened in his eyes, but there was only darkness. Still, Jenny wondered, if for only an instant, if she had judged him unfairly.

Maybe, in all honesty, he did feel something for her—something more than needless lust.

But it wasn't love. Mustn't fool herself about that. Most certainly not.

❧

Thankfully, due to Meredith's performance's miserable failure to impress, the evening was drawn to an early close, much to Jenny's relief.

While the widow and Callum were each handed their hats and wraps by the glow of a lone candle, Jenny enfolded herself in the shadows once more.

"Lord Argyll." The Widow McCarthy slipped her bony arm around his. "You will be so kind as to escort me next door, won't you? Being alone, as I am, I have a fear of venturing into the night—the thieves you know. Why, they attacked Mrs. Potswallow this just morn. Got away with her miser bag, I heard, but left her with a goose egg on her skull the size of a fist." She feigned a body-rattling shiver. "I own, I fear they may be waiting just outside to take advantage of a poor defenseless woman."

From the protection of the darkness, Jenny all but snarled at the wanton widow. Even in the low light of a single candle, Jenny could see the way her bulging eyes greedily devoured Callum. Jenny cocked a brow at her, sure that if anyone was taken advantage of this night, it would be Lord Argyll.

Callum's wry expression was plain too. "But of course. I shall be honored."

The widow and Callum bid Meredith and the Feathertons good eve, and as they neared the front door the odd pair paused before Jenny.

The widow squinted and leaned forward, as if trying to see her better. "I do apologize that we did not have a chance to better know each other this eve."

Jenny pressed the back of her head against the joining of walls, desperately trying to cloak her face in the deepest shadow in the entryway. Her breath came fast.

The widow held her tongue silent for a moment as if considering something. "I own, if you would condescend to join me for tea on Friday afternoon, perhaps we could discover together from whence I know you. For you do look familiar and I never forget a face."

Jenny's heart skipped like a flat pebble across a pond. There was absolutely no way she could take tea with the widow. Why, the crafty madam would realize her identity if her gaze settled upon her for yet another single unbroken minute!

Jenny's uncomfortable silence somehow urged Callum into the breach.

"Lady Genevieve has agreed to join me for a stroll in Sydney Gardens on Friday."

The breath Jenny had not realized she'd been holding slowly expelled from her lungs. "Yes, I am sorry, Lady McCarthy. Perhaps another time?"

The widow's eyes grew small as pinpricks. "To Sydney Gardens . . . in the winter? Hmm. W-well, I suppose we could take tea on—"

Callum pulled the widow's arm tight against his ribs, and her words were left poised in the air, replaced by a girlish giggle as he led her to the door. "Come along, madam, if ye please. The night grows late and I confess to an early appointment on the morrow."

"Oh, *of course*, my lord."

As Callum escorted her over the threshold, the widow shot a smug glance over her shoulder, undoubtedly meant for Jenny.

As Mr. Edgar closed the door behind them, and her mother busied herself lighting the candles in the drawing room and the sconces in the entry hall, Jenny caught a glimpse of herself in the gilt mirror in the passage.

The sight gave her a jolt right down to her slippers. Her face was a mottled blend of white powder and red skin where the facial concealing cream had dried and broken off like cracked plaster from an ancient wall.

Lady Letitia laid a hand on Jenny's shoulder. "Reducing the candles to one was the only way, but I think the evening was quite the success." She looked back at Lady Viola. "Do you not agree, Sister?"

Lady Viola tapped her cane upon the floor as she neared. "Well, 'tis not for us to say. Jenny, you and Argyll slipped into the darkness together for quite some time." She paused, and Jenny knew she awaited a recounting, but she was not about to give it. "And you did accept his invitation, it seems, for Sydney Gardens . . ."

Jenny nodded, hoping to purchase a little more time to craft her words, but the Feathertons stared impatiently. "To be honest, my ladies, I am not sure of our progress. At times, I think he harbors *some* feelings for me."

"Well, he likes you well enough, I'd say." Meredith gestured to Jenny's face. "The concealing cream is *completely* gone from around your mouth."

The two Featherton sisters chuckled at that.

"So he kissed you again, did he?" Lady Letitia brashly asked.

"Yes." Jenny sighed then and brought her palms to her swollen cheeks. "Oh, I am so confused. He has a reputation as a rake of the first order."

"Is that all?" Lady Viola laughed at that. "Well, you are right—in part. From what I know, and this information comes from a most reliable source, mind you, he has left a trail of broken hearts from Aberdeen to Cornwall."

Clearing her throat loudly, Meredith interrupted her aunt. "Not helping, Auntie . . ." she murmured through nearly closed lips.

"Darling, allow me to finish." Lady Viola took Jenny's shoulders and stared up into her eyes. "He dances with them at assemblies, or woos them at parties. But for only one night. No more. There has never been an exception to his one-woman, one-night habit—until now. Or so I've heard."

A nervous twitch fired through Jenny as she considered what she'd just been told.

Could it be? Was it possible, that like her, he was beginning to fall in love?

By the next morning the swelling and redness were gone, thanks to her mother's suggestion that before going to bed Jenny repeatedly plunge her face into a basin of icy well water.

This was good, of course, and Jenny knew she should be happy, but she wasn't.

Dread sat heavily upon her chest making even the act of breathing difficult . . . or maybe it was her new corset. Still, she now had no excuse not to visit Mr.

Bartleby as she'd promised. He would not have made his way all the way up the Royal Crescent just to discuss her account. Heavens! She didn't owe him that much, or at least she didn't think she did. Mayhap she should have looked at the last accounting notice he'd sent to the house before dropping it into the fire.

No, his addressing her as Lady Eros told her exactly the topic of conversation he wanted to pursue. Jenny wondered how he'd made the connection. It made no sense for anyone in service to expose her, for they'd be risking losing the income they made from the cream.

After waking and dressing Meredith, Jenny retrieved her gray wool shawl, for she decided it was important that she resume her lady's maid role for this particular meeting.

As she walked through the kitchen, she caught a lustrous glow from the corner of her eye, and turned. *Jupiter!* There dangling from the ears of one of the wretched scullery maids was a set of pearl earbobs. And they were from Bartleby's shop too. Second case from the far left on the top shelf. But how could the scullery maid afford—*oooh. Of course.*

"Oy, Erma." Narrowing her eyes, Jenny started for the chit, fists clenched.

When the scullery maid saw Jenny's face, she turned with a yelp and hid behind her plump friend, the other scullery maid, Martha. "Leave me be, Jenny. I didn't mean nothin' by it."

"You told him *I* was the source of the cream. Do you know what you've done?" Jenny growled while reaching around Martha for Erma, who bobbed and dodged to escape her.

Martha folded her arms and lifted her chin to Jenny.

"What do you think you're goin' to do about it? You can't do nothin', for if you do, the ladies above stairs will hear what you're up to."

Jenny lowered her hands and thought. Then she turned on her heel and headed off for the door.

"That's right, Jenny. You can't do nothin'," Erma called out after her.

Jenny stopped, and glanced back over her shoulder. "I don't *have* to do anything but go and meet with Mr. Bartleby. But once I tell Bath's service staff who cut off their income, I do not doubt they will wish to ... *discuss* it with you."

Even after Jenny closed the door, she could hear Erma's anguished shriek.

🐚

When Jenny entered Bartleby's, draping herself with a mantle of false calm, a bell affixed to a metal coil over her head drew the shopkeeper's attention.

A slow smile crept across his face. He quickly closed and locked his money box, then headed for the door and flipped over the water-stained wood sign to read CLOSED from the street.

Setting her shoulders, Jenny lifted her nose arrogantly. "Let us not delay, for I have not much time to spare. Last night you had the audacity to interrupt my ladies' party to demand I meet you this day. I wish to know why."

Bartleby chuckled and with his elbow resting on the countertop, he shifted his weight to lean upon it. "Pretty hoity-toity these days, aren't you, Miss Penny?"

Jenny glanced up at the figure scrawled next to her

name on Bartleby's account chalkboard. Then, with a curt nod, she withdrew a miser bag from her basket and tossed it upon the counter beside him. "This should be more than enough to settle my account. Good day, sir." Raising a brow, she turned her back on him and started for the door.

"Stop! Or by thunder, I swear you'll regret it."

Freezing in place, Jenny could feel her heart pounding beneath her gown. Slowly she turned her eyes toward him, with the wariness of a mouse beneath a hawk's gaze.

"I do apologize, Miss Penny, but you've got something I want, and I mean to have it."

"And what would that be, sirrah?"

"Why, we both know the answer to that, *Lady Eros*. I want an exclusive to sell your cream in my store."

Jenny forced a hard laugh. "I fear you have me confused with someone else."

"You can stop toying with me, Miss Penny. I have all the proof I require. Proof I shall not hesitate to share with others if you do not accept my terms."

The pounding of Jenny's heart became louder still, and the room began to close in about her. He was going to expose her.

Callum was going to learn the truth. Oh, she couldn't breathe. Her corset felt far too tight. Jenny tugged at her bodice. Dark spots were swirling before her eyes. She had to get out of here.

Gasping, Jenny staggered for the door. "I need air. *Please*."

Instead, Bartleby raced forward, drew Jenny to a ladder-back chair, and settled her into it. "I'm sorry. I didn't mean to frighten you, but I must have some of that cream."

Panting, Jenny rolled her eyes to the left to look at him. "W-why? Why is the cream so . . . important . . . to you?"

Mr. Bartleby knelt on one knee and cast his gaze to the floor. "I've had a run of bad luck."

But Jenny hardly heard his words. Over his shoulder, her eyes had focused on a pair of moonstone earbobs. The translucent feldspar caught the light and held it, making the stones glow with brilliant opalescence.

Her mouth went dry as she stared, mouth agape, at the sparkling bobs. She had to have them, but blast, she'd already given every last guinea she had to Bartleby.

Then she suddenly came up with an idea. She whipped her head around and stared hard at him, her breath miraculously restored. "Your financial downfall is hardly my problem." She gave him a shrewd glance. "But . . . since you seem to have me at a disadvantage, perhaps we can come to some agreement."

Bartleby came to his feet. "Perhaps. Yes, perhaps we can."

"I cannot give you an exclusive, for I employ a rather large sales force. But I have an idea that might make this venture worth both our time."

🌺

Twenty minutes later, Jenny nearly skipped from Bartleby's, she was so delighted. Pausing at a shop window, she peered at her reflection and smiled brightly at the moonstone bobs dangling prettily from her ears.

Annie, who'd been waiting outside for her, was confused. "Well, what did he want?"

"Just as we'd guessed, the cream."

"You didn't promise it to him, did you?"

Jenny winced slightly. "He threatened to reveal my identity to the newspapers if I didn't allow him to sell the cream, so I made him a deal."

Annie cringed as if she felt the guineas being snatched from her hand. "I am afraid to ask."

"Don't worry. You and the others can still sell to your mistresses and masters. But I must supply Bartleby with ten pots a week."

Clapping a hand to her forehead, Annie began to laugh. "Ten pots? Those will be sold in no time." Her countenance grew serious then. "He'll be wantin' more. And he'll press you until he gets it."

Jenny tapped her index finger to her temple. "When I discussed it with him, I realized it wasn't so much the tingle cream that he wanted, but that he needed to increase the traffic into his store."

"So?"

"So I suggested that he give the pots away."

Annie's eyes bulged in her head. "Are you mad?"

"No, silly. He would give a pot away with any purchase from his top shelf jewel case. Well, he adored the idea, and to show his appreciation, he gifted me a little something from that very case." Jenny flicked one of her earbobs playfully. "Pretty, aren't they? They're moonstone, you know."

"Well, blow me down. You are an original, Jenny, I'll give you that."

"Why thank you, Annie." Jenny took one more

glance at her reflection, smiled at it, and turned in the direction of Royal Crescent.

⚜

The next morning, Jenny awoke in the thin light of dawn to begin her duties. But when she peered out a window as the clock sounded the ten o'clock hour that morn, the day had still not brightened at all.

The sky was heavy with a ceiling of low dark clouds, and when she retrieved the order basket from outside the kitchen door, the air was so cold it almost hurt her lungs to breathe it.

Still, Jenny held out hope that Lord Argyll would hold true to his promise and escort her to Sydney Gardens that afternoon.

"I think you might want to call off your excursion for today." Lady Letitia looked up from the morning paper. "The last time I saw a sky as gray, snow fell up to my knees."

Jenny smiled back at her and gazed up at the thick sky above. "The clouds are moving quite fast. Perhaps the coming storm will pass us by."

Lady Viola chuckled. "One can always hope."

For the next few hours the blood coursed through Jenny's veins at an alarming speed, and she felt as though she'd consumed far too many cups of black tea.

As the short hand in the tall case clock neared the four o'clock hour, Jenny opened the kitchen door and peered outside. The air had warmed somewhat, but if it was possible, the sky was darker still, and the puddle at the end of the walk remained solidly frozen.

Her spirits plummeted. For certain, Callum would send word that their private outing was not to be.

Jenny walked into her chamber and began to unfasten the lacings at her back. The new walking gown she wore would not have been appropriate for such a bitter day anyway. But she loathed to remove it.

For some moments, she stood and peered down at it, then turned and glanced over her shoulder at the back. She would have looked smashing, if she did say so herself. Argyll would not have had one thought about the weather when he saw her in this gown.

The dress itself was deceptively simple for it was made of printed muslin, a cerulean blue spotted with black and bordered flounces of the same material. But between each flounce was an unexpected dart of black brocaded satin ribbon, elevating the dress to the upper reaches of style.

On her bed lay a bonnet of straw-colored gossamer satin, ornamented on the left side with a single full-blown rose of silk and a plume of white feathers. Even her slippers of pale blue kid and her washing leather gloves were perfectly coordinated.

She so wanted to wear this walking dress for Callum. Jenny sat down on her bed and sulked and wondered if anyone would disapprove if she wore the ensemble while she did her chores this day.

"Jenny," came her mother's voice from the stairwell. "You are wanted above stairs."

"Just a moment. I suppose I must change." Jenny sucked in a deep, disappointed breath and blew it out through her lips.

"Well, hurry, child, Lord Argyll is waiting to take you to Sydney Gardens."

Jenny leapt to her feet and snatched up her bonnet. Excitement surged through her limbs and fingers, making the act of tying her bonnet's ribbon and the lacing of her gown nearly impossible.

Lifting her coordinating cerulean overcoat from the hook on the back of her door, Jenny took the stairs two at a time to meet Callum.

Her heart was thudding as she entered the passage and saw him.

A smile lit his eyes and she noticed that even in this freezing weather, he wore a kilt.

She sighed with pleasure, somehow unable to believe it.

Her Highlander had come for her after all.

Chapter Ten

Sydney Gardens sat regally perched at the end of Great Pulteney Street like a sparkling emerald atop a scepter. It was not such a long way by carriage from Royal Crescent to the Gardens. Had they traveled the distance by foot in such bitter cold, however, Jenny was certain they would have resembled two icicles more than two people.

As she glanced at the frost building on the inside of the carriage window, she wondered if this outing was foolhardy. For no matter how much she had longed to visit with her handsome escort, or to wear her new walking ensemble, the weather was worsening.

It was only a matter of time before the sky opened up and blanketed the city with snow or ice.

"'Tis rather an ominous day fer a stroll, I ken, but I wanted to see ye again, Jenny." Callum rose from the leather bench across from her and settled himself by her side. Heat radiated from him like a coal-filled brazier and she felt warmer now, but no less nervous.

Jenny flattened her hand against the window and held it there until its heat melted a peephole in the thin breath of ice built up on the inside of the window. She looked up at the sky and wanted to groan.

Large heavy flakes were already beginning to fall. Still, the snow suited her purposes well enough. After all, Callum already thought her different from other women. Now was her chance to show him she was not the typical delicate English rose. Far from it. The snow would provide just the opportunity to show him her mettle.

"Oh, the weather's not so bad," she said casually. "Besides, I wore my new walking gown today and what would the Featherton ladies think if I did not even attempt to test its warmth by taking a short stroll?"

Callum's mouth twitched with amusement. "Weel, if ye're that intent on trekkin' through the snow, perhaps a wee walk then—just over the cast-iron canal bridge . . . then back to the carriage before the chill wind makes us as blue as yer gown."

She looked up at him through her lashes and gave him an impish smile, but all the while her mind was wondering just what a Scotsman wore beneath his kilt on a bitter day like this. If the answer was still 'nothing,' she had to give the Scots credit, for they were certainly more hearty than their English brothers.

Seeing through Jenny's hand-shaped portal that they had reached Sydney Gardens, Callum rose up and rapped on the carriage's forward wall.

The coachman slowed the conveyance and rolled to a skidding stop right alongside the ice-encrusted Kennet and Avon canal.

Like a ship on a stormy sea, the carriage rocked from side to side as the footman leapt down from atop and opened the carriage door to let down the steps for Jenny and Lord Argyll.

Jenny was first out of the carriage, eager to avail herself of a flattering pose for Callum. The moment her slippers touched the frozen ground she knew her insistence on a short stroll was naught but folly. Still, it would only take a moment or two for Callum to see for himself that she was not some frail society miss, but rather a strong woman—able to withstand the harsh Highland winters without so much as blinking her eyes. At least she hoped it wouldn't take long. As it was, the updrafts were making her colder than a goose sitting on a frozen pond.

As Callum descended the stairs, Jenny glanced down at her feet to gain better footing and saw her overcoat rippling in the wind, displaying its rich gold satin lining. She had to smile. Lud, she looked *fantastic* in this walking ensemble.

Smiling to herself, she took a turn and let the wind catch the center opening of her coat and lift each side into the air so they flew behind her like two regal banners.

She looked up to be sure Callum was looking at her, when her right foot slid forward, sending her into a deep lunge, as if she were dropping a deep curtsy.

Carefully, she slid her slipper back into place, but a prickly blend of fear and surprise still pumped mercilessly through her.

As she peered down to make sure no water stains pockmarked her slippers, she saw that under the thin layer of snow was an almost invisible coating of ice. This wasn't good. Why, one false move and she'd end up on her rear, ruining the enchanting image she'd worked so hard to achieve. Best head back for the carriage.

Warily, she started to push her feet forward without lifting them and inviting a fall, but the instant she moved, her slippers started to slide out from beneath her.

Her head swiveled and she glanced behind her.

Oh, God. She was too near the edge of the canal.

"Callum!"

Flailing her arms in wild circles, Jenny fought to keep her balance. But it was no use—she was falling backward.

The next thing she knew was a feeling of weightlessness and the world seemed to slow around her.

In total disbelief, she saw her feet rising up above her head, and Callum's startled eyes as his hands reached out for her, but came away empty.

She plummeted backward, slamming down upon the ice-skinned surface of the canal. The ice crunched sharply beneath her and she gasped as frigid water rushed around her, then sucked her beneath its surface.

Tumbling with the current, she struggled and battled with everything she had, but it was useless. Her coat and gown, sodden with water, held her under the racing water as surely as if they were made of leaden weights.

Jenny's lungs burned until she could hold the air inside them no longer. Her breath left her in a mass of brilliant bubbles rising to the surface, and she could do nothing but watch from below in abject horror.

Then quite suddenly everything was black.

"Jenny . . . *Jenny.* Open yer eyes, lass."

From the darkness, a low voice coaxed her forward, urged her to leave her woolen cocoon of ebony. But she didn't want to. She wanted to rest. Still that voice was calling, calling.

'Twas Callum.

At this realization, her eyelids fluttered and opened to an expansive chamber, devoid of light but for a candle on a table beside the bedstead and a hot fire flickering in the hearth.

Her fingers twitched as she awoke more fully, fluttering along the soft edges of the several thick blankets and counterpanes covering her. Flowing white bedclothes framed the massive tester she lay upon.

An urgent thought screamed in her mind.

This was not her bed. Not her room. No, it was much too spacious. Too grand.

This was all so confusing. What had happened to her? Why was she here?

Where was . . . "Callum?" Her voice was raspy and raw even to her own ears and she cringed at the sound of it.

She felt a warm nuzzle at her ear then, and the hum of his low, comforting voice beside it.

"I am here, lass."

Her gaze darted toward him. Their eyes met and a shard of panic cut through Jenny. She flung herself bolt upright in the bed. My word. She was in bed with Lord Argyll!

"What am I doing here? In b-bed . . . with y-you?"

"Dinna ye remember anything, lass?" His voice was as warm as the body she felt pressed against her underneath the covers.

Jenny struggled to think, tried to piece together some logical chain of events that would culminate with her lying in bed with Lord Argyll. But nothing came to her.

This made no sense at all!

She shivered violently, and felt her nipples harden as she shook. Glancing down, Jenny saw that she was entirely naked. At once she scooted under the blankets again.

Had she lost her mind?

"I remember n-nothing at all." Her teeth were chattering, knocking hard against each other as she spoke and she could not seem to stop them. "Callum, p-please. W-what is h-happening. Why are we h-here . . . *t-together*?"

He pulled her against the warmth of his bare chest and drew the counterpane close about her. "Dinna fash, Jenny. 'Tis all right now."

She felt him gently kiss the top of her head.

"Ye slipped on the ice, and fell down into the canal. Nearly drowned too, fer yer coat and gown drew ye straight to the bottom."

"My *gown*. Where is it?"

Callum lifted a finger and pointed through the opening in the bed curtains. "Dryin' by the fire, with me own clothes."

Jenny twisted and strained to see her ensemble. But when she saw it, she wished she hadn't looked. It was too horrible, for there everything was, propped on a wooden drying rack, rumpled and stained.

Tears began to course down Jenny's cheeks as she stared at her beloved walking ensemble.

"Och, come here, love. Ye're rememberin' now, aren't ye? 'Twas a horrible accident, to be sure, but 'tis over now."

Jenny nodded. He was right, she was remembering.

"Shh, just stay close, lass. Stay warm. 'Tis the only way."

And then, as she became more lucid, she realized she was lying naked in the arms of an equally naked man! She tried to push away, but his arm tightened around her.

"We can't do this. 'Tisn't right!" she croaked, realizing only then that hugging Callum's warm body had cured her teeth of chattering.

"Aye, '*tis* right. 'Twas the only way I knew to keep the both of us from freezin' to death."

Jenny stared blankly at the draped curtain that formed a ceiling over the bed. The room was dark. 'Twas night! Her mother would be worried. Mr. Edgar too. Oh, no. Her employers!

"I have to get h-home. What must the ladies be thinking? They must be ever so worried." She paused her rant and her eyes surveyed the chamber. "Callum, just where *are* we?"

"In Laura Place. In the house I've taken fer me stay."

"*Your* house?" Jenny swallowed deeply as the dire consequences of being in a bachelor's house registered. "I can't be here. I just can't." She tried to get up again, but he shifted and rolled atop her, his arms like bars on either side of her, preventing her escape.

His crisp chest hair brushed against her bare breasts, making her nipples harden and her cheeks flush. Between her thighs she felt him too, rigid and pulsing slightly against her, hastening the warmth to the most intimate part of her.

"I sent word of yer accident to the Featherton ladies. They know where ye are and sent back a note of thanks fer saving ye. And ye canna go anywhere . . . not this eve anyway."

Lud, it was hard to concentrate on what he was saying when she herself was lost in sensation. In the candlelight, Jenny could see Callum was more serious than she'd ever seen him. "Why can't I leave?" she managed.

"There is nigh on two feet of snow on the ground. And that *over* the ice that caused yer fall. So ye'll not be doing anything but stayin' in bed until the both of us are warm and weel again."

"The both of us?" Jenny looked over at her gown again, and at the kilt, coat, and lawn shirt beside it at the fire. Then she remembered what he'd said and suddenly it all made sense.

"You saved me. You jumped into the water, and saved me."

"Aye, I did."

"You risked your own life to save *me*." A smile took hold of Jenny's mouth.

"Aye," he almost growled. "Now stop repeatin' it, or ye'll make me regret I ever hauled ye from the canal."

This proved it. He could have sent the footman or coachman into the water after her, but he dove in himself. Jenny wrapped her arms around his waist and stared up into his eyes. "You fancy me, Lord Argyll. You *do*." Joyous laughter welled up inside of her and as it burst from her lips it shook her body, and she felt him grow stone hard against her.

"Christ, Jenny, ye've got to stop movin' like that when I'm atop of ye. I'm cold, lass, but I'm human too."

But that made Jenny laugh all the more.

"Jenny, *please*. Ye've got to stop movin' like that. Stop laughin'. *Jenny*. I mean it."

Then suddenly his mouth pressed against hers, and the mirth died in her throat. Instead a wanton moan welled up inside of her as she became all too aware of the growing hardness now pressing gently between her legs. Wicked excitement grew within her.

Jenny slipped her hands from Callum's lean waist and trailed her fingers along his sides, feeling the ripple of his ribs, the cords of his muscles beneath her fingertips.

And it was bliss. Her hands moved between them both, to the point where their bodies parted, and she ran her palms over the mounds of his chest, over his pebble-hard nipples.

Callum drew his mouth back from hers then, and peered deep into her eyes. "What is it aboot ye, Jenny, that makes me want ye like no other? Ye're so different."

Jenny didn't want to hear how different she was. She knew why she wasn't like any highborn debutante he'd met.

But he didn't. He didn't know she was a fake, a fraud.

A lowly lady's maid. The back of her eyes began to burn.

Still, he deserved to know and now was the time to tell him. She had to admit everything, no matter how heartbreaking it was going to be. She laid her index finger vertically across his lips.

"Hush, Callum. Please. There is something I must tell you." Her mouth went dry and her throat felt as if it were packed with wool.

Oh, how she wished she did not have to do this.

"Ye dinna need to say anything, lass." Callum gently nipped at her lower lip. "I already know."

Jenny widened her eyes to stare at him, and a tear slipped down across her temple, into her hair, and dropped to her ear. "You do?" Jenny tensed.

"Aye, I know ye love me."

She exhaled slowly.

He smiled at her. "And as much as I've tried not to, I've come to love ye as weel."

Tears raced freely from her eyes and splashed into her hair. She couldn't believe what she was hearing. Didn't know until that very moment how much she wanted to hear those words.

Callum rested his weight on his elbows and slid his hand into Jenny's damp hair and ran his fingers along her scalp. Then he drew his hand through her hair, allowing the locks to slip between his fingers.

Jenny shivered with pleasure, feeling each and every piece of hair fall from his fingers to the pillow.

She felt a wet warmth on her collarbone as he kissed a trail to her breast. The path of kisses tingled, making her arch her back upward and press her body firmly against him.

His rounded tip rose up as she did so. She felt its hard ridge move against the soft flesh of her inner thigh, and brush against her most sensitive of places, making her gasp and press down upon him.

"Tell me ye want me, Jenny, or tell me to find another place to sleep. Fer if ye do that again, I dinna know if I can stop meself from makin' ye mine."

Her heart was pounding and her body felt feverishly tight, aching. *"Makin' ye mine."* Lud, she'd never wanted anything so much.

Though a little unsure, she knew what he meant. Mostly anyway. Annie, who'd biblically known half the footmen in Bath, had told her all about it in explicit and colorful detail. She'd even shown Jenny the way to touch a man, demonstrating by running her fingers up and down a pine rolling pin.

It had sounded so wicked, but at this moment, she wanted to do nothing so much.

She looked up into Callum's dark eyes, and without breaking her gaze, she brazenly slipped her fingers between them and took him into her hand as she opened her thighs to him.

As she brought him farther between her legs, Jenny felt him flinch in her hand with anticipation and she let him touch her, just barely.

Heat rioted between her thighs as she withdrew her hand and instinctively raised her knees.

But he hesitated.

"Please, Callum," she whispered huskily. "I want you."

He stared down at her, and still he hesitated. Why, Jenny did not know. But she didn't want to think on it, she only wanted to feel.

Raising her hips, she pushed her body down upon him, taking him hard inside of her. She closed her eyes and gasped at the slightly painful sensation of his length and girth filling her, stretching her. But the sting quickly subsided and only the warmth and fullness remained.

Callum kissed her lips as he settled himself firmly between her thighs. "Och, lass, ye'll be the end of me," he said in a low heavy breath as he nudged her gently, moving deeper into her wetness.

Jenny moaned aloud, her body throbbing pleasurably

around him as he began to thrust into her. He held his weight over her, his arm muscles rigid and hard, as he braced himself upon his hands, positioned on either side of her shoulders.

Following the valleys between the rises of his tensed muscles, she gripped his arms for support and raised her hips, meeting each of his slow, patient thrusts.

Callum watched her, his dark eyes sparkling in the candlelight. His brow became damp with moisture, catching the hair that brushed there.

He was so beautiful. And he was hers.

At least for this night—a night she could hold in her memories forever.

"I love you, Callum. I do," she barely whispered, for somehow it felt almost as though she were saying good-bye. But it was important that he knew that no matter what the future brought, that at this moment in time she loved him. Truly, deeply loved him.

And in her heart, she knew she forever would.

Then, as if her words of love had unleashed his self-control, Callum began to thrust faster into her, harder. With each push, a coil seemed to tighten within her core.

Jenny writhed with pleasure as the tension building within her grew more intense. She squeezed his arms and her nails bit into his hard muscle.

Something made her want to take him deeper, hold him within her, and so she wrapped her long legs around his hips, locking them with a cross of her ankles.

Callum groaned, and suddenly his eyes went wide. He tried to pull away from her, but Jenny tightened her legs around him preventing him from escape. She ground herself against him, tightening her own feminine muscles, trying desperately to force the release lingering just outside her grasp.

An explosion of heat suddenly shot from her center through her body, and she cried out, arching her back and clinging to Callum as her muscles convulsed around him.

"Oh, Jenny, *no*." Callum's eyes closed, and he released a long exhale.

Beneath her palms, she could feel heat break across the surface of his back and the muscles of his buttocks and back tense just before he collapsed atop her.

He lifted his head then and peered down at her. "Oh, Jenny, ye dinna ken what ye've done."

Feeling horribly embarrassed, she looked him directly into the eyes, so there was no question she understood his meaning. "I think I might."

Callum leaned to his side, and reached back to unlock Jenny's ankles. He pushed away and rolled to sit at the edge of the bed, shoving a shaky hand through his damp hair. "Nay, ye dinna."

Jenny leaned to her side and with the flat of her palm ran her hand gently down his back.

He pulled away. "Please. Dinna do that." He exhaled in one great gush. "What have I done? What the hell have I done?" she heard him murmur.

Tears began to collect in Jenny's eyes. She allowed herself to fall back against the pillow where she covered her face with her forearms.

They had shared something precious. Something wondrous. But he regretted it.

An hour later, Jenny lay deathly still in the bed staring at the dwindling fire. Callum still lay next to her, though he hadn't said a word to her in all that time. She had a plummeting feeling that he thought she'd sought to trap him into marriage.

But she hadn't. *Perdition*, had she thought about the consequences of what she was doing, she certainly wouldn't have done it.

She would have never purposely put herself in the exact position her mother had been in—being with child and in love with a man who would never marry her. *Could* never marry her.

Oh, he might have consented to marry the grand Lady Genevieve, but he'd never wed Jenny Penny, the servant. And worse, a servant who secretly peddled tingle cream to his equals.

What had she gotten herself into?

Her eyes and nose tingled, making her sniffle.

"Jenny, come here, lass."

Jenny peered over her shoulder and saw that Callum, whom she had thought was asleep beside her, was propped on one elbow and was beckoning.

"I'm sorry. Ye didna know."

Jenny looked quizzically back at him. What did he mean? Of course she *knew*. She just didn't *think*!

"Come, lie down with me, and I'll try me best to explain."

Jenny hesitantly lowered her head to Callum's broad chest, and felt his arm come up around her. "If you are going to explain to me about monthly courses and how one conceives a child, you needn't bother."

Callum paused a moment before speaking again, and

she could imagine him raising a single dark eyebrow at her blunt words.

"Nay, there is more." She felt his muscles move as he swallowed deeply.

"Do ye know of Lord Lyon in Scotland—know his function within the realm?"

"Well, of course I do." Jenny, who for some selfish reason could not seem to put aside her lady's guise, did her best to sound indignant. And she did know all about Lord Lyon, didn't she? Lady Viola had explained it all to her just the other day. "Your father was elected Lord Lyon."

Callum shifted Jenny's head to his shoulder so he could look at her. "How did ye know?"

Jenny looked up at him. She lifted her fingers and traced the whitened scar crossing his cheek. "You told me"—Jenny lifted her hand and traced the scar on his cheek—"*this* came from the Lord Lyon signet ring."

"Aye." Callum brushed her hand from his scar. "Because, of his . . . *position*, the continuation of our family line was all important to him. All that mattered. And, with no other issue, the responsibility fer producing an heir—fer continuing the Argyll line—rested on me."

"Then why have you not married?" She tried to see his eyes. "I should think your father would have placed quite a lot of pressure on you to marry during his lifetime."

An odd, almost disconcerting smile lifted the corner of Callum's mouth. "He did indeed."

"But still you're a bachelor."

Callum sighed then. "After years of his abuse and loathin', I came to despise him. Came to hate everything he stood fer. And I made a decision, to extinguish what was most important to him."

Jenny's eyes rounded as she realized his intent and she sat up in the bed. "*His line.* You want to end it!"

A slow smile slid over his lips. "Aye. When I die, the family title will die with me. There is no one else left."

Jenny sat very still and considered his cold plan.

"And I've been verra careful during my manhood to ensure I never sired an heir—the verra thing he most wanted."

Jenny gulped. "Until now."

Callum nodded his head slowly.

"I'm sorry, Callum. I didn't mean . . . I just wanted . . . to hold you close." La, she was thankful it was dim in the chamber, for otherwise he might see how red her cheeks had to be—for they were burning like a torch.

"I dinna blame ye, lass. 'Twas yer first time with a man, and ye didna know what ye were doin'."

Jenny chewed the inside of her bottom lip. Perhaps it was best that she not tell him of Annie's lessons in love.

She gazed up into his dark, serious eyes. He was pensive, and she knew there was more to come. More probably than she wanted to hear.

"'Tis verra possible ye conceived this night."

She nodded. "'Tis also possible I did not," she offered brightly. "'Twas as you said, my first time, therefore the likelihood of my conceiving is about—"

"Even," Callum said matter-of-factly.

Jenny's spirits fell. "Oh." At the thought, unconsciously, she laid her hand protectively over her belly.

Callum placed his hand atop hers there. "If it comes to pass that I have left ye with a bairn, ye've got nothing to fear. I will do right by ye."

Jenny turned her face toward him and girded herself for the truth she knew she must now reveal. But before she could speak, Callum spoke again.

"I will provide a guid, clean, and safe place for ye and the bairn to live. And guineas each month, whatever ye require, so ye can continue to live in the fashion ye are accustomed."

Jenny didn't understand his talk. She cinched her brows and studied him. Why wouldn't he look at her while he was speaking?

Then it struck her as coldly as the ice atop the canal had. Jenny grew very still.

Wait a moment. Wait just one bloody moment. He wasn't offering to marry her at all! He was offering to keep her as his mistress . . . while making his own child a—*bastard.*

Well, that wasn't a fate she'd wish on any child, having carried that burden herself all the years of her life.

Callum's gaze flicked across her face for just an instant, and she knew he saw the betrayal she felt in her eyes.

"I am sorry, but I canna marry ye, Jenny, even if ye carry me child even now. I canna give the bairn me name. I canna."

Fury welled up within Jenny. He thought he could do this, did he? Impregnate her, well . . . possibly, then set her aside like yesterday's stale bread?

Who did he think he was? She was a lady after all and deserved better.

Jenny opened her mouth to tell him so when he raised his hand to halt any protest from her.

And it was a good thing too. Jenny drew her lips into her mouth and held them there. For a moment, she had almost forgotten that she *wasn't* a lady, but rather a conniving, deceitful little maid who, after her grand lie, deserved whatever she got.

"Please, I must continue, lass."

Jenny closed her lids slowly, then opened them with deliberation and looked straight into Callum's eyes.

He took a shaky breath, then expelled his next words forcefully, as if trying to make himself remember them.

"The Argyll line *will* die with me," he vowed. "It must."

Chapter Eleven

The next morning, Jenny wriggled into her uncomfortably stiff, puckered, and pitifully ruined walking ensemble. The fabric had reduced, and had she not expelled the breath completely from her lungs, it would have been impossible to fasten. But, being the lady's maid she was, Jenny was mindful of a few fitting tricks from the seamstresses she'd worked with over the years.

Silently she moved to the window and swept back the thick curtains to look out. Glancing back at the tester, she saw that Callum still slept peacefully, having managed to say what he felt he must.

Jenny barely slept at all. When she did, she dreamed of walking through the Upper Assembly Rooms, her belly heavy with Callum's child, as the *ton* collectively pointed, then turned their backs to her.

Nightmare or not, Jenny knew the dream might well be her future.

As she leaned her forehead against the cold windowpane, she looked out at the deep drifts of snow and at the lone track looping its way from house to house. Deliveries by foot. Callum had been right. No carriage or sedan chair was getting through the streets this day.

Rising up on the tips of her bare toes, Jenny tried to glimpse Royal Crescent on a mount in the distance, but it was just too far away and too many buildings blocked her view.

Lud, how was she to get back? She turned and glanced at her damp slippers beside the fire. Her shoes were quite inadequate for trudging across Bath in the knee-deep snow. When she'd picked them up a moment before, she'd found the linings still soggy with cold water from the canal. For certain, she'd freeze before she arrived on the crescent.

Yes, she could see it all so clearly in her mind. She and the baby inside of her—Richard . . . no . . . *James*, that was quite a nice name—would be found frozen midstride like a new bronze statue in the middle of Queen Square.

Everyone in Bath, or at least the loyal service staff, would mourn for her and her unborn babe. And Callum would stand over their grave in the Bath Abbey Cemetery, and place flowers on their simple tomb every Sunday, knowing that his damning words had driven her into the snow, and that their deaths were entirely his fault.

Jenny placed her hand on her belly, her breath catching as she succumbed to her own fanciful story.

Callum heard her whimpers, for from the edge of her vision, Jenny saw him climb from the bed and walk to her.

He wrapped his arms around her from behind. "Oh, Jenny. Dinna cry."

Jenny daren't turn around, for she knew full well he was fully naked in the daylight. And from the slight unintentional prodding against her behind, he was in a curiously aroused state.

It was so hard to be a lady — and not look at him. He was impossibly beautiful, this Scotsman.

Turned as he was to the side, the sunlight illuminated his flawless body and Jenny found she could study his reflection in the window without him being any the wiser.

And so she let her eyes wander where they would. Her gaze followed the dark hair of his sculpted chest to where it trailed off between his legs. At once she felt an insistent throbbing between her thighs, and it was all she could do to resist the urge to drag her naked Highlander back to the tester bed.

Seeing her hand atop her middle, Callum slid his palms protectively over her belly. "No matter what happens, 'twill be all right, lass. Ye'll see."

"'Twill be all right?" Jenny jerked her head around and glared up at him, knowing that growing rage sparked in her eyes. "How can you say that to me? *You* are not the one whose life will be forever changed. You will not be shunned by society, and forced to live your life with your eyes cast down in shame." Her voice shook, and this truly surprised her.

Callum trembled slightly at her words, and she knew she had struck a chord with him. And yet, she was not pleased. She didn't want to say these things, but she felt so horribly betrayed.

If he loved her, as he claimed, he would put aside his vendetta against his father and offer to marry her! Of course, she could not accept, she being a lady's maid and he a viscount, but he should at least *make* the offer.

Unbidden tears erupted in her eyes.

"I am sorry, Jenny." When Callum looked down at her, his eyes glistened slightly in the cool light coming through the window.

Jenny stared silently up at him for several seconds as a tear rolled down her cheek and dripped from her jaw. "As am I, Callum, for until this moment, I believed you were not the rogue you claimed to be, but instead a good and true gentleman. But now I see I was horribly mistaken."

Callum blanched, and Jenny knew her words had carried the force of a balled fist. But she hadn't lied. She'd meant every word. Her eyes started to sting again. She had to leave now. Had to put space between her and the viscount, for it pained her too much to even look at him.

Jenny pulled from his embrace, crossed to the hearth and retrieved her overcoat, and then stepped into her mushy slippers. Without another word, she solemnly left the chamber and started down the stairs.

She heard Callum's bare feet on the Scots carpet above in the passage.

"Jenny, dinna be daft. Ye canna walk to Royal Crescent in the snow. Ye dinna even have yer stockin's."

She stopped and grasped the newel post at the landing and squeezed it for support. "I cannot stay." Jenny looked down at her soiled and rumpled coat, and at her muddied slippers. "I'd rather face my ruin in the harsh light of day than cower here."

Behind her, she heard Callum coming toward her. But knowing he could not follow her, naked as he was, she hurried to the door, plunged into the knee-deep snow, and started for home.

"What could you have been thinking, child, walking all the way from Laura Place in the snow?" Mrs. Penny poured another kettle of steaming water into the copper hip bath where Jenny soaked.

Jenny lolled her head back against the balled sheet behind her head and closed her eyes. "I was thinking that I made a grand mistake and 'twas better to leave with my pride than stay and agree to accept his charity."

"'Tis your overblown pride, gel, that got you into this predicament. Perhaps 'twas better that you stayed, accepted what he offered, and left your pride in Laura Place." Her mother grunted her disapproval and tossed a pot of soap into the water.

Water splashed Jenny's face. She slowly opened her eyes and stared back at her mother as the water dripped in clear strings from her chin. "Mama, though nothing is for certain yet, I may be in a real hitch. I need your compassion now, not your disapproval. You of all people should understand what I am enduring."

The moment the words came out of her mouth, Jenny wished she could have sucked them back in.

Her mother's face paled, then two angry red sunbursts burst upon her cheeks. She narrowed her eyes at Jenny. "Our circumstances are nothing alike, gel. *Nothing.*"

Jenny stared at her mother. She'd never seen her this upset before. Though she appeared angry, for some reason, she was shaking too. "What do you mean, Mama?" she asked hesitantly.

Her mother stared back at her and for a moment Jenny was convinced she was about to explain herself. "Never you mind," she finally snapped, then turned and left Jenny's bedchamber.

Jenny was sitting in the cooling bathwater, dumb-struck, when Erma walked into her chamber with the harvest basket and plunked it down on the floor.

"When the snow started coming, Mrs. Penny brought your basket inside, but it's getting in me way in the kitchen so I'm bringing it to you, Miss Miser Bag . . . or should I say *Lady Eros*?"

Jenny grimaced. "You better not say either one again if you know what's good for you."

Erma crossed her arms over her chest. "I ain't afraid of you none, Jenny."

"Really?"

"That's right, because I know it'll only take a few words to those newspaper fellows that 'ave been snoopin' around—least I 'eard that's who they are—and your fancy 'I'm a Great Lady' game is over for good."

Jenny looked up at the pearl earbobs dangling from beneath Erma's mobcap and a sly smile skated across her lips. "If my identity is revealed by your doing, I have no doubt Mr. Bartleby will be most displeased. In fact, he might rethink any gift he might have given you for giving him access to my tingle cream."

Erma's fingers flew up to the pearl earrings and stayed there. "You wouldn't dare tell him."

"Of course I would. *If* I were given no other choice."

"You are a wicked girl, Jenny Penny."

Jenny rounded her mouth and her eyes. "I am not wicked at all, Erma. But I am a shrewd merchant who will protect her business. I should think you'd want me as your ally rather than your foe."

Jenny scrutinized the scullery maid. Erma was a real threat. And though Jenny gave not a hoot about her cream business, she had to admit the money was very, *very* nice. Still, being exposed as Lady Eros could deeply hurt a number of people, including the dear Featherton ladies . . . and Callum. She felt a twinge in her heart at the thought.

Then an idea came to her and she fashioned a bright smile for the scullery maid. "Erma, how'd you like to make a few bob?"

The next day, Jenny quietly came to stand next to her mother beside the linen-dressed breakfast table, having been summoned above stairs by the Featherton ladies, who had only just heard of her return to the house.

Not noticing Jenny's arrival, Lady Letitia propped her lorgnette on her nose and stretched the hand that held the newspaper to arm's length. "I say, 'tis almost like living in London. I would not have believed it possible that so much purse-snatching, violence, and thievery would have ever occurred within the walls of Bath."

Taking a sip of chocolate, Lady Viola nodded in agreement. "Just Thursday last, Lady Avery was hit in the head and her rings were snatched right from her fingers. It's true, I tell you. I saw the cut on her brow and I own it was as long as my little finger." She wiggled her pinkie in the air. "To think, this all occurred just outside the Upper Assembly Rooms. Then at the Ash rout on Monday, the countess's jewel box was stolen from her bedchamber. Her own *bedchamber*. Imagine that!"

Lady Letitia let out a long sigh. "I daresay, there is a thief among our ranks."

"Indeed. Frightening, just frightening. Why I am

feeling light-headed just talking about the horrors." Lady Viola waved her hand weakly. "Mrs. Penny, my vinaigrette, please."

As Jenny listened to the Featherton ladies, her thoughts became centered on the little man she'd seen outside the Pump Room and then later at the Bath Abbey.

Why, he was small enough to slip right by a person, sneak up the stairs, and make off with a fortune in jewels.

She wondered again if the magistrates ought to hear of her revelation, for if they already knew of him, he wouldn't be scurrying around highborn Bath snatching up treasures, now would he? She really should report him to the authorities.

But wouldn't it be better if she were to find the baubles he'd taken and turn those in as well? She'd be a heroine and they'd throw a parade in her honor. Of course, everyone would be so grateful for her quick thinking that they would probably gift her with a jewel or two in thanks.

Besides, a few bob or a sparkler might really come in handy if she was with child—but of course nothing was for certain yet.

"Ah, Jenny, there you are. Come, sit down." Lady Viola patted the empty seat cushion beside her.

Jenny dolefully glanced at her mother, who shot her a sullen look as she settled a silver and crystal vinaigrette before her ladyship, then politely excused herself from the room.

"We received word from Lord Argyll about your unfortunate accident, but Mrs. Penny has informed us that you are perfectly well now. You undoubtedly have a strong constitution to have survived with nary a chill."

"Yes, my lady." Jenny couldn't seem to raise her eyes and look at her employers. If she did, she knew the tears would start again. Lud, she'd tried very hard to block the heartache of Callum's betrayal from her mind. And had actually succeeded in thinking of other things for a full quarter of an hour. *Blast.* They were going to dredge the whole painful event to the surface again.

"Oh, dear. Such a glum face." Lady Letitia clucked. "Viola, I think our gel is not nearly as happy as she would have us believe. Just look at the poor pup."

Heat began to rise into Jenny's cheeks as she felt two pairs of faded blue eyes scrutinizing her.

"Oh, my, you are right, Letitia." Lady Viola set her cup into its saucer and leaned toward Jenny. "Didn't Lord Argyll afford you the attention you desired when you left for your stroll in Sydney Garden?"

"Oh, yes, my lady. Much more than I *ever* imagined." Jenny glanced up from the floor to see the two old women exchange concerned glances.

"Darling child," Lady Viola began hesitantly. "Do you mean to say he . . . well, certainly the two of you did not—"

But Jenny was already nodding her head. Why lie to them now? After all, if she was with child, they would learn of it soon enough. Secrets never lived long in the Featherton household. Lud, she was surprised word of her tingle cream sales hadn't yet drifted above stairs.

There was a collective gasp from the Feathertons, then abject silence as they considered her silent admission.

"Of course, afterward, he offered for you. Yes, of

course he would have." Lady Viola beamed and clapped her hands excitedly. "When may we begin to plan the wedding?"

But Jenny only stared mutely back at her.

Lady Letitia raised her hand, stopping her sister's merriment. "My, my. It seems our Lord Argyll is not quite the gentleman we had hoped he would grow to be." She leaned so close to Jenny that their noses nearly collided. "Sweeting, after the two of you . . . well, what did he say to you *exactly*. Perhaps you are merely confused."

Jenny released her breath and a watery whimper slipped out. "No, my lady. Sadly, I am quite clear on the matter. I believe his exact words were 'I canna marry you.'"

Lady Letitia nodded as if she suddenly understood. "Oh, this makes more sense. You told him the secret of your position within our household."

"No, my lady. He still believes me to be Lady Genevieve."

"Then why will he not marry you?" the two Featherton sisters chimed as one.

And so, in a hail of tears, Jenny explained everything. Told them about Lord Lyon, his lie, the abuse Callum suffered at his father's hand, and finally of his frightening vow to end his family line.

Lady Viola seemed as disturbed as she was confused. "But . . . but . . . if you are with child, his line has not been extinguished."

Lady Letitia rose from the chair, her red cheeks puffing in outrage. "Oh, Viola! Do you not see? If he doesn't marry our Jenny, the child, if there is one, will be a *bastard*. In the eyes of the new Lord Lyon, and the law, when Callum passes on without legal issue, the Argyll line *will* have been extinguished."

Putting her meager weight on her cane, Lady Viola raised herself to her feet. "Dear, dear. Of a certain, he will come around, and whether there is a child, or there is not, I know my Callum—err . . . *Lord Argyll* will offer for you whether you be Lady Genevieve or Miss Jenny Penny."

Jenny pressed on a weak yet hopeful smile for the ever optimistic Lady Viola.

In her heart, however, she knew better. For in the darkness of Laura Place, she had stumbled upon the ugly truth of her situation.

The man who honored truth above all things, the man who allowed himself to trust her when he would no one else, would never be able to accept the grand lie she had willingly perpetuated about her identity.

Never.

"Jenny," Erma, the scullery maid, shrieked, "you're spillin' the emuls—the emuls—oh, bugger it—the bloody melted cream all over the table. Where is your head this eve?"

"Sorry," Jenny muttered. "But do try to keep your voice down. Lady Letitia rang for my mother twice now, so I know she is not yet abed."

"Well, you mightn't care if you waste the cream, but you pay me a shilling per pot and you've already burnt a batch this eve, so I can't afford to lose none to the table and floor. 'Ere, let me pour it into the gallipots."

Jenny handled the iron ladle to Erma, then plopped

down on a stool and tried to center her thoughts on her business . . . instead of on Callum, and her possible baby.

"How many pots does Bartleby need?" she asked Erma softly.

"Well, he said as many as I could deliver. Told me your idea about givin' the pots away with a posh purchase was brilliant. Said ladies of the Quality actually queue up to buy his baubles now. Oh! I completely forgot." Erma released the ladle and let it clatter to the worktable. "Hold on a tick. He sent a parcel over for you."

"For me?" Jenny perked right up.

When Erma returned, Jenny watched impatiently as the scullery maid set a small red leather box before her.

"What is it?" she asked eagerly.

"I dunno. Go on, open it."

Jenny bit her lip and she slid the tiny gold clasp aside and opened the lid of the box. There, inside, were the pearl earbobs he'd refused to let her put on her account. The earrings she'd seen the very day she first met Callum.

"Blimey, them are a lot grander than the pair he gave me for offering you up. Why, they're as fat as hazelnuts."

But Erma's words were scarce more than a buzzing to Jenny. She could not take her gaze from the magnificent pearl drop earbobs. "Blimey is right." She looked at Erma. "They're gorgeous! But why did he send them?"

"He said 'twas for the customers you've brought him. All it took was a notice in *The Bath Herald* and in *The*

Bath Journal, and there was a queue clean down Milsom Street before opening time."

Erma leaned on the table and reached out to finger the earrings. Jenny snatched them out of her reach.

"Where'd you learn about the merchant trade, if you don't mind me pryin' a bit? I never would have come up with an idea like that—free pots to make customers buy more."

Jenny shrugged. "I just imagined what might encourage me to buy from the top shelf—I mean, were I a lady of course."

Erma grinned at her. "For a shilling a pot, you are a real lady in my mind . . . *Lady Eros.*"

"L-Lady Eros?" came Lady Letitia's low voice from behind them.

"Oh, dear," Lady Viola uttered within the same breath.

A pang of horror propelled Jenny to her feet. She and Erma slowly turned around to see their employers standing just inside the kitchen door.

Erma dropped a quick curtsy, then hurried out of the kitchen, leaving Jenny to their mercy.

"My . . . my ladies. What are you doing below stairs?" Jenny managed to stammer.

"We smelled a queer odor drifting up the stairway and since we could not sleep, we decided to track its source." Lady Letitia's thick white brows were drawn so close in the middle that they reminded Jenny of a furry V.

"The question should be, my dear, just what are you doing—*Lady Eros*, is it?" Lady Viola asked.

Oh, goodness. Here it comes now. She was going to be sacked. They wouldn't care that she was with child, or might be anyway. *Blast!* She would be on the street before morning, she just knew it.

"I . . . um . . ." *Criminy. Just tell them the truth, Jenny.* "I was making the tingle cream. And yes, I am Lady Eros, and this is the . . . below stairs cream that for some reason every member of the *ton* must have."

Stealthily, Jenny closed the lid to the red leather box from Bartleby's and covertly slipped it from the table and into her apron pocket.

The two ladies studied her for a long moment, then burst into laughter, startling Jenny so that she lurched. Tripping backward over the harvest basket, she slammed against the floor.

"Oh, Jenny, are you injured?" Lady Viola clucked as her sister knelt next to Jenny and began to help her to her feet.

Jenny shook her head dazedly, confused when Lady Letitia, of all people, assisted her to the stool once more. "I am fine."

"Oh, good. Wouldn't want anything to happen to my great—" Lady Viola broke off and looked fearfully at her sister.

"Our . . . *greatly* entertaining lady's maid," Lady Letitia concluded with a grand smile.

Hmm. Somehow Jenny got the impression that wasn't at all what Lady Viola had meant to say.

"You are not angry?" Jenny asked guardedly.

Lady Viola shook her head and brushed her question away with a wave of her bony hand.

"Y-you are not going to dismiss me?"

Lady Letitia, who had a distinct twinkle in her eye, laid a pudgy hand on Jenny's shoulder. "Of course not, gel. There is nothing wrong with showing a bit of pluck—especially given your new condition."

"*Possible* condition," amended Lady Letitia. Then she paused a moment as she and Lady Viola exchanged conspiratorial glances. "Though perhaps now we might be able to acquire a pot . . . or even two *tonight*?"

Though Jenny was still quite gobsmacked that her employers didn't seem to care a lick about her tingle cream business, she had to grin at the Feathertons' request. Stifling a guffaw as she lifted a gallipot in each hand, she watched her two elderly employers snatch them from her with gusto.

Lady Letitia gave an exaggerated yawn. "We'll just be off to bed then, I think. I for one am quite sleepy suddenly."

Lady Viola nodded her head in agreement, sending the wattle at her throat wobbling. "As am I. Do get some rest, Jenny. I am sure tomorrow will bring us better news."

"Yes, my lady." Jenny rose and bobbed a curtsy as the snow-capped twins started for the stairway.

That night, heavy, driving rain poured over Bath, but the next day, the sun shone brightly, warming the air. By late afternoon, but for slushy mounds of snow nestled in shadows between houses, the icy blanket that had paralyzed Bath for two full days had melted.

Jenny had greatly needed those two days. It had been a blessing that she had been unable to leave the house. She had needed the time to think about the course her life should take—if she was indeed with child.

She could live out her life in service, this she knew. But Jupiter, that would be hard, especially after tasting the sweet life of her betters.

Her tingle cream business had taken Bath by storm, and she had earned quite a lot of blunt in the past weeks. That was good. But she'd spent every bit, right down to the last half crown, on gowns and adornments. That was bad.

Why, Miss Meredith had said her lady's maid possessed a far better wardrobe than she, and though Jenny denied it profusely, she felt quite satisfied in the knowledge that the statement was completely true.

Still, the ways of the *ton* were fickle and Jenny knew her fortune, and therefore her clothing-buying expeditions —and indeed her future—was limited by their whims, which of a certain would turn to some other diversion within time. Yes, her guinea-gaining days were limited. How much longer did she have? Another month? Two?

"What about a shop of your own?" Annie suggested as they walked to Trim Street for needles and silk thread that late afternoon. "You know, the old Upperton Dry Goods place on Milsom is still unoccupied. Has been for at least a year. I'm sure you could let the shop for a pittance."

Jenny kept walking. "Well, I haven't got any money, Annie, and besides, what would I sell?"

Annie scoffed. "What indeed! The tingle cream of course."

She stopped walking as an image erupted in her mind. A store brimming with luxurious fabrics and trims, fans and modish bonnets, fragrant scent bottles from France and her own blends of powders and beauty creams. And of course there would be earbobs, pendants, bracelets, and brooches . . . maybe even *tiaras*. A dreamy sigh flowed from her lips.

Annie chuckled. "There you go. You're seein' it now, aren't you? Let's go and take a peek through the window."

Jenny looked back at Annie, considering.

"It won't hurt none to peek. Come on, Jen. Just a quick glance and I'll stop pestering you." Annie tugged at Jenny's arm.

"Oh, very well." Jenny looped her arm around Annie's. "But this is folly, you know. Pure folly."

Several minutes later, Jenny stood with her nose pressed to an empty shop window, her hands cupped around her eyes like opera glasses. It was a narrow shop, far deeper than wide. And it reminded Jenny of her own bedside drawer where she kept her trinkets and treasures.

There was a long, horribly dusty glass front counter near the wall to the right, and cobwebbed shelves bracketing the wall behind it.

All Jenny saw was its carnival of potential, and for the first time in days, her blood began to pump madly through her veins. Pastel blue and cream satin would line the walls and a cheval glass would stand in the corner near two cream settees. Esteemed ladies would sit there and drink tea, while shop girls draped swathes of the latest fabrics over their arms and a modiste counseled them in the latest fashions from Paris.

"Oh, Annie . . . I must do it. I *must* have this shop.

Think of all the beautiful things I can fill it with—and they'd all be mine. Mine! Well, until someone bought something, of course."

Thoughts swam through Jenny's mind like spring salmon in a stream. It would take quite a lot of money to open her dream shop. At least three hundred guineas. Hmm. Maybe more.

Immediately she began ciphering the number of pots needed, less expenses . . . Erma and supplies of course. *Criminy.* She needed to get started producing tingle cream right away!

"I've got to go now, Annie. Mustn't tarry. Good-bye."

Before Annie had managed to utter a word, Jenny's boots were clicking double time for home. But not two hundred yards down Milsom, as she habitually glanced in a shop window to check her appearance in the reflection, she saw she was being followed.

Stopping abruptly, she whirled upon the little man who trailed her not five paces behind. "Hello there . . . can I assist you with something?" she asked warily.

"No, miss. I'm just walking and enjoying the sun." Though she expected a speaking tone quite higher, the little man's voice was deep and soft.

She looked at his coat and saw that it was tattered and dirty, and though he was possibly the thief of Bath, her heart went out to him. She jammed her hand into her reticule, but felt only the needles and silk thread she'd purchased on Trim Street. "I haven't any money," she muttered to herself.

"I haven't asked for any," the little man replied.

"Oh, I know." But he could use a shilling or two, that was evident. Odd though, with all the baubles he'd lifted recently—for she was sure it was he—that he hadn't taken care to buy himself some new clothes. That's the first thing she would have done. "I am sorry if I have offended you in any way."

The man smiled up at her, his kind eyes glistening in the waning sunlight. "Be assured, my lady, you haven't."

"I am so glad." With a careful eye, Jenny studied him then. Why, he didn't seem capable of committing the brutal robberies of late. Why, he scarcely even came up to her hip. Yet, if indeed he was the thief, here was a prime opportunity to investigate. She'd be safe enough, surely, if she remained on the alert. "Perhaps you might condescend to assist *me*."

The man tilted his head to the side and waited for her request.

"Dear sir, with all the reticule-snatching in Bath, I was wondering if you would be so kind as to escort me home. 'Tisn't so far, I assure you. Just a few streets farther . . . Royal Crescent."

The little man smiled warmly and offered up his arm. Jenny touched her fingers to his forearm to avoid stooping as she walked, and the pair headed down the flag way.

"Royal Crescent," he repeated. "Quite the direction in the Bath."

"I suppose it is. My ladies are quite grand indeed."

The little man stopped walking and his great blue eyes blinked up at her. "You are not the mistress?"

Jenny laughed. "Oh, heavens, no. I am but a lady's maid." She gestured to her apron jutting from beneath her pelisse.

The man urged Jenny into a walk again, but he was

pensive. "I'm sorry, if I seem a little confused, but I thought I saw you inside the Pump Room not a week ago."

"Oh, yes, I was there. My ladies . . . needed some assistance, and I was only too happy to oblige them." Jenny focused her eyes upon his. Where was he going with these questions?

Sizing her up as a mark, was he? She'd already told him she had no money. "I've seen you about Bath too. Outside the Bath Abbey was the last time, I believe." Jenny quieted for a moment, then added with a wry smile on her lips, "You were not following me just now, were you?"

The little man grinned cheekily up at her and perhaps it was the sun in his eye, but she could have sworn he winked at her.

"Would it be so wrong for a man in his prime to enjoy the sight of a pretty woman?"

Jenny chuckled at that. Had he been any other man, Jenny might have turned and walked in the other direction, but she felt no threat from this interesting man . . . though she certainly should.

"I am Hercule Lestrange. But I am known to all simply as Hercule."

"*Hercule?*" Jenny glanced down at the tiny man with such a improbable name. "I am very pleased to make your acquaintance. I am Miss Jenny Penny."

Hercule looked up at her and chuckled with such deep infectious laughter that Jenny could not help but giggle as well.

"I suppose our parents gave us each a cross to bear with our names," she said.

Hercule laughed again, and Jenny realized she quite liked this little fellow. Too bad he was a scoundrel.

A few minutes later they arrived at the wrought-iron rail leading down to the kitchen door.

"Well, we have arrived," Jenny told Hercule. "I do thank you for your company and protection."

The little man removed his beaver hat and held it in his hands. "It was my pleasure, Miss Penny."

At that moment, Jenny felt so at ease with her escort that she totally forgot her investigation and an invitation slipped from her lips. "Would you like to come inside for some tea?"

A tremor shook her. *Oh dear.* She couldn't ask a possible thief into the house. Was she mad? She opened her mouth to rescind her offer, but it was already too late. He was at her side, beaming. "Thank you, miss. I'd greatly enjoy that."

Jenny opened the door to the kitchen and, thinking quickly, made a show of hurrying to the servants' stairs. "It's only me," she called out.

Hercule's brows crunched together.

Jenny forced a smile. "With all the violence of late, my ladies have engaged two burly chairmen to watch over the house," she lied. "Didn't want them to rush down and mistake you for an intruder, now did I?

"Please take a seat while I set the water to heat." Jenny set the kettle to warm, taking keen note of the position of the fire poker, then turned around in time to see Hercule still standing beside the door. He was intently staring at something.

Curious as to what he seemed to find so fascinating, she stepped forward and saw the harvest basket on the floor, filled with twenty gallipots.

Oh, perdition!

Hercule reached down into the basket and lifted a pot up toward her.

"Lady Eros, I presume?"

Chapter Twelve

Jenny stared, transfixed by the little man's words. "W-what do you know of Lady Eros?" she asked rather shakily.

Hercule lifted the lid from a gallipot and breathed in the fresh peppermint scent. "All of Bath has heard of the tingle cream, though I admit, this is the closest I have come to a pot. Bartleby's cannot keep them in stock, and I have no connection below stairs to acquire a cream pot by other means."

"Why would *you* need a pot?" Jenny crossed her arms over her chest, suddenly feeling uneasy with the man. He was a study in contrasts. Though his clothes were grubby, Hercule's well-chosen words and impeccable manners now sparkled with a genteel polish Jenny hadn't noticed earlier.

"Curiosity, I suppose. 'Tis amusing, is it not, to see the *ton* clamoring of a simple pot of cream." He extended a finger as if he meant to sample a bit for himself.

"*Stop!* You'll ruin it," Jenny snapped. "Those pots have already been spoken for."

The little man smiled and waggled his unruly brow. "So you *are* Lady Eros."

"I told you, I am Miss Penny."

"Ah, yes, but I am quite sure that Miss Penny and the mysterious Lady Eros are one and the same." Hercule returned the lid to the pot and settled it into its place in the basket.

"See here," Jenny began. "It is clear that you *think* you know who I am."

She took a full breath into her lungs, knowing that the words she uttered next might plummet her into great danger. "Mr. Lestrange, I'll have you know that I am wise to *your* true identity as well. Reveal my game and I shall reveal yours, sirrah."

"*My* identity?" Hercule was shaken, and even took a step backward to regain his shoddy balance. "But h-how? I've taken great care to conceal it."

"Not enough care, for it took me no time at all to realize who you really were," Jenny countered, suddenly feeling she had regained control of the situation.

The little man walked slowly to the table and using the stool's foot rungs as a ladder, climbed atop the tall chair and sat down, bringing him eye level with Jenny. "It seems we have reached an impasse, you and I."

"Not an impasse at all." Jenny shook her head and leaned toward him. "'Tis simple, really. We both forget what we know about the other. The success of our business ventures depends on our silence, does it not?"

Hercule nodded his wide head. "You are a shrewd woman, Miss Penny."

"So we have a bargain?" Jenny extended her hand to the little man for him to shake.

As he squeezed her hand, he chuckled softly. "I suppose we do."

⁂

Miss Meredith came racing below stairs but a moment after Hercule Lestrange closed the kitchen door behind him on his way out.

"Oh, Jenny," she huffed, being completely out of breath. Meredith looked her up and down and grimaced.

"Oh, that won't do. You've got to change your clothes. Hurry. Put on something fine!"

Jenny took hold of Meredith's arms and sat her down upon the stool. "Slow down. Tell me what is wrong."

"Now that the streets are clear again, he's *here*."

"What? Who is here?" Jenny asked.

"*Lord Argyll.*"

Jenny's heart skipped a double beat, then thudded hard in her chest, making her a little light-headed and faint.

"He's talking with the ladies right now, and from what I overheard, Aunt Letitia is none too pleased with his treatment of you."

Jenny felt a tremor of weakness in her limbs. "Really? How did he seem to you?"

Meredith seemed confused by the question. But it was simple really. She needed to know if he might be here to resume his courtship of her. If he was, she ought to wear the scarlet, for it was the color of love.

However, if he only wanted to explain his ungentlemanly behavior to the ladies, then the cream dress, that made her look so innocent and angelic, really would be the only choice. Lud, how she wanted to just race up the

stairs and throw herself into his arms. Despite everything, she missed him horribly.

"Come on . . . how did he *seem*?" Jenny's heart
pounded unnaturally loud in her ears.

"Oh." Meredith thought about it. "He looked tired, I
suppose. Really weary, as if he hadn't slept in nights."

Meredith's observation brought a smile to Jenny's
lips. His conscience had been plaguing him—and well
it should after what he said to her. Perhaps then, after
seeing her, he would regret his decision and recant. Oh,
yes, the cream gown was exactly the one to wear.

When Jenny appeared in the doorway, Lady Viola,
who stood behind and just off to the side of Callum,
shook her head violently and waved Jenny away.

Jenny crinkled her brow. Had she not been summoned?

She started to back away from the door, but somehow
Callum sensed her arrival. He went to her and reached
out for her hand. But Jenny guessed his intent and
pulled it away before he could touch her.

"Jenny, nay. Please dinna leave. 'Tis *ye* I came to see."

Jenny looked past him to Lady Letitia for direction,
who begrudgingly beckoned her into their fold.

She walked solemnly into the drawing room and
stood before the settee, where both Featherton sisters
joined her, one to her left and the other to her right.

The sisters each grasped one of her hands, and as if
arranged by a dance master, on the eight count they all
sat down at once.

Ever in control, Lady Letitia gestured for Lord Argyll to take his ease in the japanned chair directly across from them. Callum's eyes never left Jenny's as he silently seated himself on the edge of the chair.

Lady Letitia gave Jenny's hand a quick squeeze as if to urge her to speak. But la, what was she to say . . . the first words that entered her mind? Yes, that was it. *Do not think. Just speak.*

But she knew the words in her heart, her lowly lady's maid heart, *I love you, Callum,* were not to be uttered now, but rather held painfully to the breast. And so Lady Genevieve, her glittering alias, spoke in her stead.

"Has your intent changed, Lord Argyll? For if it has not, I do not understand the purpose of your visit this day." Jenny cringed inside. She could see the turmoil in his eyes. See how his decision had tortured him.

And for heaven's sake, she could not fault him for not wishing to marry her—she was a lady's maid. If he only knew the truth.

"It has, lass." He swallowed. "In part."

But Jenny was so gobsmacked by "It has" that she hardly heard the conditional he'd added to it.

"W-what did you say?" she stammered. Her heart pounded deafeningly in her ears and she leaned forward so as not to miss his next words.

"I've changed me mind, in part." Callum came to his feet.

Jenny watched, unable to move, as he came toward her, kilt swaying gently, and knelt before her. Reaching forward, he opened his palm to her.

She knew he wished to take her hand, and though she tried to offer one to him, neither lady would release her grip.

Lowering his hand, Callum laid it far too intimately atop her knee. Jenny needn't look around to know that the ladies were scowling. Whatever he was about to tell her, they were not pleased.

This made Jenny even more of a victim to her nerves.

As if gathering his courage, Callum dropped his chin toward his chest. By degrees, he slowly raised it again. There was a purpose in his gaze now.

"Jenny, I ken the ladies are aware of what happened when ye stayed with me in Laura Place."

"Yes." Jenny nodded. "I saw no reason to lie."

Callum's breath left his lungs, almost as if her statement had knocked it from him.

"Och, just let me say it," he finally managed. "If ye are with child, Jenny, I will marry ye. I will not condemn ye to a life of embarrassment and dishonor."

Lady Letitia grunted. "How magnanimous of you," she muttered.

From the corner of her eye, Jenny saw Lady Viola shaking a finger of disapproval at her sister.

Jenny considered his words carefully, wanting to make sure she understood him. "But if I am not carrying your child . . ."

"Then I canna marry ye. Ye ken my purpose. I will put an end to the Argyll line." There was a break in his voice, and she knew all of this was killing him inside.

She knew too that she alone could release him from the conflict he had been facing since they shared his bed.

"Lord Argyll," she began, "before you say another word, there is something I must confess to you."

Suddenly both Featherton ladies came to their feet.

"No, Lady Genevieve, you do not," Lady Letitia

broke in, cutting off Jenny's words. "Lord Argyll has not presented an honorable offer, and therefore you are under no obligation to explain anything whatsoever to him!"

Jenny looked up at Lady Viola. Why were they doing this? She must tell him the truth. She must release him from his pain.

But as her eyes met with the watery blue of Lady Viola's, she saw an urgency in them that confused her.

"No, Jenny, not another word. Not now. *Not yet*," the old woman said in a slight voice, barely more than a whisper. She began to waver and grow unsteady on her feet. Oh, heavens, she was going to have a spell.

"Please, what did ye want to tell me, Jenny? I am here, listenin'." Callum's hand tightened over her knee.

Lady Viola crumpled and crashed down in a sitting position upon the settee. As she struck the backrest, her frail body seemed to lose solidity and she tipped to the side, careening with the firm seat cushion. But strangely, the old woman's grip on Jenny's hand remained ever tight.

Callum jolted as Lady Viola toppled, but having witnessed her spell before did not take his attention from Jenny.

"No, not another word!" Lady Letitia snapped, thrusting her free hand forward and whisking Callum's palm from Jenny's knee.

Jenny's gaze darted from Callum to the sleeping Lady Viola and back again.

"In fact, Lord Argyll, since my sister is unwell, I must ask you to away. *Please*." The stern look in Lady Letitia's eye made clear her seriousness.

"*Jenny*." Callum's gaze held hers firmly.

"No, I am sorry, Lord Argyll, but I must insist." Lady Letitia shot a glance at Mr. Edgar, who had been standing sentry in the corner of the room. Taking his cue, he shuffled forward and stood over Lord Argyll.

Callum slowly came to his feet.

"I meant what I said, Jenny. If ye carry my bairn, I will marry ye. *I will*."

Jenny looked helplessly into his eyes. She wanted to run to him and beg his forgiveness for her grand lie. She knew she could break away from the two old ladies' firm grasps and go to him if she truly desired. But there was a part of her, a selfish part, that did not wish to confess her true identity. The childish, greedy part of her that wanted Callum so much that she would live a lie forever to retain his love.

Callum took his coat and gloves from Edgar and with one long, meaningful parting glance at Jenny, he left the Featherton household.

Meredith, who had slipped into the drawing room unseen and had hidden behind the thick curtains, made her way around the settee to Jenny and began to sputter.

"Are you mad, Jenny? Why didn't you tell him who you really were? You started to do it, and you know by now he certainly deserves the truth!"

Jenny lowered her eyes and stared down at the gold and cream sunburst pattern in the center of the Aubusson carpet. She said nothing.

But Lady Letitia did. "Because it was not yet time." Jenny looked up for her to continue. "He has not acknowledged the depth of his feelings for our Jenny yet."

Lady Viola opened her eyes and quickly sat up. Her supposed spell was clearly a ruse.

"Once he has, he will offer for Jenny no matter the

circumstance," Lady Viola said, adding, "and it will not matter if she is a lady's maid or a fine lady."

Meredith did not seem convinced. "You are putting quite a lot of faith in a man—no, *a rake*—you barely know."

Lady Letitia opened her mouth to speak, but very uncharacteristically, Lady Viola raised her hand to quiet her and spoke in her sister's place.

"We knew his mother well, and though he is unruly and does not conform to our society's rules and expectations, he is his mother's son and his heart is warm. You will see, Meredith, he will not disappoint young Jenny here."

"I wish my faith in him matched your own, my lady," Jenny said to Lady Viola. "I truly do."

"Mark my words, he shall marry you, Jenny. He shall."

Jenny looked into Lady Viola's eyes, and saw the Herculean strength of her faith in Callum. And for a brief moment, she actually believed it could be true.

Meredith plopped down on a footstool and stared up at her aunt. "So a rogue with a warm heart is . . . redeemable," she murmured to no one in particular. "But how does a lady learn these things?"

"Sadly, gel, through trial and error." Lady Letitia bobbed her head solemnly.

Meredith wrapped her arms around her knees and hugged them to her chest. "Well, someone should write a guidebook on dealing with rakes, scoundrels, and rogues, so young ladies will know what sort of men they are dealing with, and will not be so easily deceived by their charming ways."

The two Featherton ladies laughed at the absurd comment, but Jenny noticed that Meredith did not join them. No, instead the right corner of her mouth lifted, and Jenny could see the machinations of a working mind in her shifting eyes.

Oh, dear.

Later that evening, Jenny pocketed a guinea and slipped next door to check Molly's progress on her second project, a velvet pelisse she'd quietly assigned her a week before. Since she was trying to put aside a few bob each day for her shop, she had dismissed the notion of lining the garment with beaver fur for warmth, and instead settled for wool. Horrid, rough wool.

She'd never be able to step into a wind, for she would be sickened to have the plain wool exposed. It would ruin the effect of the pelisse. And how lovely and luxurious would *fur* have been? She sighed, for there was no use lamenting over it. What was done, was done.

To appease herself for the cost-cutting measures she was forced to accept, Jenny had convinced Mr. Bartleby to supply her with a dozen gleaming onyx buttons. In exchange, she only needed to add two gallipots to his next order. That was a bargain, for the buttons were worth at least . . . hmm. Not two pounds. *Not anywhere near that.*

The pleased smile dissolved from her face as she realized her mistake. Maybe it wasn't such a grand arrangement after all. No wonder Bartleby was so eager to seal their deal. She'd have to watch that man. He was far cleverer and half as trustworthy as she'd first thought.

Jenny rapped three times on the servant portal and Molly opened the door, appearing more than a little nervous.

"Come with me," the girl whispered. "But don't say nothin'. The mistress has been scaring the pudding from the service staff by surprising us below stairs all eve. She's havin' a grand guest tonight, and is giving Cook fits about the menu. She's changed it three times already! Imagine the waste."

"Who is the guest?" Jenny asked softly as the two of them slipped into the bedchamber Molly shared with a parlor maid.

"Oh, some sotted highborn, I don't doubt. What was his name . . . *Argyll*? Yes, I think that's it."

Jenny began to cough and choke.

Molly slapped her on the back. "Are you well, Miss Penny?"

"Y-yes," she croaked. "Are you sure—*Argyll?*"

"Sure as I can be. The widow hasn't had a gentleman visit the house since before her husband died. She's been primping all day. Never seen her in such a condition. Why she's acting like a love-struck chit."

Jenny sat down on the edge of the bed and watched the maid's cat wind an eight around her mistress's ankles. Molly could not possibly be right. Callum had no interest in the widow. Heavens, anyone could see that.

"Here's your pelisse. It's so beautiful, miss. But if I were makin' it for myself, I would have lined it with fur. Why go to the expense of using the softest velvet, satin trim, and real onyx buttons, then go and line it with commoners' wool?"

"For warmth, of course. Utility is far more important than style." Jenny roughly took the pelisse into her hands and spread it across the bed to view Molly's work. "And besides, I do not condone the killing of innocent creatures simply to strip them of their fashionable fur."

Molly wrung her hands before her apron. "Oh, *yes*. I hadn't thought of that."

Jenny suddenly felt almost heroic. Yes, she might have saved countless beavers' lives by her decision. "It would be like . . . killing your cat because it has such lovely fur, wouldn't it?"

"Oh, Miss Penny, don't say that. Why, I'll never be able to look at a fur collar or muff again."

A little twinge of guilt pinched at Jenny as she remembered the bear muff sitting inside her wardrobe. But as she caressed her lovely new pelisse, the feeling vanished just as quickly as it had come.

"Molly! Molly!" came a harsh female voice from the other side of the door.

Molly's eyes filled with terror. "It's the mistress. What do we do?"

Jenny jumped to her feet and scanned the chamber. There was no way to escape. No windows. Not even a wardrobe in which to hide.

"Open this door!" came the widow's screech again.

A moment passed, during which neither Molly nor Jenny dared even to expel a breath.

"Very well, then . . ." The door swung open and the widow barged inside. Her eyes swung from Molly to Jenny.

"Who are you?" she demanded, but then, as she studied Jenny for a moment longer, her gaze softened. "Wait a moment. I *know* you!"

"I—I . . ." *Goodness.* She was going to faint. Sweat

began to burst at her temples and blood pulsed in her ears.

The widow looked at Jenny's cream-colored muslin gown with tiny embroidered sprigs of gold ringing the hem. Clearly, this was not a lady's maid's costume. *Blast!* Why hadn't she changed into her brown frock before coming next door, and pulled a snowy mob cap over her perfectly coiffed hair?

Run, her mind screamed. *Just run!* There was nothing else to do, so Jenny tucked the pelisse under her arm and started for the door. She could push her way through the spindly widow if she needed to. Certainly, Lady McCarthy wouldn't be expecting such a bold move.

But as she neared, a smile broke over the widow's otherwise pinched face and she extended her hand. "Lady Genevieve," she crooned. "So lovely to see you."

Jenny stopped a mere breath away from the widow. She forced her shaking hand forward and dropped a curtsy as she became Lady Genevieve.

Then the widow's brows cinched tightly. "But what are you doing here . . . with my maid?"

"I—I—" Jenny's mind began to spin through options, finally, miraculously pulling one plausible explanation from the jumbled mix in her mind. "I needed these onyx buttons sewn onto my pelisse."

More, Jenny. Something more.

"But after hearing that you were stabbed by the Feathertons' completely *mad* lady's maid, why, I feared for my life if I were to request her assistance." She waited a moment, unsure if the widow was eating the lies she fed her.

The widow's eyes widened. "Yes, yes! She is mad,

that one. Why I couldn't walk for days after she stabbed my ankle down to the bone—*the bone*, I tell you. Can you imagine?"

What a huffing liar. Why, Jenny saw her dancing at the Fire and Ice Ball at the Upper Assembly Rooms that very evening!

"I remembered how kind you were to me, and since I needed the pelisse this eve—for it is exceedingly bitter this night—I stopped by to ask your girl if she might quickly stitch the new buttons for me. And she did."

Jenny turned to Molly and pressed the guinea into her hand, taking care to fold the girl's fingers over the gold coin so her mistress would not see its high denomination. "This *shilling* is for you, Molly, for doing me the favor so quickly."

"A whole shilling for stitching buttons?" The widow appeared appalled. "I think not. Molly, give it back."

Jenny raised her hand. "Madam, I do insist. And I must commend you on the training of your staff. For though I pressed, they insisted I not disturb you for you were about to receive an esteemed guest."

The widow flushed with color. "Err . . . yes. A . . . just a gentleman friend."

Jenny smiled at her. "Really? Well, he must be quite handsome for you look positively radiant this eve."

The older woman gave a nervous half laugh, and surveyed her flame-hued gown with a matronly green turban. She looked like a huge orange.

"Oh, he is somewhat tolerable, I suppose."

Jenny fought the impulse to sneer. *Tolerable, indeed.* If 'twas Lord Argyll paying her a call, tolerable was not a word she would ever use to describe such a devastatingly handsome man.

"Well, I do thank you for the use of your girl. I must away. Good eve, Lady McCarthy." Jenny dropped a deep curtsy, then with a parting glance at a totally confused Molly, she exited the chamber.

At a mad dash, she shot through the service door and headed back to the Featherton household.

After placing her new pelisse in her wardrobe, Jenny crept up the stairs and slipped into the drawing room. By luck, the room was unoccupied, though candles glowed in the two sconces above the hearth where a low fire burned.

She was relieved, for now she could step behind the thick curtains and watch for Callum through the great windows facing the crescent. For nearly an hour, she stood with her forehead and her hands, spread like two fleshy stars, pressed against the cold glass.

Though Molly and the widow had all but confirmed his visit, Jenny could not make herself believe it. And so she stood, waiting, until, just as the tall case clock struck eight in the eve, a familiar town carriage drew up before the widow's home.

Holding her breath until her lungs burned, Jenny watched as the footman let down the stairs, and Callum, so ruggedly handsome in his fine dress kilt, stepped out into the night. He was holding a gathering of hothouse roses in his gloved hand.

Roses. How she loved roses. In fact, they were her absolute favorite flower.

Her brows drew together and she felt a sudden tightness in her chest. He'd never brought her roses. Heat washed across her eyes. Why was he bringing them to the widow? Had he dismissed her, er . . . Lady Genevieve, already?

Callum stopped before continuing up the walk and turned to stare up at the Feathertons' house, at the same window where Jenny stood. For some moments, he did not move, but looked up, waiting.

Jenny's body jerked involuntarily, though she was sure he could not see her.

"Who is in there?" came Lady Viola's voice from the direction of the high-backed wing chair.

Jenny froze. She hadn't noticed her when she came into the drawing room. The lady must have entered only belatedly. And so, for a moment, Jenny thought not to answer, in hopes that the old woman might think she had imagined the movement she evidently saw behind the curtains.

"Hello. Is that you hiding in the draperies, Meredith?"

Reaching out her left hand, Jenny pushed the curtain aside and stepped out from behind them. "No, 'tis Jenny," she answered guiltily.

"Whatever are you doing behind there? It must be dreadfully cold standing so close to the glass. Come away from there, child, before you catch your death." Lady Viola coaxed Jenny forward with a crook of her finger.

Jenny came to stand before her lady, her eyes scraping the floor. "I—I saw Lord Argyll just now."

Lady Viola sat up straight. "Argyll, *here?*"

"No, my lady. I believe he meant to have an interview with the widow."

Lady Viola brought her fingers to her lips, and her

eyes began to shuttle back and forth in her head. "This is not good, child. Something is afoot."

Something about the frail woman's tone unnerved Jenny. "What do you mean, my lady?"

"Letitia suspected something after all of the widow's odd questions yesterday, but I told Sister she was just chasing a feather in the air. But she was right all along." A walking stick shot up from beside the chair and plunged into the carpet. "Some assistance, please, Jenny. Help me stand."

Jenny looped her forearms under the old woman's armpits and hauled her from the wing-backed chair. "Is something amiss, my lady? Please, you'd let me know if there were."

A pale, withered hand sluiced through the air, dismissing her question outright.

"Letitia!" Lady Viola cried, startling Jenny so much that she nearly fell backward into the fire.

"My lady, *please*. What is wrong?"

But Lady Viola was already halfway into the passage, screaming for her sister every second step. "Letitia! *Letitia*, come quickly, Sister! We've got trouble. Immense trouble!"

Chapter Thirteen

Within minutes, both Featherton ladies were bundled in their wraps and charging, in their own way, out the front door.

Jenny and Meredith rushed down the passage to catch the two old women. Instead, they snared only a scattering of words trailing behind the ladies in the frigid night air on silver scarves of vapor.

"Never you fear, Viola, she'll not turn us out into the cold. So we'll just remain until Argyll takes his leave," came Lady Letitia's booming voice as the two made their way to the widow's front walk.

"What do you suppose is wrong?" Jenny asked Meredith, hoping that she, with her tendency to accidentally overhear private conversations, might have gleaned some enlightening bits and pieces.

Meredith's blue eyes glowed like cut sapphires in the candlelight and Jenny knew at once she had not been wrong. Meredith knew something.

"The widow came by yesterday and most urgently wished to see my aunts. When I sat down to join them for tea, she made it quite clear that she had a private matter to discuss with the ladies and that matter *did not* include me." Meredith gave Jenny a charged look.

So Jenny reacted as she guessed Meredith wanted her to. "How incredibly rude! Casting you out of your aunts' own drawing room."

Meredith smiled puckishly. "I wasn't about to give her the satisfaction of treating me like a child, so I left the drawing room, walked down the passage and straight into the dining room, where I listened to everything that was said through the open door."

Jenny took Meredith's hand and led her to the chairs, where they settled themselves, on either side of the drawing room hearth. "What did you hear?" she asked.

Meredith hesitated, which was very uncharacteristic of her nature. "I do not know what it all means. Her words were naught but a pile of puzzle pieces to me—but to you, Jenny . . ."

"I do not know the widow at all, so I am sure her words will mean little to me as well." Jenny grinned conspiratorially. "Still, I do love a good secret."

Meredith grinned back at her. "Very well. She was asking a number of questions about a woman named Olivia Burnett."

Jenny felt her eyes widen, and when they did, Meredith paused.

"You *do* know her," Meredith charged. "I knew it!"

"No, I do not. But I know *of* her." Jenny exhaled and looked back at Meredith. "She was Lord Argyll's mother."

"His mother?" Now Meredith looked astounded. "No, no, that doesn't make sense."

Jenny reached across the slate hearth and took Meredith's hand. "Why not?"

Meredith's face screwed up as if she were straining to carry a heavy parcel. "The widow was saying something about this Olivia Burnett woman being a relation of my aunts. A *very close* relation."

She released Meredith's hand then and sat upright. "When you say *very close* . . ."

"You needn't ask. I don't know what she meant. But Aunt Letitia got roiling angry and told the widow she ought to get her facts straight before she dared make such accusations again."

"Really?" Jenny leaned near, and widened her eyes. "What happened next?"

"I don't know. Edgar walked into the room behind me, and . . . well, he gave me that look of his. You know, the one that sets your knees to quaking."

"Oh, I know it all too well."

"So, I had no choice. I had to leave." Meredith's eyes grew round and her pupils expanded, until the blue surrounding them was little more than a thin ring of vibrant color. "Do you suppose my aunts are hiding something important? A horrible secret maybe, or the locking key to a mystery, mayhap? Wouldn't that be terribly exciting?"

"I haven't a notion what is afoot." Jenny rose slowly, walked to the window, and peered outside toward the widow's house. "But something is not being said. Of that I am all too sure."

That night, Jenny forced herself to remain awake in her bed until she heard the front door close and the sound of footsteps and cane knocks on the marble entry floor.

Lifting the hem of her shift, she padded across the cold floor and crept up the servants' steps so she could watch and listen through the back passage door, which she had purposely left ajar before heading to bed.

"Do you suppose she told him anything before we arrived?" Lady Viola was asking as she handed a weary-looking Edgar her wrap.

"There was no time. Besides, would he have been so gentlemanly and civil to us if he knew the truth?" Lady Letitia asked.

"I suppose not."

"Well, on the morrow, I'll send a few coins over with that scullery maid, Erma. She's a crafty one, and if anyone can buy us a spy among the widow's ranks, it will be she."

"Oh, Letitia, not a spy."

"I fear there is no other way. We must know if Argyll has been enticed over to Lady McCarthy's residence again—this time preferably *before* he arrives."

"Of course you are right, Sister."

On the other side of the door, Jenny sat down on the wood-planked floor and wrapped her arms around her knees for warmth. What was all of this about? She was aching to know. And blast it all, those old ladies should confide in her. For if it concerned Callum it also concerned her . . . what with she possibly being the mother of his child and all.

Well, in the morning she might ply the scullery maids with a few bob as well. Yes, she'd have her own spy at the McCarthy residence.

Just then, the door edged open. Jenny's head shot up and met the angry gaze of Mr. Edgar.

"Shouldn't you be abed . . . *my lady*? You have an early morning tomorrow, if you've not forgotten."

"Uh . . . yes, Mr. Edgar. I haven't forgotten." Jenny stood up and scampered down the stairs. But with all this hullabaloo concerning Callum, she *had* completely forgotten.

Bloody hell.

She had to try to get some sleep. There was so much to do in the morning. Lud, she had sleeves to attach to Meredith's gown and yards of satin skirt yet to hem.

For tomorrow was Miss Meredith's eighteenth birthday.

꧁

"Morning, dove . . ." sang her mother from the darkness. "Time to wake. Lots to do this morn. Up, up, up!"

Jenny groaned and covered her head with her feather pillow as her mother lit the stub of a candle at her bedside to break the darkness.

"Still no visit from your *friend*?" her mother asked sweetly.

"*No*, Mother," she murmured from beneath the pillow.

"What was that, dear?"

Jenny yanked the pillow from her head, causing her hair to stand on end from the friction. She scowled up at her mother's smiling face. "*No*."

"That's fine, dear. You shouldn't worry about it. I've learned that worry might delay visits at times."

"Please, Mother, do stop asking me about this every

morn. I do not *feel* as though I am with child. I haven't lost my breakfast even once, and I am as strong as a chairman. Does that satisfy you?"

"Oh, of course, darling. Whatever you say," she said softly in a placating manner that made Jenny's blood sputter and bubble hotly as tingle cream over the fire.

"But if you *are* with child, remember, Lord Argyll did say he would offer for you."

"Not you too?" Jenny pressed the pillow atop her face and screamed into it. Then she sat straight up in her bed, letting the pillow fall to her lap. "Are the ladies awake yet?"

"Goodness no. 'Tis still dark."

"What about . . . Erma? Is she about?" Jenny asked casually.

"Indeed, tending the fires in the kitchen just now." Then her mother's left eye began to narrow. "I hope you haven't got any idea about getting her to help you with the cream this morn. Like the rest of us, she has work to do—and so do you, my clever miss."

"Oh, I would not dream of potting any cream today, not with it being Meredith's birthday. I just wanted to have a word with Erma, that's all."

Jenny pulled open her bedside drawer, palmed two gleaming guineas, one for each surly scullery maid, then pecked her mother's cheek and hurried into the kitchen.

❧

That eve, the Featherton house glowed like a lantern, with nigh on eight score beeswax candles lit, some in sconces, others hoisted to the ceiling in sparkling crystal chandeliers, to help make Meredith's birthday rout bright as it could be.

"I can't bear this," Jenny complained as she laced Meredith into a horrid black evening gown.

Jenny could not abide black bombazine. She didn't care if it was all the crack. It looked awful. She opened Meredith's tiny jewel box and withdrew a pair of ear pendants of deepest jet. And while her mistress attached these to her ears, Jenny swept up her curly red locks in a bandeaux, allowing several tendrils to fall prettily about her face.

"You do realize," Jenny began as she tossed black silk gloves to Meredith, "the eye is naturally drawn to color. Though I know you, like all of England, grieve the death of our princess, can't you forgo swathing yourself in ebony? It is your birthday after all. 'Tis a time for celebration, not mourning. Other ladies will certainly wear lively color this eve, and I do not believe you would wish to remain unnoticed."

"You are wrong about that. I *do* wish to remain un-noticed, so that I may observe the rogues and rakes in action."

Jenny's mouth fell agape. "But it's *your* rout. Please do not spend it spying . . . I mean *observing* others."

Meredith chuckled. "While I do enjoy spying from time to time, tonight I am conducting research for my guidebook for ladies. I might even try a few social . . . *experiments*." The edge of Meredith's pink lips lifted mischievously.

Jenny rolled her eyes. Meredith's plans were not her concern, but rather the Featherton ladies' problem. She, after all, had to prepare for the rout herself. "There you are. You look stunning—despite your color choice."

And she did. With her creamy ivory skin, startling blue eyes, and brilliant copper hair, Meredith had been blessed with enough natural color to balance the solemn weight of the wretched ebony gown.

"Oh, Jenny. It's just a small rout. I swear I'll don the emerald gown for my birthday ball next week." Meredith pulled a few more tendrils of hair from the bandeaux. "While tonight will be utterly dreary, I own that the ball will be wickedly exciting."

Jenny had started from the chamber, but turned around. "How shall this ball be any different from others?"

"Oh, then you've not heard!" Meredith rushed to Jenny and grabbed up her hands. "My aunts wanted to share my celebration with the world . . . and I daresay garner a little attention for themselves. My sisters, you see, are both too far along in their confinements to travel to Bath for my ball. So, my aunts, thinking I would be greatly saddened by my sisters' absences, distributed a public invitation to *all* of elevated Bath. Staid old matrons and horse-faced daughters won't be the only guests ringing the floor at my ball. But people we've never met before. Rogues, *viscounts* . . ." Meredith winked at Jenny. "Maybe even the mysterious *thieves*! Won't it be exciting? La, I simply cannot wait!"

Jenny could not believe what she was hearing. If the Feathertons had truly issued a public invitation, of course the thieves, and their likely ringleader, Hercule Lestrange, would attend. Every member of the *ton* would be at risk of being bludgeoned and robbed.

Jenny sucked her lower lip into her mouth and bit into its soft flesh. "The thieves might well attend." She looked into Meredith's glittering eyes. "Therefore you should wear paste jewels, nothing more."

"I agree, but you will never convince my aunties. They love their baubles too much to miss a chance to wear them," Meredith said. "Now, you'd better go and dress. Take care to look your best this eve," she called out as Jenny strolled down the passage. "I saw Lord Argyll's name inked on the rout's guest list."

🕸

Every crystal bob, dripping like ice from the chandelier in the Feathertons' drawing room, glowed as if lit from within, Jenny noted as she entered the room.

The gold damask silk on the walls reflected the light and warmed the wan complexions of matrons, while gilding the rosy countenances of those of fewer years.

Jenny smiled to herself, for her opulent ivory gown drank in the flickering light. She looked luminous and she well knew it.

At once her eyes swept the room for Callum. It was yet early in the eve, but she had hoped to see him by now. Butterflies tumbled inside her stomach and her skin tingled in nervous anticipation. Somehow, if only she might speak with him privately, Jenny knew she could bridge the gulf that had opened between them. She had to. Her heart would have it no other way.

"You look right fine this night, Jenny. Delicious in fact," buzzed a hoarse whisper near her ear. "Good enough to eat."

She looked up to see George, one of the footmen, standing beside her with a sterling salver of crystal glasses filled with amber sherry. Jenny reached out and lifted a small glass from the tray, not bothering to reply.

A bloody rake in footman's garb, he was. Why, Meredith's guidebook could devote an entire chapter to George alone.

"Later, though, I suppose," he added, raising a brow as if he truly thought she'd take a roll with him.

"Thank you for the sherry, George," she murmured, then walked across the drawing room to the marble mantel. As she waited for Callum, Jenny turned her body three-quarters to the room—for it was important her gown catch the light properly—while she nervously fingered the plumed hat of the Chelsea figural candlestick.

It was foolish to anticipate Callum's appearance so eagerly. It was not as if she had any idea as to what to say to him. Nothing had changed in her situation, or his. Still, she had to speak with him. Had to try to set things to right.

As Meredith played the fortepiano, quite well in fact, Jenny soon found herself tapping her slipper in time.

"Were we in a larger gallery, lassie, I would ask ye to dance."

At the sound of Callum's voice, a thrill trickled up inside of Jenny and she turned her head to find him bowing low to her. He looked wickedly handsome in a dark cutaway coat, which brilliantly picked up a repeated line of azure in an understated dress kilt she'd never seen him wear before. On his lapel was a silver dagger topped with a rather large cabochon sapphire. La, he looked impressive.

Turning more fully to the light, she eased into a

curtsy, taking care to tilt her head just enough to send her pearl bobs to swaying.

His gaze darted to them.

Jenny grinned inwardly. Then all at once it struck her that perhaps she was being too forgiving, too kind. Were she a lady true, as he believed her to be, she would be seething about the situation he'd left her in.

She arched an accusing brow. "Have you something to say to me, Lord Argyll, for I should join Meredith at the fortepiano. I've found," she lied, "it exceedingly difficult to play while turning the music one's self."

But when she looked up at Callum, she saw the deep despair in his warm dark eyes. Suddenly she wanted nothing more than to take him into her arms, kiss him, and forgive him anything.

In the brief seconds that this thought breached her mind, it was as if Jenny had accidentally left a door open, a door through which Callum had peered and saw what truly lay in her heart.

And something within him changed . . . evolved.

It was there in his eyes, in the shift of his shoulders, in the confidence in his stance. All at once, he had come to some decision.

Jenny took a deep breath and held it in her lungs, afraid to breathe or even move.

"Jenny, will ye come with me to the study where we might be alone."

"Oh." Jenny looked across the drawing room at the Featherton ladies.

Lady Letitia was laughing, in her deeply contagious way, while standing in the company of two older gentlemen. But Lady Viola had a distressed expression on her face, one that cinched her thin lips and white brows. With her, stood the widow.

Something wasn't right, and a little voice inside Jenny's head told her to go to Lady Viola, but then she felt Callum's hand brush the top of her glove.

"Please, Jenny. I must speak with ye now."

There was need in his eyes, and she could not refuse. With one last glance at Lady Viola and the widow, she silently followed Callum into the passage.

Out of habit, she snatched a candle from a sconce and as Callum opened the door to the study, she hurried around the room lighting the candles, then bent to see to the fire.

Callum reached down and took her hand, and she dropped the candle into the barely glowing embers in the hearth.

"The candle!" Jenny blurted, forgetting momentarily that at this moment she was not a maid concerned with household thrift, but a refined lady.

"Leave it be." Callum led her to the chair before the mahogany bureau bookcase and with a sweep of his hand bade her to be seated. "Please."

As she settled herself in the chair, Jenny searched Callum's eyes for any hint of what he was about. But she could not read what she saw there, for in those swirls of deepest brown lit with flecks of gold was a tumult of emotion.

Argyll knelt on one knee before her. "Jenny, can ye ever fergive me? Ye gave yer love, yer heart, yer body to me—and I thrust it back at ye as if it meant nothing." He took a long cleansing breath. "But being with ye that night, Christ, it meant everything to me. More than ye'll ever know. And I hope to prove that to ye now."

And suddenly Jenny knew what he was about to do. A twist of dread pinched at her.

"Please, Callum. *No*."

Callum shook his head slowly. "I ken I've hurt ye badly—"

Jenny came to her feet. "No, 'tisn't that at all."

Do it, Jenny! Tell him. Tell him who you really are.

"I—I . . ." she sputtered. *Tell him.*

Just then, the door flew open and the Widow McCarthy stood staring at the sight of Callum on bended knee before Jenny.

"Lord Argyll, I must speak with you," the widow pressed.

Callum sighed. "I shall attend to ye presently, Lady McCarthy, but I am indisposed at this moment."

The widow looked nervously down the passageway to her left. "I beg you. There is something you must know, and when you hear what I have to say, I believe you will be most grateful for my interruption."

Callum slowly came to his feet and faced her.

The widow lowered her voice almost to a whisper. "I have some information that cannot remain wrongly hidden from you any longer."

The widow looked straight at Jenny. "Will you please excuse us?"

Jenny looked at Callum. "No, Callum, I *must* speak with you first."

He tried to ease her worry with a gentle smile. "We have quite a lot to discuss, ye and I. But that will take time. Please, let the widow have her say, then I will devote myself to ye entirely."

"But, Callum, you don't understand. I—"

"'Tis all right. Please, go on, lass. I willna be long."

Tears began to burn in the backs of Jenny's eyes as she walked past Callum, the smirking widow, and into the passage.

She turned around and looked back into the room as the widow shut the door in her face.

"Lord help me now," Jenny whimpered.

Chapter Fourteen

Wretched corset! She couldn't get a single bleedin' breath.

Jenny closed her eyes and leaned her forehead against the door. What was she to do? The wicked widow was going to expose her. Oh, why hadn't she told Callum she was a maid sooner? This was all her fault—her own foolish fault!

For a few moments, Jenny paced stiffly just outside the study. The widow was taking much too long. She just had to be telling him something more.

Jenny gasped. *No. The tingle cream.* Someone must have told the widow about the Lady Eros's cream!

Lunging forward, she pressed her ear so hard to the paneled door that it throbbed as she strained to hear. A murmur of voices, dulled by Meredith's incessant forte-piano playing in the drawing room beyond, was all she could discern.

The tapping of a cane alerted Jenny that someone had entered the passage. She swiveled her head and saw Lady Viola staring back at her.

"Oh, my lady. Something dreadful has happened."

"I thought as much." Lady Viola hurried up the passage toward Jenny. "'Tis the widow, is it not?"

Jenny nodded feebly. "She's in the study with Lord Argyll."

Her employer's frosty brows shot skyward. "Oh, heavens! Find Lady Letitia and bring her here at once. Do hurry!"

Lifting her hem, Jenny ran down the passage and straight into the drawing room, where, heedless of the rankled partygoers she left in her wake, she hurried through to reach Lady Letitia.

Moments later, she and the two Featherton ladies stood poised outside the study door.

"She's telling him who I really am," Jenny whimpered. "What shall I do?"

The two ladies looked quizzically at one another, then back at Jenny.

"No, dear. I do not believe it is *you* they are discussing." Lady Letitia turned away and took Lady Viola's left hand. "Are you ready, Sister?"

"Yes," Lady Viola muttered, her eyes glistening with unshed tears. "As ready as a body can be in such a situation."

"Well, then . . ." Reaching her hand slowly forward, Lady Letitia pressed the door latch and released it, allowing the door to inch open of its own accord.

As a unit, the snowy-haired pair moved into the study, positioning themselves directly before Callum.

Jenny slipped just inside the door and leaned against the blue verditer painted wall for bodily support. Oh, how she hoped the ladies were right and the widow wasn't revealing her secret, but what else could it be?

The widow sat in the ribbon-back chair beside the

hearth, her face obscured to Jenny by the needlework-embroidered polescreen. This suited Jenny quite well, for the smirk on the widow's face as she entered the room only minutes ago was still vividly emblazoned in her mind.

Callum's shocked face was plainly visible to her, however. His gaze was solemn and unyielding, but to her astonishment, it was not Jenny who held his attention. No, 'twas Lady Viola.

"Why?" he stammered in a voice so wrought with anguish that had Jenny not seen him speak, she would not have recognized it as his own. "Why dinna ye tell me? Why did ye leave me to believe ye barely knew my mother . . . when all along—"

Lady Viola walked slowly toward Callum and laid a quaking hand to his shoulder. He pushed it away with unnecessary brusqueness.

"My dear boy." As Lady Viola began, her voice shook. "I was unmarried when I learned I was with child. I wanted to keep her, to raise her, but Father would not allow it."

She turned her eyes to her sister, who nodded for her to continue. "In Father's eyes, I had shamed him and the family name. I was sent to live with my cousin in Cornwall. She was barren, and when the child was delivered into the world, she and her husband took Olivia and raised her as their own."

"Please try to understand." Lady Letitia lowered herself to the petite chair near the hearth. "It was a different time then."

As Jenny stood quietly in the background, listening to every word, she was very confused. Lady Letitia had been right, this *wasn't* all about her. Lord above, what a blessed relief.

But Lady Viola—Callum's *grandmother*? She could not have heard correctly. Her ladyship had a child without the benefit of marriage—and she was an earl's daughter. Not a lowly maid, like her. Lud, how could this be?

Still, she could not summon the least bit of happiness at this fortunate turn of events. Not when those she loved were clearly leveled by the widow's ill-timed revelation.

Callum turned his eyes to the frail old woman, and Jenny could see the redness within them.

"Why dinna ye tell me? Ye knew I searched for any news of her . . . any record of her last days."

The widow stood then and lifted her chin haughtily. "Such an important revelation should not have been left for *me* to report. But it was, and Lord Argyll is only too grateful that I have come forward with the truth—since evidently you were not about to offer it."

Shooting to her feet, Lady Letitia plowed forward, her cheeks puffing with rage as she grabbed the widow's bony arm and flung her toward the door. "Out! Get out of this house. Have you not done enough damage to this fragile family?"

Recovering her balance, the widow's lips opened wide, and an image of the mouth of a great cave came at once to Jenny's mind.

"*I* did what was right! I know Lord Argyll appreciates *my* honesty." The widow's eyes gleamed with fury. "Though the two of you may not."

Lady Letitia glared at the widow. "Jen—Lady

Genevieve, please escort Lady McCarthy to the front door."

Jenny instinctively bobbed a quick curtsy and shooed the horrid widow out of the room as her employer had bade her to do. She could feel every skeletal bump in the widow's lean back as she pressed her forward at near trotting speed toward the front door, where Mr. Edgar awaited with her wraps.

After leaving Lady McCarthy in his capable charge, Jenny dashed back down the passageway for the study, for she did not want to miss any part of the unfolding drama.

But by time she returned, clearly the most interesting snippets of conversation had passed. Callum stood, his towering frame in complete contrast to Lady Viola's tiny body, which he hugged tightly to him.

"Shhh, dinna cry," Callum said softly into her hair. "Ye cudna have known what happened to me after she left."

Lady Viola tilted her head all the way back to look up into his eyes. Tears cut trails of white through her heavy face powder. "I would have come for you. I swear it. You must believe me."

"I do believe ye. But ye must stop the tears. This day should be joyous, fer today I learned that I wasna alone in this world. I have blood kin. I have a grandmother."

"And an aunt!" Lady Letitia added exuberantly, rushing forward to join her sister in hugging Callum.

Though Jenny had remained in the shadows and had said not a word, Callum seemed to know she was there. He turned around and looked straight at her.

"Jenny, did ye know of this?" he asked her. The two Featherton ladies turned to look at her.

"On my honor, I did not." As soon as the words had sailed from her mouth she regretted her choice. On her *honor*. Bah. What honor had she? She was living a lie—and enjoying every day of it!

"Come, lass." Callum lifted his hand from Lady Viola's back, releasing her and Lady Letitia as he beckoned to her. "Please, Jenny."

Hesitantly, she went to him and when she stood before him, the two old women drew back, taking Jenny's place in the shadows.

Callum lifted Jenny's hand in his. "I had come here this eve with a purpose."

The Featherton sisters looked at each other, clearly perplexed.

Settling Jenny in the same chair he had placed her in earlier, Callum knelt down on his knee as he had done just before the widow had so rudely interrupted.

"Jenny, I have not yet discussed this with Lady Letitia and Lady Viola, but I must approach ye now. I've left this too long already." He paused but an instant before bringing her hand to his lips and gently kissing the tops of her gloved fingers. "Jenny, would ye do me the great honor of becomin' me wife?"

Jenny's eyes flooded with hot tears. She could not agree, could not scream *yes*, though it was what she wanted most in this world. "Callum, I—"

Lady Letitia hurried forward, and Jenny glanced up to see her violently shaking her head and placing her index finger vertically across her lips.

Lady Viola, hands folded over her heart, was beaming. "Oh, Jenny, say *yes*! You love him, and he loves you. Now is the time to listen *only* to your heart, dove.

Nothing else matters at this moment. *Nothing*." Her gaze that held Jenny was crystal clear in meaning.

Jenny looked at Callum, and at the Featherton sisters, all watching for her reply with joyous anticipation.

Listen to her heart? Golly, could it be so easy?

Say yes, embrace this glorious moment, and make everyone happy. Or should she do what her conscience dictated . . . and confess.

"Young Callum has had such a difficult hour, love. Make this moment one he will recall happily 'til the end of his days." Lady Letitia stared hard at Jenny, her eyes pleading with her to accept his troth.

But how could she when their entire relationship was based on a massive lie?

Jenny thought silently for several moments, until Callum withdrew a brilliant ruby ring from his sporran. As he peeled back her glove and slipped the ring onto her third finger, Jenny gasped at its beauty.

The facets of the bloodred center stone caught the candlelight, its brilliance enhanced by a circlet of sparkling diamonds.

And all at once, that little scolding voice in her head started to fade away.

It made no sense, but for some reason, when she looked at the ring, that stunning ruby and diamond ring, she could barely hear that nagging little voice at all.

Jenny raised the ring before her eyes and blinked at it. And then it happened.

Four words slipped past her lips before she could bite them back.

"*Yes*, I'll marry you!"

Late that night, as Erma toiled in the kitchen filling two dozen pots of cream, Jenny sat on her small bed, head dropped forlornly to her chest.

"Heavens above, child, how could you have accepted Lord Argyll's troth, his ring, when you've still not told him who you are?"

"Because I love him, Mama."

Her mother grabbed Jenny's hand and, bending her fingers toward her palm, forced her to look at the ring. "Look at that, Jenny. Here is proof that he loves you. If you truly love him as well, you owe him the truth!"

Pulling her hand away, she let her back fall across the width of the horsehair mattress. Her feet tapped nervously on the stone floor. "I know 'twas wrong. You needn't remind me. And I was about to admit everything to him, really I was, but then the ladies started shaking their fool heads and signaling for me to shush. 'Listen to your heart' they told me. And so I did."

Her mother folded her arms across her chest. "I repeat, gel, you owe Lord Argyll the truth."

"I know. I *know*. I just love him so much and the instant I tell him—" Jenny sat up and sadly rested her head in her hands, but the moment she felt the smooth cool band of the ring against her cheek, she had to lean back and take a quick peek.

But Jenny's mother knew where she was headed. "You must give the ring back and tell him who you really are. If the ladies are right about him, your true identity will not alter the way he feels about you. He will still love you, still honor his offer, and still marry you."

"Can't I wait, for just a week . . . until after Meredith's

ball at the Upper Assembly Rooms? I swear, I will tell him then."

"Waiting will only make it worse."

"Heavens, Mama, don't you think I know that? But you should have seen the look in his eyes. Had I not accepted, I would have destroyed him."

"The viscount is stronger than you know. Do what is right, Jenny. And you know what that is." Then her mother turned her nose upward and sniffed the air. "Best check on Erma too. Something's burning."

Erma. Bleedin' Erma.

She'd paid both the scullery maid and her spy inside the widow's lair, and did she get so much as a whisper that Lady McCarthy was about to expose dear, harmless Lady Viola's past? *No.*

Well, Jenny wanted to know why.

With hands clenched into fists, she charged into the kitchen to find Erma capping the last of a dozen gallipots.

"Oh, there you are," Erma said the moment she noticed her enter the kitchen. But the smirk on her face melted the moment she saw the hard expression on Jenny's face.

"Why didn't you tell me what Widow McCarthy had learned? You must have heard."

"I heard, I did. Surprise it was too. The prim Lady Viola must have been quite the tart in her day. Who'd have guessed."

Immense heat boiled up into Jenny's temples and her fisted knuckles went white with rage.

But Erma didn't seem to notice, for she'd turned away and set herself to the task of placing the pots into the harvest basket. "But I didn't tell you because it wasn't none of your concern."

Placing her hand on the base of her back, Erma straightened her stiff spine. "The widow's on your trail though, Miss Penny. She doesn't like it none that you and the viscount are gettin' all sweet like, so she's been doing some pryin' into your lineage as well."

"My lineage? But h-how?" A sick feeling tore through Jenny's stomach.

"Well, from what I've heard, she's got her maids and footmen pumping our house staff for any information about you. The first one who comes forward with something interesting gets a reward of some sort." Erma sat down on the stool and rested her elbow on the table, and her chin on her hand. "If I was you, I'd be thinkin' about the value of pressin' a few guineas in the hands of the staff . . . in both houses."

"Both? But I haven't got that sort of money."

Erma scoffed at that. "Well, maybe you might consider wearing a gown more than one time once in a while. Listen, I'm tellin' you to find the money, or the widow will have your mask in her hand in no time at all. I'm serious, Jenny."

Jenny dropped her head in thought as she turned from the table and started for her chamber. She couldn't let the widow learn who she really was. She had to protect Callum, for at least another week. Until the ball.

Criminy, just where was she going to get that sort of money?

Why, she still needed to pay on her accounts at four shops on Milsom—for she'd been warned that they would cease to allow her to frequent their establishments if payment was not made soon.

But most importantly, she needed every guinea she'd earn this week to pay for her finest, grandest ball gown of all—the one for Meredith's birthday ball.

Well, she'd just have to find a way to get the money. She just had to, else Callum and all of Bath would soon be reading a great dark heading in *The Bath Herald*'s weekly *on-dit* column: *Lady Eros revealed to be Miss Jenny Penny, lady's maid and liar extraordinaire.*

She shivered at the thought.

That Saturday, Jenny was summoned by her employers to the breakfast table, where, as more often than not, she found them chatting over the newspaper's latest *on-dit* column.

"A whole day it took the columnist to scrounge up the details of Lord Argyll's betrothal to our Jenny. Imagine that." Lady Letitia chuckled. "The columnist's spies must be slipping up."

Lady Viola wrinkled her nose. "Does this not disturb you in the least, Sister? No one knew of his offer except those inside this house."

Jenny swallowed hard as she stood at the sideboard alongside her mother. A little tremor shook her bones. It was happening already, just as Erma had foretold. Information was dripping from the house like tea from a leaky pot.

Her employer gazed up at her. "Jenny, have you told anyone about your betrothal?"

"No, my lady."

"And you, Mrs. Penny?" Lady Letitia asked.

"I needn't tell a soul. All of below stairs knew of the

match before the conclusion of the rout." Her mother quieted for a moment as she organized her next words. "Begging your pardon, my lady, but George, the footman, overheard two of the party guests discussing it before the lot of you left the study."

"Dear me, Letitia!" Lady Viola's eyes lit with alarm. "Was it possible someone was listening from the passage?"

Meredith set her toasted bread on her plate and looked up. "More likely someone was in here."

Lady Letitia snapped her head around. "The dining room?"

"Oh, yes," Meredith replied as she rose from the table and walked to the south wall. "If you stand right about here, and place your ear against the wall, like so, you can hear everything said in the study."

She turned around and smiled, but seemed startled to see that everyone was staring at her with harmonized looks of shock. "What? The study is just on the other side, you know. Would you like me to go into the other room and demonstrate?"

"No, dear. We believe you." Lady Viola sighed. "Now we know how the information escaped, but we have yet to discover who the spy might have been."

Lady Letitia exhaled. "And 'tis likely we never will."

Then, bells started tinkling in Jenny's ears. "I think we must suspect the service staff."

Mrs. Penny's eyes bulged in her head. "What are you saying, Jenny," she whispered hotly into her daughter's ear. "Casting the light of suspicion upon your own."

Jenny continued, however, for here was her chance to get the blunt she needed to seal the wagging lips of the staff—both Featherton and McCarthy.

"Just last night, one of the scullery maids informed me that Lady McCarthy had bade those in her service to learn as much as possible about my lineage."

"Oh! That . . . *woman*. Why will she not just leave us alone?" Lady Viola exclaimed, her high voice wavering angrily.

Jenny knew this was her moment. "The scullery maid even suggested that the widow was paying for the information, and that if we wished to ensure that my identity remain secret, until such a time as we choose to reveal it, that we pay the Featherton staff, as well as the widow's, for their continued discretion."

The two Featherton ladies sat very quietly as they considered Jenny's words.

Then a meaningful gaze passed between them.

Lady Viola settled a spoonful of hot porridge into her mouth, and after swishing it around a bit, swallowed. "Sister, I fear we have no choice. It is too soon to reveal our gel's true identity. Why, Callum is still reeling from the revelation that I am his grandmother."

"Of course you are right, Viola. His wound is still fresh and he must have time to heal completely — before learning Jenny's secret." Lady Letitia turned to Jenny. "Our man of affairs will arrive this afternoon. I shall leave instructions that he deliver to you whatever funds you request before he leaves. You will see that it reaches the proper hands, won't you, gel?"

Jenny bobbed a quick but buoyant curtsy. "Oh, of course, my lady."

Later that afternoon Jenny walked into the kitchen looking for Erma, when she felt a bone-biting draft coming from the outer door.

Rubbing her arms for friction against the bitter chill, she caught the handle to close the door when she noticed Erma chatting with, of all people, Hercule Lestrange!

The little man, spotting Jenny at the kitchen door, tipped his hat and smiled, then bid good-bye to Erma and set off in the direction of Brock Street.

Erma started back toward the house, but she seemed anxious.

"What was that all about?" Jenny asked her.

"What, the little man? Oh, I was givin' the little beggar a few tidbits, 'tis all."

Jenny nodded slowly. Indeed, she had not seen any food in his hands, nor any parcel of any kind. She watched the little man until he turned the corner and disappeared from her sight.

Ah, she just was being overly mistrusting, she decided, due to the fact that there was a spy in the household.

"I wanted to give you this." Jenny dropped a full guinea into Erma's right hand.

Erma looked up at her in disbelief. "I thought you had no blunt."

"I didn't." Jenny smiled, lifted Erma's other hand, and dropped a small cotton bag into it. "And this is for the McCarthy service staff. Can you see the money is distributed—along with a promise to bite their loose tongues, of course."

Erma opened her mouth and gave Jenny a near toothless grin. "You can count on me, Miss Penny. From this moment onward, your secret will be safe."

From this moment onward. The words echoed in Jenny's mind as she walked back through the kitchen toward her bedchamber.

Why did Erma's parting phrase itch at her brain so?

Chapter Fifteen

Oh, Mrs. Russell." Jenny knew she was gushing ridiculously over the modiste's work, but my word, how could she possibly help herself? Tears actually welled in her eyes, for this had to be, in all honesty, the most beautiful gown ever created.

Jenny beamed at her reflection in the long oval mirror mounted upon the wall of Mrs. Russell's private dressing chamber. She fingered the fine vapor of blue Venetian gauze layered over the underfrock of white crape and sighed with pleasure. *Gorgeous. Perfectly gorgeous.*

Swirling in a circle, Jenny watched the bottom quarter of the gown sway gracefully around her. No matter how she tried, she was simply unable to remove her gaze from the elegant confection.

"And what do you think of this?" Mrs. Russell settled a stunning blue headdress ringed with a double wreath of pale roses. "There is a French trick to wearing this headdress," she confided. "One that is sure to gain the wearer much notice."

"Really?" Jenny turned to look at the modiste, dying with anticipation. "Will you show me?"

Mrs. Russell smiled knowingly as she drew several of Jenny's gold-shot brunette locks through the pale Indian roses and set her fingers to work braiding them. "Now, here is the special trick. You just twist the braids . . . like this . . . so the coils of hair mimic the shape of the roses. You see?"

Staring with awe at Mrs. Russell's creation, Jenny bounced with glee on her heels as the modiste slipped from the dressing chamber.

Jenny bit her lower lip as she admired her image in the mirror. All the ladies of the *ton* would be so envious when they glimpsed her in the gown. And well they should be.

The gown was everything she'd hoped it would it be, elegant, simple . . . and memorable. At the ball, she wanted, nay *needed*, for Callum to look upon her with love in his eyes, albeit for the very last time, and see her as the lady he made her feel she truly was.

Seconds later, the modiste returned with something white in her hands. "Surely you have white satin shoes and kid gloves, but let us slip these on so you will have the full effect."

Jenny did as Mrs. Russell suggested, then looked at herself in the glass and let out a long sigh. It was perfect.

Then, Jenny caught Mrs. Russell's reflection in the mirror. Gads, she was waiting for something. Oh . . . *her payment*, she realized belatedly. Jenny lifted a brow. She could have at least waited until she had removed the gown, Jenny thought sourly.

Reaching for her reticule, she withdrew a small velvet bag and handed it to Mrs. Russell.

The modiste emptied the coins into her hand, then looked up. "And two more guineas for the headdress."

"Two?" Jenny glanced down into her bag and saw to her displeasure that it was empty. "That's a bit dear, isn't it?"

"Do you want it, Miss Penny, or do you not?"

Jenny swallowed. "Yes, but I haven't got any more money."

"Well, then you shan't have it." With that, the modiste reached up and pulled the ornament from Jenny's head, yanking hard at the braids of hair she had worked into the design.

Jenny clapped a hand to her pulsing scalp. "But I must have it. I simply must. I—I can pay you next week perhaps."

Mrs. Russell shook her head. "Miss Penny, I have sewn for you before and though you might have forgotten about your delinquent payment history, I have not. No, I must have the money before you"—she dangled the flowered circlet before Jenny's clawing hands—"receive the headdress."

"I'll get you the money."

Mrs. Russell leered at her. "Good. I shan't wish to apply pressure, but I will do what I must, Lady Genevieve . . . or would you prefer to be called *Lady Eros*?"

Jenny gasped. "H-how did you know?"

Mrs. Russell laughed. "Miss Penny, your trio of identities are well known throughout the servant and merchant classes. 'Tis only the Quality that cannot seem to see the grand imposter before their very noses."

That night, Jenny peered into the harvest basket. *Blast*, only one stone. *One*.

It was as she feared. She'd glutted the tingle cream market. Now she could do naught but wait for the highborns to run out of their current supply.

She slumped down on the stool and let a loud sigh roll down her tongue. What was she going to do? She needed money and needed it now.

Then a single word waved for attention in her mind, like a squealing shop sign in the wind. *Bartleby's*.

Shortly after sunrise the next morning, Jenny stood shivering outside, harvest basket in hand, as Mr. Bartleby unlocked his shop door.

"Good morn, sir," Jenny said brightly. "I made up some extra pots last eve and I thought you might be able to use them."

"More pots?" Appearing confused, the shopkeeper stared blankly back at her. "Erma brought round over twenty pots just yesterday."

"What? Only yesterday?" Jenny furrowed her brows. "No, no, you must be mistaken."

"I assure you, I am not." Bartleby invited Jenny inside as he flipped open his ledger book and ran a finger down a page. "There you go. Have a look. Twenty guineas, I paid her just yesterday."

Jenny began to sputter. "B-but I didn't make any cream—" Suddenly an uneasy thought exploded in her mind.

Maybe *she* didn't make any cream . . . but Erma had

been watching her whip the emulsion for several nights now.

No, she couldn't have. But nothing else made more sense.

Erma was making the tingle cream and selling it—*herself*.

Why that double-crossing thief!

⚘

"All right, Erma. Give it over." Jenny ground her teeth at the grimy scullery maid.

Erma looked up at her quizzically as she stoked the fire in the kitchen hearth. "What are you going on about, Jenny?"

"I know you have been making the cream and selling it on your own." She folded her arms at her chest. "I want the money you've stolen from me—*now*."

Erma stilled for a moment, then slowly turned her body to face Jenny. "Figured it out, did you? Aren't you the clever one? But I ain't givin' you nothin'. *I* made the cream."

"From *my* receipt, using *my* supplies!"

"All right then, I will pay you for the supplies I *borrowed*. What would that be—all of five shillings?"

"I'll see you dismissed." Jenny glared at Erma, her fists clenching and releasing in her rage.

"I'll see *you* in *The Bath Herald*'s *on-dit* column."

A tremor shook Jenny's body. "What do you mean, Erma?"

Setting her hands on the broad shelf of her hips, Erma laughed. "Oh, nothin' . . . except if I was you, I'd

make bloody sure I enjoyed the ball tomorrow eve—
because it's the last one you'll ever attend."

Jenny tried her best to sound strong and sure, but inside she was shaking like a mouse under a cat's paw.
"You had better explain yourself."

Erma stretched out her arm and pulled something
from a nook in the overmantel. She turned and dangled
Lady Letitia's bag of coins Jenny had given Erma to silence the widow's service staff.

"Y-you never paid the McCarthy service staff,"
Jenny muttered in shock.

"Why should I? There is more blunt here than I'd see
in five years. And now that I know how to make the
cream . . . it won't matter a lick if I get sacked."

A cold finger swiped down Jenny's spine. "Oh,
Erma. What have you done?"

Erma smiled amusedly back at her. "Enjoy your glittery life while you can, Jenny," she said in a singsong
voice. "Because even now, your world is crumblin'
down."

The scullery maid emitted a deep throaty laugh as she
rotated her hip and strolled cockily from the kitchen.

Jenny paced the floor of her bedchamber. Just what
had Erma done exactly? She'd mentioned the *on-dit*
column. Had the wretched scullery maid truly exposed
her to *The Bath Herald*?

Oh, no. Callum. The sudden thought stopped her mid-
step.

He mustn't read of her treacherous lies in some gossip column. No, *no*, she had to tell him herself.

Raising her hand to her mouth, she bit the soft fleshy tip of her thumb as she sat down on the edge of the bed to think.

Today was Thursday, the day before the ball. But *The Bath Herald* would not be delivered until Saturday morning. She still had a modicum of time in which to think, to plot her strategy.

Jenny rose, opened her wardrobe, and looked fondly at her lovely new blue gown and sighed.

Time was short. There was no time for half measures. Jenny swallowed the apprehension wedged in her throat.

She knew precisely what she must do.

In way of preparation for the grand birthday ball, the Featherton ladies, and surprisingly Meredith herself, took Jenny's very helpful advice. They retired early to conserve their strength for the much anticipated event the next evening.

Of course Jenny had her own reason for seeing them all abed. She could not risk them creeping around the house and looking for her once she'd made her escape.

It was only half past nine, when she surreptitiously wrapped herself in her warmest pelisse and mantle, then headed off alone into the cold night.

In the bitter wind, it hurt her lungs to breathe during the long walk from Royal Crescent to Laura Place—and Callum. But she had to see him. Had to hold him, kiss him . . . one more time before her life crashed down about her.

She longed to see the tender love in his eyes as he caressed her skin, and merged his hard body with her own.

For the last time.

This idea of hers was beyond scandalous, she knew. But it really didn't matter anymore. Jenny didn't care. She would be ruined in the eyes of all by Saturday morn with the sunrise delivery of the newspaper.

Her breath puffed furls of gray clouds into the air and her strides were wide and swift. In fact, so determined was she to see Callum that she found herself standing before Lord Argyll's tall buff-colored home far more quickly than she had anticipated.

This was a problem, for though her pounding heart had made its choice by driving her out into the night, her mind still had not figured out what to say . . . without sounding like a light skirt.

One just could not barge up to the door and say, "Callum, I need to be with you tonight. Do not ask questions, just kindly show me to your bedchamber." Though, she thought, it would certainly be efficient.

And honest. And he did admire honesty.

It was standing before his front door that bothered her most. Anyone could walk by and see her, though that was unlikely on a freezing winter night like tonight. Still, why sully her name earlier than absolutely necessary?

So, she turned the corner for the alleyway between his house and the next, and scurried down a few narrow steps. With a hard shove, Jenny pushed the service door . . . and to her surprise, it opened.

Quietly, she crept through a dark cloakroom, then into the bright kitchen, where a plump cook sat drinking tea tinted near white with cream.

The older woman's eyes grew astonishingly large when she spotted Jenny, and she struggled against her own heft to stand.

"Oh, do not mind me," Jenny said confidently as she passed through the kitchen. "Lord Argyll and I need to discuss a private matter and I did not wish to alert all of Laura Place to my presence." She paused before three wide doorways and turned her head back around to the woman at the kitchen table. "Which way above stairs?"

The confused cook lifted her finger and hesitantly pointed to the door on the right.

"Very good. Thank you, Cook." And with that, Jenny hurried through the doorway and up the stairs.

It was very dark when she emerged, though a wand of light broke through the partially open door of what Jenny took to be the drawing room. Stealthily, she tiptoed forward, holding her breath as she leaned close to peer through the opening between the door and the jamb.

And there he was. *Callum.*

The chair in which he rested seemed uncommonly petite in comparison to his large, commanding form. But there he sat, his long muscle-scored legs rising from beneath his kilt to prop themselves on a tiny footstool.

A smile came to her lips as the image of a great friendly giant from a childhood faery story seeped happily into her mind.

Jenny whisked her mantle from her shoulders with one hand as she unfastened the frogs at her throat and removed her pelisse with the other. All the while her gaze remained riveted on Callum.

The strong profile of his face, and even the sinuous curve of his broad chest through the linen of his shirt, was silhouetted against the light of the roaring fire in the hearth and it was all she could do to keep from sighing aloud.

God had certainly blessed the man.

Jenny removed her velvet Bourbon hat and quietly placed it and her wraps on the foyer table. Catching notice of the looking glass above the table, she leaned forward to peer into it. Her fingers poised to return any loose locks to their places, but the faint impression of the whites of her eyes peeking back at her was all she could see in the darkness.

What was she doing? She bloody well knew she looked grand, for she'd spent a full hour on her toilet before leaving. No, she was only delaying the inevitable.

Reaching out, she touched her fingers to the raised panels and pushed the drawing-room door open. Quietly she moved inside the room, then closed the door behind her and turned the key she found poised in the lock.

Callum did not look up. "I'm weel, Winston. But perhaps another whiskey might be in order."

Jenny's eyes caught notice of the amber liquid glowing inside the sparkling crystal decanter on the table near his chair. She slowly moved toward it, lifted the decanter, and tipped it so the liquid trickled slowly into Callum's awaiting glass.

She moved to the far side of him, already breathing deeply of his smoky masculine scent. Slowly, she lowered the glass down before him.

It took him but a half breath to realize it was not Winston at his side. Before she could blink her eyes, Callum's hand shot forward and caught her wrist.

Jenny struggled to hold the drink level as he swung his head up to look at her.

"I must be dreamin'." His voice was deep and husky as he drew her around the chair to stand before him.

Smiling, she knelt before him, and leaned over and seductively sipped slowly from his glass. Moving it to his lips, she urged him to drink as well, then she set the glass on the plush carpet beside her.

"This is no dream, my love. I have come."

Callum's eyes were confused, but still he pulled her wrist toward him, drawing her forward until she hovered above his seated body. "I dinna understand, Jenny."

Shaking her head slowly, she laid her finger over his lips. "Hush now. No words. No thoughts," she whispered softly.

Raising her skirt slightly for movement, she placed one knee and then the other on either side of his hips, straddling him. Callum sucked in a breath, then moaned with pleasure as she wriggled atop his kilt to find her balance.

Through the silk of her gown and the cotton of her chemise, she felt him harden against her, and like the wanton she was this night, she pressed solidly against him.

Heat washed to her center, making her want things an unmarried woman had no entitlement to desire.

Callum caught her hips and made a start as if to lift her from him, but Jenny flung her arms around his neck and held tight.

"Jenny, what are ye doin'? Nay, lass, we canna do this again." But there was no conviction in his words. None at all. "We dinna even know if ye're carryin' our—"

"Hush, my love," she whispered warmly against his lips, nudging his mouth open with hers.

His right hand slid from her hip around to the base of her back and pressed her toward him. Cupping her jaw with his left hand, he guided her closer, into his deepening kiss.

As his tongue mingled with hers, she found herself rocking against his hardness, making him grow and pulse beneath her.

She broke the pressure of their lips and leaned back slightly to look at him. "I want you, Callum." Her voice was low and she hardly recognized it as her own.

"But why now? Why this eve? I dinna understand." Callum's eyes searched hers for the answer, but it wasn't there. At least not in a way he could ever understand. Or that he'd want to understand.

If he knew the truth.

She did not reply. How could she?

She was saying good-bye . . . privately. Saying good-bye to the man who had become her world. To the man she loved with a depth she had never known was possible.

Jenny hugged him close and felt the new, strange hardness in her belly press against him . . . and a tear came to her eye.

She was saying good-bye to the man who had given her a gift more precious than diamonds, emeralds, or rubies—his love, and possibly, quite possibly, his babe.

But it had to be.

For a man who revered truth above all else would never understand the depth of her lies.

And so, tonight, Jenny would give him the truth—*her truth*. She had to make him know how very much she loved him. No matter what else happened between them, after the ball, after the newspaper tore her wide open, she needed him to believe that her love was true.

Untainted. Pure and honest.

Jenny smoothed her fingers over his beard-roughened cheeks and looked deep into his eyes. "I love you, Callum. With all my heart and all that I truly am, I love you."

He pressed his lips softly to hers, then met her gaze once more. "And I love ye, Jenny."

Hearing her name, so tenderly spoken, sent her heart pounding within her ribs. For at this moment, there was no proper lady. No servant. Just two people, whose hearts had come together to create something new and wondrous.

He loved *her*. Not the trappings with which she masked herself. *Her*. And she loved him.

Jenny leaned closer until her lips brushed his as she spoke. Her eyes felt weighted and sleepy. "I want you, Callum. I need to feel you inside of me."

This could not have been a surprise to him, but Jenny would not have known it by the expression on his face. But within the span of breath, a look of determination spread over his face. He reached around and, cupping her buttocks, lifted her as he stood from the chair.

Jenny clung to him, wrapping her legs tightly around his waist, as he moved directly before the fire and laid her down before him on the soft carpet.

As she looked down, Jenny saw that her skirts were bunched around her hips. Her thighs were still spread wide, and Callum was standing high between them.

He evidently saw this too, and without allowing her to close her legs, he knelt down.

Heat surged between her thighs in anticipation. She could feel the sweep of his kilt atop her legs, and the prickle of the hairs above his knees pressed against the smooth skin of her inner thighs. It was too much, and she began to writhe.

She looked up into his eyes. They were glowing in the firelight, dark and primal. "Please, Callum. Don't make me wait."

But he didn't move. Instead he gazed appreciatively down at her. And so, she lifted her right hand from the carpet and slid it beneath his kilt and up his solid thigh. Higher and higher, until she felt him in her fingers. He wanted her too.

She heard his breath snag as she ringed her fingers around his girth and began to stroke him . . . just the way Annie had demonstrated that afternoon with the rolling pin.

When she looked up at his face, Callum's eyes were closed and his mouth was parted. She tightened her grip, and she saw him bite into his lower lip, then moan with pleasure.

His hands came down above each of her shoulders then, and he balanced there above her, his mouth a scant finger's width from her own. This brought him closer below as well.

She lifted her index finger and each time she moved her hand upward, she traced the ridge where his plum-shaped tip met the length of him, then slipped it higher to caress him.

He moaned her name once before he jerked in her hand. He pulled back to kneel between her thighs again.

Jenny wrinkled her brow in confusion. "Have I done something wrong?"

A deep laugh fell from Callum's lips. "Oh, no, lass. Just the opposite in fact." He leaned back down to kiss her, and when he did, she felt the three buttons between her breasts release, one after the other. And then he pulled the gown quickly over her head.

By the time her arms landed with a thud on either side of her head, the gown was gone, and she was lying before him in naught but her shift.

Clearly the man had done this before. And Jenny grinned inwardly, thinking of a new entry for Meredith's guide to rakes.

She had not worn a corset, and felt rather wicked about the omission, but she had known where this evening would end, and did not wish to delay the inevitability a moment longer than necessary.

With a sinful grin on his lips, Callum untied the ribbons that bound up her stockings, and slid the silk wisps down her legs. He bent and bit the tiny ribbon between her breasts that cinched closed her shift. Pulling it in his teeth, he finally released the tie and her breasts expanded the cotton, opening the garment to him. A moment later, the shift was gone and Jenny lay, arms on either side of her head, utterly naked before him.

Her breath came fast as he studied her body, as his fingers traced the tips of her nipples, then rode down the gentle slope of her belly until his hands rested between her thighs.

He pushed them wider, and suddenly she felt his hot mouth upon her most private of places, felt his tongue flicking her.

A sigh of delight fell from her mouth as her hands caught his head and pressed his harder against her. But this wasn't what she wanted.

"*Please*, Callum."

Callum rose up and leaned back on his heels to peel away his shirt. Jenny could not take her eyes from his supple skin, etched deeply between the curves of well-worked muscle.

He unfastened the clip of a glittering silver stag and citrine-crowned thistle kilt pin, set it aside, and began unwinding the tartan kilt from his body with unbearable slowness. When at last he dropped the tartan to the carpet, Jenny was near frantic with need.

He was so beautiful. Every bit of him seemed formed of lean muscle. Stiff and erect.

Jenny licked her lips, then eased her palms up the tops of his thighs to his waist. She pulled him down to her, and kissed him. And he her.

"No matter what happens, Callum," she whispered anxiously, "remember this moment. Remember that I love you, and always will."

"I will, Jenny, but ye speak as if our time is scarce." He kissed her again as he pressed just his tip into the moistness between her legs. "We have a lifetime ahead of us, ye and I. *A lifetime*."

Jenny wrapped her arms tightly around him, and lifted her hips. He thrust into her.

A lifetime, she thought sorrowfully as they made love.

If only that were true.

Chapter Sixteen

The next morning, Jenny awoke in her own bed, still lingering in the glow of a most blissful dream. But as she glimpsed the still-damp hem of her pelisse, which she'd tossed across the chair near her bed, she smiled. It had been no dream. Her night with Callum had been very real.

In fact, it had been only two hours past that Callum had awakened his manservant and arranged for his town carriage to convey Jenny back to Number One Royal Crescent.

The brazier on the floor of the cab had been thoughtfully lit, warming the air inside enough so their breath no longer frosted the moment it left their mouths. Still, Callum had held Jenny in his arms for warmth and kissed her mouth repeatedly during their short journey through the dark streets of Bath.

Between their kisses and lovemaking that night, Jenny had told Callum again and again of her love for him. In her heart, she knew she'd achieved her objective. Callum would know, no matter what outrageous things he read about her in the Saturday newspaper, that her love was sincere and true. That he should never doubt.

Jenny knew she should feel happy—she had done it. But as she drew back the counterpane and sat at the edge of her lumpy mattress, she sighed miserably.

For though tonight they would dance and smile and laugh, inside Jenny would be mourning the loss of the man she loved, aching at the knowledge that she would never share a night in his strong arms again.

Outside her room one of the bells rang and she heard Edgar's voice call out. "'Tis Miss Meredith."

"Yes, Mr. Edgar," Jenny called back. "Right away."

Jenny filled her basin with the contents of her ewer and splashed the astonishingly cold water on her face. She shivered as she saw to her toilet, thankful at least that the icy water would have a restorative effect on her weary mind and body. At least temporarily.

Dressing quickly, Jenny took to the stairs. It was uncharacteristically early for Meredith to ring, but she could not fault the girl for being eager to begin her morn.

"There you are, Jenny!" Meredith was beaming. "I could not rest a moment longer—for the ball is this eve! And look at this—" Meredith held up a tiny notebook with red leather carded facings. "It's for my observations—for my guidebook. Oh, you remember, don't you?"

Jenny nodded and forced a weak smile as a reply.

Meredith wrinkled her nose. "I say, Jenny, you look terrible. Did you not sleep last eve?"

"How could I sleep knowing that your birthday ball is this very eve?" Jenny pulled a pink morning frock and silk-lined corset from Meredith's wardrobe and began to dress her mistress.

"You hardly seem yourself." Meredith kept turning around to look at her, but Jenny would yank her back around by her lacing ribbon and continue fastening her corset. Then Meredith ceased her fidgeting and became very still. "You are not . . . with child, are you?" she asked softly.

"What a thing to ask. Do I look as though I am?" Jenny threw the frothy morning gown over Meredith's head and pulled it over her ribs. "Well?"

"Oh, Jenny, do not be angry with me for asking. 'Tis just that you do appear so dreadfully tired."

After Jenny fastened the last button, she sat the young miss before the mahogany dressing table and began removing the loose braids from Meredith's curly copper hair. "Of course I am tired. There are many preparations to be made before a ball."

Meredith turned her wide blue eyes up to her. "I saw your gown. It's gorgeous! I hope you don't mind that I took a peek inside your wardrobe. I just knew you would come up with something spectacular."

Jenny stopped brushing. She had so looked forward to wearing that gown, but today she was hesitant to even look upon it.

Meredith turned back around, prompting Jenny to resume running the boar's bristle hairbrush through her heavy locks. "I didn't see a hat to match though," Meredith commented. "Nor a headdress of any sort."

A frustrated groan slipped from Jenny's mouth. "I— I have . . . decided to forgo a headdress. Instead I shall affix two or three brilliants to my hair. After all, the gown is so unique, I should not wish to detract from it by overaccessorizing with a . . . with a fussy headdress."

"Oh, I see." Meredith cast a critical eye at the ringlet of silk flowers and cording sitting atop her satinwood worktable. "Mayhap I should do the same. The vibrancy of my hair is quite enough, do you not agree?"

"Hmm?" Jenny distractedly looked at Meredith's reflection in the mirror atop the table.

"That's the end of it. It is clear you are exhausted." Meredith pushed up from the dressing table and walked past Jenny for the door. "You must get some rest before this eve. I shall inform my aunts directly."

With a halfhearted level of effort, Jenny lifted her hand to prevent Meredith from her mission, but it was too late.

॰॰॰

Ten minutes later, Jenny found herself sitting in the drawing room facing the Featherton inquisition.

Lady Viola studied Jenny for some moments before coming upon the correct words. "Dear, a month has not quite passed . . . and this is quite indelicate of me to ask . . . but do you believe . . . well, that you might carry my great-grandchild?"

Golly, that was blunt.

Jenny stared down at the nails she had chewed down to the quick over the past week. "I do not know, my lady . . . but I suspect I may."

Lady Letitia elbowed her sister in the ribs, who yelped at the painful surprise. "Did I not tell you, Viola?"

A smile like Jenny had never seen illuminated Lady Viola's face. "And you have told him, yes?"

"No, my lady. And I shall not."

The Featherton ladies stared at each another, sputtering meaningless sounds.

"But why, dear?" Lady Viola's eyes blinked rapidly, betraying her agitation.

"Because I will not use his babe to bind him to me."

"What are you talking about, gel? He has already offered for you." Lady Letitia folded her thick arms beneath her large breasts, unconsciously pushing them higher until they nearly reached the rolls of her double chin.

"He has offered for Lady Genevieve, not *me*," Jenny reminded them. "And once he knows that I have lied to him, he will not wish any sort of connection with me."

"I do think you are judging the lad unfairly," Lady Viola told her. "For he loves you, completely. In the coming weeks, you will find the right moment to tell him the truth of your position in our household. And when you do, he will not desert you simply because you are not of society. You will see."

If only she had the luxury of days and weeks to admit the truth to Callum. But she didn't. She must confess all this very eve. For by tomorrow morn—*oh, perdition*. She might as well tell them. After all, their names would be connected with her scandal when the newspaper column swept elevated Bath tomorrow morning.

"My ladies, I have heard that on the morrow, Saturday, *The Bath Herald* will reveal everything about me. *Everything*." She raised her eyes to see their reaction.

They were sitting wide-eyed and motionless, mouths positively agape.

"By morn, I suspect all of elevated society will know that Lady Genevieve is but a lady's maid in your employ. And that this lady's maid, Miss Jenny Penny, has the dual distinction of being Lady Eros, maker of the popular tingle cream."

Rising up from her seat, Lady Letitia came to stand before Jenny. "But I do not understand. Who supplied this information to the *on-dit* columnist? I assume it is he who shall report this gossip. No other journalist would find interest in such society drivel."

Jenny's eyes remained trained on Lady Letitia's wholly unfashionable, lace-fringed lavender slippers that jutted from beneath her wide and equally dated lavender mantua.

"I learned just last eve that the guineas meant to silence the service staff of the McCarthy and Featherton households were never distributed by the maid set with the task," Jenny muttered.

The Featherton ladies looked pointedly at each other, then spoke one world in unison. "*Erma!*"

"And if I know her, and I do, she is likely the *on-dit* columnist's mole." Lady Letitia's cheeks reddened and her face was filled with anger. "I declare, that gel has been nothing but trouble since she arrived at the house. I shall see that Edgar dismisses her immediately!"

Jenny shot to her feet. "Beggin' your pardon, my lady, but mightn't it be wise to retain her until after the storm has passed?"

"The gel is right, Sister," Lady Viola said evenly. "Once Erma is gone we shall have no control over her. She might share . . . *other* private matters that could damage our family . . . and my grandson."

As Lady Letitia stepped from the edge of the carpet,

the force of her high-heeled slippers clicking on the wooden floor left no question as to her mood. She yanked the bellpull and almost as if by magic, Mr. Edgar appeared instantly in the drawing room.

"See that Erma does not leave this house. Furthermore, no one but you, sir, shall speak with her or listen to her. Am I understood?"

"Yes, my lady. Entirely." Mr. Edgar bowed and backed from the room to make his way below stairs.

An afternoon nap was a most civilized institution, one Jenny wished she had opportunity to observe more often. Thanks to Meredith's concern for her well-being, the Featherton ladies had shooed Jenny to her bedchamber to restore her energy before the ball.

She awoke refreshed and rested, and begrudgingly began her toilet. But she was not at all eager for the ball to commence. For its beginning marked the end of her grand love affair with her beloved Callum.

Mrs. Penny entered Jenny's bedchamber just in time to fasten the two pearl buttons at Jenny's back and to witness for herself the ethereal beauty of the gown.

Trying to raise her own spirits, Jenny whirled in a circle to demonstrate Mrs. Russell's clever stitchery. "Do you see how the overskirt floats when I turn? This gown was made for dancing, Mama."

Jenny forced a pleased laugh, but it quickly died on her lips and even the most elegant and beautiful gown in all of England could not revive it.

She slumped into a small wooden chair, prompting her mother to race toward her, hands waving in the air.

"Goodness, child, do not sit like that. You'll crush the gown!"

Drawing in a long breath, Jenny exhaled a sigh. "I don't care."

"You don't care? Is attending this ball not your grandest dream come to life?"

Raising her eyes to her mother, Jenny nodded solemnly. "Tonight, a lifetime of impossible wishes will come true." She turned her head slowly to her mother. "Except, I no longer desire such things. I do not care about this dress, or jewels, fashionable bonnets, reticules, and handfuls of gold. My only desire is to spend my life with the man I love, Callum."

Just the sound of his name on her lips was enough to bring down a torrent of tears. *Oh, perdition.* Love had completely muddled her emotions.

"I know this is difficult, darling," her mother said very softly. "Perhaps you should not attend the ball this eve."

Raising the back of her hand to her face, Jenny scrubbed the wetness from her cheeks. "No, I must be there. 'Tis the last time Lord Argyll and I will be together. I must go."

Her mother withdrew something glittery from her apron pocket and held it out to her.

Jenny stared at it with amazement. Why, it was the brooch her father had given her when she was but a child.

"Take the brooch and wear it this eve." Her mother urged her to take it, but Jenny could not seem to obey.

Criminy. She couldn't believe it. Her mother was going to let her wear the brooch.

This was unbelievable. For nearly twenty years, her

mother had been unable to bear the sight of the brooch. Seconds after her father had given her the pin, her mother had snatched it from her dress, leaving Jenny to stand teary-eyed, with a hole in her frock, as her father's gleaming carriage rolled away, never to be seen by either of them again.

Jenny looked down at the pin, then again at her mother. "Are you sure, Mama?"

"He meant it for you. 'For his little lady,' he said when he pinned it to your dress. Do you remember?" Her mother lifted Jenny's hand and placed the brooch in her palm.

"I do . . . somewhat." Jenny's hand shook as she lifted the brooch by the clasp. With utmost care, she affixed it upon the satin band beneath her breasts.

"Looks lovely, it does." Her mother sniffled. "I thought by hiding the brooch from you, you would forget your father, forget the life you might have had . . . were I not in service. But you never did forget. Being denied his brooch only made you want it all the more."

"What are you talking about, Mama?"

"Don't you see? This brooch is the reason you are utterly obsessed with lovely things. As if by acquiring baubles, gowns, and the trappings of a society miss, you will become your father's 'little lady.'" Her mother knelt before her and took her hands into her own.

Jenny sat very still. Lud, it was true. On some level, she felt she knew this somehow. Until tonight, though, she never connected her passion for pretty things with the brooch and her father's words "my little lady."

A light rap summoned her eyes to the door. There Mr. Edgar stood, his hands folded behind his back. "Mrs. Russell was here earlier for you."

The headdress. Oh, no. Jenny stared back into Mr. Edgar's stern face.

The modiste had warned her that if she did not pay, there'd be trouble.

"I apologize, Mr. Edgar." Jenny swallowed. There was a queer look in his ancient eyes—something akin to sadness. He must be so very disappointed in her. She'd brought him nothing but mayhem to his tightly run ship the past month.

"I did not have the money to pay her," Jenny muttered.

Then, her astonished eyes nearly leapt from her. For Mr. Edgar, dear Mr. Edgar, withdrew her gown's matching headdress from behind his back and held it out to her.

"Oh, my word." Jenny could scarcely stand, but somehow she managed to reach the tall manservant and take the Indian rose headdress. "I don't understand . . . how?"

"Cook told me that Erma stole your receipt and therefore your business with Mr. Bartleby. So I . . . I paid the modiste in your stead."

The ever stalwart butler stumbled over the words that betrayed his warm heart. "There you have it. I know this eve is very special to you. The headdress matches your gown, so you should wear it. Only makes sense." His old blue eyes welled up, startling him so, that he turned swiftly and made to leave.

"Wait, Mr. Edgar." Jenny thrust the headdress at her mother and threw herself into the tall old gent's arms. "Thank you, sir." She looked up at him and saw the merest hint of a smile on his thin lips. "You have no idea what your gift means to me." She stood on the tips of her toes and kissed his cheek.

Mr. Edgar broke from her embrace, his wrinkled face turning the most adorable shade of crimson. "Now, now, Jenny. Your thanks is more than adequate." He turned, trying in vain to obscure the tiny smile on his lips, and hurried from the room.

Darling old Mr. Edgar. Were she to know her father, she always fancied that he would be exactly like him.

As her mother looked on, Jenny settled the headdress atop her head like a crown and began to swirl several locks into braided roses, which she mingled with the crape blooms.

When she finished, Jenny stood and turned around. "H-how do I look, Mama?"

Her mother's eyes brightened the moment she spun around. "Oh, my dear Jenny, you look . . ."

Jenny found herself holding her breath—needing her mother's approval more now than ever before.

"You look beautiful—every bit the lady."

A single tear ran down Jenny's cheek as her mother took her in her arms and hugged her tight. "Thank you, Mama. Thank you."

🌸

The orchestra stopped playing the moment they entered the assembly room. And as Jenny had dreamed, everyone on the dance floor turned and stared as the Featherton party was announced and regally entered the ballroom.

Jenny held her head high and shoulders back as she walked beside Miss Meredith toward the front of the grand assembly room. Her ear seemed especially attuned to the appreciative observations made about her appearance, and to the sprinkling of suppositions that she was a grand French lady of royal descent.

And lud, she felt like royalty this eve—like a princess in a faery story. Of course, were this true, she could count on a happily ever after ending.

But she knew her story would not end that way.

Still, until black Saturday, she made a promise to herself to smile and to live her life to the fullest. To drink in every sight, sound, and sensation and store them safely in her memory for the bleaker days to come. What good would it do to rob herself, and indeed Callum, of one last evening of pleasure?

This promise was all well and good, but inside she was screaming—for tonight she was going to lose Callum and there was naught she could do to stop it.

And then she saw him, smiling excitedly at her from the edge of the dance floor. He walked toward her, his long legs carrying his towering body at twice the speed of any ordinary man.

But he was no ordinary man, was he? He was her betrothed—her prince—at least for tonight.

Callum politely greeted Miss Meredith and the Featherton ladies, then without a word to her, extended his hand to Jenny. She laid her hand atop his and allowed him to lead her to the floor for the waltz that had just been announced.

The music filled Jenny's ears, and happiness welled in her heart as he turned her about the ballroom floor. They made a striking pair, Jenny thought, and so did the assembly, for couples seemed to fall back to dance the perimeter, leaving the center floor to Callum and herself.

Jenny tilted her head back and looked up at him.

"Ye are the most beautiful woman I've ever seen." Callum's eyes seemed to sparkle as he gazed upon her.

A blush crept across Jenny's cheeks and swept the sensitive skin rising from her low neckline.

The edge of Callum's kilt brushed her thighs as they moved, and his sporran, heavy with tooled leather and silver studs, bounced upward a bit as they danced, drawing her eye to its movement—and her wanton thoughts to what lay beneath it.

"I have never seen you look so handsome either, my love," she said just loud enough that he could hear her above the sweet swell of violins. Still, as she gazed wistfully at him, she felt a burn at the back of her eyes.

"Is everything all right, Jenny? Ye dinna seem quite yerself this eve." Callum's face filled with a look of real concern.

Caressing his hand as they waltzed, Jenny looked up at him through her long lashes and gave him a small but convincing, she hoped, smile. "Everyone is staring," she told him. "I feel a bit as though we are on stage at the Theatre Royal."

"Staring are they? Weel, let us give them something interesting to watch." He waggled his dark brows at her and grinned.

Jenny couldn't help but laugh at the devilish curve of his lips. "What are you going to—*oh, my heavens!*"

In that instant, with one strong arm, Callum hoisted Jenny against his chest so their eyes were level and her feet, thankfully shod in new, gleaming white satin slippers, dangled.

Faster and faster he turned, never missing a four-count step. The rotation sent Jenny's legs flying backward behind her.

Starting to feel a little dizzy, Jenny trained her gaze on the crowd surrounding the ballroom floor to steady herself.

Bath society was indeed staring. But not with looks of shock in their eyes, as she might have expected, but with amusement. To them, they were but a young couple foolishly in love.

Lady Letitia and Lady Viola, clapping with delight, had turned to watch Callum and Jenny as Meredith excitedly recorded her observations in her notebook.

"Lord Argyll, they will think you mad!" Jenny quipped, giggling between her words.

He only laughed. "Madly in love with you, Jenny, and I dinna care who knows it."

An uneasy jolt shot through Jenny, and she knew Callum must return her to the floor. He mightn't care now who knew of his love for her, but come morning, his feelings would be different.

"Please, Callum, I cannot breathe. Do set me down."

"Verra weel, my lady. Yer wish is my command."

His eyes twinkled with happiness as he loosened his grip on her waist and allowed her to slide down his chest to the wooden floor. Even this was far too intimate an act, but the Highlander seemed oblivious to the fact. And this sort of scandal, while guaranteed to generate comment, was of little concern to Jenny. Oh, how she wished that displaying affection in public was her only shame.

When the music ended, Callum, his eyes still alive with the excitement of the dance, offered Jenny his arm and together they left the floor to return to the Featherton ladies and Miss Meredith.

Jenny smiled pleasantly at all those she passed, until from the corner of her eye, she caught notice of a man bowing to her—a very small man.

She jerked her head around to be sure. How had *he* managed an entrée to this esteemed event? But then Jenny remembered the Featherton ladies' public invitation.

Oh, my word. Hercule Lestrange was here . . . and no doubt already hard at work.

Chapter Seventeen

Squeezing Callum's gloved hand gently, Jenny bade him to rejoin the Featherton ladies, and with a few mumbled excuses for leaving his side, promised to join him again a few minutes later.

At once, she picked her way back through the churning crowd until she came upon the guest she sought. "Ah, we meet again, Mr. Lestrange." She hung a bright smile on her lips for him. "I had not truly expected to see you at the Upper Assembly Rooms this eve."

He seemed surprised. "Where else would I be? Gatherings such as these are how I make my living. But then, you know this."

"Quite right." Jenny covertly stole a glance at Hercule's deep coat pockets, searching for any signs that he had already been slipping baubles and rings from unsuspecting guests.

"Since our last discussion, *my lady*," he said, intoning the last two words a bit louder, "I wondered how you came to discover my true identity. Over the years, many have tried, but none successfully. That is, until you."

Jenny was a little stunned by the question. "I don't

know really. Maybe it was the way you always seemed to haunt the locales where society gathered. And you were always watching, your eye tuned to detail."

Hercule Lestrange nodded thoughtfully, then lowered his voice to a private level. "You have a very keen eye yourself, as well as a clever mind, to have inferred from so little that I am Bath's mysterious *on-dit* columnist."

What? A rolling shudder seemed to throttle Jenny from within. Hercule Lestrange wrote *The Bath Herald*'s *on-dit* column? *Lord above!* But suddenly it all made sense. He wasn't the leader of the swell gang at all. He was a bleedin' gossip columnist!

Schooling her features, Jenny tried very hard not to let on that she had had it all wrong.

"I have a bone to pick with you, Mr. Lestrange."

"You do?"

"Yes, for we had an agreement."

A look of bewilderment came into his eyes. "Of course we do. And have you kept your half of the bargain by keeping my identity a secret?"

"*I* have." She pulled her shoulders backward. This just *had* to work.

"And I have kept my half." He beckoned for her to lean down. "I have not reported your identity, *any of them*, though I could have."

"But I have heard that tomorrow's *Herald* will reveal Lady Eros."

"Ah, I see." Hercule smiled with new understanding. "You've had a chat with Erma Soot."

Jenny rose up to her full height and set her hands on her slim hips. "As a matter of fact, I have. And here I took you for a man of honor," she added, hoping her teeth wouldn't fall out of her head for her lies, as her mother had warned her when she was a child.

Hercule Lestrange was clearly taken aback. "I have honored my vow to you." He crooked his finger and urged her to his level again. "Tomorrow, the usurper of Lady Eros's throne, the scullery maid, Erma, will be revealed and your business will be returned to you."

Jenny stared into the little man's wide eyes, and saw truth in them.

She was not going to lose Callum by morn after all. This little man, this beautiful little man, had saved her!

"I could kiss you, Hercule," she exclaimed. "In fact, I shall." And then, taking his oddly shaped head into her hands, she kissed both his cheeks.

Hercule Lestrange blushed fiercely. "My lady, people watch."

"I don't care. I really don't care. You are *wonderful*." She quieted suddenly as a very large question posed itself in her mind. "Why would you do this for me?"

The little man extended his hand to her and she took it, allowing him to lead her to a row of empty chairs at the floor's perimeter.

Hercule laid his chest upon the seat and swung his foot upward to pull himself upright in the chair. He patted the chair next to him, urging Jenny to join him. She did.

"Because, though I was dirty and my clothes were tattered—a look I often don to remain unnoticed by the *ton*—you treated me with great kindness—like a *man*. Not a small man, but a real man. You talked with me, allowed me to escort you home, then you invited me inside for something to eat. I don't know why you did that, and I don't care. For the first time in many years, someone saw the man inside this small, mangled body. And for that," he lowered his voice to a whisper, "I am grateful, Miss Penny."

Jenny's eyes were filling with tears again and she hugged Hercule to her breast.

"Here now, careful there, miss. Or you'll learn just how much of a real man I can be."

When she pulled abruptly back, he gave her a wicked smile, and she laughed. There was a nudge at her back, knocking Jenny forward in her chair. She turned and looked up to see Meredith rising from a chair behind her. Until that moment, Jenny hadn't noticed that the girl was near.

Certainly, Meredith had heard every word, for as she walked across the dance floor, Jenny saw her busily scrawling down the little man's roguish words in her book of observations.

When Jenny returned her attention to Hercule, she saw him gazing at the opal brooch she wore. In fact, he was studying the sparking bauble most intently.

His ruddy brows shirred for a moment. "Where did you get this?" he asked, looking up at her face.

"'Twas a gift from my father when I was a child."

"A gift, you say? Might I ask your father's name?"

"You might ask, but I cannot answer." Jenny shrugged her shoulders. "My mother will not say."

His eyes shifted to the brooch, and narrowed slightly. "May I?" he asked, reaching for the opal pin.

"How queerly you look at my brooch. Is it familiar to you? Perhaps you've seen one like it before."

Releasing the brooch from his thick fingers, Hercule looked up at her with a distracted smile. "Perhaps." He exhaled a long breath. "It is quite lovely. Guard it well this eve."

"Guard it?"

Hercule glanced about the room until he found what he was searching for. "Look there. The woman and the two men."

Jenny followed his gaze. To her surprise, she found herself looking directly at the woman in red—whom she'd seen in the Pump Room and then at Bartleby's—along with her two dandy escorts.

"Yes, I've seen those three before. Something is not right about them. They . . . they don't *belong*."

"Very astute, Miss Penny. I've been watching them too. I believe they are the swell gang responsible for the thefts in Bath these past weeks. Still, I've not been able to prove it."

"I'll be wary of them. You can be certain of that."

Hercule patted her hand. "Forget them for now. Go back to your man. I see he is waiting for you."

Jenny looked up and briefly met Callum's warm gaze. She smiled back and acknowledged him with a slight wave of her hand.

Though it would be difficult to simply forget about the swell gang prowling the ball, she had far more important things to worry about.

She came to her feet. "Thank you, Mr. Lestrange, for everything."

"And thank you, my shiny penny. Until we meet again." Hercule Lestrange tipped his head to her.

Jenny smiled once more at the strange but wonderful little man, then walked a few feet before turning again to wave good-bye. But when she did, he was gone. Perplexed, she glanced around the ballroom. Lud, he had absolutely disappeared.

With a confused shrug, Jenny had just started through the milling throng when someone slammed into her, knocking her breath from her lungs in a great whoosh.

She clutched her ribs, gasping for air. When the dark specks dancing in her eyes finally cleared from her vision, she noticed with horror that her father's opal brooch was missing!

The swell gang. Spotting the woman in red hurrying away ahead of her, Jenny raced through the crowd. Catching the woman up, she grabbed her wrist and spun her around.

"Give it back," she hissed, before dropping her voice to a low, menacing tone. "I know what you are and shan't hesitate to expose you."

The woman smirked at this and pulled her own wrist close so quickly that Jenny was hauled against her.

"I see you and the dwarf have become quite close. But just as the two of you can see we do not belong here—we have been watching you as well. You, Miss Penny . . . or shall I say *Lady Eros,* have not the standing to be in this assembly room either. And I shall not hesitate an instant to expose *you* . . . if I must."

Jenny shook so violently that she feared the ties of her corset would unthread. "You wouldn't dare it," she managed, surreptitiously glancing at her opal brooch clutched in the woman's hand.

"Darling, I would. So be an obedient maid and leave us be—we have work to do." Seeing the path of Jenny's gaze, the woman tightened her grip around the brooch.

"Return the brooch to me." Jenny glared at the

woman with a level of loathing she'd never felt in her life.

Her intensity seemed to unnerve the thief, and the woman's gaze darted about the room until she found her cohorts. Then a cold smile iced her lips.

Jenny couldn't help but turn to see what the woman had seen. There, walking between the two dandies toward the open doors, dripping with every jewel she owned, was the frail, tiny Lady Viola.

Heavens, why was she leaving the ballroom with them? Jenny's eyes scoured the ballroom for Callum, but when she finally glimpsed him, he was standing just below the blaring orchestra preparing to join in an English country dance with Meredith.

Even if she shouted for his assistance, he'd likely never hear her.

Jenny became light-headed. She was frantic. "Please. Take the brooch. It's yours. But leave Lady Viola alone," she begged. "*Please.*"

The woman laughed. "Oh, I'll keep the brooch. And whatever we get from the old hag." She hoisted Jenny's chin up with her middle finger. "And you won't say a bleedin' word. Or I'll tell the entire assembly who you *really* are. What will your viscount think then? Or does he already know?"

Heat suffused Jenny's cheeks at the comment, but she said nothing.

"Hah, I thought not."

Swallowing very hard, Jenny glanced at Lady Viola who had paused to chat with a friend before crossing the threshold with the dandies. She had only seconds to do something.

"Call off your snakes *now*." There was a strange determination in Jenny's voice; a cool calmness. A new strength.

"I don't care what you say about me, but I will not allow those men to leave this ballroom with my lady."

The woman sneered back at her. "I don't believe you."

Jenny held the woman's wrist tight in her right hand as she shot an accusatory finger to the dandies, who even now were trying to urge Lady Viola through the door.

"Thieves!" Jenny shouted until the last breath in her lungs was expelled. "Stop those thieves!"

The orchestra ceased playing and the entire assembly seemed to turn to stare.

"Stop them!" Jenny screamed again. "The dandies by the door—and this woman *here*!"

A distinguished, gray-haired gentleman snapped his fingers and two burly footmen rushed forward to seize the two dandies.

The collective audience gasped as the gray-haired man closed on them and withdrew ring, after pendant, after watch from the dandies' deep pockets.

Shocked cries of ownership bubbled up and burst through the crowd, as ladies and gentlemen pushed forward to retrieve their stolen belongings.

Two men stepped forward and took hold of the woman in red. Jenny pried the brooch from her fingers, and didn't care a whit that the pin poked the thief's hand as she retrieved it.

"You've made a grave mistake, gel." The woman glowered at Jenny. "And now you will repent."

Callum rushed forward and took Jenny into his arms.

She clung to him, knowing in all certainty that this was the last time he would hold her ever again.

"Hear me, good people of Bath! I wish to confess," the woman shouted and at once a hush washed over the assembly.

Even Callum released Jenny from his embrace to listen to what the thief would say.

"Callum." Jenny tugged pitifully at his sleeve, and he turned to look down into her eyes. Jenny worked the muscles of her throat to swallow her dread and eased Callum's betrothal ring from her finger. "Know that I love you. No matter what happens, my love is true."

The skin around Callum's eyes crinkled. "I do know, Jenny. But why are ye tellin' me this now?"

Taking his hand in hers, she pressed the ring into his palm. "I'm sorry, Callum. I love you . . . but . . . I'm so sorry."

Callum's dark brows cinched. "Jenny, what's wrong? Why are ye givin' back me ring?"

A dark, seething grin spread across the thief's pointed face. "Because of what I am about to say."

At her words, Callum turned his gaze to the thief once more.

The crowd continued to gather ever closer, heating the still air. Jenny gasped for breath.

"A thief I may be, but I do not lie," the woman stated with a strength and clarity of voice that allowed her words to touch every corner of the expansive assembly room.

This is it.

The thief arched a sardonic brow at Jenny. "I have stumbled upon a truth that might interest you all. This woman before you is not the lady she pretends to be."

A rumble of voices rose up like dust around Jenny. Her head began to spin and she began to swoon.

The woman leveled a sneer her way. "No, this woman is Miss Jenny Penny, a lady's maid within the Featherton household."

Jenny could not make herself look up at Callum, even as she felt his gaze burning down upon her.

A dull roar of conversation welled up from the two hundred people swarming around her, all jockeying for a glimpse of the imposter.

Then the thief's voice grew louder still. "But she is no ordinary lady's maid. She is famous. Yes, yes, you all have heard of her." She paused then, until the room fell into utter silence.

Jenny squeezed her eyes shut. *Air.* She needed air, needed to breathe, but her corset was too tight, the room too warm, the crowd was too close.

"For you see, good citizens of Bath . . . she is none other than *Lady Eros*!"

The mob roared, forcing Jenny's lashes to fly open. To her horror, she found herself staring straight upward into Callum's face.

His eyes were blank, the muscles in his cheeks had fallen lax leaving his mouth half open with shock.

Reaching out to her, he desperately grasped her shoulders.

"Tell me 'tisna true." Callum's voice. "Tell me, Jenny, and I will believe ye. *Please.*"

Jenny looked up at him and channeled every bit of strength she had into uttering three simple, yet damning words. "'Tis true, Callum." A tear ran down her cheek. "I wanted to tell you. I truly did."

Suddenly she could not breathe at all. Perspiration

speckled her skin, darkness crowded her vision, and all at once, she felt herself falling.

She was swaying to and fro, almost like a babe rocked in a cradle.

"Jenny," sang a voice just beyond the reaches of her conscious grasp. "Wake, dear. You're almost there. Just open your eyes."

The voice was so very peaceful and comforting that she did as asked and lifted her heavy lids.

Three huge faces hovered just inches from her own: the ladies Letitia and Viola, and Meredith.

"W-where am I?" Jenny asked as her mind cut its way through a thick fog.

It was Meredith who answered. "We're in the carriage, headed for home. Are you well? For you don't look it. You're as white as the ice on the canal."

"That's quite enough, Meredith," scolded Lady Viola. "Give Jenny some fresh air. That's right." It was then that Jenny realized that her head was resting on her ladyship's lap.

She bolted upright. "I beg your pardon, my lady."

Lady Letitia laughed. "Whatever for? You were lying precisely as Sister bade the footmen to place you."

"I am deeply indebted to you, child. Had you not cried out when you did, I would have been lured from the ballroom and likely bludgeoned and robbed."

Horrible pale memories began to float to the surface like dead fish on a pond as Jenny slowly became able to focus. Then one thought enveloped her mind, blocking out all others—"*Callum.*"

The two old ladies exchanged disappointed glances.

Lady Letitia patted Jenny's hand to calm her. "Well, as you might recall, he was properly gobsmacked by the news of your identity. For a moment or two, I thought he was going to lose his hold on consciousness too."

Jenny was alarmed at this bit of information.

"Don't worry, dear. He is well enough," Lady Viola told her soothingly. "Though once we had you inside the carriage, he charged off from the assembly rooms without so much as a word, headed, I believe, for Laura Place."

Jenny glanced over at Meredith, who was sitting quietly with her shoulder bumping against the wall as the carriage drove slowly down the road toward Royal Crescent. "Oh, Meredith," Jenny began. "I am so sorry for ruining your ball with scandal. Will you ever forgive me?"

"Ruined?" Meredith looked confused. "What are you going on about? My ball was bloody wonderful!"

Lady Letitia scowled. "Your language, Meredith!"

"I am sorry, Auntie, but lud, I have never had such an exciting evening in my entire life." Meredith grinned impishly. "Why, if society balls are anything like mine was tonight, I shan't allow myself to miss a one."

"The question is, ladies, what do we do now to bridge this schism between our two lovers?" Lady Letitia asked.

Jenny waited, hoping someone might have an answer, but instead the carriage filled with a stifling silence. Her spirits fell into despair.

What had she been thinking? There was nothing the Featherton ladies could possibly do.

Nothing anyone could do.

She had lost Callum . . . forever.

❧

"You cunning cow!"

The sun had just begun to rise, judging from thin light breaking into the bedchamber, as Jenny opened her eyes to find the scullery maid standing over her.

"Get out of here, Erma," Jenny snapped. "I've had a dreadful enough night and don't need to start my morn by dealing with yet another thief!"

Erma shoved something forward, and Jenny saw that it was the morning paper. "Cook read it all to me, and by the time she had finished, Mr. Bartleby had called to tell me he would be doing business only with you—and no other."

Jenny took the paper from Erma and quickly scanned Hercule's *on-dit* column. Why he'd even mentioned her ordering system. She looked up at Erma. "Everything in this column is true. Why are you here trying to quarrel with me? I am the wronged party, after all."

Erma glowered at her. "I want to know how you did it—how you turned the bloody story around to swing the hatchet at me!"

Jenny pushed the newspaper back at the scullery maid. "Shall we just say that I have friends who look out for me, and leave it at that?"

Erma let out a sound remarkably similar to a cat's hiss. "When the ladies read this, and Cook told me they always read *The Bath Herald* at Saturday breakfast, I'll be sacked, and it will all be your fault."

Jenny scoffed at that. "You listen to me, *Erma*. If you are sacked, it will have nothing to do with me, but rather with your disloyalty to the family. By trying to ruin me, you very nearly hurt the Featherton ladies." She folded her arms and narrowed her eyes at the maid. "So if I were you, I'd keep my head down and mouth closed—and hope, just hope, that the ladies, in their great generosity of spirit, will overlook your shortcomings and keep you on at the house."

Erma just stared at her.

"Now please, leave my chamber. Haven't you got some pots to scour or something?"

"You haven't heard the last of this, Jenny."

"Oh, I think I have."

Erma threw the newspaper back at Jenny, then stomped from the room.

Picking it up, Jenny's eyes skimmed the column again. Lud, after the way she was exposed last eve, she began to think it would have been far more preferable to have been revealed in *The Bath Herald*.

At least she wouldn't have had to look into Callum's eyes when he learned the whole awful truth of her lies—*from another*.

Folding the paper in half, she crawled from her tiny bed, washed, and dressed herself in preparation for another day. Jenny sighed. For though her world collapsed under the weight of her lies last eve, today was a new day and life would go on.

Jenny rested her hand atop her belly.

Yes, life would go on.

Later that afternoon, Jenny descended the stairs to retrieve her hat and cloak, intending to walk to Trim Street for some ribbon to update Meredith's flower-festooned straw bonnet.

It was something to do to occupy her mind, since the ladies had given strict orders that Jenny was not to see to her daily duties. Under normal circumstances, Jenny would be dancing with glee that she was excused from her work, but not today. She needed to remain busy if only to diminish the pain of last eve.

As she passed through the kitchen door, out of habit, she walked forward to peer over the edge of the harvest basket by the door.

She didn't know why she bothered, for who would buy a pot of cream from her now that all of Bath knew the whispered-of Lady Eros was naught but a lady's maid?

What she saw inside nearly made her faint. Her breath came fast, and she slapped her hand to her chest to steady herself.

The basket was full. More than full. At least eight stones had fallen out and lay against the woven carrier.

She clenched her fist. If this was Erma's idea of getting back at her . . . but then she opened her palms. Tiny notes were bound with strings, thread, or colorful wool to the stones. She bent and removed one.

"Two pots for Mrs. Potter, Fifteen Great Pulteney Street," she read aloud. She opened another note. "Mr. Higgins, Six Lower Borough Walls, requests one pot please."

She read three others, but realized there was no need to continue. These were all legitimate orders—but not from the *ton*. No, these were from ordinary folk. A smile lifted her lips for the first time since the previous night.

Chapter Eighteen

Each morning for the fortnight following the fateful ball, Jenny awoke to discover her harvest basket bulging with stones.

So, after a day's work blending concoctions for the Feathertons and seeing to the sartorial needs of Miss Meredith, Jenny split her time between the stillroom where she extracted the Mitcham peppermint from her herbs, and the kitchen, where she would stir the creamy emulsion and fill the awaiting gallipots.

Her hands remained busy, though her mind was left to ponder the mistakes she made during her short time with Callum. She knew her betrayal pained him deeply. He'd not even come to call on his grandmother, Lady Viola, as had become his habit just before the ball, and Jenny knew how much that hurt the old woman.

How she wished she could live those weeks over again.

Not that she would have done much differently, for she was who she was after all. Except she would have told him the truth when the opportunity first presented itself, instead of waiting 'til nearly every granule of sand had sieved through the pinch in the hourglass. For had she been honest with him, her life might have been so different today.

Distracted by such somber thoughts, Jenny failed to notice that the pot over the embers had overheated until it began to sputter and pop, sending globules of cream into the hearth where they ignited into flames.

Scolding herself for her inattention, she yanked the crane toward her and quickly hoisted the pot from its hook, completely forgetting to insulate the handle with a folded cotton cloth. *Blast!* The metal handle seared her hand, and she dropped the pot onto the slate hearth.

The fatty cream slowly seeped from the lip of the fallen pot and progressed toward the fire. Lifting her hem, Jenny ran across the kitchen pavers to fetch a broom to whisk the emulsion back before it could reach the fire.

The service door swung wide, nearly striking Jenny down, as Annie walked into the kitchen.

"Help me!" Jenny pleaded, frantically waving her finger at the hearth and the steaming cream.

Annie followed Jenny's finger and when she saw the pot on its side, her eyes nearly leapt from her skull. "Great God in heaven, Jenny, are you tryin' to burn the house down?"

Annie flung her basket to the floor and raced to the hearth. Catching up the ember shovel in her hands, she quickly built a dam of ashes to prevent the cream from reaching the fire.

Jenny's heart pounded in her ears. Thank heavens Annie had come when she did.

A few minutes later, Annie had wordlessly scraped the sputtering emulsion back into the pot and had turned back to Jenny.

"What is in that head of yours, hmm?" Perspiration laced Annie's hairline and her cheeks were flushed from exertion and the heat of the cooking fire.

Jenny slumped to a low stool. "That's just it. I can't concentrate on anything . . . but the pain I've caused everyone."

Annie came over to her and wiped a smudge of soot from Jenny's face with the hem of her apron. "Look at those rings under your eyes. Haven't you been sleeping none?"

Jenny shook her head. "Whenever my eyes close long enough to sleep, I seem to relive Miss Meredith's ball. All I can see is Callum's stricken face when I have to admit that all those damning words hurled by that thieving woman were completely true."

Lifting an empty gallipot to her lips, Jenny blew into it to remove the flecks of ash from the hearth. "And so I come in here to work until I can barely stand. Only then can I claim a dreamless sleep. But by then, 'tis almost morn."

Annie pulled Jenny into an embrace and hugged her. She leaned back and raised Jenny's chin with her palm. "You can't keep this up. 'Tisn't good for you . . . or your babe."

The warning startled Jenny. "I—I never said my condition was for certain."

"No, but you didn't need to neither. Because for the first time since I've known you, you haven't been whining about the pain in your belly at month's end. And you ain't just late neither. Why the moon itself sets its month by you."

Jenny pulled away from Annie and dragged the pot of ruined cream toward the door so she could dump it outside come morn. But Annie was right. She was never late, and now had to admit what she'd avoided acknowledging all along.

She leveled a sullen gaze at Annie, not wishing to discuss her condition with anyone. Best to keep it quiet for as long as possible so as not to impact her cream business. For now more than ever, with the babe coming, she'd need every spare shilling she could earn.

Annie had just settled herself before the long trestle table when Jenny pulled up a stool and sat down for the first time all eve. She looked quizzically at Annie. "What are you doing here so late anyway? Shouldn't you be thinking of heading abed yourself?"

"'Tisn't that late, and besides, I've got some news that might brighten your spirits." Annie's eyes were large and she bit her bottom lip with excitement.

"What? Has a new footman come to Bath?" Jenny grinned and raised her brows in anticipation.

"*Better*. And you are going to thank me, Jenny Penny." She paused a moment more, until Jenny's curiosity had her ready to shake the news loose from her friend.

"Well, on Saturday next, you and I have an interview with Mr. Malcolm Lewis."

Jenny just stared back at Annie. "The name means nothing to me. Why should I wish an interview with this fellow?"

"Because, ducks, he owns the empty shop on Milsom. You remember. We peered through the window one afternoon."

Yes, she did remember that day, but lud, those happier times seemed like years ago now. "An interview, you say?"

"What with all the orders you've been gettin' from the regular folk, you're certain to have the blunt to let the place now, or at least you will have soon enough, I reckon." Annie stared patiently back at Jenny as if waiting for some reaction.

Then it happened. The dullness that seemed to cover her like a wool cloak these past two weeks began to lift. There was an excitement building within her, something she had not felt in a very long time.

"Ah, there we go, ducks. I can see it now. 'Tis in your eyes, bright and shiny as a new guinea." The grin on Annie's face was contagious, and Jenny found herself smiling as well.

"All right. I'll do it!"

"Knew you would. Well, must be off." Annie retrieved her basket and headed for the door. "I daresay, it mightn't be too soon to start thinking about what you will sell, besides the tingle cream of course."

Jenny nodded, and as soon as Annie had gone, she raced to her chamber. Flipping open her scientific journal, she thumbed through the pages until she found her extensive plans for her very own shop.

The next morning, Jenny did the impossible. Taking her earnings, she paid her accounts in full. Yes, she settled up with every merchant she owed in Bath.

This process took nearly an entire day to achieve, even with Annie's assistance, but it was worth it and necessary—for her future and the babe's.

For if she was to open her shop and fill it with glorious trinkets, creams, and balms of her own making, she would need to be able to do business on account with a number of merchants in Bath.

Especially the draper. For her latest brilliant idea for her shop was to create a selection of ready-to-wear gowns created in the height of modish Paris fashion.

Annie had scoffed at the idea, for everyone knew that ladies of the *ton* habitually visited the draper for fabrics, then had a modiste craft the gown. The process took days or even weeks.

Yes, this was the inefficient way gowns *had* been sold. But what were the ladies to do when an unexpected invitation arrived to a glittering social event? They had to condescend to retrieve an old gown from their trunk or wardrobe, when in their heart they longed to impress with a new gown.

Until now, this was impossible. No modiste could fashion a high-quality gown so quickly. Jenny knew this for certain, for she had tried during her courtship with Callum! And even then, on short notice, the best she had been able to hope for was a remade gown.

Hardly the same. Remade gowns didn't make the body shiver with pleasure, now did they?

So Jenny decided that her shop would carry several gowns, drawn straight from *La Belle Assemblée*, made to fit women of average proportions. She, herself, being handy with a needle, would see to the final fitting.

When Jenny returned to her chamber after paying off every debt she had, she almost felt giddy. This was really going to happen. Though it was going to take every shilling she had left, she was going to meet with Mr. Lewis on Saturday and the shop was going to be hers. *Hers*.

Jenny could already see herself standing inside the

elegant silk-swathed shop. A stack of her tingle cream would fill one of the narrow windows, for the product was her mainstay. In the other window would be fantastic collections of baubles, fans, and slippers, all guaranteed to make even the most sensible lady drool like a hound beneath a supper table.

And each day, she would wear a different piece of jewelry or maybe a new mantle. Well, it only made sense. For how could her customers truly see the magnificence of a quality piece when it was stuffed into a glass case? It just wasn't the same, was it?

Happiness budded within her at the thought of her future, but somehow the feeling never blossomed, never wiped away the sadness aching in her breast.

She missed Callum.

Just then Miss Meredith came racing into her chamber and leapt on her bed like Cook's marmalade cat.

"Hurry, you can't wear your service clothes—you've got to change into something more suitable." Excitement coursed through every fiber of Meredith's being.

"Something more suited to . . . what?" Jenny asked warily.

"For an interview." Meredith shook her hands in frustration. "Lud, Jenny, he's come to see you."

"Oh, for goodness' sake." Jenny rolled her eyes in exasperation. "*Who* is here?"

"Please, Jenny. I only race down here when *he* comes to call for you. And he has." Meredith grabbed Jenny's hands and squeezed them. "Lord Argyll is above stairs right now."

Jenny did not change into a more appropriate frock. It was befitting for his lordship to view her as she really was—a maid.

As she approached the drawing room where he waited, she glanced into the mirror to double check her appearance. Every hair was in place, and in the golden afternoon light, her citrine earbobs perfectly accented the green in her eyes.

She gave a quick thought to removing the earbobs—so that he would see nothing but a lady's maid. But leaving her earlobes unadorned conveyed no more the "true" Jenny than entering the room in a beaded ball gown would.

No, *this* was who she was—the lady's maid with the earbobs. She'd even heard the staff below stairs refer to her as such—except it was the maid with the *bleedin'* earbobs.

Oh, perdition, she was stalling again. For more than two weeks she'd waited for this moment and now that it had arrived she could scarce move her feet toward the door.

Just move one foot forward. That's right. Now the next. You're nearly there. Hand on door. Press down. Now push.

There was a whine from the hinges as the door swung open.

Callum was sitting beside the roaring fire, his elbows on his knees and head resting in his palms. He looked up at her when he heard the door. Slowly, he came to his feet, giving Jenny the distinct impression that at this moment he was every bit as given to nerves as she herself.

As she closed the door behind her, and turned back

around, Jenny did not miss his sweeping gaze, that seemed to pause curiously on her citrine earbobs. But she could not fault him for that. They were extraordinarily lovely.

"Lord Argyll," she said, her tone cooler than she had intended. Jenny bounced a curtsy. It was not a fluid motion, such as the sort Lady Viola had taught her, one conveying grace and manners. Rather it was an obligatory gesture, such as the sort a maid gave her better.

Callum, his eyes almost squinting in confusion, belatedly bowed to her, sending his kilt swaying. "Will ye join me beside the fire, Lady . . . *Miss* Penny?

The gaffe was not meant to humiliate, she could see that. He was simply trying to be correct, in a very difficult situation.

Jenny hurried to the settee and sat down. Callum sat on the edge of the chair across from her, resting his elbows on his knees in the very same way he had done when she first had entered the room.

"We need to discuss what happened, ye and I." He stopped speaking for a moment and looked down at his steepled fingers. "I should have come earlier, but as ye might have guessed, I required time to think and come to terms with yer . . . weel, with everything."

Jenny folded her hands in her lap to quell the shaking of her fingers. "I understand, my lord."

Just then the door swung open again. Both of them turned their heads and looked, but there was no one there. Jenny rose, meaning to close it again.

Callum waved her back. "Leave it, lass, please. This shanna take long."

Jenny slowly lowered herself onto the settee, waiting for the question she knew he would eventually have to ask—*why?* Jenny prepared the answer on her tongue and waited.

Callum exhaled and stared down at his hands for what seemed like hours to Jenny. At last, he looked up again.

"Jenny, I made ye a promise once before. That if ye carried me bairn, I would marry ye."

Jenny started. This was not what she expected him to say at all. "My lord?"

"Oh, Jenny, must I ask it?"

"I suppose you must ask it, for I am not entirely sure what you are expecting me to say." Jenny leaned forward and patiently waited for him to continue.

Callum rose and, turning away from her, placed his hands atop the marble mantel and gazed down into the fire. "Are . . . are ye with child?"

He didn't even look at her. Which, in hindsight, Jenny decided was a good thing, for at once her hand flew protectively over her belly, before she had the good sense to remove it.

Jenny came to her feet, girding herself as best she could. "You needn't fear, Lord Argyll. You need not be concerned that my condition will impinge on your plans to see the Argyll title extinct." Golly, she almost sounded like a real lady.

Then, she heard his breath hitch. Moving his elbows atop the mantel, he propped his head in his hands and exhaled slowly.

She felt cold all over. She had not said the words, but it was a lie just the same. Still, she would not use her babe to maintain her hold on Callum.

How could she? She did not wish to spend her life

seeing the resentment in his eyes when he gazed upon her . . . and their child.

No, she would carry on and fill her child's life with love, the way her own mother had. Though she would raise their babe alone, she would open the shop, work hard with the babe on her hip if need be. She would bring the babe to visit the Feathertons, for they were bound by blood. She'd give her child the life he or she should have had. Might have had . . . had she confessed the truth to Callum weeks ago.

She looked up and saw that he still faced the hazy mirror on the overmantel. Her heart sank for she knew he would not utter another word.

Tears began to itch the backs of Jenny's eyes, until she knew she had to leave the room, had to leave Callum before he saw through her and realized she did in fact carry his babe.

Turning on the ball of her foot, she started for the door, when to her shock, she saw the two Featherton sisters crouched on the floor behind the settee.

Lady Letitia, not the least concerned at being spotted by Jenny, quietly raised a finger to her lips, while her sister shooed Jenny back in the direction of Lord Argyll.

Eyes wide, Jenny turned and returned to Callum, hoping to give the ladies adequate time to crawl from their hiding place and through the drawing-room door unseen.

There was a thickness growing inside her throat as she reached out her hand, wanting so much to touch Callum. Instead, she let her hand hover there above his shoulder for several moments, before slowly returning it to her side.

He was aware of her proximity for she could see the change in his stance. But still he did not turn to her.

"Callum," she said, her voice strained and thin. "If you believe nothing else . . . believe that I loved you." She turned then and started for the door.

The Feathertons were no longer hiding behind the settee, and so she made to leave the drawing room. As she reached the threshold, she halted and slowly turned back to gaze at Callum.

"And I love you still," she whispered.

Callum's back stiffened at her words, and she knew for certain that he had heard her.

In the reflection in the overmantel mirror, she saw that his eyes remained closed, but his lips moved.

Jenny remained rooted to that spot and stared in disbelief as his lips mouthed the words she longed to hear: "And I love ye."

Her heart sprang into her throat. She ran from the room and retreated down the passageway, where at its end she found her mother awaiting her with open arms.

Chapter Nineteen

A moment later a flash of movement lured Jenny's eye. Wet-cheeked, she raised her head from her mother's comforting shoulder just in time to see Callum stride from the drawing room.

"Lord Argyll?" Lady Viola stepped from the study and into the hall. "I would have a word with you, if I may."

Jenny and her mother stepped back into the thickly shadowed alcove beneath the stairs so as not to be observed.

"Of course, my lady." Callum turned and followed his grandmother into the study. The door closed behind them, and the click of its brass lock reverberated down the narrow passageway.

What, pray, was Lady Viola going to say to him? Jenny wondered. Lud, she felt a little wobbly just considering the possibilities. Well, there was no sense waiting around and wondering. She meant to find out.

Remembering Meredith's demonstration of how conversation in the study might be overheard through the dining-room wall, Jenny broke from her mother's grip and started for the next open doorway.

"Jenny, you can't. Leave them their privacy." Her mother's eyes pleaded with her.

Jenny quirked her lip. "I might have considered doing so had the ladies given me the least bit of privacy only moments ago. But they did not. Besides which, whatever Lady Viola says affects me, you can depend on that. So, I own, I feel I am justified in listening."

When Jenny stepped into the dining room, she was quite startled to find Lady Letitia already standing with her ear to the wall.

The old woman beckoned her forward. "Sister is about to begin, hurry, *hurry*." Lady Letitia pressed the side of her head to the wall once more, and as she concentrated, her eyes wedged in the corner nearest the wall, her mouth fell open, and the tip of her tongue lifted to touch her top row of teeth.

Jenny hesitantly moved forward and, resting her hand on the dado chair rail, settled her ear against the sand-colored wall.

"Please come and sit beside me, dear boy," came Lady Viola's soothing voice through the wall.

Jenny stared with amazement at Lady Letitia. Every word was perfectly clear. "I daresay, it's as though we're in the room with them."

Lady Letitia hushed her. "They may be able to hear us as well," she whispered harshly.

"Oh, right." Jenny eased her ear to the wall again.

Lady Viola began tentatively. "You have spoken with Jenny."

"I have . . . briefly. Though before ye utter another word, ye should ken that nothing has changed since I . . ."

No sound came from the wall for several seconds,

until Lady Viola filled the silent gap. "Since you learned that she was a lady's maid."

Again, there was a long pause and both Jenny and her employer pushed their ears flat to the wall, straining to hear his reply. But none came, for it was Lady Viola who next spoke.

"Do I have it right, lad, that you feel she betrayed you?"

"Aye, and she did."

"But you trusted Jenny."

"I did. But 'twas more than that. I believed in her. Christ . . . I *loved* her." Callum's voice was thick with rising emotion. "But still, she lied to me."

There was a tinkling of glass and sound of liquid filling a vessel. "Dinna ye see. She's just like my mother."

"Jenny is like Olivia? How so?" came Lady Viola's terse reply.

"Because she claimed to love me—but still she lied, even though she knew why honesty and truth mean everything to me."

"You oversimplify, Argyll, but still I do not see how Jenny and your mother compare."

"Dinna ye? My mother loved me too, or said she did, but she still lied . . . lied in a way that tore my heart from my chest. When I saw her leaving, she kissed me and promised she'd come back and I believed her, because she said she loved me."

Again a heavy silence met the wall that stood between Jenny and Callum. "From the day I realized that me mother was never comin' home, I vowed never to trust another. Never to open myself up to the depth of pain betrayal brings. *And never to lie.*"

"But was Jenny's lie so grand? She only pretended, at

Sister's and my bidding I'll have you know, that she was
a lady. Does it matter so much that she is in service—
rather than a lady true? I would think you, a man intent
on seeing his family's title made extinct, would not be
so concerned with the blueness of another's blood."

Jenny sucked the seam of her lips inside her mouth
and waited with bated breath for what he would say
next.

"Nay, ye've got it all wrong," Callum said, his words
hitting the wall as though they'd been exhaled with
some force.

"I dinna give a damn if Jenny is a maid or the queen
herself."

Callum must have risen. For the heavy sound of
boots pacing the wooden floor edging the room was
plain.

"You forgave me for keeping my identity from you.
Is there not room enough in your heart to forgive Jenny
as well?"

"'Tisna what she lied about, my lady. God, 'tisna that
at all. She lied to me, knowing that someday I would
learn of her deceit. And still she did not confess."

The rap of a walking stick tapped the floor on the
other side of the wall. "Why do you suppose that was?"
Lady Viola asked.

"Because she never really loved me."

Jenny gasped and her heart twisted in her chest as his
damning words reached her ear.

"Oh, do you really believe that? If you do, you are
not half the man I thought you to be." The walking stick
clicked thrice, then stopped just at the point where Callum's voice emanated. "Because I happen to know that

the opposite is true and if you trusted your heart, you would know this."

"What do ye mean?" came Callum's confused voice.

"That Jenny did not confess, at first because we begged her not to . . . but later, because she loved you so deeply. She knew, after learning your deep-seated requisite for truth, that the moment she told you who she really was, a maid, you would leave her forever."

"Nay, I wudna have."

"Oh, really, Argyll? What have you just done?"

Jenny couldn't endure another word. This was all so painful. When she looked up and met Lady Letitia's eyes, her employer reached out a hand and squeezed her shoulder gently.

"I'm sorry, gel," she whispered. "I had hoped Sister would be able to talk some sense into the lad by now. But it seems his wounds go far deeper than we knew."

The smile Jenny returned felt feeble on her lips, but that was all she could manage just then.

"Oh, there now. I own, Viola may still turn his coat. In fact, I am confident that she will. Won't you stay?"

As Jenny shook her head, a pin flew from her hair and clattered across the sideboard. And that was it, all it took to send the tears cascading down her cheeks again. Averting her face from her employer, she snatched up the hairpin, then turned and quietly left the dining room.

For the next three days, Jenny threw herself into her work. Come spring, the family would return to London to prepare for Meredith's presentation. And though she had not yet confessed her intentions to anyone, for she did not wish to be talked out of beginning her life anew, she would not be making the trip with them.

Still, Meredith would require an appropriate wardrobe for her debut and it would not do to leave the girl in a fashion lurch. Therefore, Jenny spent every afternoon with a draper or modiste, fashioning a workable ensemble of clothing for a young miss of Meredith's elevated standing.

She scoured the shops of Bath for the perfect accoutrements for each frock, right down to jewel-headed hairpins.

Efficiency was her primary goal with each outing, for each trip held a dual purpose—outfitting Meredith and taking inventory of available items for her own shop. When possible, she even quizzed the shop owners for their sources—and they would actually tell her! Of course, they had no way of knowing they were aiding their own competition.

By the second day, Jenny had made a game of how much information she could glean from each merchant. She'd push open the shop door, and from the moment the bell clattered overhead, she timed herself to see how quickly she could encourage the shopkeeper to part with supplier information. Soon, her belly did a little flip each time she heard a bell.

On the third day, quite by accident, Jenny found herself on Upper Milsom Street and decided to take a look at her shop. For in her mind, it already was hers. She had the blunt she needed for the first six months, but decided she'd only offer payment for the first three. After all, she needed money to decorate and fill the place, didn't she?

For the first time in days, her step was light as she

neared the shop. Until she saw a man outside *her* shop, turning a key in *her* lock.

"Excuse me, sir," she called out, not giving a fig if such a display was not ladylike. "I say, is this your shop?"

The man was tall and lean with a long, narrow face, which immediately brought to mind a horse. His clothing was neatly pressed, but his coat was made of coarse wool, and his shirt of cotton. No fine gentleman, this. But what bothered Jenny was that he held the TO LET sign in his gloved hands.

"Ah, yes, it is. May I assist you with a matter, miss?" His voice was raspy—and good God if he didn't sound as much like a horse as he looked.

Her eyes alighted on the sign again and her spirits and the smile on her face plummeted.

Oh, no. How could this have happened? She had an interview with a Mr. Lewis on Saturday. She had been so close. So blasted close to realizing her dream.

It was clear her feelings were transparent. "Is everything all right, miss?" the man asked. "Name's Lewis, Malcolm Lewis. I own this building."

Mr. Lewis, did he say? Her attention was pricked. Well, that changed everything, now didn't it?

Jenny spread her lips and flashed him a gleaming smile. "I am very pleased to know you, sir, though I daresay, I find our meeting quite the coincidence. For we were to meet Saturday to discuss this very property. My name is Miss Jenny Penny."

Now it was Mr. Lewis's turn to appear crestfallen. "Oh, dear. I do not know what to say."

Any sentence that begins with "Oh, dear" cannot finish

positively. The smile melted from her mouth and dripped away into nothingness.

Mr. Lewis looked her squarely in the eye. "I do beg your pardon, Miss Penny, but there is no longer a need for our interview on Saturday."

Oh, blast! Here it comes.

"You see, miss, I just finished meeting with another gentleman who has agreed to purchase the entire building."

Jenny's mouth fell open. Just like that? A gentleman buys the whole bleedin' building and her dreams—her future—dashed?

"So . . . I am sorry to advise you that this property is not available."

Jenny heard sounds coming from her mouth then, but only a few seemed to make any sense. "But . . . there are n-n-no more shops to let on Milsom." And even those words wobbled nearly incoherently.

He manufactured a forlorn look for her. "I am sorry, Miss Penny." Tipping his hat and bowing ever so slightly at the waist, he walked past her and continued along Milsom Street.

All strength seemed to leech from her body. The three parcels she had been carrying fell from her arms to the walk. She bent to retrieve them, but her legs went to jelly too, and lest she fall, Jenny sat down on the ground and stared up at the empty shop, *someone else's shop*, as her skirts billowed around her.

So what are you going to do now, Jenny? What will you do now?

The next morning, the sky opened up and released upon Bath a hail of sleet and freezing rain. Walking was treacherous, but despite her aunts' protests, Miss Meredith left the house shortly after her midday meal with a dutiful Edgar at her heels.

With Meredith absent, Jenny spent the day planning the girl's trousseau, which she had been remiss in building sooner.

By tea time, the sun peeked through the gray clouds and fell upon Royal Crescent, though the rest of the spa city remained bathed in gray.

When daylight shone through the window in Meredith's chamber, Jenny peered out at Nature's selective illumination and marveled at what she saw. The dark bare branches of every tree behind the crescent's grand sweep of houses were coated with a finger's width of ice, and they glistened like a sparkling wreath of Austrian crystal in the golden light.

"Jenny!" came the sound of Lady Letitia's strong voice from the passageway.

She turned her head just as her ladyship entered Meredith's chamber.

"Meredith has taken it upon herself to visit Lord Argyll in Laura Place."

Jenny was stunned and doubted she heard Lady Letitia correctly. "I—I beg your pardon, my lady?"

"Yes, 'tis true. I only just learned of this myself. Edgar sent a message back with a footman. Thank heavens I sent him along to walk with her for safety, what with the ice on the flag way."

Just where was this discussion going, Jenny wondered with more than a little trepidation.

"I own, I do not know what Meredith's concocted in

that mischievous brain of hers, but she refuses to return unless you, my dear, retrieve her."

"Me?" Jenny gaped at this.

"Yes, *you*. And I do apologize, dear, but she is required to play the fortepiano next door in two hours' time, so you must go and fetch her."

"Right away, my lady." *Oh, please. Anything but this!*

"Oh, do not look so shaken. Though young Meredith insisted on walking all the way to Laura Place, likely for the folly of sliding on the ice, I have sent for the carriage to convey you."

Jenny bobbed a curtsy. "Thank you, my lady."

Lady Letitia turned to leave, then stopped and looked back at Jenny. "It is quite bitter. Do take care to bundle up—in fact, why don't you take Viola's fur-lined cloak. I will let her know you shall be borrowing it. She will not mind in the least. Don't want you and the babe to—" Her words cut off then and she stared at Jenny. "Well, we wouldn't want *you* to catch a cold upon your chest."

"No, my lady. My thanks."

The moment Lady Letitia left the room, Jenny returned to the window and gazed out onto the ice-covered landscape. Of course there was another scheme afoot. But she could not disobey her employer.

No matter. A sad little smile crept over Jenny's lips. Whatever it was, it would be worth enduring, if only to wear Viola's fabulous ermine-lined, royal blue cloak. She turned and hurried down the stairs.

It was nearly dark as the town carriage arrived in Laura Place. As the door opened to the footman's knock, Lord Argyll's man, Winston, led Jenny through the house to a wide set of French windows.

"There you are, Jenny!" came Meredith's excited voice as she bounded down the passageway with Edgar at her heels.

Jenny cast a serious gaze at Meredith. Perhaps if she hurried, she'd not even see Callum, and thus spare her heart a modicum of pain. "You are wanted at home, Miss Meredith. I have come to retrieve you."

Meredith just laughed. "Actually, no, Jenny. You have come for an interview with Lord Argyll. I was merely the means to bring you here."

"What?" Jenny's muscles tensed as she felt the Feathertons' well-oiled trap spring closed upon her.

Meredith slipped her arms around Jenny's waist and drew her close. "I will be leaving now, but Edgar shall stay here, below stairs . . . you know, for propriety's sake."

Jenny's eyes went wide. "But I can't . . . not now."

But it was too late. Meredith was already on her way out the front door, waving good-bye as she hurried toward her aunts' carriage.

"Miss Penny," said Winston, gesturing to the French windows. "My lord awaits you in the courtyard."

In the courtyard? What, in this weather?

Still, when Winston opened the glass doors, she dutifully stepped over the threshold. Flickering light to the right caught her eye and she turned her head to see a most amazing spectacle.

White votive candles, the sort Jenny knew were only to be had at the premier chandler on Trim Street, lined either side of a pathway that led to a shimmering center circle ringed with nigh on twenty flaming wood-filled cressets.

The flames in the cressets burned so high that a glowing opaque wall of bright golden light prevented her from seeing inside the wide circle.

Her curiosity overtook her apprehension, and she crunched carefully down the sparkling ice-encrusted pathway, through the narrow opening between cresset baskets, and finally into the circle of light.

Oh . . . my . . . word. Jenny's voice left her and she could do naught but stare at the faery story world before her.

Four ice-coated cherry trees, filled with tiny glass lanterns, created a brilliant starlike canopy of winking light above a table set for two.

The candlelit table was strewn with the perfect snowy petals of white hothouse roses, and if her nose did not fail her, fragrant orange blossoms ringed two crystal goblets.

Could she be dreaming? She blinked her eyes, then a small giggle slipped through her lips.

"Jenny," came Callum's deep voice from just behind her and she quivered within as she gradually turned about to face him.

Reluctant to see the sadness in his eyes, she slowly lifted her gaze to meet his. But instead of the pain she expected, she saw hope.

He brought a single white rose from behind his back and lifted it to her. She took it, as emotion welled up in her breast.

The thin skin around Callum's dark eyes crinkled as

he smiled down at her. "Jenny, I have been a thick-headed fool. Can ye ever fergive me?"

What was this? He was asking for *her* forgiveness?

"I do not understand," she confessed. "I am the one who must beg absolution. I deliberately led you to believe I was a lady . . . when I was only a—"

But he pulled her to him gently and hushed her by moving his lips over hers. She felt his fingers in her hair as he kissed her, and she shivered with pleasure.

He lifted his mouth from her lips and looked deep into her eyes for several seconds without saying a word. Then, he raised the ruby betrothal ring before her, just as he had done in the study once before.

"Jenny, to me ye *are* a lady. If ye do me the great honor of accepting my troth once more, and tell me ye'll be my wife, ye'll be *my lady*."

Tears seeped into her eyes and thickened the wall of her throat. "But can you ever forgive me?" she sputtered.

"There is nothin' to fergive, lass. My grandmother told me how it all came to be—"

"But even when I could have confessed, I didn't." Her wet cheeks grew chilled in the cold air and he cupped them in his hands, warming them.

"Why, lass?" he asked her.

She looked quizzically up at him . . . for he was still smiling. "Because I loved you and I didn't want to lose you."

"Aye. Not to hurt me. Ye did it because ye loved me. And fer that reason, there is nothin' to fergive. Ye only wanted to love me and be loved by me a while longer."

"Yes," Jenny said softly.

"So take my ring, lass, and tell me ye'll be my wife.

And we'll both have that love forever." Callum knelt on one knee.

Jenny peeled off her white kid glove and held up her hand to Callum.

He took her hand and slowly slid the ring over the knuckle of her third finger. When the ring reached the base of her finger, he looked into her eyes. "Tell me, Jenny. Tell me what I want to hear. What I *need* to hear."

Jenny smiled and laughed through her ridiculous tears. "I love you, Callum. Nothing in this world would make me happier than becoming your wife."

Callum came to his feet and nodded, and from the corner of her eye, Jenny saw Winston, who appeared as if from nowhere, begin to fill the two crystal goblets with wine.

Then, Callum swept her into his arms, and as he pressed his lips to hers, a small sigh slipped from her mouth.

Above them, the ice-slicked branches swayed in the winter breeze, clapping together, as if applauding.

Jenny opened one eye and looked upward at the heavens.

Annie was never, ever, going to believe this.

Chapter Twenty

It was the most perfect of perfect days.

Bells were ringing, and the sun shone brightly through the massive windows of Bath Abbey, warming Jenny's cheeks as Mr. Edgar escorted her up the long aisle to stand before the altar with her beloved Callum.

Jenny sighed with happiness.

It was actually happening.

She and Callum Campbell, the Sixth Viscount Argyll, were to be married on none other than Saint Valentine's Day.

Everyone said that a wedding held on such an auspicious date was a good omen. For Saint Valentine's Day, according to the all-knowing Lady Letitia, was the singular day of the year that birds of like feather chose their lifetime mate.

As Jenny approached Callum at the altar, she was quite overwhelmed by the sight of silk festoons in muted Featherton purple and hundreds of ribbon-bound lavender stalks that seemed to fill the abbey.

It was a lavender-hued dream, not quite the color Jenny would have chosen, of course—a fashionable blush would have been more the thing—but neverthe-less, it was a dream come true.

Standing nearest the altar was her mother, her face aglow with happiness; Miss Meredith, who seemed still to be taking copious notes, and the Featherton ladies, who stood waiting with wide expectant grins.

The church also held a dozen of Jenny's friends, service staff all, who'd somehow been clever enough to beg the day off. But most surprising to Jenny was the at-tendance of Bath's elevated society, highborn ladies and gentlemen, who, Jenny reckoned, had accepted the Featherton sisters' invitations merely to see if the vis-count was truly marrying the scandalous Miss Jenny Penny, Lady Eros.

Jenny only smiled at this thought. Because, indeed, he *was* marrying her.

Still it hardly seemed real. Hardly seemed possible. Yet, here she stood, her hair simply arranged yet wreathed in brilliants, artfully shaped into sparkling rosebuds.

Jenny concentrated hard to focus only on Callum, even as her wedding gown all but called for her atten-tion. Its design was by her own hand, and even if she did say so herself, it was certainly the most beautiful cre-ation ever conceived.

Her gown was an overdress of silver lama on net, worn atop a silver tissue slip drenched with embroi-dered shells and flowers. The bodice and sleeves echoed the embroidery at the hem, but was set apart with a breath of elegant Brussels lace.

The manteau was of silver tissue lined with shim-mering white satin. It was trimmed with a border of em-broidery to answer the handiwork on the dress, and was perfectly fastened in front with the opal brooch her father had given her so many years ago.

She felt every bit the princess—*the lady*, and for certain she would be by hour's end, as unbelievable as it all seemed. For as she clasped Callum's strong hands— those of the man she truly loved—he swore before God and England to love and cherish her all the days of his life.

She peered down at her hand as Callum pushed a band of gold onto her third finger, until it abutted the ruby and diamond betrothal ring.

A tear trickled down her cheek. But Jenny didn't care. This was the happiest moment of her entire life.

Her most precious dream had just come true.

She and Callum, the man she loved with all her heart, were married.

🌹

Late that afternoon, after the Saint Valentine's Day wedding breakfast and festivities at the Upper Assembly Rooms had concluded, Jenny returned to Royal Crescent to pack the rest of her clothing and her abundance of accessories for transport to Laura Place.

"Oh, do not cry, Mama. It is not as though I am leaving Bath to move to Scotland."

"Not yet, anyway." Her mother made no attempt to silence her tearful sniffs as she slipped three pairs of gloves inside Jenny's bear muff and placed it in the open portmanteau. "Argyll will not wish to stay in dreary Bath forever."

"Well, we shan't be going anywhere until after the baby is born." Jenny gave her head a confident nod.

Her mother's eyes brightened at the mention. "So you've told him? What did he say?"

Jenny bit her bottom lip and diverted her eyes from her mother. "Well, I haven't exactly told him . . . but I will. Tonight in fact."

"Oh, Jenny! How could you have waited so long?"

Jenny exhaled as she pinned her opal brooch between her breasts for safekeeping, then closed her new leather traveling jewel case and placed it inside the portmanteau beside the bear muff. "What with all the excitement of the wedding, I completely forgot." She glanced sidelong at her mother to see her reaction.

"You . . . *forgot*? Jenny, do not mistake with whom you're speaking. I *know* you." Her mother took Jenny's hands and led her to the bed, where they sat down together. "Darling, he loves you. He will not be cross with you. But you must tell him."

"I shall." Jenny quieted until her mother's forceful glare set her tongue in motion again. "I shall tell him *this eve*."

The servants' bell sounded and both women looked up.

"You're wanted above stairs," her mother said. "Argyll must be here with the town carriage."

Jenny rose and closed the portmanteau.

"Go to him now, dear. I'll send George with your belongings." Her mother pecked her cheeks and drew back with a smile. "There you go. Off with you now."

Jenny dashed up the stairs and into the passage ready to greet her new husband. But instead, her eyes met with those of Hercule Lestrange.

She smiled broadly. "Hercule! There you are. How

good of you to come. Though I had expected to see you at my wedding breakfast."

The little man removed his glossy beaver hat and settled it on the table in the passageway. "I had an investigation to complete . . . Jenny," he said hesitantly. "I have someone with me who I would very much like for you to meet."

Jenny tilted her head, wondering what Mr. Lestrange was up to. "Very well . . . but I shall be leaving for Laura Place soon."

Hercule's brows lifted high over the bridge of his nose. "Ah, but this person is already waiting in the drawing room with the Featherton ladies." He offered up his arm to her. "Shall we?"

A dreadful blend of confusion and anticipation built inside of Jenny, but still she placed her hand over Hercule's arm and walked with him into the drawing room.

As they entered, Jenny could see Meredith and her two aunts sitting on the settee all but staring at the gentleman who sat with his back to her. Upon hearing their arrival, the gentleman rose and turned to face her.

He was a handsome man, tall and dark-haired with slashes of gray at his temples. His nose turned up slightly at the tip, not unlike her own, and his green eyes seemed to dance as he smiled down at her.

But it was his clothes that caused Jenny to marvel. He was dressed impeccably in the height of Paris fashion. The lines were clean, and the fabric was nothing less than the finest quality.

His valet must truly be a wonder, for no man could dress so well without extensive study of current modish fashion.

The Featherton sisters rose as well, and as Lady Letitia pulled Meredith to her feet, Lady Viola stepped forward.

"Lady Argyll," she began, gesturing to Jenny.

Golly. Lady Argyll. For some reason, hearing herself referred to as such sent a giggle into Jenny's middle and she had to fight to prevent it from leaping from her mouth into their guest's face.

"May I present Lord Trevor of Amhurst."

The gentleman smiled again, and honored her with a truly gallant bow.

Jenny stared at him. My word, he looked familiar somehow. Still, she couldn't quite place him.

Lady Viola, likely having spotted the puzzlement in Jenny's eyes, stepped beside her. "Dear, Lord Trevor is an old family friend. He was otherwise engaged, and therefore unable to attend your wedding festivities."

Lord Trevor spoke then, his voice as smooth and silken as his ivory waistcoat. "I do regret not bearing witness to the event, but 'tis my fondest wish to offer you a gift to celebrate your union with Lord Argyll."

Jenny watched with excitement as he withdrew a small leather box from his coat and held it out to her.

Her brows lifted as she looked at it. Everyone knew that the absolute best gifts came in tiny packages like the one in his hand. Her heart began to pound.

She glanced at Lady Viola, dutifully feigning a request for permission. Then when her employer gave a nod of assent, she took the box into her right palm and lifted the lid.

Two diamond-ringed fiery opal earbobs glistened inside. Jenny caught her breath.

Lord Trevor gave an appreciative sigh as well. "They were my mother's."

"Your mother's?" Jenny turned her eyes up to his. "Oh, my lord, I could not possibly accept such fine—"

Lord Trevor reached out and folded her fingers down atop of the earbobs. "But I insist. And besides, they complement your pin so well, my lady," he said, gesturing to her opal brooch.

My lady. My lady? There was something about the way he spoke those two words. Jenny pinned him with her gaze.

This seemed to unnerve the gentleman and he looked to Lady Letitia and her sister. "Well, must be off." He started past Jenny for the door, then turned and kissed her cheek. "Be happy," he said softly, yet earnestly. "'Tis my greatest wish for you and your husband." With great haste, he stepped into the hallway.

Everyone rushed through the doorway and into the passageway. They watched as he lifted his hat from the table, then gave himself a quick appreciative look in the mirror, before turning to face them all. "Good afternoon." Then with a click of his perfectly polished boot heel, he left the house.

Jenny was utterly stunned. She turned to Hercule, who leaned against the doorjamb grinning. "He . . . was my—"

"*Oui.* Your father."

Jenny's eyes flashed upon the Feathertons. They nodded back at her.

"But, Hercule," Jenny stammered. "How did you . . . I mean . . . I didn't even know his name."

Hercule straightened and moved before her. "'Twas the brooch. When I first saw it at Miss Meredith's birthday ball, I knew I'd seen it before. It only took some

time for me to realize 'twas in a portrait of Lady Trevor
at Amhurst Hall."

Jenny wrinkled her nose. "Lady Trevor?"

"Your grandmother, dear," Lady Viola explained.
"Your mother was engaged as a parlor maid at Amhurst
Hall before she came to us. 'Twas there that she met
Lord Trevor."

"But why did she never tell me this?" Jenny turned
around just as her mother emerged through the door to
the servants' stairs.

"Because, my darling girl, I loved him. But he was
not the man your Lord Argyll has proven himself to be.
And so I left Amhurst Hall in the past, where I hoped the
painful memories would remain, and took away the very
best part of him—*you*."

Jenny rushed to her mother and embraced her. "Oh,
Mama. I am so sorry."

"Bah, girl." Her mother took her by the shoulders and
pushed back, smiling through her tears. "Today is a joyous day for me. For my daughter has married the man
she loves, and is about to start her life anew." She
looked up as something over Jenny's shoulder caught
her notice.

Jenny turned to see Mr. Edgar open the door for Callum and usher him inside. The young lord was smiling
from ear to ear.

"Are ye ready?" he asked Jenny, very nearly hopping
from foot to foot in his excitement.

Jenny was still half mute from the shock of meeting
Lord Trevor. "I—I believe so . . ."

"Shall we all head off to Laura Place then? My staff
have prepared a feast we shallna ever see equaled in this

lifetime." He looked from the ladies Letitia and Viola, to Meredith, who all rushed Edgar for their wraps.

Jenny slowly approached her husband, then rose up on her toes and brushed her lips across his. "Whatever are you on about, my lord?" she asked suspiciously.

"Who me?" he asked, then pulled her into his arms and kissed her the skin-tingling way Jenny decided a husband ought always kiss his wife.

ॐ

The caravan of two fine conveyances left Royal Crescent just before four. But rather than thrilling at the prospect of being alone with her handsome new husband, Jenny was distracted by thoughts of the news she swore she would share this eve.

And so, instead of recounting the clothing choices of the wedding breakfast guests, a topic she would otherwise delight in exploring, Jenny gazed pensively out the carriage window as they rounded the Circus and started down Gay Street. But then the carriage turned left on George Street, then abruptly onto Milsom.

Lud, not Milsom Street. Not when her wound was so fresh. In fact, for the first time since she'd arrived in Bath, Jenny hadn't set foot on Milsom Street for four whole days.

It was simply too painful to see the empty shop that was almost hers, knowing that someone else would soon open the doors . . . probably to sell tools or something else completely unnecessary.

The carriage wheeled ever closer until . . . *there it was.* Jenny closed her eyes, unable to even look upon it. But then to her immense consternation, she felt the carriage stop. She snapped her eyes open as the footman let down the stairs.

"Why are we stopping here? I thought we were going to Laura Place." She tried very hard to avoid sounding bitter, but it was too difficult. She heard the bile flavoring her every word.

"Just need to stop inside a shop for a moment." Callum playfully pulled her from the carriage. "Come with me, lass. I know shopping is yer passion."

"No, *you* are my passion, Callum. Take me to Laura Place and I'll prove it to you." Jenny smiled wickedly at him, hoping he would take her bait and forget his blasted errand.

But by now, the Feathertons had already disembarked from their carriage and were headed toward them. Lady Letitia looked up at the linen-draped shop sign above *her* shop's door, swaying lightly in the chill breeze. "Looks like a new shop is to open, eh?"

Meredith glanced up too. "I wonder what it will sell?" A broad smile appeared on her face. "Perhaps antiquities; mummies packed in sarcophaguses, and temple jars filled with metaphysical elixirs."

Jenny turned to Callum, to share a roll of eyes, but he had simply vanished.

Then there was a rattling of keys, and the sound of a door opening. She spun around. There stood Callum in the open doorway of the shop wearing the largest, most foolish grin she'd ever seen.

"Callum," she began, creeping forward. "What are you doing . . . in that empty shop? The new owner won't be amused."

"Ye're not amused? Hmm. Somehow I thought owning yer own shop *would* amuse ye."

A wild jolt raced through Jenny's limbs. "What did you say?"

Lady Letitia laughed. "Oh, don't be such a goose. He bought the shop for you, Jenny."

Meredith grinned. "Well, as Lady Argyll, you can't very well go on selling your creams from the kitchen door."

"Go inside, dear. Have a look around." Lady Viola snickered and covered her mouth with her gloved fingers.

Callum reached out his hand for hers and together they walked into the shop. Once inside, Jenny's mouth fell open. She couldn't speak. Couldn't do anything but turn in a slow circle and stare in complete disbelief.

Somehow her sketches for her dream shop had materialized. There were the silk-wrapped settees where grand ladies would sip tea while being shown the latest designs. A long brass bar, where her ready-made gowns would hang, ran along one wall. Blush satin swathes lined the walls and crawled all the way up to the wonderfully high ceiling.

Near the windows was a sparkling glass case where jewelry and brilliants would catch the light, and wink at Milsom's passersby.

"B-but how?" Oh, blast, her eyes were getting hot.

Setting her hands on her hips, Meredith proudly lifted her chin and stepped forward. "When I came down to your chamber to fetch you, your scientific journal was lying open on your bed. And you know how I am, Jenny. I had to take a look, and when I did I was amazed. I had no idea you were such the *entreprendre*."

"Oh, dear, you should not have done such a thing." Lady Viola waved a finger at Meredith.

"Well, I daresay everyone should be quite happy I pried, for when Lord Argyll asked for suggestions for a wedding gift for Jenny, I immediately told him about the shop in every glorious detail." Meredith stepped before Jenny and looked deeply into her eyes. "You do . . . like it?"

Jenny nodded mutely as tears breached her lashes and spilled onto her cheeks.

Callum cuddled Jenny to him. "Now dinna ye go and cry. Ye should be happy."

"I am . . . I just seem to cry at the slightest shift in wind." But as Jenny looked up, she saw the concern in Callum's eyes. "Lud, you don't need to worry. Nothing is wrong, it's just the babe—" *Oh, no*! Jenny sucked in her breath and clamped her lips closed.

"Did ye say . . . *the babe*?" Callum stared at her. "But ye told me . . . Christ, Jenny, ye must tell me true. Are ye carryin' me bairn?"

Meredith and the ladies seemed to be drawn round her by invisible threads. Everyone was staring at her. Her heart played a riotous tattoo in her ears until she could withstand it no longer.

"Yes, Callum. By autumn we'll have a child." She drew in a deep cleansing breath as she fortified herself for the next words she knew she must utter. "And Argyll will have its heir."

She winced, prepared for a harsh retort. Even the Feathertons seemed to hold their collective breaths in anticipation of Callum's reply.

But instead of words, a smile came to Callum's lips, and a look of boundless happiness rode from his mouth to his deep brown eyes.

"Oh, lass," was all he said before he swept her right

off the floor and into his arms and he kissed her as never before.

When at last he allowed her to slide down his chest until her slippers touched the floor, Jenny gazed up at him. "I don't understand . . . I thought you wanted . . . you intended to see the Argyll line extinct."

Callum led Jenny to one of the elegant settees and waited for her to settle into it. "Aye, I was an angry man, filled with pain borne of a lonely, frightened lad. But now I have ye, and love fills those empty hollows. I am whole again, because ye are in my life. Ye, and our babe."

He bent and kissed her softly then and laid his large hand over her belly. Jenny gasped an absurd gurgling sob as more tears streamed down her face.

"Come on, 'tis time, 'tis time," Meredith cried from outside the door. "I'm ready!"

Another surprise? A little grin pushed through the tears to take hold of Jenny's lips. "She's ready for . . . what exactly?"

"Weel, ye'll just have to come with me outside and see fer yerself." Callum reached out his hand to help Jenny rise.

But Jenny was on her feet already and halfway to the shop door before realizing she really ought to have taken her husband's hand. It would have been the lady-like thing to do after all—and she was a lady . . . at last.

As she stood in the open doorway, the sunlight streaming into her eyes, Meredith pulled a rope attached to the linen over the shop sign. The linen dropped away and fell in a dusty heap at Jenny's feet. Lifting her slipper over the linen, she moved onto the flag way and squinted her eyes to read the sign.

Miss Penny's Miscellany
All a Lady Desires

"What do you think, Jenny? Wickedly clever, don't you agree?" Meredith asked excitedly. "I wouldn't be the least surprised if you expanded to London . . . or Edinburgh . . . or—even America!"

Jenny's felt her eyes grow round as the idea took. Why not? For surely the shop would be a resounding success. Why, already it promised to be the toast of Bath.

But the name . . . it might be a little long for the American market. Well, she'd just shorten it. She could call it . . . ah, yes. Jenny smiled.

Penny's.

Epilogue

Scientific Diary of Lady Argyll
20 December, 1818

I have made an important scientific discovery—one that, as a mother, will change my life and those of mothers everywhere—forever.

By crossing two particularly soothing varieties of comfrey and goldenseal, then blending them with the oils of sweet almond and Norwegian cod liver, I have produced a cream for babies' bottoms of unmatched effectiveness for curing rashes. However, the healing strength of the cream allows it to be applied to any sort of chafing, kitchen and sun scorches, as well as small cuts. No doubt this cream will rival the popularity of the tingle cream, but purely for its healing powers of course.

Thus far, there have been no ill side effects during my careful tests on our own wee James's bottom, and scrapes and burns of the house staff here at Laura Place. Therefore I shall commence blending a dozen gallipots of the bottom cream and begin selling it in my shop immediately.

I am very optimistic about the future of this cream and to prepare, have decided to order one hundred new gallipots from the dispensing apothecary. I shall place my order at once, for as I have learned through experience, if you need something, do not tarry, but rather buy the item immediately before it's no longer to be had.

And so I shall be off directly, for not two shops down from the apothecary, I glimpsed the most exquisite sterling baby rattle with a gleaming ivory handle, a trio of tinkling bells, and an attached whistle. Wee James truly needs it and what sort of mother would I be to deny him such a basic necessity of life?

About the Author

KATHRYN CASKIE has long been a devotee of history and things of old. So it came as no surprise to her family when she took a career detour off the online superhighway and began writing historical romances full-time.

With a degree in Communications and a background in marketing, advertising, and journalism, she has written professionally for television, radio, magazines, and newspapers in and around the Washington, D.C., metropolitan area.

She lives in Virginia in a two-hundred-year-old Quaker home nestled in the foothills of the Blue Ridge Mountains with her greatest source of inspiration, her husband and two young daughters.

Kathryn is also the author of *Rules of Engagement*, winner of the Romance Writers of America's prestigious Golden Heart award for Best Long Historical Romance.

Readers may contact Kathryn at her Web site www.kathryncaskie.com.

Imperative One

*It is inadvisable to approach a possible rake
without first observing him from a distance,
where his seductive charms cannot overwhelm
a lady's gentle sensibilities.*

The maddening heat from the aged balloon's fire sent sweat trickling beneath Meredith Merriweather's corset, making her flinch. Still, she held the lens of the spyglass ever firm, focusing squarely on the impeccably dressed gentleman who strolled along the bank of the rippling Serpentine, some forty feet below.

"Oh dash it all, can't you bring the basket any lower?" she shouted to her pilot. "Look there, he's getting away!"

"I'll be seein' what I can do, Miss Merriweather, but I'll not be promisin' a thing," the Irishman droned.

Meredith wasn't at all convinced, but movement caught her notice then. Abruptly, she shifted the glass to a sable-haired woman who approached from the north, swinging her hips seductively as she walked. "Go to it, Giselle," Meredith urged quietly. "Work your charms."

Meredith held her breath and waited. Surely he could not resist the French courtesan's dark beauty. No man could. Her allure was studied. Perfect.

A huge onion-shaped shadow fell over the gentleman as the balloon passed between him and the sun. He turned, and cupping the edge of his hand to his brow, peered upward, squinting at the balloon's massive silhouette.

Meredith's muscles tensed briefly, but then relaxed. Even if he saw her, she had nothing to fear. Balloon ascensions in Hyde Park were commonplace these days and seeing a great floating orb, while extraordinary, was nothing to warrant suspicion.

She turned the glass on Giselle once more. "Oh, *no*." Why was she beckoning him into the trees? That wasn't the plan. Meredith whipped the spyglass from her eye, quite unable to believe what she was seeing.

Hadn't she bade Giselle to keep to the footpath—*in plain view?*

Meredith jerked her head around to be sure the balloon's pilot understood the urgency of the situation. "We're going to lose sight of them! Bring us lower, *please*."

The leather-faced pilot stared back at her with his queer, unblinking insect-like eyes.

"Beggin' yer pardon, miss." He shot a nervous glance over the edge of the basket's frayed woven lip. "But another few feet and we'll be sittin' in the oak tops—or worse. How badly do you need to spy on that bloke? Is it worth crashin' through the bloomin' branches?"

Meredith gasped at his effrontery. "How dare you accuse me of spying! I am conducting a scientific experiment—one which you, sirrah, are about to ruin."

Tipping her gaze over the edge of the basket, she peered down at the jutting branches, then turned and looked hard at the impertinent pilot. "We have at least six feet to spare. Drop her three, *please*."

With a resigned shake of his capped head, the pilot waved to his tether handler below and raised three stubby fingers.

The basket jerked and Meredith's hip struck the wall hard. "Thank you," she growled, leveling a narrowed eye at the pilot, who was working quite diligently to conceal the amused grin on his lips.

Spreading her feet wider for balance, Meredith rested her throbbing hip against the foremost corner of the basket and raised the glass to her eye once more.

This was the closest she'd ever been to London's most notorious rake, and even floating above the treetops was too close for her comfort.

Having had her own heart and reputation shattered by one of his ilk just two years past, Meredith knew what sort of damage Alexander Lamont and his kind were capable of wreaking.

She rested her elbows on the lip of the basket rail and trailed her gaze down the gentleman's well-shaped form.

Good heavens, even from this height, the rake's appeal was plain. His jaw was firm, angular, and lightly gilded from the sun. He was taller than most men, certainly. His muscular shoulders were broad, his waist trim and—*oh, dear*. Swallowing hard, Meredith hurried the spyglass downward, not stopping until only his thighs, his delightfully sculpted thighs, were safely in her sight. Well . . . she had to admit, without question he was the perfect physical specimen of the human male.

Still, if tearoom chatter was to be believed—and when was it not?—he was also the perfect example of a rogue . . . and the absolute worst sort at that.

Not for a moment did Meredith believe, as others seemed to, that Alexander Lamont had given up his rakish ways and truly reformed.

It wasn't possible. And she would prove it.

That is, if the stubborn pilot would move the great monstrosity of a balloon closer. She had to observe Giselle's progress in bringing out the rake's *true* nature.

Lud, now she was leading him to a bench beneath a massive oak!

"*Please,* just a little lower," Meredith implored the pilot.

He shook his head solemnly. "Not wise."

A growl pressed through Meredith's lips as she crouched down to the flooring and removed three gold coins from her reticule. It was all she had left, damn him—she had already paid him four times the normal fare. Rising, she pressed back her shoulders and made her final plea. "Another guinea per foot you manage to lower this contraption."

The pilot hesitated for nearly a full minute, but it was clear by the tattered condition of the basket and the way he kept licking his withered lips, that he could already taste the money.

With her thumb, Meredith moved the coins around in her palm, making them clink together irresistibly.

"Oh, very well. Three feet," the pilot called out to the man below. "Not a finger more."

As if hearing the pilot's reply, Alexander Lamont looked up at the great red balloon, which now hovered a mere thirty feet above.

Meredith hid her spyglass low inside the basket, and had just gazed out over the Serpentine, as if studying the waterbirds on its glistening surface, when she felt a horrifying scraping sensation beneath her feet.

The basket began to descend into the treetops. Her gaze shot upward in time to see a limb gouge the red bulb of fabric above, tearing savagely into it. There was a deafening, flatulent outpouring of air and the basket lurched and fell. Sharp protruding branches shot up around her.

With a frightened squeal, Meredith dropped low and cowered down deep inside the basket, protecting her face with her hands.

"The skin's been punctured. She's comin' down." The pilot's voice was thin with fear, heightening her own terror. "Hang on!"

"Hang on?" Meredith whipped her hands from her eyes and frantically searched the innards of the basket. There was nothing to grip. "To what, sir?"

"The rail, you fool. The rail!"

Crawling on her knees toward the pilot, Meredith slid her hands up the rough hewn wicker wall, scrabbled for the rail's lip and clung to it.

But the shift in weight was too abrupt. The basket, already deep inside the tree canopy, tipped to the side, pouring her out of its pot like the last drop of tea.

Her back struck a thick limb and pain sucked the breath from her lungs. She gasped for air as she slipped from the branch and plummeted downward at a horrific speed. Branches tore at her gown and scraped her tender skin as she shot through the tree toward the ground.

Below she registered the wide-eyed shock in Alexander Lamont's eyes as she careened toward him. *Heaven help me!* She squeezed her eyes shut.

Bloody hell.

His ribs were cracked. Maybe his spine too.

At the very least his new cutaway coat was ruined. He was lying in the dirt after all.

What in Hades had happened?

Alexander Lamont lifted his head from a clod of grass and focused his eyes on a most intriguing sight—a pair of bare female thighs traversing his middle.

Damn it all. No sooner had he vowed to remain celibate, to remain the veriest picture of decorum until marriage—or his father's passing—when women bloody well started dropping from the sky.

Lying flat on his back, Alexander Lamont shoved a heavy branch from his shoulder and blew at the dew dampened leaves sticking to his cheek. Every muscle smarted.

Slowly, he raised himself a bit on one elbow to marvel at the shapely woman laying in a crumpled mass of dark blue silk across his body.

She wasn't moving, and for a clutch of seconds, Alexander was quite certain that she had died right there atop him. But then he noticed the rapid rise and fall of her chest, and was able to breathe easier himself.

"Miss?" He gave his hip a bit of a buck. Still she didn't budge. "Darling, you've cut off the blood to my legs. I say, can you move?"

No answer. This was looking worse by the moment.

He raised his right hand, and found it caught in a fine web of copper ringlets. Unable to disentangle himself, he wrenched his fingers through the hair, but his golden signet ring caught and snagged a long tendril.

He heard a groan, and suddenly he was looking into the bluest eyes he'd ever seen. Glaring blue eyes, the color and hardness of polished sapphires.

"Sir, do you intend to rip every strand from my head, or might you leave me a few?"

He didn't reply. He knew better, for there was no correct answer. Women were shrewd that way.

Besides, already her delicate hands, the color of sweet cream, were working to free her hair. Finally succeeding, she pushed up from his chest, with what Alexander decided was unnecessary force, for unbelievable shards of pain knifed through his ribs.

Leaning back on her boot heels, she stared down at him, biting her full, pink lower lip. Framed by her vibrant flaming hair and startling blue eyes, her oval face seemed unnaturally pale, save a scarlet scrape traversing her left cheek.

"Can you stand?" Her voice was soft with concern now and she lifted a hand to him. But there was anger in her eyes. Indeed, as well as something more palpable. Loathing?

How curious.

Planting his freed palm in the soft earth, Alexander bent at his waist and raised himself to a sitting position, willing himself not to wince.

A look of relief eased across the young woman's delicate features. "I . . . I thank you for . . . cushioning my fall." At the snap of a twig, she raised her eyes to a point behind him and he heard his new French acquaintance's lilting voice.

"You are lucky to have been spared, mademoiselle. Look at the balloon."

Alexander glanced up into the guts of the oak, where he saw a large wicker basket skewered by a thick limb.

There was a sudden thrash of leaves, and a weather-worn man dropped down from a wide branch and thudded down on a patch of damp earth behind him.

"I told ye we were too low," the pilot snarled at the fiery haired lass, then shook a wild finger at the basket and the deflated balloon blanketing the tree's soaring canopy. "And look at my Betsy now! Ye owe me, miss, owe me quite a lot!"

The young lady turned her frantic blue eyes from the pilot to Alexander.

"I . . . I—Oh, dear." She brought a hand to her head, then crumpled back down atop him.

Forgetting his own pain, Alexander lunged forward and cradled her limp body in his arms. He looked from her wan features up to the pilot. "Do you know her name? Where she lives?"

"'Er name's Miss Merriweather," the pilot offered. "Hails from Hanover Square or somewhere thereabouts."

"*Mon Dieu,* is she going to die?"

Alexander looked up at the French woman as she collected, then handed over, what he took to be the miss's belongings. "No, my dear. But I fear she requires assistance without delay." Digging into his coat pocket, he fingered a cool coin and flipped it to his lovely new acquaintance. "This should see you home. I am sorry that I cannot help you with the stone in your boot, as you requested."

"*Merci, monsieur.*" The dark-eyed mademoiselle

caught the coin and, with a grin, stuffed it into her boun-
teous cleavage. "And do not worry yourself about my
boot. The stone will dislodge itself." She flashed a co-
quettish smile his way. "But then, perhaps it won't.
Maybe you will be so kind as to come to Ten Russell
Square later this eve and check for me, *oui*?"

Alexander grinned, but kept to task and lifted the
pale young lady into his arms. Stepping over the clutter
of broken limbs and leaf-sprigged branches, he started
down the footpath.

"*Monsieur*, where are you taking her?" the French
woman called out, a tinge of worry licking her thickly
accented words.

"Home," Alexander shouted back over his shoulder.
"I'm taking her home."

Home, he'd said.

Sweet heavens, Meredith only hoped he meant *hers*
and not his own beastly lair. Lud, what a pickle she'd be
in then.

Meredith held her eyes tightly closed and continued
feigning unconsciousness.

Yes, it was deceitful, but there was no help for it.
Only, she wished she had thought to fall backward, instead of straight onto Alexander Lamont.

But the balloon pilot was about to expose her experiment, wasn't he? She had to do something to stop him,
and unfortunately, fainting was the first method that
came to her mind. Her great aunt Viola, a kindred spirit
if ever there was one, used the method whenever necessary and with great success.

Of course, Meredith hadn't taken the time to think

what other events her fainting episode might set into motion. And now here she was in the arms of the most dangerous man in London——*oh, no.* She sniffed the air, and now sure of what she sensed, cringed inwardly.

Horses. She smelled horses. Heard the grunts and scuffle of the beasts. Her heart began to pound a terrified tattoo inside her chest.

He'd taken her to a stable, of all places! Well, this little folly of hers had gone on long enough. She must end it this very instant!

In a most calculated manner, she allowed her head to loll lazily forward, until it struck a heavy button. *Time for a murmur.*

Add a little sigh. Lovely, lovely.

Eyelids flicker and . . . open.

Oh, hellfire.

As she lifted her lids, Meredith found herself staring into dark mossy green eyes, ringed with a tea-hued band. The combination was not unique. Meredith had seen it before, she was sure she had. But somehow the welcoming warmth of these particular eyes made her want to plunge into their depths and wade there a while longer.

"I see you've come back to me." Alexander Lamont's lips lifted and he leveled her with an equally moving smile that made her blood fizz in her veins and her body go all wobbly.

A jolt of nervous realization skated through her limbs. Heavens! It was happening. She was being taken in by a rake—*again!*

Well, she wasn't about to give herself over so easily this time. She glared up at him through narrowed eyes. "Sir, I implore you. Return me to my feet at once, please." She snapped her fingers twice, as she'd seen her great aunt do when the servants were dawdling, but this only earned her an amused grin.

" 'Ere ye are, my lord. Brushed him down for ye, just how ye like."

Meredith turned her head to see a stable hand leading forth the most gargantuan horse she'd ever seen. Its black hide gleamed almost blue, and even Meredith, who possessed an unnatural wariness—all right, a horrible *fear*—of the beasts, had to admit this one was . . . well, rather spectacular.

In the next instant, Alexander Lamont raised her up as if she weighed no more than a feather—which with her heavy thighs and plump bottom, was far from the truth—and settled her upon the great equine's back.

"N-no!" Her hands shot outward and her fingers frantically clawed Lamont's sleeves before he could lower his arms. *Oh, blast*. Her lips were quivering now.

"There, there, miss. You shan't ride alone." With that he cuffed his foot in the stirrup, swung a leg over the horse's back and came down on the saddle behind her. Then the rake scooted close and pulled her tightly against him.

Against *him*. Yes, *that* part of him. Why she could feel every . . . *curve* through those tight deerskin breeches men favored these days.

Heat washed across Meredith's face, and given the milky whiteness of her countenance, she knew her cheeks glowed like hot embers in a hearth.

Instantly she clung to him, lest she fall. Her body was shaking. La, how she wished horses did not petrify her so.

He smiled down at her and sat up straighter in the

saddle. At that moment she noticed, beneath his hat, that his hair was every bit as black as the horse's swishing tail.

"Hanover Square, is that correct?"

The deep tone of his voice rumbled inside Meredith's chest, sending a vibration clear through to her . . . well, never mind.

"I am quite capable of walking, sir. So if you'll just let me—"

"Wouldn't think of it, Miss Merriweather. I've made it a practice: whenever a woman tumbles out of the sky into my lap, I always see her home to the safety of her family." He turned his mesmerizing gaze upon her. "And the name is Lord Lansing."

"I know who you are." Meredith cocked her head and met his gaze straight on. "All of London, those of the gentler sex anyway, knows of you. You, my lord, are London's most notorious rogue."

He laughed at that. "I fear you have me confused with another."

"I daresay, I do not."

"Ah, but you do. The Lord Lansing you refer to no longer exists. For you see, Miss Merriweather, I have reformed."

Meredith snickered at his gall. "Well, nevertheless, my aunts would think it imprudent to allow you to escort me home. So if you will just stop and let me down—"

"I do apologize, Miss Merriweather, but I *will* see you to your home. Remember, women falling from the sky?" He poked a single finger into the air. "It is a rule with me. I cannot divert."

There was laughter in his voice, and in any other

circumstance—and were he any other man—she might have smiled. But not now. She was intimately pressed against London's worst rake, riding toward Mayfair, and there was nothing she could do about it!

"When you were in the balloon, I heard you urging the pilot into the trees. What were you doing up there?" He said nothing more, but instead remained quiet and awaited her answer.

"W-what?" As Meredith readied a plausible excuse on her tongue, the rake reached beneath his coat and withdrew her brass lens. The minute the sun glinted on it, the blood inside her veins stopped flowing and for an instant, she was sure she really would faint from the shocking evidence.

"This telescope was beside you. Where you perhaps *spying*?"

"C-certainly not! I was . . . bird-watching. Yes, and I thought I saw a very rare species in the trees."

His lip twitched upward. "Really, I have done a bit of *bird*-watching in my day. What species do you mean?"

Heat pulsed in Meredith's earlobes. "The, um . . . the scarlet rogue . . . finch." Hesitantly, she glanced up at him and caught the last remnants of a grin.

"I can't say that I am familiar with the *rogue finch*."

Meredith diverted her gaze and instead studied, with utmost fascination, a narrow row house they were passing. "Well, as I said, it is quite rare."

Criminy. Did she just see Lady Ashton peering through her parlor window at them? Why, if she had not already had her reputation all but ruined, this would certainly do it.

As the massive horse trotted into Hanover Square, Meredith at last felt a modicum of relief, which heightened the moment the rake stopped before number 17, and leapt from the horse.

That is until she realized she'd been left atop the great beast, *alone*.

Her fingers scrabbled for the saddle's pommel and there she sat, trembling even as Alexander Lamont raised his broad hands to her.

"Allow me to assist, Miss Merriweather. Just let go of the saddle."

Her eyes went wide in her head. "I . . . I . . . cannot," she stammered. The horse was going to bolt, she just knew it.

Suddenly, she felt his warm hands encircle her waist.

"I've got you now. Just relax your fingers."

But Meredith could not reply. She shook so violently that her teeth were chattering inside her head.

Just then the front door opened and her two great aunts, the ladies Letitia and Viola Featherton, stepped outside.

"Good heavens, gel!" her turnip-shaped aunt Letitia quipped. "What are you doing atop that huge horse, Meredith? Come down at once!"

Still Meredith could not manage a single word in reply. Instead she stared mutely back at her aunts and clacked her teeth at them.

"Sister, look at her fingers. They're as white as frost. The poor child is frozen with fear."

"I can see that, Viola. Which is why I wish for her to dismount." Then her aunt Letitia caught the rake in her sights. "You, sir. You're a big fellow. Will you pull her from the saddle? Just give her a good hard yank. We've seen her like this before. I fear there will be no talking her down."

Alexander Lamont gave her aunt a curt nod then looked at Meredith. "Are you prepared?"

Meredith's teeth played castanets in response. *Lud, how mortifying!*

"Very well then, off you go." His fingers tightened around her waist and with one clean jerk, Meredith's grip on the saddle broke.

An instant later, she was standing on her own two feet on the flag way before her aunts' fashionable Mayfair townhouse.

In perfect rakish form, Alexander Lamont offered Meredith his arm, which she had no desire but little choice to take. Then, appearing the most well-mannered of gentlemen, he escorted her up the few steps to her aunts.

"My ladies, allow me please to introduce myself. I am Alexander Lamont." He bowed before the two old women, and they each bobbed a quick curtsy in response. "I believe you are acquainted with my father, the Earl of Lansing."

"But of course. I vow, it has been several years since our paths have crossed." Aunt Letitia turned to her sister. "Viola, of course you remember young Lord Lansing here."

"I do indeed. And I daresay, you are the mirror image of your father in his youth." Viola smiled brightly. "How do you do, my lord?"

"I fear that my visit this day is not a pleasant one. Your—" He nodded toward Meredith then.

"Our *grandniece*." The snowy-haired pair replied together.

"Of course. Your grandniece suffered a tremendous fall less than thirty minutes past, and I am convinced she did sustain some degree of injury." With great bold-ness, he reached out a hand and laid it, comfortingly, upon Viola's bony arm. "You see, she fell from a hot air balloon, through an oak tree."

Both aunts snapped their heads around to Meredith.

"Are you injured, dear?" Aunt Viola asked.

Meredith opened her lips and, to her great relief, her teeth were no longer marching. "No, Auntie. I am per-fectly well. This gentleman cushioned my fall with his body."

"Oh, how gallant you are, Lord Lansing!" Her aunt Letitia exclaimed. But then, she took note of the man's earth-marred coat and grimaced. "I do hope young Meredith did not cause you any distress, my lord. I dare-say, she is a spirited gel and is always getting up to some mischief or another."

Meredith softly groaned her displeasure, but quieted when her aunt Viola gave her a hard, covert pinch.

"Why after all you've been through, my lord," her twig-thin aunt Viola began, "you must come inside and join us for a restorative."

"As much as I would enjoy joining you, madam, I am afraid that another pressing matter requires my atten-tion."

No doubt, Meredith mused. Pressing a certain French courtesan to a mattress would be her guess. Oh, she knew his sort all too well. No matter, Giselle would tell her all about it the next morn.

Then, Alexander Lamont pulled a visiting card from a concealed pocket in his dirt-encrusted coat and pressed it into Meredith's hand.

"Should you have further need of my services, Miss

Merriweather, please do not hesitate to send for me." He flashed her a brilliant, knee-weakening smile.

With a nod to her and to each of her aunts, Lord Lansing the rake bid them all farewell, leapt upon his massive horse and galloped from the square.

Her elderly aunts released pleased sighs.

Aunt Letitia caught Meredith's shoulder and hobbled along beside her toward the door. "My, he is a handsome devil, isn't he?"

"Indeed he is," Meredith murmured. "But then, they always are."

"Still, I feel I must caution you against forming any sort of connection with the gentleman, for I have heard rumors that in truth he is no gentleman at all."

Aunt Viola wrapped her thin fingers around Meredith's upper arm, but as they entered the house and turned into the parlor it was her sister she addressed. "What a thing to say, Letitia. You must have heard, Lord Lansing has reformed. And you know what the ladies say . . . a reformed rake makes the very best husband."

"Nonsense!" Meredith exhaled her breath. "I for one do not believe it for a moment."

Aunt Letitia widened her faded blue eyes then shook her head at her sister, who winced when she took her meaning.

"Of course a good, sensible gentleman, like your Mr. Chillton, dear Meredith, should always be a lady's first choice." A wisp of a giggle slipped through her lips then. "I only meant that a reformed rake, might know how . . . well . . . to please his wife."

Aunt Letitia chuckled heartily at that, until she toppled back against the settee beside her sister and gasped for breath.

Finally, as the two elderly ladies quieted, Meredith crossed her arms over her chest and raised her chin proudly.

"That may be, Auntie, but I am afraid no woman will ever know for certain because there is no such thing as a *reformed* rake."

Aunt Letitia lifted her thick white brows. "You seem quite sure of that, my dear."

"I am." Meredith gave herself a secret little smile.

"And with Alexander Lamont as my subject, I intend to prove it, to the satisfaction of all, before the season ends."

Her aunts' widened eyes met nervously and their lips moved in shocked unison. "Oh, dear."

THE EDITOR'S DIARY

Dear Reader,

Whenever life throws lemons at you, make lemonade, right? But even the best lemonade isn't any good without a little sugar to sweeten things up. So grab our two Warner Forever titles this January—I promise even the sweetest of sweet tooths will be satisfied.

New York Times bestselling author Cathy Maxwell raves **Kathryn Caskie's** writing "sparkles with wit and humor" so prepared to be dazzled. Pick up her latest, **LADY IN WAITING**, and you'll never look at facial cream the same way. Jenny Penny is a lady's maid to the matchmaking Featherton sisters and a lover of all things fine—and expensive. But soon her debts pile up, forcing her to secretly sell her homemade facial cream. Jenny could never have anticipated the sensation it would cause...or that women in the ton would use her tingle cream in the most intimate of places to boost their libido. As if that weren't enough, the Featherton sisters have made Jenny their project. Passing her off as Lady Genevieve, they are determined to see her wed sexy Scottish marquis Callum Campbell. Being wooed by day and churning out tingle cream by night, Jenny is leading a double life and she's about to get caught. But will Callum's feelings change when he learns she is not a lady but an entrepreneurial lady's maid?

How far would you go to protect your daughter? Lady Johanna from **Shari Anton's AT HER SERVICE** would risk anything to protect her little Ivy. The plague devastated the village, killing Johanna's abusive husband and two of her three beloved children. Determined to keep Ivy safe from harm's way, Johanna has pledged her life to her daughter. So when outlaws raid her village, threatening their safety and injuring Ivy, Johanna is forced to hire a fearsome mercenary to stop them. Though she dreads the presence of a hulking, aggressive, and completely uncivilized man in her home, she has no choice. But when Logan Grimm arrives, he's nothing like Johanna thought. With his broad shoulders and kind eyes, she sees a gentleness she never expected—and one that she fears more than anything. For while Logan is protecting them against the outlaws, who, pray tell, is guarding her heart? *Rendezvous* calls Shari Anton a "master who weaves magic onto every page" so get ready to fall under her spell.

To find out more about Warner Forever, these January titles, and the author, visit us at www.warnerforever.com.

With warmest wishes,

Karen Kosztolnyik

Karen Kosztolnyik, Senior Editor

P.S. Here are two reasons to believe in true love again: **Annie Solomon** presents a powerful romantic suspense about a blind man and the sole witness to his attack who must save themselves from the assassin on their trail in **BLIND CURVE**; and **Candy Halliday** delivers the hilarious and outrageous tale of a woman determined to create the perfect virtual soulmate and the very real man who starts to seem more perfect every day in **DREAM GUY**.

Look for
Rules of Engagement
by Kathryn Caskie
(0-446-61423-8)

When two elderly aunts mistakenly use the military strategy handbook *Rules of Engagement* to secure their headstrong niece a fiancé, London's ballrooms become battlefields in a war of wits, matchmaking, and mayhem.

"Top Pick! A smart and sparkling romance that quite simply captivates. Make room on the keeper shelves!"
> —*Romantic Times BOOKClub Magazine*

"A delightful debut!"
> —Julia Quinn,
> *New York Times* bestselling author

"Her writing sparkles with wit and humor."
> —Cathy Maxwell,
> *New York Times* bestselling author